Sacrifice of the Faithful

Book XI of The Quietus of Fate

By Brian C. Kershner

Acknowledgements

The key themes that the *Quietus of Fate* series seeks to address are perspective and perception. This extends not only from the author to the characters, but from the characters to the reader.

Ramifications of choices are on display from the very first chapter of *Worlds Shadow*, and how those choices are perceived and the information that shaped those choices. Every character at some point has had to make choices based on misinformation, disinformation, or outright lies, and the ramifications of some of those choices are still being felt ten novels later. Some of these ramifications are extremely personal, while others are felt across the whole of the world.

One of the choices made near the end of *Effigies of Faith* that will have clear ramifications on the whole of the world, and that is Kaitain Lorien's banning of the worship of the Creator. As a disclaimer, some portions of *Sacrifice of the Faithful* will deal with those consequences, and some could be considered at least off-putting and at most offensive.

Writing terrible things is a difficult process, and sometimes I feel like I need to take a shower after writing some of the things that I have written. But I am consistently encouraged that whatever darkness I can dream up, there is light enough to more than balance the scales.

B.K.

Table of Contents

Chapter 81

Chapter 82

Chapter 83

Chapter 84

Faith must be tested to be true,
Service and Devotion themselves are not enough,
For the soul darkness seeks to imbrue,
And every vestige of divine light snuff.

The powerful and the plain alike,
Seek love in the bosom of belief,
And against the wages of sin to strike,
So their souls may find eternal relief.

To this end the Creator has spoken,
And touched one whose life was wrapped in shame,
He removed the blight and has awoken,
His Chosen ruler, His world to reclaim.

The Divine Empress her past transgression shed,
Stands ready to answer His call,
To banish the shroud of fear and dread,
And Salvation deliver unto us all.

- *The New Verses of The Word*
  From Reverend Mother Amallia
  Spiritual Advisor of the Divine Empress

Prologue

A Soul's Passing

Year Four of the Just Emperor Kaitain "Dragonsbane" Lorien,
Creator's Calendar Year 1871

Logan Ranthall sat at the edge of his bed and did his best to try to quiet his mind. So much had happened over the past few days, and his mind still reeled from much of it. The betrayal of his brother, the acceleration of the war against the Cadarians, the new followers of Dorovar, Jerah, Jillian, Aerith, his father being alive… If he hadn't been through so much on Onea, his head probably would have already exploded. But there were comforts to be found in the quiet moments. He thought of Elwyne, thought of her smiling face, how she would hold him late in the night when he could not sleep and make him feel that everything would be alright. She would never have to say a word, she simply would look at him with those beautiful eyes, and the fear and trepidation would just flee from his body. Her touch could restore him and calm his racing heart. Now though, there was not truly a heart to calm. Ever since he had touched the Blaze and become a member of the phasia, his heart had beaten the same calm cold rhythm every moment of his life. No matter the trial, no matter the exertion, the same unperturbed beat. Part of his mind said that he should lie down and try to get some sleep. Now that the war was joined in earnest, there would be very few pockets of peaceful rest left. Just as he was reaching down to unlace his boots; there came a knock at the door. Jerrard had been generous in providing rooms, but as usual, the chance on actually using them uninterrupted for a night was consistently low. Smiling despite himself and shaking his head, Logan made his way to the door and opened it. When he saw Rhain's tear streaked face, he knew that something bad had happened. The red-haired girl was trying her best to keep her emotions in check, but she wasn't doing a very good job.

"Sabrina wanted to see you."

Though his heart's beat would never reflect the feeling that passed through him, he imagined it skipping a beat. Something was certainly wrong, and it was the something that Logan had been dreading since he learned of Sabrina's inheriting of Halicon's powers. Without a word, Logan nodded and stepped out of the room behind Rhain. The much younger woman didn't wait and continued to a different part of the royal palace on another errand. Logan didn't need an escort anyway; he knew exactly where Sabrina was. One of the first things that inheritors of Aerith's mantle learned, once things became complicated, was to shut out the thoughts of the others connected to the annoying man's legacy. Much like Aerith's personality, his thoughts were intruding, crude, and usually mistimed. But for all of the things that made Aerith the most meddlesome and infuriating man in the whole of Creation, it was his loyalty and love that endeared him to those that truly understood. Out of the corner of his eye he saw a door crack open. Jillian's head emerged a moment later, but it looked as though she had just gotten out of bed upon hearing the sounds in the hallway. In a lot of ways Logan had been impressed with the manner in which the woman had been able to keep up with the madness that was suddenly swirling around her. She emerged from the room, her white nightshirt hanging loose around her.

"What's wrong?"

Logan did his best to smile.

"I wish I could explain, but I have to go say goodbye to an old friend. Sabrina is dying, and I need to be with her."

There was a momentary look of shock on Jillian's face but she quickly suppressed it and the look of genuine concern filled her eyes.

"Do you want me to come with you? I can be dressed in a minute."

Logan smiled and took her hand in his.

"It's alright, Jillian. She's family, and she waited until it was late to avoid people fawning. She wants to do this on her own terms, and I respect that."

Jillian hugged Logan and held him tightly. For a long moment, he didn't know what to do. But after several more moments he returned the hug and then when she pulled away from him, she looked up into his eyes and smiled.

"Wake me up when you come back. You shouldn't be alone."

A single tear ran down her face, and before he realized what he was doing, Logan reached up and wiped the tear from her soft cheek. He said nothing but nodded before turning to walk down the hall. So many thoughts were whirling in his mind, but he did not have time for any of them. He thrust his hands in his pockets and tried best to quiet his mind as he walked through the twisting halls. He was vaguely aware of the turns he was making and finally he realized that he had stopped in front of a door. The door opened without any prompting from Logan, and when he stepped inside, he looked up and saw Sabrina sitting on the edge of the bed, Alderin leaning in the corner closest to the door, and Rhain kneeling beside Sabrina, with concern painted on her face. Sabrina looked up briefly and fixed her eyes on Logan. He could see the exhaustion there, the kind that came when all strength is ripped from the body, and all that is left is the will. But the strength of her will was fading, and Logan knew just looking at her that time was short. There were no words that passed between them; Logan simply shut the door and stayed there, waiting. Sabrina took a deep breath, closed her eyes for a moment and then stood. She gingerly made her way across the room to stand in front of Alderin. Her smile did not comfort.

"I'm not sure how much I can help you, Alderin, but I will do what I can. Your powers were ripped from you differently than Gwydeon's were, but I was able to give him a measure of his abilities back. Through your father you know about the Blaze, you know what it is capable of, and you know what it means to touch it. Through Logan I know the depths of commitment it takes to surrender to the Blaze, that is why I wanted him here. Things were different when I imparted abilities to Gwydeon; he still had some measure of the powers of the Brother of Angels. You however, you are just a man, your immortality notwithstanding."

Alderin stood up straight.

"Just tell me what I need to do."

Sabrina grimaced, but Logan came to her rescue.

"It's simple, Alderin. Everyone in theory can touch the Blaze, but not everyone can control themselves enough to perceive that the Blaze is there, and fewer still can open themselves to it without killing themselves. Those of us who have been touched by the Creator in one form or another have better chances than most. What Sabrina is going to do is to pierce the veil, and allow you to see the Blaze without trying. The first instinct you are going to have is to reach for it, to try to take control of it. But the more you reach, the more it's going to flee from your fingers. Imagine standing perfectly still, your hands at your side, and just let the Blaze find you. No matter how long it takes, just keep your consciousness fixed on it, and let it come to you. Once it touches you, your next instinct will be to try to hold on to it. Don't. Let it fill you. It won't hurt you if you just surrender to it. The people who try to drink it in, to let it permeate them so completely are the ones who are consumed by it."

Alderin nodded. Sabrina took another step toward Alderin and looked up into his brilliant blue eyes.

"Just keep your mind clear. If you have to think of something, think of Darrien. Think how much you love her and how you are doing this for her. Let the Blaze find you, and let it become part of you."

Alderin nodded once more, and in turn Sabrina took a deep breath and laid her hand on Alderin's chest. Alderin closed his eyes, but wasn't sure whether it was of his own volition or something that Sabrina was doing to him. There was only darkness behind his closed eyes, but after what seemed like minutes there was a faint glow just on the edge of his perception. As Logan had said, his first instinct was to turn toward it, to chase it, but Alderin resisted that urge. He held his ground, stood still as Logan had suggested, and kept his hands at his sides. The bright green glow grew around him, and before long he began to see the peaks of dancing flame at the edge of his vision. Ever so slowly, the living flames grew, filling his field of vision until the Blaze was all he saw. Again, the urgency of the moment made Alderin want to lunge for the Blaze, to wrap his arms around the writhing fires and engulf himself within it. He needed the power to be able to help Darrien, to stand by her side and protect her from all danger. But again his restraint won out. How could he help Darrien if he were dead? How could he stand by her side if he failed now? In his mind he pictured peaceful moments with Darrien. The quiet stolen moments when they would sneak out of the Citadel together. The thoughts calmed his breathing, calmed his nerves, and held his actions at bay. Finally the Blaze itself reached out and touched Alderin. It wriggled across his skin, latching into every pore and duct. He began to feel the burning all along his arms and legs, moving inward, across his stomach and chest until they met at his heart. For many long moments it felt as though his heart was being held in a bubble of fire, but then the edges of the bubble solidified and started to squeeze. Each beat of his heart was labored, tortured, and filled with pain. Then the beating stopped. Alderin felt like he was holding his breath, but then realized he wasn't truly breathing at all. Nothing moved through his lungs. Nothing moved through his heart. He was dead. Alderin felt as though he were floating in the space between life and death, the place that could be confused with dreaming. Moments later, a faint beat resounded in Alderin's chest. There was a slow, cold, calculated rhythm, one that settled in as though it had always been that way. Alderin was one with the Blaze, it was neither his master nor his slave, it was his ally. It was no different from his arm or his leg. It was an appendage, an extension of his will, so long as he respected its power.

Alderin opened his eyes, and immediately felt the change. He looked at his damaged arm, and reached for the flows of the Blaze that now circulated within him. After a matter of moments the stump began to glow. Bright green flames erupted from the severed stump and began to form something akin to a forearm, wrist and hand. But the form was much thicker. In Alderin's mind's eye, he imagined the way that his father looked when he wore his famous golden gauntlet. Finally, the flames began to solidify, as though they were being frozen into place, the bright green cooling into a black, almost obsidian color and structure. Alderin tested his new appendage, flexing the fingers and could not help but smile at his handiwork. He felt whole again, in more ways than one. Sabrina took a step back and almost faltered, but Rhain helped her keep her feet. Once Sabrina was safely seated back on the bed, she closed her eyes and then took a deep breath.

"Alderin," Logan said calmly, "you should rest. I know you feel like you can move mountains, but by the morning it's going to feel like a couple dozen mules kicked you in the head and chest all night long. Take a few days. The powers you had as a Dark God are similar to what you have now, but the application is different. I'm sure you'll get the hang of it, but don't rush."

Alderin nodded and started toward the door. When he put his new Blaze-constructed hand on the handle, Logan put his hand on the man's shoulder.

"And be careful with portals," he added, "they're pretty tricky at first. When you were a Dark God, you could just picture where you wanted to be and the portal would take you there. With the Blaze, you won't have that kind of precision. When in doubt, aim high."

Alderin forced a smile, gave a curt nod, and then headed out of the room. Sabrina raised her head and looked at Rhain.

"Would you give me a moment with Logan, Rhain? Just wait in the hall, and he'll come and get you in a moment. I promise it won't be long."

Rhain nodded. She knew that other than Aerith, Logan was the closest thing that Sabrina had to family, and if there was anyone that she was going to spend her last moments with, it would be him. Rhain started to walk past Logan, and he stopped her and put his hand on her shoulder and looked her in the eyes for a long moment before leaning in and kissing her on the forehead. Rhain's first reaction was to pull away. She wasn't used to genuine emotion. But despite herself, she surrendered to the embrace and then when he pulled back, she quickly left the room. Alone, Sabrina and Logan just looked at each other. There was so much to say, but no time to say it. Logan moved across the room and sat beside Sabrina. She moved down the bed slightly and lay down so that her head was in his lap. He gently stroked her hair and the two stayed there for several long minutes, just letting the emotion of the moment go. There was nothing that words would do, nothing that could have been conveyed that was more powerful than just that simple quiet expression of love. When Sabrina finally sat up again, Logan expected to see tears in her eyes. But there were none. She had come to terms with what was about to happen, and was at peace with the choice that she had to make. Logan wasn't sure that he would come to terms with things that quickly. His family was small, and Sabrina was an important part of it. After a nod, Logan got up and moved toward the door to fetch Rhain. Sabrina's hand found his, and he turned. There was now a sorrow in her eyes.

"I was in love with Gwydeon. I would have done anything for him."

Logan looked her in the eyes, but there was nothing for him to say. For so long Sabrina and Gwydeon had been together, in the Heavens, on Espre, and during the time when Gwydeon was in hiding. Sabrina was Gwydeon's lifeline for almost two thousand years, and there was no way that there wasn't closeness there. But Sabrina knew that Gwydeon was wholly dedicated to Midarin, no matter their distance. So Sabrina, for so long suffered with unrequited love, a love that she buried so deeply that even Aerith never would have been able to discover it. Logan reached down and put his hand on her head, stroking her hair once more before turning again toward the door. This time though Sabrina didn't restrain him. When he opened the door, Rhain was waiting just on the other side. She moved past him without a word and returned to the chair that sat facing the bed. Sabrina looked at Rhain and then slipped gently off the bed and knelt before the red-haired woman.

"I know you don't want to do this, Rhain, but it's the only way. Maybe someday you'll believe that, and maybe someday you'll forgive me. But no matter what, you are going to have to stand tall in the days to come. Protect the ones that still call themselves phasia and bring those corrupted by Emries' touch back from the brink before they do something so horrible that there is no possible redemption. I know it will make things more awkward with your mother, but that can't be helped. Between you and Wolf, I hope you can bring a peaceful resolution to all of this."

Rhain's eyes went wide. She had never thought of how things would change between herself and Bryn, but perhaps for once she would be able to get the upper hand on her mother, or at the very least have a better understanding of who she was and what motivated her to be the way that she was. Maybe it would even give Rhain a deeper understanding into the nature of the relationship between her mother and father, something that had always mystified her. The two were so different, so combative, but at the same time a love held between them that defied explanation and it was a love that had shaken the Cosmos. Perhaps if Rhain could understand that kind of love, she would be able to find love for herself. A real love that meant something more than the physical parts her mother had taught her to use as a weapon. She wanted to feel what Bryn felt for Aerith. She wanted to feel what Marlae at some level felt for Gabriel, though she never would have admitted that fact.

"You are about to become the master of the Blaze, the true wielder of its power, and the protector of all who can touch the brilliant green flames. It will be your life force, as much as your beating heart is. You may extend this power to others as I have done with Alderin and Gwydeon, and as Halicon did with the phasia. I trust your judgment in this Rhain, and I give you everything that I am, and everything that Halicon gave me. Always remember that we do this to protect your father, and to protect those that wear his mantle. Work with them, and help them to accomplish our ultimate goal. We must save those who cannot save themselves, and protect those who cannot understand the true nature of what swirls around them in the darkness and in the spaces between light and shadow."

Sabrina reached out and put her hand on Rhain's chest. She closed her eyes and all expression faded. Green flames appeared like a halo around Rhain's body. Over the next few moments the glow intensified and started to pulsate rhythmically. The pulses became shorter and shorter until finally there was one singular bright flash. The flames instead of surrounding Rhain danced across her skin for long moments before finally disappearing. When Rhain opened her eyes, they glowed a brilliant green. Sabrina collapsed backwards, but Logan was there to catch her. Her breathing was labored and became shallower and shallower. Finally her head rolled back and she fixed her eyes on Logan's. A weak smile came to her lips, and Logan smoothed her hair back gently and held her as tightly to him as he could. Logan bent down and kissed Sabrina gently on the forehead, and when he pulled back, her eyes had closed. The last shallow breaths slowed and then ultimately stopped. Sabrina Binosear, the daughter of Cairyn Binosear, the granddaughter of Anabel Binosear and the great granddaughter of Aerith Seth had left the living world. As the moments passed, Sabrina's body began to grow insubstantial. The light in the room passed through her as though she was made of smoke. Finally the last bits of her faded from view, and she was gone. Silence held between Logan and Rhain for several long moments before Rhain got to her feet and started toward the door.

"I need to go talk to Taya. I know the process of taking Emries' influence from her, and we need to do that as soon as possible. I trust you'll be leaving in the morning?"

Logan got back to his feet.

"It's probably best if I keep moving, at least for now. We're still unsure of so many of the other players, and I have a sinking suspicion that once I start digging, I'm going to find out that many we counted among the dead, aren't so dead. I still have contacts in the Brotherhood of the Flickering Flame, and I've been gone long enough that I can drop in without attracting suspicion. Plus I promised Aerith that I would look in on the Snags. I think it may be time that we start mobilizing them. And I'm sure that having me around makes Jerrard nervous."

Rhain nodded.

"Taya and I will be leaving tomorrow as well. Sabrina believed that there may be a key to Talisia's schemes in Oradrim. Besides, I need to look in on Jeroch and Saurn, especially now that I know exactly where they are."

Logan frowned.

"Taking Bryn along?"

Rhain sighed.

"You know that my mother is a delicate issue. But this is phasia business, so I suppose we should travel together. At the very least she may be able to keep Saurn from doing something rash."

Rhain stood silent for a long moment, and Logan knew there was something else that Rhain wanted to say. Finally she cursed to herself and locked her eyes back on Logan.

"I would like to ask a favor."

Logan cocked his head.

"Well, since we're basically family, how could I refuse?"

Rhain turned fully to face him and put her hands on her hips, shaking her head.

"No, Logan, not for something like this. It's too important and probably too dangerous to just be taken on faith."

"Alright," Logan said finally, "what's the favor?"

Rhain swallowed hard.

"No matter what you may think, you need to stay as far away from Tess Annis as possible. She is out of your league, and she is more dangerous than anyone knows. There are steps being taken to deal with her one way or another. You should be focused on Pike. He is your main concern now. But in the meantime, I would ask that you find and look in on Marlae. She's important and I have a feeling that she needs you now more than ever."

A puzzled look came to Logan's features.

"Marlae? The spoiled little would-be Empress?"

Rhain bit her lower lip.

"She's much more than that Logan, even if she doesn't know it. Please look in on her, and help her if you can. I think she may become very important in the weeks to come. If anyone can unite this empire under a single banner again, it's her."

Logan nodded and smiled.

"For you, I will, Rhain. And if you need me, you know how to find me."

Rhain tapped the side of her head.

"Yes, Phoenix, I do."

* * * * * * * * * * * *

An hour had passed since the death of Sabrina Binosear, and Logan finally made his way back to his room. Dawn was only a couple of hours away, and if he didn't sleep now, it was doubtful that he would have another chance to sleep in a comfortable bed for quite some time. When he got to his door, he stole a glance over his shoulder to Jillian's room. He knew that he said he would wake her when he returned, but it was late, and she needed her sleep. There would be plenty of time to talk in the days ahead, and eventually she would forgive him for looking out for her instead of worrying about his own needs. He opened the door quietly, entered the room, and closed it again behind him. When he turned to face the bed, he was shocked to see Jillian lying there looking at him, a gentle smile on her face. "I had a feeling that you wouldn't keep your word," she said with mock annoyance. "So I thought I wouldn't give you any choice."

Jillian sat up slowly, letting the thin sheet slip away from her naked form. She patted the spot on the bed beside her.

"Hurry up and come to bed. It'll be morning soon."

Chapter LXXVIII

Forging New Doctrine

Year One of the Divine Empress and Child of the Creator Marlae Tamerlane, Creator's Calendar Year 1871

Marlae Tamerlane sat forward in her chair, and could hear the bells of the church tower ringing in the distance. Three bells, three o'clock in the morning. They should all have been in bed, fast asleep, but there was no time for that. There was still so much to discuss, so much to decide, and volatile elements within the Kingdom of Hedorah that needed to be bent to a single temper. The longer that the rival elements continued to think that their own wills and their own schemes were the proper course of action, the harder it would be to focus that will to Marlae's ultimate agenda when the time came for it. Terrance Aldora had returned to the chair opposite the bed on the far side of the room, while the new arrival, Anabel Binosear sat in the larger chair close to the bed. Isabella remained standing by the door waiting for an indication as to what she should do next. Marlae didn't notice Isabella's discomfort immediately, but eventually her mind caught up and she smiled to herself. Isabella was going to be good for her, that much was obvious. Her value was clear, and it was time to make the girl aware of exactly what that value was.

"The four of us, represent the beginning of my council, and though I cannot begin to think how we will craft this new government, we have the mandate of the Creator, and we have the Creator's own angels to lead my armies. But that does not solve the greater problem."

"The greater problem?" Terrance asked.

Instead of the Divine Empress responding, it was the mysterious Anabel Binosear.

"The greater problem is that even with divine mandate, Marlae here is a woman with a bad reputation among the people, a worse reputation among the nobles, no leadership or combat experience, and the previous attempt at rebellion ended up with the Heart of the Stone falling in battle with damage that had never been seen in the structure's history. None of the royals are simply going to lie down and turn their kingdoms over to Marlae, no matter what mandate she says she has. There are bargains that need to be made, and her posture for bargaining is weak to say the least."

Terrance was shocked and slightly appalled. Not only did this woman call the Divine Empress by her first name and not her title, but she also had the audacity to question not only the Empress's abilities but also the divine mandate of the Creator. He could not hold his tongue any longer.

"Your Grace, forgive me, but who is this woman to be questioning your abilities, your motives, or the mandate of the Creator? How can she show you such disrespect by using your name and not your title? It's disgraceful bordering on insulting."

Marlae raised her hand and did her best to quiet Terrance's discomfort.

"Though I have never met Lady Binosear before this evening, I know her credentials and her experience well. It is her frank appraisal of my abilities as well as her insight into the needs of a capable ruler that will make her invaluable in the weeks and months ahead. She has seen rulers come and go, of all shapes and kinds. I cannot go into this with my eyes closed thinking that my reputation means nothing. I cannot proceed on the notion that simply because the Creator has touched me means that those who value gold above blessings will simply bow to me out of their better natures. Please, Anabel, go on."

Anabel nodded.

"As I said, bargaining will be difficult. What is it that you have to offer? You have no great treasury like your father does. Even were Lordhill willing to support you, you have no means of securing it without taking Aldere. You have no military strength to barter with, either for mutual defense pacts, or to defeat rival kingdoms. The only natural resources that you have are the foundries and shipyards, but without forests and mining, eventually the hammers will fall silent. All you will have are the ships that have been produced, but with no experienced crews to man them. There is only one commodity that you have to offer."

Marlae grimaced.

"How did I know that was going to become a topic of conversation? Alright, we might as well get this out in the open. I don't care how my ancestors did it, but I will not under any circumstances prostitute myself for the sake of a treaty, an army, or a crown. I will marry for one reason only; I will marry for love."

Terrance smiled, but Anabel's face remained passive.

"That is all well and good, Marlae, but there are other ways. And I applaud you for acting like a grown-up for the first time in your life. You have started to name your advisors and that is a start, but your rule will not be respected as a leader if you don't act like a leader. Who is your high councilor? Who will ensure that the business of the Empire will continue to run regardless of what happens? In the days of your forefathers, a member of the family would take the position. One of the reasons that your father has become such an unstable ruler is that he pushed away every opportunity he had for assistance. His Voice, his High Councilor was nothing more than a puppet that could do nothing but spew his hatred. You must name a High Councilor that will convey trust, that will convey confidence, and will be willing to argue with you when necessary. The High Councilor cannot be beholden to you. There is a place for lackeys, but that cannot be the role of those whom your truly wish to help you rule."

Marlae kept her eyes focused on Anabel.

"How could I find anyone more willing to argue with me than you, Anabel? You come to me highly recommended, and I can think of no one who has better credentials to serve in the capacity of High Councilor. I know it is a bit of a step down from the type of position you are used to holding, but perhaps in time, when more kingdoms have given their loyalty to me, I can invest you as the Lady of a Kingdom once more."

Anabel stood, smoothed her dress, and curtseyed low.

"My time of ruling is done, Your Grace, but I would be doing a disservice to everything I was raised to believe in if I were to refuse your offer. I shall gladly fulfill the role of High Councilor, until I am dead, or until you have found someone more fit to serve you."

Anabel returned to her seat, and immediately felt Terrence's eyes upon her. She knew what his question was, what his concern was.

"It's an old oath," Anabel answered the silent question, "one that dates to a time before this world to a kingdom that once was ruled by the strength of the Lion. Those who served him had no lineage, had no claim to authority, but were trusted with such power. They would give the ruler their oath, to serve him, to love him, and to honor him, no matter the cost or the trial, until their death, or until they could no longer serve their purpose and someone was found to replace them. Over time the oath was simplified and radiated out from the Lion's direct followers to every man who could hold a sword that served in his army. He was a beloved ruler, a trusted general, and perhaps one of the greatest heroes his world had ever seen. Men served him and his grace because they wished to, not because they were forced to by any type of mandate, divine or otherwise. He was a man, a good man, and was due the honor shown him. Marlae should be due that same honor, but only if she shows honor to those who wish to serve her."

Marlae nodded and turned her attention to Isabella who was still standing at the door. The girl had done well to keep her mouth shut, and to keep her ears open. It was a talent that Marlae intended to put to good use.

"Isabella, please approach. I wish to ask your opinion of things."

The girl moved tentatively across the floor and went to one knee, her head bowed. She was still getting used to being noticed by anyone, let alone someone in a position of power.

"Isabella," Marlae said quietly, "how do you feel about what has occurred?"

Isabella remained silent, looking at the floor. She heard the question and understood, but didn't have the first clue how to answer. Finally Isabella raised her head and looked Marlae in the eye. There had been a point in her life, probably right up until that moment, when she should not have dared to be so brazen. However, the Isabella she had been, the ignored and terribly shy servant girl, was no longer needed if she intended to serve this Divine Empress.

"I wish I knew how to make sense of all of this your Grace. We are taught that those who are of royal blood are our betters, that they make decisions that affect the life and death of thousands. And that their lives are so important and have so many responsibilities that they could never possibly notice those who are lowborn. But now, kneeling here, knowing that you are wishing for me to speak with you and share with you my thoughts, I am overwhelmed. I was never reared in the teachings of the Creator, nor was I taught to worship His name. But that does not mean that I do not fear the gods and angels that walk in this place."

Marlae blinked softly.

"Why do you fear them, Isabella?"

Isabella hesitated for a long moment before responding.

"In the time that they have been in Hedorah, I have walked by the angels many times. I have felt the power bristling across their wings, the heat of the divine fire from their burning blades. No matter whom they claim to serve, they are terrible creatures possessed of terrible power. That power will not be restrained when the time comes. And though they serve you now, Empress, they truly serve the Creator. How can you trust such power when it does not truly serve you?"

Marlae's satisfied smile beamed. She turned her attention back to Terrance.

"You see Terrance. There is value in listening to all people, regardless of their status. Isabella chooses to be honest with her Empress, a quality that very few have. The ability to speak truth to power is rare, and perhaps the most valuable commodity that anyone could ever have. For Anabel it is easy. She has been in power; she has lived in the halls of it for her entire life. For Isabella it is different. Depending upon her words and whom she speaks them to, it could mean the very end of her life. So despite that, despite the danger to her life and welfare, she has put her life in my hands, her faith in me, and has done me the honor of telling me the truth. That, Terrance, that is what I need to make this new Empire a reality. Not the old foundations of lies and patronage. Not the system that was corrupted by its own power. No, the only way forward is to remove the stigma of the past. To forge a new way, a new doctrine by which not only the common people will live, but also how the royalty lives and treats those whom they have providence over. There must be a new doctrine of faith that permeates all levels of life and being. More than just worship of the Creator and adherence to his laws. It must be a dedication to the betterment of all within Cadaria. And it must come from us, not from the Creator's words, not from the booming voice of a Servant, and certainly not at the point of an angel's flaming sword. The voice must be mortal, and all mortals must benefit from that voice."

Anabel applauded softly which was quickly echoed by Terrance. But Marlae's glance did not leave Isabella. There was more that she intended for the young woman, so much more.

"Isabella, you have walked these halls, and you have seen naked power. In the days to come, you will be my eyes and ears within the walls of this palace. There is no rumor, no innuendo, and no half-spoken conspiracy that you will not ferret out for me. An Empress can only rule as effectively as the information she has. My father had the whole of the Shadow Guild at his command, and his only thought was how to use that power to eliminate his rivals and to keep himself in power. I too would use information to keep myself in power, but not at the expense of others. I must embrace all that claim to serve me, whether those claims be proved or not. There may be times perhaps that such information will lead to uncomfortable choices, but I would rather have options than to have them forced upon me. You shall enlist others of your station in life, but a small number, those who you can trust absolutely. These Eyes will report to you, and you will report to me. No matter who it is you recruit, you may not inform them it is at my behest. If they must have a name, give them Terrance's name as he is ultimately in charge of this palace's security, no matter what role Ayden may take. Do you understand and accept this charge I give to you?"

Isabella remained on her knee and bowed her head.

"I would be honored, your Grace. If there is anything that I can do to benefit you and this new Empire, than I shall. You need only ask, and it shall be done. For now I shall be your eyes and ears, I shall make sure that you have all information that you need, no matter how difficult it may be to acquire. I shall hold this position until I am dead, or until you have found someone to take my place. I give you this oath willingly, and I shall keep it in the same fashion."

Marlae could not help but smile.

"Then rise, Isabella, my Mistress of Secrets. You have joined my circle of advisors, but never openly. Aside from this group here, everyone in the palace shall know you as my loyal chambermaid, and you shall comport yourself as such. I know that the position comes naturally to you, and it must continue to be as natural to you as breathing. There is too much to risk otherwise."

Marlae placed her hand on Isabella's shoulder and the woman finally rose back to her feet and returned to the place where she had stood by the door. Relaxing back in her chair, Marlae sighed. Exhaustion was starting to creep into her bones and muscles. She looked first to Terrance and then to Anabel.

"I will introduce Anabel to the others in the morning, but there is one final order of business that I wish to make clear. I shall not be appointing a Court Sorceress. That position has already been filled. For me to go back on that word now would undo everything that I stand for. It would tarnish my name and the new reputation I hope to build. The rest shall fall into place as it must. Terrance, please arrange for a meeting of the war council for first thing in the morning. There is much that must be addressed if we are to stem the tide of madness that wants to crush Cadaria under its weight. It is time to see just how much authority I have. Also, make sure that Anabel is well bestowed. She deserves the best."

Terrance and Anabel rose almost in unison and bowed to Marlae, though Anabel's bow was much shallower and certainly for show only. The thought of Anabel bowing to Marlae must have amused the woman almost as much as it amused Marlae. When they ushered themselves out of the room, Marlae was left alone with her thoughts. She felt pride in her words of the evening, but wondered and feared as to whether or not she could live up to them. Her thoughts drifted to Rhain and to Gabriel and how much she longed to have them both at her side during these trials. She may have been trying to re-forge herself in the divine fires that surrounded her, but no matter the heat or the pressure, it would not change the deepest parts of her heart. In that place, she loved Rhain, and she loved Gabriel. What those loves were, what form they took and ultimately what they meant were still a mystery to her, but Marlae would continue to hold on to those emotions as long as she could. In the dark days ahead, they would be her guiding light, and her reason to continue to push on. She had made a promise to never lose her way again. To never put her own interests above the interests of those whose very lives rested on her words and deeds. But in the same turn, she could never abandon or betray her heart. What good would the promises of compassion and care be if she sacrificed the very part of her that made those promises matter? As Marlae sat in the darkness she realized that living the life of a selfish spoiled princess was so much easier than walking the path of a righteous woman. That Marlae, that flawed self-absorbed Marlae was dead, and she hoped that the new Marlae had the strength to truly live in the light.

* * * * * * * * * * * *

When Marlae entered the war room, the argument looked as though it had been in full swing for quite some time. Terrence had ensured that Reverend Mother Amallia, Azure, and Ayden had arrived several minutes before the Divine Empress would make her entrance, and she had to admit that it pleased her to watch the whole room pause, mid argument, and turn to the door and fall to one knee in deference to her. Before her transformation, it would have felt as though the entire world should act this way, that it was her birthright as the sole inheritor of the Cadarian Empire. But this was different, and the fact that the angelic guards in the room made no move at all reinforced that. She was in a tenuous position to say the least. With the wave of one hand, she dismissed Isabella, much to her chagrin, and moved into the room with Anabel Binosear at her back. Isabella would not go far, standing just outside the door waiting to be summoned as someone in her perceived position should. Anabel stood a pace behind Marlae and when the Divine Empress beckoned everyone to rise, she made eye contact with each and every person in the room. There was understandable puzzlement on Amallia's face, and acknowledgement on the face of the Will. But the look in Azure's eyes could not have been called anything other than contempt. Marlae moved quickly through the room to her chair and sat, with Anabel keeping her position at Marlae's side. When everyone turned to face the Divine Empress, Marlae spoke.

"In keeping with some of the traditions of my forefathers, I have a number of internal policies and decrees that will be in effect starting this morning. First and foremost, is that Anabel Binosear will be from this moment forward, the High Councilor to the Divine Empress of Cadaria."

Anabel held her position and made no move except for a curt and somewhat mocking nod in Azure's direction. This caused Azure to take a step forward and speak.

"With all due respect, Divine Empress, I believe you are making a grave error by having this woman with a cursed name at your side. Her family name is a scourge upon the Heavens and uttering it should be considered blaspheme."

Azure's words were met by a sly grin from Anabel. Though Marlae wanted to scoff, she kept her tone even and her face without expression.

"Reverend Mother, is there anything in the sacred texts to support this claim that the name Binosear is cursed and should never be uttered?"

Before Amallia could answer, Azure's face turned red, and he practically yelled.

"You would take the word of a mortal over the word of a god? How do you expect to rule this world without the input of the Heavens? How do you expect to fulfill the position that the Creator has given you if you will not follow the mandate of Heaven?"

Ayden's jaw tightened and he fingered the hilt of the blade that was strapped to his hip. This caused the angels at both doors to tense. At that moment Azure realized that he had raised his voice, but he was too arrogant and confident to back down. After a moment Marlae returned her attention to Amallia.

"I'm waiting for your answer, Reverend Mother."

Amallia bowed slightly.

"I have studied the sacred texts every day from the moment I could read, your Grace, and never in all of my readings have I ever seen the name Binosear or read any interpretation that recognizes that name as blaspheme or anything else."

Marlae continued, her eyes never leaving Azure.

"And would the lessons being taught at the Heart of Stone agree with your interpretation?"

Amallia nodded her ascent.

"None of my readings or interpretations varies from those spoken by the High Priestess or any other member of the Church of the Creator."

Marlae then directed her words back to Azure.

"Do you intend to share any of these new revelations to the sacred texts, Azure? Who will carry the new words of the Creator to everyone who has studied the sacred texts their entire lives as Amallia has done? Would not the newly minted Divine Empress, touting to be serving the will of the Heavens look dubious arriving to rule with new sacred texts in hand that speak of blasphemes and demons? Would I not look like my father who instead of outlawing worship of the Creator is altering it to fit my own needs?"

Azure's features were unreadable.

"The sacred texts by many are considered the Word of the Creator, and as such are immutable. Those are the words that the mortals as you call them are familiar with, and therefore are the ones we must use to keep them faithful. Whatever your personal grudge with the Binosear family does not have a place here. Do we understand each other, Azure?"

Finally the god relented.

"Of course, your Grace. My only thought is to protect you from danger."

Marlae waived a dismissive had.

"Of that I have no doubt, Azure. Anabel will serve at my right hand as my Voice. She will be afforded the proper level of deference, and when I am not in the room, she will speak with all of my authority."

Marlae waited for several moments before continuing.

"Reverend Mother Amallia, has there been any word from Albitonin as to the fate of Hannah Ironheart? Has the Church of the Creator named a new High Priestess?"

Amallia tried her best to keep the frown from her face.

"Lady Ironheart has not been heard from since her disappearance after the Fall of the Heart of Stone. It is a great worry for the people of Albitonin. But in her final few days before the Fall, Lady Ironheart took steps to invest a new High Priestess. It was one of her disciples that had been with her since her infancy. The new High Priestess's name is Baeata Catrinel. She has yet to make any public statements and I know from correspondence that she struggles with Kaitain Lorien's decrees. There is much fear in the hearts of the faithful."

Marlae nodded.

"Ayden, you will take Reverend Mother Amallia to Albitonin to meet with this High Priestess Catrinel. Amallia, invite the High Priestess here for a conversation. I wish to have the Church of the Creator at my side in these days to come, and if the Heart of Stone can do without her for a day or two, it would please me. However, if she is unable to break away from her duties to meet with me here, then I shall come to her."

Amallia bowed.

"But tell her this as well," Marlae continued, "if I am forced to come to Albitonin to meet with her, it shall not be a quiet appearance. I shall walk down the center of the city, flanked on each side with angels. I shall walk up the steps of the Heart of Stone, and walk into its largest chapel during high mass, and I shall announce myself. Ask her what would happen then. Ask her if that is how she would want her tenure as the High Priestess to end."

Anabel leaned down and whispered something in Marlae's ear. Marlae could not keep the smile from her face.

"Very good. Tell her also, Amallia that you will take up the position as High Confessor in service of the Divine Empress. You shall be my chief advisor on matters relating to the Church of the Creator and the actions of the faithful. No one in the history of the Empire has held such a position, and that I believe has caused an unnecessary division between the Throne and the Church. We can have no such divisions in the days to come."

Amallia fell to her knees.

"You honor me far beyond my place, Divine Empress. I shall not fail you."

Marlae motioned for Amallia to rise.

"We shall attend to your formal ordination upon your return. But for now, that oath will do."

Marlae rose, and all fell to one knee save Anabel and the angelic guards.

"This last before I leave the remainder of this meeting to my High Councilor. Let it be heard from every herald that spreads the news of my rule. I offer a general amnesty for all surviving members of the Knights of the Flashing Blade. Hedorah will be a safe haven for them, and no action will be taken against them for deeds done in my father's name. If they would serve me, I will find positions for them. And send an envoy to the royal palace of Iltorp. Tell them that the Divine Empress of Cadaria will be coming, and it is up to them whether I come in peace or with a flock of angels and an army at my back."

Legacy of a Lion

Year Eight of the Just Emperor Ender "Just Hand" Lorien, Creator's Calendar Year 1790

Leonora awoke with a start, feeling the cold water dripping across her forehead. As usual, Cedric had awoken before her and also as usual, Leonora had overslept. Over the years, Cedric had continued to find interesting ways to awaken her, and this morning's choice was an overhanging limb that had collected rain from the night before. The collected rain water was still cold from the evening before, and made for perfect motivation to return to wakefulness. Though they slept outside most evenings Leonora had not shaken the habit of wearing only a short nightshirt that only covered to her navel, and as she jumped to her feet away from the heavy blankets, she immediately felt the cold crisp wind on her exposed skin. Winter was approaching, and it was thick in the air. There was a wry smile on Cedric's face, one that Leonora had come to know as amusement, and she crossed the distance between them quickly, punching him with mock fury in the middle of his chest. She knew he would already be wearing his simple armor, so to hit him any harder than she did would cause her more injury than it would him. He pulled her to him after a moment and held her close. After a long moment his arms relented, and he took a half step back.

"Get dressed, Leah," he said sharply, but without intending to be harsh, "lessons this morning."

Leonora gave her best annoyed smile.

"You are more demanding than any teacher I ever had," her look changed to something akin to the soft and seductive looks she would see her friends give to boys, "but at least they are more rewarding."

The look brought a wider smile to Cedric's face and he could not stifle a laugh.

"I'm sure fighting in that lack of dress would garner some distraction, Leah, but in the end, discipline wins out over passion."

The words made Leonora feel more naked than she truly was, and she rushed to find and put on her clothing. Cedric realized almost instantly that his words had not contained the humor that he intended, and he had to keep reminding himself that Leonora was still very young and did not even have the same amount of experience that he had at her age. Despite her upbringing, she had many of the traits of common girls her own age. She was strong, passionate, but still wandering through the world without the slightest idea of what lay ahead of her. But Cedric intended to change all of that. Every day was spent with one manner of lesson or another, all focused on giving her the ability to see past her own limitations; to make tomorrow a goal and not a formality. When he was finished with her, she would be able to see tomorrow and yesterday as they were intended to be, words that held more opportunity than meaning. He watched as she fumbled with the ties of her simple armor. He had procured for her a simple shirt of light chainmail, but for sparring and lessons, she did not like to wear it. No matter how many times he told her that the more she wore it the more she could make the armor part of herself, she ignored him, preferring the reinforced leather that they had made together. Though Cedric didn't have the talent of master armor smiths, he did know enough to make functional pieces, or to repair those that he had. At times he would barter his skills as armorer, blacksmith, or weapon smith for food and lodging, but since he and Leonora had been traveling together, those times were few and far between. Most nights they would sleep out under the stars, and Cedric would hunt and gather for their meals.

Leonora had never liked hunting, had never enjoyed the idea of taking the life of one creature to serve the needs of another, but hunting with Cedric was different. He did not so much hunt as he did feel the wind and the ground. Together they would sit in silence, listening to the wind as it whipped around them, waiting to hear the movements of a rabbit or a deer. At first she didn't believe him when he said that he could hear the heartbeat of the animal nearby, but in time, she too could hear it. She could close her eyes and see the movement of the creature, knew where it was, where it would be, and how long between the two. At first Cedric allowed her to use a bow, first sighting with her eyes, and then finally sighting with just what she heard and felt. Before long she was taking down deer and rabbits at a full run from hundreds of yards away with her eyes closed. But then Cedric taught her to use only a dagger, which required new types of lessons. Sneaking, using the wind to disguise her scent, using the shadows to mask her approach, the moment before the strike when she had to quiet her heart to prevent detection and to steady her hand. What she thought were simply survival skills eventually were folded into her combat training. Cedric always taught her that the first thing that created defeat was the inability to control one's heart. The less one was able to control that, the more likely it was to betray at the moment of truth. Cedric spoke often of opponents that he had fought who never had to worry about the beat of their heart, whether it would race, or beat so loud that it obscured all sound. He called them the most ruthless and efficient killers that he had ever known. In time he taught her their names, and her eyes were opened to the wonders and terrors of the abilities of the people that Cedric called the phasia. He respected them greatly.

Once Leonora was dressed and ready, Cedric recovered a thin-blade rapier with a simple basket. She had seen the weapon before but had never held it. He had said that when she was ready to learn her true lessons, it would be there for her. He held it gently in his hands, and slowly approached her. Finally Cedric extended the blade to Leonora. She didn't know why, but she hesitated before reaching out with her right hand to take hold of the hilt of the sword. The fine golden mesh of the basket was not as ornamental as some of the rapiers she had seen in her time, but it was not as simple as the solid steel guards either. It was fine workmanship to be sure. Taking the blade finally from Cedric, she held it out in front of her as Cedric had taught her, testing its weight. She was surprised at how light it was, how responsive to her every move. Even the moves she did not intend, a subtle shiver or spasm of the muscle would cause the blade to miss its target. Leonora understood why Cedric had waited so long to give her this blade. It would require the use of every lesson of control and patience he had ever taught her. This weapon was not as clumsy as a broadsword or as demanding of strength as a claymore. It was an agile weapon, more like a dagger, but as deadly as a spear at range.

"In my land, that weapon was known as a Hornet's Needle. Only the most skilled sword masters would carry such a blade. In battle it was formidable as it could seek even the smallest gap in the heaviest and most well-made armor. This one has been called Heartseeker, or Throatripper. For you, it is today's lesson. Now, take a stance."

Leonora regarded the sword once more before sinking back into one of the practiced defensive stances that Cedric had taught her. She kept all the weight on her back foot, with her front foot just barely touching the ground. Her left hand she kept raised, at the height of her chest, while her right she held at the level of her hip, the blade of the sword jutting outward from there at a slight incline. The stance felt good, but not quite natural. She knew from her lessons that this stance favored a light weapon that had some range to it, but the weapon seemed almost too light. As though Cedric was reading her thoughts, he smiled and nodded.

"Do you feel how the weight of the blade unbalances you? This is not like any weapon you have ever held, and to use a common stance robs the weapon of the properties that make it special. This is true of weapons, of armor, and of people. Knowing what makes them special allows them to be used to their best effect. In turn, knowing what makes your opponent special can mean the difference between living and dying. No opponent is beyond you, and you are beyond no opponent unless you think it is so. Anyone can be defeated, and thus anyone can defeat you. Understand this. Give yourself over to it, and embrace it."

Leonora couldn't take all of the words in, and before she could form even the first intelligent question, Cedric's hands were on her. Whenever he touched her, even in correcting her posture or her stance, she would lose her concentration. She knew it was silly, and she knew he would chide her for it, but it did not change the fact. His hands first went to her hips, twisting her so that her sword shoulder was away from her opponent, and also changing the distribution of her weight so that it was more even between her feet. Her left arm he lowered to the level of her waist, while her right he pulled up to the level of her shoulder. Standing behind her he put his head to hers, and together they looked down the length of the blade.

"The rapier is an extension of your arm, but also an extension of your eye. Treat the rapier like an arrow ready to leap from the string of a bow. Keep it here, at your shoulder, primed and ready to strike precisely at your target. You will score no lucky strikes with a rapier of this quality. Use your cunning, use your vision, find the weaknesses to exploit. Keep your weight moving between your front and back foot, do not settle. When your feet become heavy, your arm becomes slow. Control your breath, control your heart, like you do with a bow. With this weapon you are a snake, needing but one piece of exposed skin to sink your fangs. You have the speed for these precise strikes, but unlike other swords, you cannot block the blows of heavier weapons. An ax or a heavy broadsword will break your weapon on most strikes. You can parry, using momentum and weight to move around blows. The rapier is a dancer's weapon."

Leonora could not help but smile.

"I can't picture you dancing."

Cedric laughed despite himself.

"Which is why I don't use a rapier."

Before Leonora could retort, Cedric pulled away and took up a position opposite her, drawing his own heavy broadsword and taking up a dueling position.

"Tell me what you see."

She sized Cedric up in a split second, but she tried hard not to rely on information she already knew. That was one of his earliest lessons when they were dueling. No matter how many times you face an opponent, treat it as though it were the first time. You can learn tendencies and tactics, but relying on them once swords are crossed will leave you open to the unexpected. You will unconsciously eliminate possible tactics, and you will not see the strike that kills you before it's far too late. Familiarity can breed complacency.

"Your weight is on your back foot. You'll be slow your left side because of the way you hold your blade. But your sword is heavier than mine, I can't block, I have to move and parry. But you're not wearing heavy armor. Its light and flexible, meaning even with your increased sword weight, you can move and counter faster than most. But your throat is exposed. That would be a prime target. Your first strike should be to your right, crossing hard so that you can close the distance and use your strength. If I'm fast enough, I should be able to counter left and have a shot at your neck or shoulder. Or if you close faster than you can control, I can spin away and aim for your inner thigh or knee."

Cedric was on her before she knew what was happening. He moved faster than it should have been possible for him to move, bringing the flat of his blade down hard on the back of her hand, causing her to drop her blade. His next move brought his sword to her throat. His eyes held hers for a long moment before he stepped back and sheathed his sword. Though she was irritated with what had occurred, she bent down and recovered her blade. She was fuming on the inside and could not help but let it show in her eyes.

"You think it was unfair?"

Leonora nodded without a word.

"Why?"

Leonora looked down at the ground and then back up at Cedric.

"Because you made me think we were going to duel. That you were teaching me how to use a new weapon."

The left side of Cedric's mouth twisted into a smirk.

"So I cheated. I used the abilities that I had to win the duel. But you knew I had those abilities. You knew I could move faster and hit harder. Why didn't you factor that into your answer?"

Leonora frowned.

"You asked what I could see."

Cedric nodded.

"Yes, I did."

Suddenly Leonora understood. She reached back into the back of her mind and found the softly flickering green flames that Cedric had taught her about. He had called it the Blaze, and said that it would make the difference between her living an ordinary life, and learning to make that which was inside of her extraordinary. It took some effort, but eventually she was able to touch the bright and fickle flame, letting its power rush through her like a great wave. When she reached for it now, she let it fill her mind. Her eyes opened, and she could see the wreaths of green fire around Cedric's body. He had filled himself with the Blaze and channeled it into his legs and hips, greatly increasing his speed and agility. Had she not been so focused on the moment, she would have used those lessons to see how he had manipulated her. He knew that she would fail his test. He had distracted her with his touch, with the pretty new weapon, with the talk of tactics and strategy, and that had made her forget his first lesson. Never forget that what you are capable of is more important than anything your opponent may do. You must always know your limits, your limitations, and use all of your abilities to the fullest, for if you do not, then it gives your enemy something to exploit.

When he saw her eyes narrow with frustration, he approached her and put his hand on her shoulder and looked deeply into her eyes.

"Leah, I'm not training you to fight ordinary men. You are a match now for even the best sword masters on this world. I'm training you to fight against monsters. Monsters like me. Monsters that shake the world around them and thrive on blood and death. You will have to stand against those that know no fear, that have known no challenge for thousands of years, and can kill with a single wave of their hand. This is the legacy that I leave you with, Leonora. This is the trial that stands before you. When your training is complete, you shall make those monsters know fear. You shall use their own weapons against them. You were not touched by the

Creator. You were not touched by one of His Children or one of His Servants. It is your mortal blood and your mortal birth that make you special. It's alright to be afraid, Leah. Just don't let that fear ever rule you, or turn you into the monsters that you fight against. That was my failing, and one I will make sure you don't repeat. Now, let's try it once again."

Leonora tried her best to process the words, but she could not. She had always known that Cedric's lessons were for something more than living a life at his side. He often spoke of the war that was coming, the last great war that would consume the whole world. But no matter his conviction, no matter his pride, there was always a darkness that held him. In the deepest parts of the night, when he slept, he still mumbled and cried out. One night, listening and watching as he slept she came to the sudden realization; he was not her salvation, she was his. She would not fail him again.

* * * * * * * * * * *

Year Four of the Just Emperor Kaitain "Dragonsbane" Lorien,
Creator's Calendar Year 1871

Leonora Wastri awoke with a start. She knew she had been dreaming, and though it had been a good dream born out of a memory, her mind was not comforted. She tried to sit up, but felt the pain radiate through her. Suddenly the memory of the battle outside the Academy of Arcane Arts in Jelan started to flood back to her mind. She had fought against men, knights, monsters, gods, and dragons, and still she drew breath. Her body ached from head to toe, but for the first time in many years she felt whole.

"You should be careful," a woman's voice said from the doorway. "It took quite some time to bandage all of your wounds, and even with your accelerated healing it will take a few days before you are at full strength again. I did what I could, but healing was never my forte."

Leonora looked to the woman standing in the doorway and was immediately aware of her identity through the Blaze. Her red hair and brilliant eyes were a rarity among the phasia, and her normally white wardrobe brought further attention to those characteristics. Though her features seemed much softer than in those memories.

"I know you," Leonora said, doing her best to get to a seated position. "You're Trece Starlin, the Lady Tiger of the Brotherhood of Phasia."

Trece nodded.

"Very good. It seems your command of the memories of the Blaze has not fled from you during your slumber. I know you as well, Leonora Wastri of the Knights of the Flashing Blade. But it is not our names or our titles that is important now, is it? It is all of the things that the name cannot tell you that should define us. And I certainly know that is true about you."

Leonora instantly did not trust the woman, but there was something about the tenderness in her voice, the earnestness of her nature that Leonora didn't expect. This Trece was a member of the phasia, a ruthless order so violent and self-absorbed that they would kill thousands on a whim. They ground whole kingdoms into dust, and could prey on human weakness as easily as breathing. But then Leonora remembered that there was something different about the twin phasia Rael and Trece Starlin. They had walked away from the phasia, turned their back on their duties as nightmares of man. Instead they chose to live simply, to live together, and to be at peace. Those were qualities that demanded respect. Leonora had always been taught that one was not defined by who they were alone. Who they were was just a factor, no different than who they are or who they will be. Being able to see into the soul of the person and the deeds that they had done gave the true measure of their humanity.

"You have some powerful friends, Leonora," Trece said, coming a few steps closer, "and that more than anything is why you are still alive. So many did not return from that battlefield, including several of my own children. And yet, you still live."

Leonora could feel the pain resonating from Trece's voice, a pain that Leonora knew could not be quantified. But there was something under the pain, something that Leonora could not put her finger on.

"I'm sorry for your loss," Leonora said, trying to sound as earnest as she could. "I've never lost family, but I've lost someone I loved. Though I know that nothing can measure up to the loss of a child. Whatever quirk of fate has led to my survival, I thank you for your hospitality and for your mending of my wounds. But I would like to know why you saved me. Before today we had not set eyes on each other, and everything inside of me tells me that we should have been enemies. You were in Jelan for the Academy, as was I."

Trece sat on the bottom edge of the bed, away from Leonora and looked into her eyes.

"We were invited," Trece said quietly, "unlike the armies of the Moonstone Knight, and unlike the Jade Army. We were invited to help preserve the Academy's neutrality. To keep it from being compelled to be a weapon by either Kaitain or Marlae Lorien. And yet, you fought against the Moonstone Knight, turning your back on one of your own in favor of what?"

Leonora could not hold Trece's gaze. So much of that battle was jumbled in her mind. Bernhardt had given her no choice. He served Kaitain Lorien, and the Academy could not be allowed to fall into the Emperor's hands. Leonora had not wanted it to come to a fight, but Bernhardt made that impossible.

"Not that it mattered in the end," Trece continued. "Talisia and her dragons saw to that. Luckily Jerah arrived. Though I am sure you are shocked to hear that I was relieved that one of Dorovar's chosen proved to be our salvation. But Jerah saved not only the two of us, and our remaining children, but also ensured that you were not left to die on the battlefield."

Leonora looked up, and suddenly felt like a little girl once again.

"Why would Jerah care about me?"

Trece smiled.

"Jerah was once very fond of your mentor. One might even say that she loved him, if Caris could have loved in those days. But it was never to be. Cedric had a destiny, and that destiny would not allow love to find a new place in his heart. He became a hard and broken man, and it was that dedication that caused him to stray from the path of a hero. But let it never be said that Cedric was not a good man. So, in recognition of what Cedric was, and what he tried to impart in you, Jerah wanted to make sure you were protected, and that we conveyed you to someone that can help you make sense of your new place in this world."

Leonora tried to sit up straighter.

"Cedric always said that he trained me to fight monsters. Monsters like him. I never believed that he was a monster. I never believed that those things were really as dire as he made them sound. But seeing you. Seeing Jerah. Seeing the dragons and that Talisia. It's all true isn't it? The Dark Gods, the Creator, the Servants, the war. It's all just the way Cedric taught me, isn't it?"

Trece patted Leonora's leg through the covers in a very maternal way, and tried to smile her best smile despite the tears forming in the corners of her eyes.

"Cedric taught you to be everything he wanted to be. Everything he thought he should have been before he was dragged down by our treachery. It was one of us that set him on his path, and that is why she saved you."

Trece stood and came closer to Leonora, helping her back into a prone position.

"You need rest," she said pulling the covers back up around Leonora. "In the morning you will feel stronger, and we can talk more. But as soon as you are ready to travel we must take you to see Logan. He'll be able to tell you what comes next. Until then, consider this your home. We are all wanderers here, and in some ways, you are a part of our family."

Though Leonora didn't feel tired, as soon as Trece passed her hand over Leonora's face, her eyes became heavy and she felt as though she could drift off to sleep. There were so many more questions that she wanted to ask, so many more uncertainties that needed resolution. But sleep would not relent, and Leonora found herself fading back into the darkness. The darkness where the man that she loved with all of her heart still waited for her.

Covetous

Year Four of the Just Emperor Kaitain "Dragonsbane" Lorien, Creator's Calendar Year 1871

The Kingdom of Night Galateria earned its name for two reasons, one functional and one more ceremonial. They were both easy to understand, the first could be seen with the eyes, the second would only take understanding the history of how the Kingdom came to be. The Kingdom was founded after the end of the First Shadow War. It was part of the treaty with the Dark Gods that ensured that the creatures fallen from the Heavens would never move against the Cadarian Empire again. Perhaps it was fitting that the kingdom was constantly gripped in a veil of shadows, blocking out the sun for most of every day, only allowing the briefest glimmers. As a swirling black portal opened deep in the wilds outside of the capital city, Pike Rhuiden stepped into a place that suddenly felt very much like the way home should have. He felt as though he was cloaked in night, but that he was seeing the sunlight for the first time in a long time. He had a clear purpose. He had something that he had not had since the destruction of Onea. A plan that was his own. Yes Dorovar told him how to execute the plan, but the plan was his. He would tear down every member of the Children of the Creator, wrap his hands around their throats and watch the light go out of their eyes. Then he would ensure that the Servants of the Creator fell, then Dorovar's other servants, then the warped followers of the Cadarian empire, and then finally, if need be, the other

Dark Gods, before finally taking the fight to the Creator Himself. Death would surround him, and he would be up to his neck in blood. For all of the years he had remained restrained when he could have ended the war in a day, he would now be recognized for the hero he truly was. He would be able to step out of Gwydeon's shadow. He would be able to step out of Logan's shadow. Finally he was able to do things his way.

From the time he had left Aradon with Logan all those millennia ago, he was never able to be his own man. He followed the orders of Aryx Terian, Logan Ranthall, and eventually Korrd Ranthall. But even they were not in control. The monster Emries was secretly pulling the strings from behind the scenes, lying to them with every word and breath. And who had distinguished themselves during the lie that was their quest to destroy Shau-ling? First it was Logan, the so-called savior. After the ordeals at the Island of Mist he returned as a sainted hero, the savior of the world, the man who faced down the demon born of man's nightmares, Shau-ling. But again, it was all lies. Logan wasn't the hero. And neither was Korrd. Korrd was a barely reformed villain who had no choice but to accept his role in the larger narrative, and Logan was a pretender who went through the motions and was lauded for participating in one of the greatest frauds ever committed. Then there was Gwydeon Sandar, the darling of everyone who saw him. Good with the sword, calm-headed, and what everyone thought of when they thought of a hero. A mortal, wading into the depths of darkness with no powers against odds he eventually would be unable to outrun. But that was the old Gwydeon, the Gwydeon that Pike respected. The one that stared down Rael on the Island of Mist and Jeroch in the Hall of Terrors. But that wasn't the Gwydeon that Pike had been reunited with years later. No, this Gwydeon was part angel, part saint and all self-important. The Brother of Angels had replaced the humble young man that Pike had admired. Tainted by the power of the Heavens, the new Gwydeon was nothing but an extension of the will of the Creator, and everything that followed was Gwydeon's fault. He was the one that led the rebellion against Emries. He was the one that forced them to side with Shau-ling. He was the one that practically invited Aerith Seth into their lives and brought their world crashing down around them; he and that spoiled rotten former princess turned queen of his.

However, those petty matters no longer held sway. Onea was dead and gone, and those who were responsible would be brought to justice in Dorovar's crusade, the same way Dorovar would punish those responsible for the death of his world. Now the politics of the Heavens had intruded onto a new world, and the stupid pettiness and jealousy was about to rip apart another world and condemn hundreds of thousands more people to their graves. The Dark Gods were only a means to an end for the Creator and his Children, and yet again Pike was cast in the role of a supporting character, a pawn in another's game. Even when Gwydeon sacrificed himself to keep the peace with the stupid and arrogant Cadarians, Pike was denied true leadership. He was denied the ability to truly show what he was capable of. For thousands of years, across two worlds and the Heavens above, Pike had been involved in battles that would shape the direction of the whole of reality. Most of the time it was not by choice, but by necessity of the situation, and Pike had not sought out the means to become more than the sidekick to greater warriors. But with the new powers that Dorovar had bestowed, and the new clarity of purpose, Pike would be stepping into the light, and not only would Emries be made to pay for what he had done to them all those years ago, but so would the Creator.

Pike looked toward the horizon and spied a small town on the edge of the larger capitol of Galateria. Despite the rage that continued to boil in his heart, Pike could not keep his thoughts from drifting back to the months before the quest that would consume the lives of so many. Before Logan became an outcast vagabond hoping to prove himself to the father of the woman that he loved. Before Gwydeon Sandar became one of the most feared duelists in the world. Before Aryx Terian, Midarin Rice, and Gideon Viruci entered their lives and became more than friends and more than family. Pike was nothing more than a blacksmith's apprentice; spending his days at the forge and his nights at the tavern. He could see himself sitting at a simple wooden table with a flagon of ale in his hand and a song springing from his tongue. In his mind's eye he looked around the room and saw all of his friends, the ones that he loved in a way that he could never put into words. First was Talon, Pike's best friend, harmony in spirit and harmony in song. In the tavern he was so full of life and vigor, but a blink of the eye later, all Pike could see was the young man's body broken and bleeding on the floor of Shau-ling's throne room. A casualty of lies and deception. Eldar Merin, the woman that Pike loved above all others, cut down in the prime of her life for nothing. Lane Toridon was next, a victim of his own loyalty. Loyalty to a friend who would never be able to live up to what was being asked of him.

Logan Ranthall was a fraud. He was nothing more than a paper dragon, an imitation of a savior who could manage nothing more than to wring his hands as all of his friends died around him. His indecision and hatred cost them the lives of two more of their company, Alexander Mealon when Logan had fallen under the charms of Caris, and Talos Berder when he failed during the game of the gods on Mount Tantis. In one version of the story even Pike and Gideon had fallen in Shau-ling's throne room. Gideon when he tried to save Elwyne's life as Lane had, and Pike when Cedric Binosear and Aryx Terian had been revealed as exactly what Pike believed they were all along, traitors. But in true selfish fashion, Logan had put the needs and desires of his own heart above the well-being of those he called friends. The Ranthalls were more important than anyone else. That was why Elwyne had to be saved above all others, that's why Gwillim was pulled away from the final battle, that's why so few walked away from that den of hell. But here on this new world it was the same. The Ranthalls were still making everything difficult. Logan, Korrd, Wolf, Lissa, Mirana, Liara; they were nothing more than irritants to the situation. They would see the whole world burn if only to save themselves. Pike would not allow that to happen, not again. Another world would not be sacrificed for the glory of the Ranthall family.

But the Ranthalls would wait for another day. In time they would all be made to pay for their crimes, and even if it was not directly at Pike's hand, Dorovar would ensure that they would fall one by one. No, Pike's errand was different. Pike was going to take on the Children of the Creator, but this time he needed to make sure he had the upper hand. When he had been mortal he had battled against Emries and Halicon, and when he had been in the Heavens he had crossed swords with Talisia. Even though those battles had been ultimately won, there was a great price to be paid, and the victory was only temporary. If Pike was going to serve his new purpose as Conquest, and advance the goal of the destruction of the Creator and all of his servants, then he needed the power of the dragon's treasures. It would start with two of the dragons that called Galateria home, and then would grow to include others across Cadaria. Once Pike had enough power, he would be able to face down all of the Children and bring them to justice for the death they had caused.

Tracking dragons had proved to be a difficult task for the mortals of Cadaria, and once the so-called Emperor Kaitain Lorien began his war against the beasts, thousands had died in the attempt. While there had been casualties on both sides, the greatest share had been suffered by the underprepared and under-equipped mortals. But their failure would prove to ultimately lead to their redemption. As a quiet breeze began to whip around Pike, he closed his eyes and focused on the land around him. Warmth radiated through him, and Pike tapped into the gift that Dorovar had bestowed upon him. The gentle murmur of the wind changed as the seconds passed, first becoming something akin to a whisper and then finally to a growing cacophony. But there was something else there, something beneath the discordant strains of moaning and the sounds of death brought too soon upon the soul. It was as Dorovar had taught him. There was a song, a beautiful and alluring song. It entered Pike like a cold chill, but once inside burned him as though he had swallowed liquid fire. The song was so sweet and powerful that for a moment Pike felt as though he were going to fall to his knees and weep. Dorovar had allowed Pike to hear the song once, but now, bathed in its purity, Pike knew what Dorovar was fighting for. The beautiful music, the music of the soul, it had to be saved from the Creator. Those poor creatures who had given their lives for nothing had to be redeemed, and that redemption would come as they lifted Dorovar to the Heavens as part of his Chorus of Souls, and gave him the power to topple the worthless Creator that had ignored their pleas at the moment of their deaths.

Now though, Pike listened to the stories of the souls, and used them to learn the location of his quarry. Only a few hundred yards away was the den of one of the murderous creatures that had been breathing since the birth of the Creator's worlds. It was one of the treacherous creatures that had presided over the death of Dorovar's idyllic society, and it was one of the creatures that would not be satisfied until all humans had burned in the fires of their own ignorance. Now, Pike would seek retribution for his new master as well as for all the souls that had been displaced by the overgrown lizard. Following the trail of souls and the voices on the wind, Pike easily found the massive cave that sat in one of the great mountains of Galateria's

Range of Long Shadows. Most of the entrance was obscured by dense hanging moss, and someone who was not looking for it probably would have dismissed it entirely. But as Pike stood looking at the entrance he could see the ghostly apparitions, the forms of the fallen soldiers and common men and women who had been the victims of the monster that dwelled within the cave. They pointed and gestured while crying out in sorrow and pain. Feeling the need for vengeance filling him, Pike pushed through the thick moss and vines and entered the cavern.

Barely three steps into the cavern, the thick smell of smoke and sulfur clung to Pike like oil. It threatened to overtake his senses and send him to the floor of the cavern choking and gasping for air. Perhaps if Pike had been mortal he would have been so easily overwhelmed. But he was not. He was not even a Dark God any longer. He was so much more. Pushing through the haze of noxious gasses, Pike traversed the winding cavern passage until it opened up to a much larger space. Here the sulfur was so thick that it was visible to the naked eye like a veil of yellow particles that floated in the air and coated every surface in the cave. In the center of the chamber, lying on a pile of skulls and bones was the monster known as Agathys Smokespitter. While the creature was not the most massive of the dragons that Pike had ever seen, it was still much larger than Pike, and it could easily hold him fully in the palm of one of its clawed hands. Unlike most dragons, Agathys did not have wings, but that did not mean the beast could not take to the air. Through the sheer force of its undulating serpentine body it could guide itself across the currents of the wind as though it were swimming, and its powerful back legs with their wide base and three thick toes, as big around as Pike was tall, were strong enough to allow the creature to leap high into the air. Agathys' scales were a dark gray with mottling of white splattered across them. A ridge of razor-sharp scales flowed down the center of its back like a fish. Gouts of flame rolled across the dragons body like sweat, and as the dragon breathed, the noxious sulfur it exhaled would catch in the sparks and create massive plumes of smoke. Agathys' aged face turned toward the interloper into its domain, the long horns on the back of its head scratching against the scales of its neck causing more of the sulfur hanging in the air to ignite.

"Another foolish mortal comes to claim my head?" the dragon's deep angry voice thundered. "The arrogance of your breed never ceases to amaze."

The voice was like an assault. The force threatened to knock Pike off his feet, but the stench of the sulfur was greater even than what hung in the air. Pike's stomach lurched, but he concentrated his powers to resist the urge to vomit. The dragon raised its head slightly and turned one malice-filled white eye toward Pike.

"But you're no ordinary mortal, are you? I feel strength in you. Perhaps you will provide a little more entertainment than most of my prey."

Pike's lips curled into a frown.

"Dorovar sends his regards."

The dragon roared and the whole cavern shook with its fury. Pike began to charge, his hands still empty, but several feet before he could reach the dragon, he leapt backwards, avoiding a swipe by one of the dragon's front feet. Again Pike charged, but the dragon was changing positions, bringing its huge tail around for a swipe at the interloper. Pike was able to slide under the blow and when he came back up to his feet, the dragon had incredibly turned fully around again, and Pike found himself nearly crushed by Agathys' massive jaws and razor-sharp teeth. Again Pike leapt backwards, trying to get out of the way of the blow, but Agathys was prepared for the tactic, and it caught Pike it one of its massive hands, and began to crush him. Knowing that he had no time left, Pike channeled all of his power inside of himself, creating massive spikes of stone that burst simultaneously from dozens of points on his body. The sharp stone pierced the flesh of the dragon's hand, and the reflexive recoil from the pain allowed Pike to break free. But freedom was not enough, Pike wanted another measure of the dragon's blood. Pike leapt high into the air and landed atop the dragon's head. Channeling all of his strength, Pike took hold of one of the long horns on the back of Agathys' head and ripped it free from its skull. Thick blood poured everywhere, and the dragon roared in pain and horror, shaking its head and sending Pike soaring through the air back toward the opening of the cavern. When Pike got back to his feet, the angry eyes of the dragon were turned back toward him.

"You shall pay for that impudence! Burn!"

The dragon opened its massive mouth and a burst of white-hot flame hit the air. However, Pike was not prepared for what happened next. Instead of a single coherent stream that Pike could dodge, the flame ignited all of the sulfur in the chamber, turning the whole of the cave into an expanding fireball of such heat and intensity that it engulfed everything. Pike was barely able to erect a defense, but even he was not sure it would hold against the inferno. Once the sulfur had finally burned itself out, the dragon looked to where the mortal had been, expecting to see nothing left but dust. However, out of the bank of smoke the mortal strode, Agathys' horn still clutched in his hands, and only his clothes showing the slightest marks from the fires. Pike was on Agathys a second later, the long horn plunging like a dagger through the center of the dragon's head, stealing its life and extinguishing the fires that still rippled across its body. The dragon's body thrashed and convulsed and Pike held on to the horn that pierced the dragon's head, forcing it down into the cave floor, and then leaping free as the creature went through its final death throes. After one final violent tremor, the last burst of smoke, sulfur, and breath escaped the creature's jaws and its white eyes stared a final violent hatred toward Pike. Ignoring the indignation of the fallen beast, Pike went to his gruesome work, flipping the dragon on its side and then ripping open its chest and exposing its still heart. Ignoring the gore and gushing blood, Pike plunged his hand into the massive organ, and after rooting around for several moments pulled his hand free with a single common looking brass ring clutched in his hand. Though the simple band looked common, from the power that it was radiating, it most certainly was not. Pike wasted no time in slipping the ring onto his finger before turning back toward the entrance of the cave. The taste for blood had filled his heart with a new sense of purpose and a new sense of urgency. The quicker he dispatched the other dragon that Dorovar had targeted, the quicker he could turn his attention to gutting the Children of the Creator. That thought alone filled his mind as the swirling portal opened that would take him to the far side of Galateria, and to his next target.

* * * * * * * * * * * *

As Pike Rhuiden plunged through the small waterfall that hid the entrance to Abysm Nightwalker's lair. Only a few steps into the cave, all light except for a few broken beams that came through minor cracks in the ceiling had been extinguished. From deeper in the caverns, completely obscured by the darkness and the shadows of the chamber, Pike could hear breathing. The deep rhythmic sound shook the ground but the air was still and there was no apparent movement within the shadows. Stopping dead in his tracks, Pike let his voice break the stillness.

"I've come for your treasure, dragon."

Pike waited, but no sound came from the shadows except for the low rhythmic breaths. As the moments passed, Pike's hands balled into fists.

"I've just come from ripping the treasure from the heart of your fellow, Agathys Smokespitter. He put up such a meager fight. You could simply surrender your treasure to me, but I would rather pull your heart out too."

Pike's taunt went without answer, and still the breathing continued. Finally, after several long minutes, a low gravelly voice broke the air. But instead of coming from in front of Pike, the voice seemed to come for every direction all at once. It felt to Pike as though he were surrounded.

"Agathys was old and weak. I'm surprised he lasted this long. But if you think you have enough power to take my treasure from me, by all means. I'll gladly start you on your road to oblivion."

The next sensation that Pike felt was a massive set of claws ripping through his back. Reflexively Pike rolled forward, and as he popped back up to a knee and turned around, he saw nothing, but felt the stream of hot blood streaming from the gaping wound. It took barely a second for the flows of power to knit the wound; however, he did not dare concentrate more power than for a temporary fix. There was a chance that the wound would open again if the combat became strenuous, but better that than losing his head while he was concentrating on healing. The claws flashed out again, this time from Pike's right, ripping through his shoulder and leaving his arm hanging limp and useless at his side. For the briefest moment, Pike thought he saw the flick of a tail running in and out of the shadows, but it was not enough to use as a target. He needed to buy some time.

"Fight me fairly beast!"

The rhythmic breathing answered.

"Why?" the voice whispered from all directions. "Had you the advantage, would you fight fairly against an overmatched opponent. I think not. I know you Pike Rhuiden. I know of your crimes. But you shall account for them here. With blood."

This time the claws came from below Pike, ripping through his leg and driving him down to his knees. From somewhere in front of him, the shadows began to ripple and from the darkness emerged a shape. The dragon's head was sleek, but because of the shadows it was almost impossible to make out a definite shape. All Pike could truly make out was the violet eyes that stared through him. From behind Pike there was a sound, and suddenly the dragon's tail darted out of the nothingness and wrapped around Pike's throat.

"I have ended your petty challenge, boy," the dragon hissed. "You were a fool to tangle with a dragon in his den. I'll be sure to send Dorovar your regards when I rip his head from his shoulders. Let me show you what it will be like."

The tail tightened around Pike's throat and he could feel the muscular appendage begin to pull upward as the dragon tried to rip his head from his shoulders. Reaching into the depths of the new powers that he had received from Dorovar, Pike stretched out his awareness to the spirits of the victims of the dragon. They began to appear, faint and translucent first two then a dozen and then a hundred. The more that appeared, the more the darkness in the cavern began to recede. But Pike was running out of time. The corners of his vision were beginning to darken and his breaths became shorter and shorter. The light from the spirits grew; an eerie green light that pushed back the darkness. One hundred became two hundred. Pike could no longer see anything but the mass of souls pressing in on each other, filling every part of the cavern. Finally when the chamber could hold no more, the green light flared brighter than the sun, burning away all the shadows. The dragon roared in pain, and the pressure around Pike's neck relented. The tail thumped the ground, a reflex reaction to the pain. When Pike's vision cleared, he could see the dark form of the dragon against the back wall of the chamber, its violet eyes squeezed tightly shut, and its claws digging into the dirt. Blind and furious the dragon lurched forward, sending is mass hurtling toward Pike. Filling himself with all of the power he could manage, Pike reached out his hands, and as the two collided, Pike took hold of the dragon's massive neck. The maneuver caused the dragon's body to tumble through the air where it struck the wall of the cavern threatening to bring it down on top of them. But Pike cared little for what would happen next. Instead he put his foot down on the neck of the massive beast and pulled with all of his might. The ripping sound was grotesque in his ears, but in a matter of seconds Pike had succeeded where the dragon had failed, and he had ripped the creature's head free of its body. Blood sprayed in all direction, and soon Pike was covered from head to toe in gore. Another few minutes saw the end of Pike's gruesome deed, and a second ring, this one a brilliant silver graced his hand.

Pike emerged from the cavern and he stood under the flowing waterfall, letting the cool crisp water free his body from the mixture of his own blood and that of his prey. It took little effort now, out of the heat of combat, to heal his extensive wounds, and inwardly he cursed himself for letting the dragon do that much damage. The sound of a pair of clapping hands pulled Pike away from his self-judgment. When Pike looked skyward, he saw only a brilliant light. However, when it receded, the massive form of Gregor Quicksilver, the new Voice of the Creator hovered above him.

"Pike Rhuiden," the former Knight of the Flashing Blade's voice boomed, "Dark God, criminal, harbinger of the abomination known as Dorovar. You have been judged guilty of crimes against the Laws of the Creator and against Creation itself. I am here to make you pay with your blood."

Chapter LXXIX

The Gathering Storm

Year Four of the Just Emperor Kaitain "Dragonsbane" Lorien, Creator's Calendar Year 1871

When Midarin opened her eyes, she wasn't sure whether she was awake or dreaming. Right before her eyes was the man that she loved with all of her heart, the man who she had just recently been reunited with after an eternity of separation. Just beyond him, but still within her field of vision was their only child. At least, that was what Midarin had convinced herself of after all these years. And even though she had just been face to face with a demon wearing her dead son's face, nothing would ever convince her that the twisted puppet that Emries sent to destroy them was her child. Camille was now their only child, touched by a combination of the divine and the tenacity of their mortal lives. She had been born in the Heavens, the first child to have been born there in generations. Her father's nature as the Brother of Angels, a being who was already walking the line between the ascended and mortal worlds blessed her from birth with angel's wings. She had nearly limitless power, like that of the very few gods who had called the Heavens their home from the day of their birth. But all but one of those beings had been destroyed during Talisia's rebellion, and the last had disappeared without a trace. Some said that she too had been killed, but Midarin had always doubted that fact. Beings like Camille, and like Wolf and Lissa's twins were rare and special, and their capabilities seemed at times to be without measure or equal. At this moment though, Midarin didn't see a divine being, or even the limitless potential. All she saw, and all she wanted to see, was her little girl and the reunification of her family. When Gwydeon took her hand and helped her to her feet, all she could do at that moment was envelope him in a long hug. A moment later Camille added her own arms to the embrace and for what seemed like forever the three stood there, complete once more. Midarin knew it couldn't last forever, and tried hard not to feel like something had been broken when Gwydeon finally pulled away. He kissed her gently and then turned his attention to where Felicia was pulling a man out of the rubble. Midarin had seen him fighting during their confrontation with Nathan and the two returned members of the *Erieal* from Onea. He looked vaguely familiar to her, but she could not place him. What was clear was that he was completely in over his head and the fact that he was still alive was more attributable to luck than anything else. In the rubble, she could also see the unconscious forms of Storm and Taya Mystic, two people who should have been long dead. Of course, there was only one thought that kept coming to her mind over and over again, and she could only express that thought in a way that would suit her emotions.

"Would somebody mind telling me what the hell is going on?"

The question brought a smile to Gwydeon's lips, but only briefly. The truth was far too horrible for any prolonged levity. Too much had happened, too much was still to happen, and it was obvious that the end game had begun.

"First thing's first," Gwydeon responded. "Camille, Felicia, make sure that Storm and Taya remain unconscious. As long as they are under Emries' control they'll be a threat. We have to get them to Sabrina as quickly as possible so that she can remove Emries' influence. If the influence can't be removed, we may have no choice but to eliminate them. But that would be my last choice. It's not their fault they've come to this, so they shouldn't be made to suffer unnecessarily."

He then turned his attention to the approaching man.

"And what is a Knight of the Flashing Blade doing out here at the site of one of the greatest massacres in the history of Cadaria?"

Orren Eldrath pulled his shoulders back and stood as straight as he could.

"This is my home," he said, irritation filling his voice. "I grew up here. I played in these streets as a child before I was bundled up and carted off to Jelan. But Rashaleb will always be my home, and I weep for its loss. But you know all about losing your home, don't you, Gwydeon Sandar?"

The statement made Gwydeon clinch his teeth. There was a light in the man's eyes, one that was unmistakable to anyone who had seen as much as Gwydeon had in the days before and after his ascension.

"So, you are the one the old man has cursed," Gwydeon said rubbing his chin softly. "I should have known it wouldn't take Aryx and Diana's souls long to be reunited once they left this world. I can only hope that Midarin and I are as fortunate when our time comes."

Gwydeon's words trailed off as he half-turned away from Orren and back to his wife. It had been so long since they had been together for any extended length of time, and he kept expecting her to disappear. For quite some time he had felt the end coming, and now that it was upon him, he didn't know if he had the strength for what was to come. But he could not change the person that he was. He would face everything head-on as he always had. And perhaps in the end he and Midarin would be able to find some of the peace that Aryx and Diana had carved out for themselves. Now though, there were more important things to attend to than a fragile future. Gwydeon raised his voice so that everyone in the clearing could hear.

"Emries has made his move. It's not going to be like it was on Onea. He's not desperate, and he's not overconfident. He's been preparing for this for a long time, and he waited until we were all off-balance before he struck. He's fighting more like we did back then, covert war with no clear strategy. Which also means that Nathan and Korrd will be on the board for him, as well as anyone who ever carried the powers of the *Erieal*."

Out of the corner of his eye, Gwydeon caught a look between Orren and Felicia. He wasn't sure that they had ever met one another, but the memories and emotions that they had inherited connected them in a way they would never be able to deny. Almost at once, the two spoke.

"Lissa."

A look of horror came to Midarin's face, and when Camille and Felicia returned from ensuring Taya and Storm's slumber, Gwydeon could feel the uncertainty and fear. He shook his head slowly, a great weight descending on his shoulders.

"This is exactly what Emries wanted. He wanted us jumping at shadows, suspecting assassins around every corner. It would make us too cautious and too focused on protecting what we had built. If we were only dealing with Talisia, things would be different. She only knows one way to attack, straight forward. She may try to disguise things and make it seem like more is going on than really is, but in the end her tactics are clear; advance and destroy. But Emries…"

Gwydeon's voice trailed off. He looked around his assembled allies, some new, some old, but all family in one form or fashion. All of the Dark Gods and their progeny would have to be united if they were to win this war, much as they were in the Heavens during Talisia's rebellion. It should have ended there. None of this pain and suffering should have been necessary. But the Creator wanted to prove a point, to everyone, his children and those touched by his children. What that lesson was, no one could yet say. But the implication had become painfully clear. There was only one right answer to this puzzle.

"We hurt Emries," Gwydeon said, his voice thick with his uncertainty and fear, "and now his only aim is to hurt us. Luckily as much as he hates us, there is at least one person he wants dead more than us."

"Aerith," Camille offered.

Gwydeon nodded.

"For now Emries will just be satisfied sending his pawns after us, but if I know Emries anywhere as well as I think I do, all of his focus will be on destroying Aerith, his family, and the remaining *Chosen Ones*. Which means we have old friends in the line of fire."

A sudden light came to Midarin's eyes.

"Logan."

Gwydeon hung his head for a moment.

"Logan has another path. As much as he may want to get his revenge on Emries, he knows that he is on a collision course with Pike. Only one of them will walk away from that confrontation, and that is the only way it could have ended for them. Pike has toiled in darkness for too long, and there is no way back. His chance to turn away from the darkness has come and gone, and people like Pike do not get third chances to do the right thing."

Midarin put her hand on Gwydeon's shoulder.

"I know he was your friend. I can't imagine how hard it will be for Logan considering you all grew up together."

Gwydeon tried his best to force a smile.

"Our friend died on Onea," Gwydeon answered curtly trying hard not to sound cold, "the thing that wears his face now is a monster, like the creature that Emries is calling our son."

Before he would let the gravity of the situation or the conversation drag them all down, Gwydeon cleared his throat and turned to Camille.

"The priority is to nullify any of the weapons that Emries has at his disposal. We have to get Storm and Taya to Sabrina. Can you do that?"

Camille began to nod, but it was Felicia that stepped up.

"I think it would be better if I took them," the Cadarian Princess said. "Sabrina may not be in Celidar any longer, and as you say, time is of the essence. Because she has Halicon's abilities, I can use Nightwing to find her wherever she is. Besides, I could use the practice with portals."

Gwydeon nodded and Felicia turned her attention to Orren.

"I could use the help," she said softly, "care to tag along?"

Orren Eldrath could not help the smile from coming to his lips and nodded without words. He was feeling a little worse for wear after the back to back battles, and he could use a respite within friendly confines. It took only a few moments for Orren and Felicia to gather Taya and Storm before Felicia opened a portal and the four stepped through. This left the Sandar family alone in the desolate wasteland that had once been the prosperous and flourishing capitol city of the Kingdom of Rashaleb. Gwydeon was just turning to face Midarin when there was a sound like thunder coming from the mountain range to the north. There was something about the sound that struck a chord inside of Gwydeon and he felt the prickly sensation of danger racing up his spine. Gwydeon was just able to channel enough power to let a crystalline sword appear in his hand before two massive shadows flashed across the ground and two huge dragons crashed to the ground just feet away from where the trio stood. Midarin was thrown into the air, and Gwydeon had to move quickly to catch her, with his wings allowing him not to be impacted in the same way. Camille also let her wings catch the air and push her backwards, but instead of touching back down on the ground, she hovered a foot above, letting twin crystalline blades appear in her hands. Gwydeon set Midarin gently back onto the ground several hundred feet from the massive winged beasts, and she had her bow in hand seconds later. Gwydeon and company did not have to wait long before one of the creatures roared and let its terrifying voice be heard.

"You are intruding upon our domain," the smaller of the two dragons growled. "Already the forces of darkness have wrought devastation upon the humans that called this land home and now you bring more destruction in your wake. We tolerated the humans because they did not have the power to threaten our homes, but now you, you so-called Dark Gods, shake the mountains with your recklessness. Frigia Shatterbreath is the ruler of this domain, and together with my mate, Glaciarium Magnus, we must ensure that this land is safe."

The smaller of the dragons, Frigia Shatterbreath, had a light blue almost white coloration to its scales that shimmered in the sunlight and gave the appearance of ice. The scales themselves were also not smooth but ended in sharp-looking points that had icicles dripping from them. The creature's wings were covered in frost and ice, but the heavy coating did not seem to impact the creature's mobility. Long sharp spines ran down the length of the dragon's back from the back of its head all the way down to its tail, and three gleaming sharp claws adorned each of its surprisingly narrow feet. The creature held itself upright more like a bird of prey than any dragon Gwydeon had ever seen, perching like a great hawk ready to lunge in and strike at any moment. Bony protrusions adorned its head down the length of the lower jaw all the way back to the neck line, forming a collar that looked like a lion's mane of spikes. The sockets of the creatures eyes were elongated along each side of the dragon's head, giving the creature a much larger range of vision, and at the back of each of the eye ridges was a massive spike that swept back and must have allowed the wind to careen across the creatures body in flight giving it incredible speed. The dragon's tail also seemed much more delicate and thin, but its rippling muscles were visible under the scales. It was clear to Gwydeon that in the sky, this monster would have unparalleled maneuverability and would be able to take turns at breathtaking speed. Prey would not stand a chance of out running or out turning this beast even at its huge size.

The larger of the two dragons, Glaciarium Magnus, looked as brutish as its companion looked agile. The scales of the hulking creature were light gray while the scales of the belly and underside of the tail were an eggshell white. There seemed to be something that looked like glowing blue crystalline formations that were growing in random patches on its scales. A frost-like smoke wafted from each of these patches. Its feet were wide and sturdy, tipped with four gleaming black claws. Razor sharp black bone spurs emerged from the tips of each wing, its long serpentine neck, and impossibly long coiling tail. Bright gleaming white teeth were visible from the wide gaping maw of a mouth, and a haunting glow burned in the creature's eye sockets. This dragon stood twice as tall as its companion, and easily was twice the girth. Its tail was as long as the entirety of its companion.

"We meant no disrespect," Gwydeon said as he folded his wings back and let the weapon disappear from his hand, "we were merely defending ourselves from a threat. We will gladly leave here and are no threat to you. We wish no conflict with you."

"You know where we live, you know where our nest is, you will tell the hunters," the smaller dragon raved. "You will lead the destroyers to us, the heralds, the abomination. Our leader is dead because of creatures like you. You must be made to pay for your crimes."

The sword reappeared in Gwydeon's hand the next moment.

"This doesn't have to happen," Gwydeon said taking a step back. "Please see reason. We mean you no harm. We are not threat to you."

The larger dragon rumbled.

"It's too late for that. You have trespassed on our land. You must be made to pay, and you must be silenced."

Frigia charged the next moment, her lithe and compact form quickly covering the distance between she and Gwydeon. Without thinking, Gwydeon shoved Midarin hard, sending her sprawling away, and then threw himself to the ground. Frigia barely passed over Gwydeon's back, razor-sharp claws just catching some of the feathers of his wings and ripping them free. Instead of banking around for another pass, Frigia pulled up, burying her claws into the ground, coming to a complete stop, and then turning back in the direction of Gwydeon. It was a maneuver that should not have been possible for a creature of Frigia's size. However, Gwydeon was faster, his long-trained combat reflexes pushing to the surface. Before she could charge again, Gwydeon was on his feet with a weapon in hand, ready to defend himself. Midarin too had her feet back under her, and had her bow in hand and the bowstring drawn. It took only a matter of heartbeats to channel enough power to create three arrows made of pure flame, and less time to let the arrows hit the air. Each of the three hit Frigia in the chest, but seemed to have no effect. It certainly didn't dissuade Frigia from pushing off the ground and barreling toward Gwydeon. Claws flashed, and Gwydeon was able to catch one set of claws with his sword, but the other set dug hard into his shoulder. The force of Frigia's charge pulled Gwydeon off his feet, where he was dragged across the ground for nearly a hundred yards. A long crater was left the entire length that Gwydeon was dragged, but he hung on to consciousness despite the intense pain that wracked his body. Even though he had an incredible measure of power at his disposal, it seemed that the dragon's strength was more than enough to shatter his resolve.

While Gwydeon and Midarin were distracted, Glaciarium took the opportunity to strike out at Camille who hovered only a few yards away. He opened his massive jaws and let out a gout of rippling blue flame. Camille felt the attack long before she saw it, diving below the stream, but she misjudged the speed at which the attack was traveling. The breath caught her right ankle, and while she expected searing heat, she instead felt an intense cold that threatened to shatter her bones. Banking away, she retaliated with a beam of bright white energy, heat as intense as the twin suns themselves. The blow struck Glaciarium full in the chest, but the massive dragon ignored the attack as though it were nothing more than an insect bite. The massive creature continued to breathe its chilling breath in Camille's direction forcing her to accelerate to breakneck speed, swooping and diving through the barest of spaces to keep from being frozen solid. Despite his incredible size, Glaciarium seemed to be able to move his head and jaws very quickly to keep the pressure up on his opponent. Camille tried to bank around the dragon in an attempt to flank him, or at the very least to draw clear of the range of his attacks, but it took only subtle shifts of his bulk and his long neck to crane around to keep her in sight. As she ducked out of the way of yet another blast, she could not believe how the dragon was able to keep up the pressure. It seemed that the creature was barely having to inhale before letting another strike billow from its maw. There was only one option left if Camille was going to survive the encounter with the fearsome ancient creature.

Camille banked around the edges of another blast of frigid flame, feeling the cold pass through her and shaking her to the core. Pulling up, she climbed high, trying desperately to leave the dragon behind her, depending on her heightened senses to help her avoid the blasts of cold that continued to pursue her. Her quick climb looked more like a tight but erratic spiral, as her evasive maneuvers slowed her retreat. When she heard the massive wings of the dragon finally beat against the air, she knew that she had the opportunity she had been waiting for. In the air the dragon would still be a fierce opponent, but was not maneuverable enough to prevent what she had planned. Reaching deep within herself, touching the divine power that had been hers since birth, Camille wrapped herself in divine light, the searing brilliant white light of the Heavens themselves. Wrapping the energy like a cocoon around her body, she allowed one of the dragon's attacks to strike her, and then fell through the skies as though she had been crippled. However, she had not expected that the dragon's breath would have been able to penetrate her shield of power. The strike that she had intended to only be a ruse caused far more damage, and several of her ribs cracked under the extreme cold. But she had committed to her course, and no amount of pain would deter her. Tumbling through the air, she corrected little, ensuring that she fell directly toward the dragon who hovered a mere hundred feet above the ground. Finally she turned, the ruse shattered, and dove directly toward Glaciarium. Camille redoubled the strength of the energy around her, knowing that there was no way that she could avoid a strike from the dragon's breath now. Glaciarium's strike was far more vicious and powerful than she had expected, and it washed over her like a tide of freezing cold, almost robbing her of consciousness and knocking her from the sky. The pain was far beyond anything she had ever felt before, and it was almost as if the shield that she had wrapped herself in had no effect. But still she barreled on, aiming straight for the dragon's head. At the last moment she shifted her track, letting one of the crystalline blades reform in her hand. The impossibly sharp blade caught the right corner of the dragon's mouth, ripping through scales, muscles, and bone. The strike continued down the length of the dragon's neck, but when Camille tried to bank in toward the dragon's stomach, one of the Glaciarium's claws struck her along the back, ripping at the base of her left wing, nearly ripping it from her back. She fell, but was able to catch hold of the dragon's foreleg. Pain wracked her body, and darkness tugged at the edges of her vision, but she pulled herself up and thrust the tip of her sword into the dragon's heart, and then channeled all of the power she could muster through it, burning the ancient creature from the inside out. However, that was all that Camille could muster, and consciousness fled her, and she and the dragon toppled to the ground, with Camille landing atop the dragon's corpse in the crater that was made by his fall.

Gwydeon was not fairing much better, as Frigia was slowly grinding him into the ground, her claws dug deeply into his shoulder. Midarin continued to rain arrows of fire down upon the creature, but they had little to no effect. Perhaps in time the perpetual assault would be able to pierce through the tough outer carapace, but that was not assisting her husband as she intended. Finally she dropped the bow, let long blades of pure fire appear in her hands, and she charged. The dragon felt the assault coming and whipped her head around in time to let a cloud of ice fly in Midarin's direction. She brought the blades up to block the blow, and succeeded in some measure, but she had not been prepared for the wave of force that accompanied the hail. Midarin was blown off her feet and sent flying backwards. Her defenses were quickly overwhelmed, and the small sharp projectiles ripped through her skin leaving long jagged bloody cuts all over her body. She was unconscious before she hit the ground.

However though his wife was suffering, Gwydeon found the opportunity he needed to strike back and end the conflict. Channeling the purity of the power of the Blaze, Gwydeon wrapped his hands in the living green flame and reached up to take hold of Frigia's clawed foot. Wrenching his entire body, Gwydeon burned through the scales and bones of the foot, ripping it free from the dragon's body. The dragon roared in pain and stumbled away from where Gwydeon lay. However, Gwydeon was not willing to let the creature get away so quickly or so easily. He reached up and took hold of the underside of the dragon's chest and pulled himself up. With his Blaze-wrapped hands, Gwydeon dug his fingers into the scales and soft tissues of the creature and began to rip outward. The dragon roared in pain once again as Gwydeon continued to rip and tear at the soft underbelly. Another flare of power and Gwydeon thrust his whole body into the dragon's hulking form before triggering an explosion of power. Blaze fire burst outward sending fragments of Frigia in all directions, soaking the ground in blood and gore. Gwydeon stood in the center of the conflagration, the claws of Frigia's severed foot still lodged deep in his shoulder. For several long moments he stood, not really seeing the scenery around him, only the residual green flames at the edges of his vision. Finally the flames began to recede, and all Gwydeon could see was carnage. He fell to his knees, all strength fleeing from his body. So many battles, so quickly upon one another, and he had been pushed to his limit. He only hoped that when he woke up, if he woke up, he would find that his wife and daughter were still alive. Just as he collapsed he became aware that a portal was opening somewhere nearby. As consciousness fled, a familiar voice came to his ears.

"Never met a fight you didn't like, did you Gwydeon?"

To Fly the Raven

Year Four of the Just Emperor Kaitain "Dragonsbane" Lorien,
Creator's Calendar Year 1871

Jerrard woke with a start just before sunrise, feeling as though there was a hand gripping his heart. It had been hard enough to get to sleep with all of the events of the previous day, even with his wife curled up at his side. When he sat up, Jerrard realized that he was covered with sweat, and reaching into the back of his mind where the primal forces of the Blaze resided, he knew what had awoken him, and he felt his heart sink. Once Sabrina had taken control of the Blaze, Jerrard knew it immediately. She was a bright light in the center of the roaring flame. Halicon's presence had always been more subdued, just hovering on the edges of the consciousness of those who could touch the Blaze. Sabrina had a light about her that could not be denied. Some might have said that it was a hold-over from her time as the Spirit, while others would say that she was the light to counter Aerith's darkness, but Jerrard had known the woman for so long, and she was a light in everyone's darkness. She had an indomitable spirit, a way of looking at the world that could never be dampened. Her loss was an incredible blow to anyone who ever knew her, and to the whole of the Cosmos. When Erika woke, she pulled herself to her husband and kissed him lightly on the cheek. When she saw the look in his eyes, she knew something was wrong.

"What is it?"

Jerrard said nothing, and just sat staring at the doorway. Finally he turned to face his wife and reached over to take her hand in his. He kissed her gently and then took a deep breath.

"Sabrina is gone."

Erika wanted to ask a question, wanted to understand what he meant, and then knew instantly. He didn't mean that she had left, didn't mean anything that could be considered tragic or untimely. Sabrina was possessed of a power that no person should have been able to access, and it ravaged her body so completely that it was stealing the life from her every single moment she drew breath. She had succumbed to the pain, to the exhaustion, and left the world. It would be a darker place without her, but she would no longer suffer.

"When? How?"

"Sometime in the night," Jerrard said stroking her hair. "It was peaceful. She transitioned Halicon's power to a new host. It was necessary. After Tess, the toll on her was too great. The phasia and their children have a new master now, and the Blaze has a new guardian, though I'm sure it's the last person that anyone ever expected. Though the more I think about it, the more it makes sense."

Erika had lived with Jerrard for thousands of years, and knew him long before any of the wars that claimed his attention. She knew his father, she knew his life and the way he lived it. Jerrard was a man who spoke slowly. He wanted to work everything out in his head before giving his thoughts voice. It was a quality that annoyed some, and others believed him simply secretive and detached. Erika had learned to simply wait, to give him time to work things out before pressing him for more detail than he was willing to give. She had learned to see when he was ready, when he wanted to talk, and when he wanted nothing more than just forget he knew what he knew. Finally Jerrard looked into Erika's eyes and smiled.

"All it does is makes our lives harder for now. Logan was right; the time for hiding is over. Kaitain Lorien will be on our doorstep before we know it, and if we aren't ready to defend ourselves, then all of the work we have done all these years will be for nothing. The people we love have sacrificed too much for us to let that come to pass."

Erika reached out and put her arms around her husband and held him for a long moment before pulling back. Her eyes took on a much different look, not the tender and soft look of the loving wife, but the more tempered look of a lady of a powerful kingdom.

"What should we do about our guests? When we make our proclamation, there will be many eyes on the palace, and many more people within the receiving hall than have been in many years. We can't just hide them in their rooms forever."

Jerrard smiled.

"Logan and Jillian are already gone. I can't feel Logan's thoughts anymore."

There was a questioning look on Erika's face.

"It was a trick that my father taught me long ago, once he and I were on speaking terms again. He knew as last born of the phasia that he was at a significant disadvantage. The one power that he was able to cultivate was to be able to cut through the background noise that the Blaze always generated to see the connections within it. He learned that when he was close to a member of the phasia, or anyone that could touch the Blaze, there was something within the Blaze that changed. It takes time, but you can separate out the changes, make sense of them, like a primitive roadmap. Even then, you have to concentrate hard to make sense of it. Logan, and I assume Jillian, are no longer here. Rhain and Taya too, though I'm sure Taya would have liked to have said something before she left. I think Alderin is gone too, but I'm not sure. Bryn is the only one left we would have trouble explaining. She doesn't exactly lay low, but I don't expect she will stay here for much longer. Now that she knows more about what Aerith has been up to, and now that Sabrina is gone, she will return to find out what happened with Jeroch and Saurn."

Jerrard got to his feet and started to dress, but Erika remained in bed.

"How do you want to handle Feyd?"

Jerrard turned back just has he was buckling his belt. There was so much complexity in the question, but that was why the simplest answer was the best one.

"We have to tell him the truth."

Erika smiled and finally turned to put her feet on the floor and reach for a simple nightgown that hung on the back of a nearby chair. She pulled it over her head quickly and moved toward the door that led to the joined room of the suite that served as her private study.

"That should make for an interesting conversation," Erika said finally. "And which version of the truth are we going to tell him?"

Jerrard crossed the room to her and snaked his arms around her waist, kissing her lightly on the shoulder.

"The one we both know he can handle. Gabriel will help with that. He's seen just enough to make reality of the unbelievable."

Erika turned into her husband's embrace and gave him a long deep kiss. Finally she pushed him away with a playful smile.

"Why don't you go get Gabriel, and I'll meet you once I arrange for breakfast. After all, I wouldn't want Prince Feyd being shocked into reality on an empty stomach. What kind of host would that make me?"

* * * * * * * * * * *

Gabriel Shadowfall sat quietly at the meeting room table as the servants cleared the dishes from breakfast. In his short time in Celidar, Gabriel had been impressed with the efficiency of the servants in the royal palace. He had learned after only a handful of conversations that the people working within the royal palace were not actually servants, but were hired workers. Lady Erika had insisted early in her tenure as the Lady of Celidar that the history and custom of indentured servitude to the royalty be abolished and that all those who worked at the royal palace work there of their own volition and be paid a fair wage for the work that they did. This had engendered a massive amount of good will with the people, and had also created true loyalty in those who worked in the palace. Once the last of the servants left the room, Jerrard leaned back in his chair and set his eyes on Feyd Lorien.

"Prince Feyd," Jerrard began, "I know that things have not been as you expected since you left Aldere. The assassination attempt on the road, the man you know as Wynne, all of the strange people in and out of Celidar over the last few hours. I'm sure you have more than your fair share of questions. And unfortunately what I'm about to tell you is not going to do anything other than create far more. But I promise you, by the time this meeting is over, you will have all the answers you want, and probably far more than you need."

Feyd rested his elbows on the table, but did not speak, simply beckoning Jerrard to continue. When Jerrard hesitated in his normal manner, it was Erika who piped up.

"Jerrard and I are Dark Gods."

Gabriel expected something other than Feyd's reaction. Instead of wide-eyed shock, or open-mouthed panic, Feyd simply sat back, put is arms on the arms of the chair, and fixed his gaze not on Jerrard or Erika, but on Gabriel.

"Should I ask if you are a Dark God as well?"

There was no humor in the man's voice, and he was taking the news far too well for Gabriel's liking. But Gabriel slowly shook his head but added his voice a moment later.

"No," the Knight of the Flashing Blade said softly, but with conviction. "I'm not a Dark God, but in the past few days I have been exposed to what they are capable of. The things I have seen them do, the things I have witnessed, I cannot put words to it. But I can tell you, given what I have seen, that I would put more faith in the works of the Dark Gods than I would put in the works of the Creator and his Servants. I have seen some of those works with my own eyes as well and there is nothing divine about the threats or the way in which they act with violent impunity."

Feyd gave a curt nod and returned his attention to Jerrard.

CHAPTER 79

"So, did my father know that you were a Dark God when he named you to the position of Lord of Celidar? Was it another appeasement to make up for the sins committed by the Loriens in the name of fear?"

There was no malice in Feyd's voice, but it was a valid question considering what he actually knew about the nature of the Dark Gods and their ultimate goals. And yet the question was also a reflection of what he knew about the inner workings of his own twisted family, and the fear that caused them to sometimes take rash action. It was not easy for a Cadarian Emperor to constantly live with the threat of a power the likes of the Dark Gods looming like a shadow every minute of every day. They may have been out of sight on their shrouded continent of Mythryn, but they were never out of mind. Every being that walked the lands of Cadaria knew the Dark Gods were always out there, and those who lived in the Kingdom of Galateria or one of the bordering kingdoms had a more constant reminder. The fear of that threat, the fear of that power caused brave men to do foolish things, and men in power to exercise that power with a lack of vision. Even Feyd's sainted father could not be held above such failures. After all, he allowed Kaitain to become what he became.

"No," Jerrard answered. "Ender did not know what we were, and our elevation to this position had nothing to do with the many wrongs that the Lorien family visited upon our friends and allies. He had fallen out of love with the royalty of Celidar and had no successor that he could trust. He felt that we would do right by the people and make sure that they were taken care of in the days ahead. Your father was a brilliant man, and I believe he saw the darkness coming. He wanted so much to be the guiding light through that darkness, and perhaps that is why he was one who was targeted by Dorovar and his creatures."

Feyd nodded.

"It would not have taken much investigation to know that my brother was the last person should have been in charge of anything more than his own darkness. Killing my father ensured that nothing but chaos would reign in Cadaria. I'm sure that there are many that benefit from my brother being in power, but it is clear that the Cadarians are not among that number."

Gabriel leaned in and folded his hands on the table.

"The worst part of all of this is that from an outsiders prospective, or for one who has had their eyes opened into the greater nature of things, that Kaitain Lorien is clearly being overlooked by everyone and everything that has the power to destroy him because his actions are doing nothing but giving comfort to those who are trying to destroy us."

Feyd nodded absently.

"And the news of these new proclamations and the assassination of at least one member of the Knights of the Flashing Blade makes this fact even clearer in my mind. There are multiple rebellions in play and yet no one seems to be able to gain any traction against the Imperial Legion and my brother. Now, these obvious revelations aside, I assume there is a reason for your revealing your nature to me, and the reason why there have been so many comings and goings here in the halls of Celidar's power. So please, enlighten me as to the purpose for your confession and what it means for me."

Jerrard and Erika exchanged glances, and Erika nodded to an unspoken question before turning her attention back to Feyd. She smiled gently and then began to speak in a soft and comforting voice.

"As you have just indicated, the damage that Kaitain is inflicting is only hurting the people. The threat of Dorovar and others pose are being dealt with by forces that we need not concern ourselves with. However, it does fall to us to safeguard the people while the war escalates. But in safeguarding the people, it also puts us in direct opposition to Emperor Lorien and those still loyal to him. The suffering that has been created in his name and by his hand must be stopped, and to do that, he must be stopped. To that end, we would like for you to stand with us against your brother. But we could not ask such a bold declaration from you if you did not know the truth. So, that is why we told you about our nature, and that is also why we have enlisted not only the services of Gabriel Shadowfall, but also have secured the use of perhaps the finest and fiercest navy that Cadaria has ever seen. Whatever you choose, we shall honor, but regardless of your choice we shall stand against Kaitain."

Feyd regarded Erika for a long moment. There was earnestness in her eyes, as well as absolute conviction. However, Feyd could tell that this was not a decision that was made lightly. It was not that they wanted to fight, it was that they could no longer avoid the fight that was at their doorstep. They were braver than he was. He had spent his whole life watching as Kaitain took whatever he wanted without thinking for a moment about anything but his own narrow desires. He was a bully, a vile human being, and too self-absorbed to understand that the choices he made were killing people. And that was before he had any real power at all. Now that he ruled unchecked, the power of the Imperial Legion and the Shadow Guild at his command, there was nothing that would stand against him, and yet he was too insignificant even in his power-madness for the true keepers of power to trouble themselves with. He was the king of the insects in a battle of giants. How many lives had been unnecessarily snuffed out because of his actions? Would this war be as far gone if it were not for his pathetic machinations? The cost was beyond calculation, and yet the price was still unknown. Finally, Feyd put his hands on the table and stood straight.

"This is something I should have done four years ago. Never for one day should my brother have sat on the throne of Cadaria. Never should one life have been lost because of his arrogance. I will sit quietly no more. I will be the dutiful son to a dead father no more. Any allegiance I had to my brother died with my father. So, you say it falls to us to tend to the messes created by the mortal world while the gods wage their battles. Then I say let us prove that we can remedy the diseases we have inflicted upon ourselves. I will stand with you."

Jerrard stood and though he wanted to smile, he could not shake the serious look from his face.

"We have much to prepare for, and no time to prepare for it. We shall address the people of Celidar this afternoon. I will make the speech if you wish, but I think perhaps it would mean more coming from a member of the Imperial family, a man who is universally respected."

"I know just what to say," Feyd replied, the corners of his mouth turning into a smile.

* * * * * * * * * * *

The streets were crowded with people as the twin suns were just beginning to allow shadows to stretch longer across the ground. The trails of the falling fragments of rock were starting to get brighter in the sky. There were murmurs in the crowd, everyone trying to figure out what the announcement would be. Would the Mistics be enforcing the rumored decrees about the worship of the Creator being against the law? Would they join Marlae Lorien's rebellion? Would they perhaps cast their support behind the Empress Dominique Lorien who had tried her best to hold the fractured empire together during Kaitain Lorien's slumber following the attempt on his life. Whatever the announcement would be, the people of Celidar trusted the wisdom of their ruling family. Jerrard and Erika had proven month after month and year after year that their only thoughts and only concerns were for the welfare of their subjects. For too long the people of Celidar had suffered under royals who only cared about amassing wealth and power for themselves, even if it meant increasing the suffering of those who served faithfully. After several long minutes of waiting, the doors to the royal palace opened, and Jerrard and Erika Mistic emerged. There were cheers that went up through the crowd, and it took several minutes before the din quieted enough that Jerrard was able to project his voice for people to hear clearly.

"People of the Kingdom of Celidar," Jerrard began. "You have stood like the steel of this kingdom's namesake against a great many injustices in the past, many perpetrated by your own leadership. Now it seems that you must be made to endure another indignity placed upon you by those whom you are asked from birth to put your faith and trust in. You have all heard the rumors. Emperor Kaitain Lorien has executed a member of the Knights of the Flashing Blade, a threat he had made before, only to keep in the most tumultuous time in the history of our Empire. A time when the power and wisdom of the Knights is needed the most. And then, the Emperor has decreed that worship of the Creator is against the law, that those who speak the ancient and hallowed words are criminals, and those who disobey these laws are subject to having all of their possessions stripped from them, their freedom stolen from them, and their lives forfeited. This is how the Emperor seeks to protect his people, by turning those who are against him into criminals. This is not the way of a responsible leader. This is not the way of the caring leader. This is not the way of a compassionate leader. This is the way of a monster."

There were murmurs in the crowd and the rumblings of support. Jerrard let the murmurs continue for a moment before continuing.

"The people of Celidar are not the playthings of a monster."

This brought a huge cheer from the crowd.

"Today," Jerrard said. "Today we shout together so that all of Cadaria can hear. We will not be subjugated by a monster any longer. We will stand alone, under a new banner, under a new flag, and under a new leader."

Above the royal palace, a new flag was pulled into the heights of the sky. It was a plain white flag with the symbol of a raven sewn into it. It was simple, understated, and common. Just like the people it would now represent. From the open doors of the royal palace, Feyd Lorien stepped into the light, and the already cheering crowd reacted with loving fervor. He stepped up beside Jerrard and placed his hand on the man's shoulder.

"Good people of Celidar, I stand here united with your leaders, with your beloved leaders, the Lord Jerrard and Lady Erika. Jerrard speaks from the heart, and is dedicated to protecting you all from the malicious lies my brother has told. But my brother is not the first emperor to have lied to you. For generations you have been lied to, you have been deceived, and you have been fed fear every day of your lives."

The crowd began to quiet, all trying to figure out what Feyd was saying.

"The biggest lie perpetrated on the people of Cadaria is that the Dark Gods hate all Cadarians and that they are constantly conspiring to destroy you."

There were shocked glances, and a stunned silence.

"I have stood with Dark Gods, I have met them, and I have spoken to them. I have seen how they have risked everything, including their own families to protect the rights and the lives of mortals. Did you ever believe that Dark Gods would care more about your well-being than the Emperor?"

Many tried to shout him down, many shouted in agreement.

"You do not believe me? You do not think that the Dark Gods care for you?"

Many shouted no, and there were many angry voices. Jerrard took the opportunity to step forward. He reached deep into himself and filled himself with the power that he could manage. What he was about to do was risky, but there was no other way to make the people see the truth. In a second he was wreathed in bright green flames, hovering off of the ground until he was ten feet in the air. The aura of green flame intensified, taking the shape of the wing-spread raven that fluttered on the flag that flew above the palace. Feyd seized on the confusion and fear.

"You see," Feyd cried. "This man who has protected you, his wife that has treated you with respect and love. They are what you have been taught to fear. They are the Dark Gods that you have been told will come to steal your children in the night if you do not follow the commandments of the Creator and the Emperor. But do these people demand your service? Do they bind you in chains and steal your freedom? Or do they protect you and ensure that you have money and food for your families. Who should you fear? Should you fear Jerrard and Erika whom you know? Or should you fear the Emperor who seeks to take everything from you? I stand by Jerrard and Erika Mystic. I stand by Celidar."

After a long moment, Jerrard floated back to the ground, and then silence rained. Suddenly a single cry went up from the crowd.

"Long live Lord and Lady Mistic!"

The cry was echoed by another voice, and then ten, and then a hundred, until the whole crowd chanted as one. The adulation was deafening. Feyd turned to Jerrard and whispered in his ear.

"We've started a fire, Jerrard. Now we must make it consume all of Cadaria."

Deep in the crowd, a robed figure turned away from the clamoring throng. Despite herself, Alise Modrall smiled, satisfied with how all things were coming into alignment. The traitors had all collected themselves so nicely together, making her job much easier. She was closer to one of her targets, and now she would have useful intelligence to return to her father, along with his brother's head, and perhaps the heads of two meddlesome Dark Gods.

The Front

Year Four of the Just Emperor Kaitain "Dragonsbane" Lorien, Creator's Calendar Year 1871

Arin Ranthall knelt near the makeshift grave of his recent ally and long-time adversary and could not shake the feeling that there were many who would find the shallow grave too much deference for the monster that Warron Ysamaran had been in his life. Some would find throwing any dirt on the body an insult, preferring that the carcass of the warlord be picked over by the scavengers that roamed the lands. But over the last few centuries, Warron had tried to be something other than what he was made to be, and that took courage beyond measure, and for that reason, and that reason alone, Arin could not abide the man not having at least a somewhat proper burial. From where he crouched, Arin's eyes found the other body that lie upon the plain. The remains of that man deserved no burial in Arin's reckoning. He was a traitor in every sense of the world, and had been consumed by petty jealousies and a thirst for a revenge that he could never quench. But now Ivan Quicksilver was dead, and Arin was determined to make Warron's death at the traitor's hands mean something.

Though Arin had not had much time to master the use of his powers, he had been tutored by one of the finest warriors in the personage of Cedric Binosear upon his arrival on Espre, and he also had the lifetimes of memories of not only his patron Aerith Seth, but also of his own son to draw upon. Though Logan was very different from the boy that he had been the last time that Arin had known him, Arin still recognized the way that the boy thought and could compare his own patterns to his son's. That helped a great deal when deciphering how and why Logan used his abilities. There were many, like Pike Rhuiden, which had become consumed with the powers that they had acquired. It changed them in ways that were subtle at first, but later became defining factors of their personality. The moment that powers were exercised to open a door instead of using one's hands, or the moment that a goblet is levitated across the room to save time, it starts the path toward something far more sinister. It was a path that led away from the true nature of humanity. Aerith understood that, and both consciously and unconsciously had tried to impart that lesson to those who wore his mantle. Powers were no substitute for a keen mind and sharp reflexes. Perhaps that was why those members of the phasia that did not make their powers their identity were the ones still fighting. Logan had shunned his powers during his time in the war against Shau-ling, using them only as a last resort. However, he had tried his best to learn what he could about the nature of power, and armored himself with that knowledge. That was the lesson that Arin chose to follow now.

He crossed the distance from Warron's grave to the bisected body of Ivan Quicksilver and knelt beside the man's head. His dead eyes still stared up at the sky and his mouth gaped slightly, twisted from the combination of pain and shock at the moment of his death. Closing his eyes, Arin put his hands on either side of the man's head and concentrated. He reached back into the deepest parts of his mind and found what both Cedric's teaching and Logan's memories told him was there. Sure enough, the green flames of the Blaze waited for him, but where in Logan's memories it had been a roaring fire just barely on the edge of control, for Arin, it was little more than a flickering candle flame. Tentatively Arin reached out and touched the flame, cupping his hand beneath the dancing green fire and drew it to him. Emptying his mind, Arin peered into the gentle flame, looking through it into its own memories. Each of the phasia from the moment of their birth had been granted special abilities, and those abilities had come from their unique nature as creations of a Child of the Creator. But just as the Blaze was the physical embodiment of Halicon's life force, the unique powers of the phasia themselves were also contained in the Blaze, but were not simply granted to anyone who could touch the primal force. No, those abilities were hidden, deeply secret, and available only to those with the discipline and ability to see more subtle applications of power. This was what Cedric spent so much time teaching Arin. But even the great Cedric Binosear did not understand everything about the Blaze, and it seemed sometimes as though Cedric was simply using Arin as a test subject for his teaching techniques.

The lessons had been most effective however, and now that Arin could more fully understand Aerith Seth's memories, the lessons of the two great men aligned in Arin's mind and he was able to find the pieces that would make his plan come to fruition. Still holding onto the Blaze in his mind, Arin opened his eyes and gently placed his hands on sides of Ivan Quicksilver's face, craning his neck slightly so that he could stare into the dead man's eyes. The powers of the Blaze flared inside of Arin, almost as if the flames knew what he was trying to do. That moment the image of the man in Arin's eyes disappeared and he began to see beyond, into his memories, into his ambitions, into his soul. This was the same power that Jeroch had been gifted with from his birth; the ability to bore his way into the mind of another, ferret out all secrets and all memories and to make them his own. For Arin's scheme to work he would have to know everything the dead man knew. But it would not be enough to just know facts and figures. The Blaze flared hotter in Arin's mind and the ancient man began to see more of the dead man's soul. Arin began to feel his emotions; his hatreds and loves, his disappointments and thwarted ambitions. Everything that made Ivan Quicksilver the man that he was flooded into Arin, creating a complete image of the man. Half of Arin's plan was complete, the second half however would be much bloodier and distasteful.

Taking hold of one of the dead man's arms and one of his legs, Arin dragged the body into a more secluded area behind the inn, a place where the vile work was less likely to be discovered. As quickly as he could manage, Arin stripped off the dead man's armor and clothing. Once done, Arin focused on the powers of the Blaze one again, reaching deep inside to find the powers that Erdric Yarrow had once taken so much pleasure in wielding with impunity. Letting the power flow through him, Arin felt as though every inch of his skin was on fire, and that he was being twisted and stretched by the exertion. When the burning receded, Arin didn't need to look in a mirror to know that he now looked exactly like the fallen former member of the Knights of the Flashing Blade. Complete with the man's memories, mannerisms, and appearance, Arin would be able to infiltrate the most sensitive places under Kaitain Lorien's control. Quickly Arin dressed in the dead man's clothes, and then with little effort was able to set Ivan Quicksilver's body ablaze. For the last touch of realism, Arin channeled the powers of the Blaze to create a bloody scar on his abdomen, just above the waistline, in perfect harmony with the rip and blood stain on the dead man's shirt. Once the evidence had been destroyed, Arin in his new guise limped slowly in the direction the Imperial Guard had marched, knowing that in a matter of hours he would be face to face with Emperor Kaitain Lorien and would be able to wade deep into the madness that surrounded him.

* * * * * * * * * * * *

The Imperial Guard had camped for the night just over half a day's travel from the temporary capital of the Cadarian Empire outside the ruins of the Imperial Palace. The Guard would have been able to travel a much farther distance had it not been for the Imperial retinue as well as the presence of the black clad group known as the Shroud. These groups were not accustomed to a forced march or covering great distances in a short amount of time. Instead of being able to cover the distance from Aldere to the capital city of Zevarit in a matter of four days, it would take nearly ten days at the current rate of travel. It would take longer if the army were to encounter severe weather of any kind. Arin was able to catch up with the army shortly after they had made camp for the night, and immediately made his way to Emperor Lorien's tent. He remained waiting outside of the tent for quite some time before one of the guards finally pulled back the tent flap and allowed him entrance. Part of Arin dreaded coming face to face with Emperor Kaitain Lorien, partly because Arin had always had distaste for those who abused power that they were entrusted with, and partly because from Ivan Quicksilver's memories, Kaitain was clearly a vile and abusive man. Now though in the guise of Ivan Quicksilver, Arin could possibly have the opportunity to take Kaitain completely off the board.

However, Pike Rhuiden's attack on the temporary capital may have made any attempt on Kaitain's life futile.

Stepping into the tent, one of the first things that came to Arin's mind was just how pompous this so-called Emperor really was. The massive eight-post tent was dyed a dark purple color with threads of gold weaved through it and the ceiling of the tent was littered with small silver points that made the ceiling look like a star-filled sky. There was a gilded chair set up against the far wall that served as a makeshift throne, and hanging behind the throne was a large mirror that took up almost half of the back wall of the tent. On the other tent walls there were various tapestries, including one of the Imperial family. However, this version of the tapestry had been significantly defaced. The tapestry depicted Ender Lorien's family in the days before his death, perhaps the last time that the Imperial Family could have been considered whole or stable. The image showed Ender standing behind his two sons, Kaitain and Feyd, and standing beside Kaitain was his late wife, and standing beside Feyd was his daughter Felicia. Sitting in front of Kaitain and his wife was their only daughter Marlae. The defacement was obvious. Someone, most likely Kaitain himself, had slashed across the neck of Feyd Lorien, and had put a single rip diagonally across the face of Felicia. Marlae's whole face had been removed from the tapestry, a clear indication of how much malice the Emperor had for his daughter after her supposed treachery.

After taking in the scenery for only a moment, Arin moved half-way down the long golden carpet that ran from the entrance of the tent to the throne, before falling to one knee to acknowledge the Emperor. Kaitain Lorien sat back on his throne, in front of him stood two heavily armed and armored guards. To his left stood a man in black robes, his face completely covered, that Arin knew immediately was Yaron Telsin, the leader of the Black Shroud. To Kaitain's right stood a woman that Arin didn't recognize, and there was no memory of her face in the information that Arin had taken from Ivan Quicksilver. It took several long moments before Kaitain chose to acknowledge his servant, and Arin hoped that the answers that he had rehearsed would be enough to prevent Kaitain from sensing that something was wrong. There were many things that could be said about Kaitain Lorien, but one that could not be said was that the man was a fool.

What made Arin's position even more precarious was the natural ability of the Lorien bloodline to detect falsehoods.

"I expected you long before now, Ivan," Kaitain said with annoyance in his voice, the hideous mask that covered his face giving every word an unconscious tone of displeasure. "What kept you? Did you find some bauble to play with, or were you simply picking flowers?"

Arin let a cruel smile come to his face. He knew from Ivan's memories that the taunt was more playful than it sounded.

"I did in fact find myself a bauble to play with," Arin said, letting some venom come to his voice. "Two Dark Gods were lying in wait near the inn. They must have been there to spy upon our movements, but they sensed an opportunity when they saw me alone, disposing of the inn staff."

Kaitain leaned forward at the news, slamming his fist down upon the arm of the chair. It was more a reaction of frustration than anger.

"The cowards come at us when we sleep, they will not fight us face to face because they know they cannot win. I hope you punished them for me."

Arin bowed his head.

"One of the Dark Gods fell, and the other managed to get away. The one who died, Warron, was powerful but overconfident and fell easily. I did not recognize the one who ran away from the fight, I have never seen him before, and in my time in the Dark Citadel I never encountered any information or descriptions that matched this man."

It would have been too much for Arin to affirm that he had killed two Dark Gods, but in staying with a version of the facts that had the most amount of truth to them he had the best hope of fooling Kaitain's finely honed senses. Ivan had killed Warron, and Arin had walked away from the battle. Arin simply hoped that there would be enough truth in his words not to tip Kaitain's ability to feel lies. After a moment Kaitain leaned back on his throne again.

"The Dark Gods once again prove themselves to be cowards. But this latest act shows just how desperate they are. Perhaps they are not as large a threat as we envisioned. They are off-balance, that much is clear, and that should allow us the time we need to take back our Empire before we take the fight to them."

Arin kept his head bowed and waited, but the woman at Kaitain's side placed her hand on his shoulder and leaned down to whisper in the Emperor's ear. There was a short wave of concern that passed through Arin, but when the Emperor laughed softly to himself, the concern was allayed.

"Ivan," Kaitain said coldly, "I don't believe you have yet had the pleasure of meeting my new Mistress of Secrets. It has come to my attention over the past few months that the Shadow Guild was no longer interested in pursuing my best interests, but were more interested in ensuring their own. For that reason I can no longer trust their council, nor can I have their representatives spying on me and my actions. So, the members of the Shadow Guild have been added to my list of those who will be arrested on sight and stripped of their possession. They will be forced into servitude or they will forfeit their lives."

The woman leaned in once more and whispered in the Emperor's ear. When she leaned back, there was the barest hint of a smile that came to her lips. For the first time, Arin took a moment to take in the features of the mysterious woman. The first feature that struck Arin was the woman's long white hair. The long strands from the top and sides of her head were braided and threaded through with crimson ribbon, while the rest of her hair hung loose down the back of her neck and stopped just past the level of her shoulders. The woman wore form fitting crimson leather armor that stretched from her shins all the way to her throat, and the armor had flecks of silver and gold sewn through it that created a slight shimmer with every movement. Her arms were covered by not only the leather armor, but also by cold iron bracers that covered the woman's arms from her forearms to the top of her biceps. Most of the woman's face was obscured by an opaque veil, but the woman's eyes were still visible. Her features that were visible hinted at the fact that she was closer to middle age, but that was only a guess in Arin's mind. Perhaps her most striking feature was her eyes. They were bright and haunting, a brilliant hazel color that bordered on gold.

"Calindria was good enough to remind me that I have yet to reward you for your bravery against the Dark Gods, as well as for bringing me the wife of the leader of the Dark Gods. Hannah Ironheart's sister will prove to be a very valuable bargaining chip in the days to come. You are the reason that I have her, you are the reason the Dark Citadel is in ruins, and now you are the reason that one more of the Dark Gods has fallen. In our march across the countryside, we have captured quite a few heretics, and Calindria believes that you deserve to have at least two slaves to make your life easier. Take what you want, you deserve it. We will camp here for a day and continue to Zevarit. Tomorrow you and I shall discuss our strategy for the invasion. Now go, enjoy yourself. I have much to discuss with my advisors, and then I plan to pay my little hostage a visit. She is far more amusing than I gave her credit for. I find her screams far more satisfying than I ever did Dominique's."

Arin rose, bowed once more, and then turned to leave the tent. Just before the guard opened the tent flap the Emperor spoke again.

"There are many rumors, Ivan, that my daughter has reemerged, and that she has once again proclaimed herself as the rightful ruler of my Empire. More than that, she has proclaimed herself as the Creator's chosen ruler of Cadaria. The little bitch continues to defy me at every turn. But she has placed herself in Hedorah, and has enough defenses now that we cannot act directly against her. At least not with military force. We must consider ways to make an example of her."

Arin turned and bowed.

"I look forward to the challenge."

Kaitain waved his hand in dismissal, and Arin turned to leave the tent. As soon as Arin was back under the night sky, he felt his stomach turn. Being in the proximity of Kaitain Lorien was nauseating at best, and Arin could almost feel the slime oozing across his skin. And as much as he detested what was going to happen next, he knew he could not prevent it if he wanted to keep his stolen identity intact. One of the soldiers outside the

Emperor's tent indicated the way across the compound to the makeshift prison tent. Walking across the open area, Arin steeled himself for what he was about to see. The guard at the entrance of the prison tent bowed slightly to acknowledge his superior officer, and then held the flap open slightly for Arin to move through.

Whatever Arin was expecting, the environment within the prison tent was so much worse. The first thing that hit Arin was the stench. The prison tent was more like a cattle barn than a place where people were being held. One side of the tent was roped off, and a large group of men seemed to roam aimlessly between the wall of the tent and the rope line which was held by closely spaced guards. Each of the men was dressed in tattered clothes, looking more like common beggars than whatever they were before they ran afoul of the Emperor's new laws. The other side of the tent was the most disheartening. A group of roughly twenty women huddled together in the center of the cordoned off area, trying desperately to keep their exposed flesh covered. They had been stripped completely and shivered from both the cold night and the abject humiliation of it all. To deepen the horror of the situation, three of the women had hideous looking iron collars bolted around their necks. After several moments of standing and looking around the prison tent, the man who must have been the warden of this perverse jail approached Arin. He nodded his head in acknowledgement of his superior and then spoke with a vile grin painted on his face.

"Have you ever seen such a glorious sight, Sir Quicksilver? We were waiting for you to return before we started passing around the spoils of victory."

Arin's stomach was in knots, but he let his lips curl into a smile.

"And where did you find these juicy little morsels?"

The warden took a step forward and pointed at the huddled group of women.

"We came across a small village half a day's march from the inn. The only large building was a Temple of the Creator in the center of town. A detachment of the Imperial Guard seized everything in the temple, arrested the men working there and burned it to the ground. One of the buildings attached to it was apparently a refuge for women who were taking their vows to become priestesses. There were sixteen of them, so under the law they were seized, stripped of all possessions and are now servants to the throne. We had to kill two of them because they would not submit, but after that object lesson, the others came much more willingly."

Arin gestured to the collar on one of the women's necks.

"And what is that?"

The warden laughed.

"That was Emperor Kaitain's idea. He picked the three that he wanted for his personal servants, and that is how he chose to mark them. He sent orders that once you returned to camp you could claim two for your own, and then the rest would be used to entertain the men between marches."

The words from the warden caused the mass of women to shiver and huddle in tighter to each other. One of the women caught Arin's eye, looking at him unabashedly with a spark of defiance. Arin pointed at her.

"I like that one," he said in his most menacing tone.

The warden laughed harder.

"You have good taste, my lord. That's the High Priestess from the refuge. The one to her right there is her sister who was an acolyte. Why don't you take the matched set? Should keep you entertained, they look fiery enough."

Arin wanted to vomit. His heart was racing and all he wanted to do was reach out and crush the warden's throat and help these poor souls escape their captivity. As strong and as powerful as he was, he could probably inflict a great deal of damage on the Imperial Legion, but the threat of the Black Shroud, and now this mystery woman who was advising Kaitain made the chances for escape very slim. There would be a way in time to help these people, but the time was not now. He would have to play along. At least in some measures. Arin put his hand on the warden's shoulder.

"Have them prepared for me, and I'll take them to my tent. But I'm a little concerned about the security here. With all of the movement, I don't want our soldiers or some of the rebels to come in here and steal our prizes. Let's discuss it."

The warden smiled and nodded, motioning for three of the guards to deal with the two women. After that, he followed Arin out of the prison tent. Arin made sure that there was no one in ear-shot, and then reached deep into himself and grasped hold of the Blaze. At first the power resisted his touch, but finally Arin had the power he needed, and from the memories of the power of the Blaze, he adopted yet another of the phasia's unique powers. Arin put his hand on the man's shoulder and looked at the entrance of the prison tent. He pushed the power of the Blaze into his words and let the power worm its way through the ears of the warden and into his brain.

"In the middle of the night, during a change of watch, you will begin a rebellion. You will scream the name of Marlae Lorien and kill as many of the guards in the tent as you can. No matter what happens make sure that the prisoners get away. Give them as much time as you can."

The warden's eyes went wide, but finally a cruel smile came to his lips and he nodded.

"I think those changes will make all the difference in the world," Arin said as he stepped away.

By that time, the prison tent flap opened, and two guards emerged with the two former priestesses, silver collars bolted around their necks, and leather straps in the fashion of leashes connected to them. The warden's malicious smile widened.

"These guards will take your prize to your tent. Do whatever you want with them. The Emperor has decreed that they can live as long as they are useful. But once that usefulness has been exhausted, they'll be sent to meet the Creator that they love so much."

Arin followed behind the guards, his fists clenched in hate, plotting the moment when he could bring an end to the perversions that Kaitain Lorien had unleashed on the world.

Chapter LXXX

The Way Forward

Year Four of the Just Emperor Kaitain "Dragonsbane" Lorien, Creator's Calendar Year 1871

For what was supposed to be a safe place, Kiara Aren did not find any comfort as she stood in the dining hall of the estate of the Serpentine Knight of the Kingdom of Steam, Iltorp. The rustic estate looked as though it had seen a great battle, and smears of dried blood littered the room much the same way as the broken furniture. However, the walls and the ceiling were all intact, and Kiara could not sense any danger lurking. However, to be safe, the Masters had sent several of the older students scouting through the estate to ensure that there were no hidden assassins waiting in the shadows. It took quite some time to check all of the rooms, as the estate was surprisingly vast, but within two hours the whole of the estate as well as the grounds were pronounced safe, and the students were settled in for their stay. The four Masters as well as Kiara retired to what must have been the Serpentine Knight's private study. Jastra Mythryn had long since recovered from her altercation with Hannah Ironheart, but she was no better for the experience. She stood in the corner of the room near the door fuming. Ashinica Maupin stood examining the books on Vallic Ultiv's bookshelves, running her fingers over the old spines, occasionally removing one from the shelf and regarding the cover before putting it back. Aris Ebonsight sat in a chair near the fireplace, absently drumming her fingers on the armrest. Kiara did her best to stay out of the way, and let her eyes drift back and forth between the three women as they waited for Fiona Ebonsight to return from meeting with the oldest acolytes from the Academy. When finally the door opened, Jastra sprang from her position near the door and did not wait for the elder member of the Masters to find her footing or give her report on the state of the students.

"What are we doing here Fiona? How can we trust Hannah or her little confederate here? And how can we trust that the Serpentine Knight is even someone that can be counted among our allies? We must return to the discussion about the disposition of the Academy of Arcane Arts, and invocation of the final covenant lest our students fall into the hands of some horrible force that will use them for ill purpose. The vote was two to two, and thus I have the deciding vote."

Fiona recovered quickly from the verbal ambush, but before she could voice her displeasure, her daughter Aris stood from her chair and glowered in Jastra's direction.

"The vote was not complete," Aris growled. "While I had discussed my reasons for a vote in favor of invocation, I had not formally cast my vote in the manner required by our laws. If you insist on reopening the question on this matter, then I will formally cast my vote against invocation of the final covenant. Our situation has changed."

Jastra put both fists on her hips and glared at Aris.

"Our situation has changed only in the fact that we have gone from being at the mercy of one foe to being at the mercy of another."

Ashinica clicked her tongue.

"Alistair always taught to never judge a situation before you knew which side you were on. How can we know who are enemies and allies are if we do not even know which side is the right one?"

Jastra opened her mouth to speak, but closed it just as quickly. Ashinica's simple words had defeated her for the moment, but the lull in accusation gave Fiona her opportunity to speak.

"Ashinica has always been very astute, and I only wish that we had more of Alistair's wisdom to rely on now. The world is spinning out of control so quickly, and it seems that everywhere we turn there is someone who wishes to use our power for ill. How can we trust that Emperor Kaitain will not violate his oath as the Emperor of Cadaria? He has already forsaken the Church of the Creator, and rumor has it that he has also gathered fallen students from the Academy to create his own arcane cabal. Then which way shall we turn? To the wife, Dominique, the mistress of the fallen Seraph Kore who attempted to assassinate the Emperor? To the daughter, the usurper whose reputation is so putrid that even standing with the two holiest people in Cadaria could not suppress the smell? The Dark Gods, who seem more and more to be the victims in this war? Or shall we instead put our trust and faith in the seemingly disgraced Knights of the Flashing Blade, who have done nothing but protect the Empire as they were tasked to do since its inception? However you may personally feel, Jastra, Hannah did help us get out of harm's way."

Without looking at Fiona, Jastra let out an exasperated breath.

"Even devils have pleasing faces," the Master of Energy mumbled.

Though her voice came out unsteady and uncertain, Kiara Aren broke the uneasy silence.

"Masters, I know that you have no reason to trust me, or my words, but I can assure you that if you had seen what I have seen over the last few days and weeks, you would not doubt the purity of Lady Ironheart's motives. There is so much to this war that no mortal eyes have seen, and I scarcely believe the little that I have been there to witness. Please, Masters, at least reserve your judgment until such times as you have the opportunity to speak at length with Lady Ironheart and she can explain more than I can. For now you must be content with having a safe place to hide until Lady Ironheart returns. And I promise you, she will return. Whether it is here or in Albitonin, she will keep her word. One who speaks with the grace of the Creator cannot do anything else."

Aris smiled as she returned to her seat.

"Your faith in your mistress is admirable," the youngest of the Masters said softly, "but you must understand that we don't have the luxury of such faith, at least not yet. But your devotion does make our decision to come this far much less frightening."

"But this place may not be as safe as Hannah believed," Fiona cautioned. "There is no sign of the Serpentine Knight or his companion, and the state that the estate was found in upon our arrival fills me with dread. In order to assure our safety here in Iltorp, I am afraid that we must appeal directly to the royal family. If, of course, that is the consensus of the Council."

Aris nodded, followed by Ashinica. Fiona turned her head to Jastra and waited. The woman closed her eyes and bowed her head for a long moment before giving a curt and minimal nod. Fiona knew that was the most she could expect from the volatile woman, but it was more than enough. With the Masters agreed on a course of action, Fiona turned her attention back to Fiona.

"We shall leave at first light for the capital. If luck holds we should be able to meet with the royal family before mid-day. As much as I would like your company, Kiara, I am afraid that we will need someone to stay behind and watch the students, as well as await Lady Ironheart's return from Jelan. I'm sure you understand."

Kiara bowed slightly. She had been a follower of one form or another all of her life, and she was accustomed to taking orders from those who could be considered her betters. This time however, the request did not seem like an order veiled by a question, but more like a genuine request. It was something that would take some getting used to.

"Then it's settled. Let us hope that the royal family is as amenable as our new allies are proving to be."

* * * * * * * * * * * *

Of all the Kingdoms of Cadaria, Iltorp was one of the most mysterious and insular. Very few people traveled into Iltorp who did not already live there, except for the traders that used the southern trading road that ran between Aldere and Saldarine. The majority of Iltorp, with the exception of the southern reaches, were dominated by forests, with some grasslands that served as farm and grazing land. There was very little industry to speak of in Iltorp, unlike the majority of the Cadarian Kingdoms, though what industry that did exist was restricted to harvesting trees for one purpose or another. The one large port on the northern coast was primarily used for barges that transported either whole tree trunks or some processed wood planks to different areas of Cadaria, though the greatest majority found their way to the shipyards of Hedorah. While the majority of the harvested trees were sent to other kingdoms, some remained within Iltorp, used by the master fletchers of the kingdom to produce the greatest bows and arrows made in the whole of the Empire. However, a great many of the bows and arrows produced in Iltorp were earmarked to be shipped to Aldere to outfit the archers of the Imperial Guard. Not many civilians, even those born and raised in Iltorp, could claim to own a masterwork bow from an Iltorp fletcher.

The royal family of Iltorp was the perfect reflection of the people and landscape of Iltorp. They were reserved, private, and dedicated to the good of the Kingdom. More often than not, the royal family took their cues from the member of the Knights of the Flashing Blade that called Iltorp home, and that course of action has allowed Iltorp to remain prosperous, and more importantly out of the line of fire that constantly flowed between their neighboring kingdoms. Because of its common borders with Saldarine and Thorigald, Iltorp often found itself in the unenviable position of neutral ground in the peace talks between the kingdoms after a skirmish had broken out. Though more often than not, the neutral ground was utilized for each side to set up makeshift medical camps as close to the front lines as possible without being in danger. Of course the royal family always allowed these camps to be set up, and found themselves rewarded with favorable trade agreements and safe conduct for their diplomats, merchants, and shipments.

Rarely in the history of the Cadarian Empire had more than two Masters of the Academy of Arcane Arts travelled to any of the Great Kingdoms, including the Imperial Province of Aldere. Only once had so many been in the same place at the same time outside of Jelan. Even the Emperor had to travel to Jelan to gain an audience with all of the Masters. That was the boon afforded to the Masters' Council ever since its formation under the rule of the first Cadarian Emperor, so Fiona was not surprised at the looks of shock from the royal herald when she announced herself and the other Masters and requested an audience with the royal family. Though this special standing also did not prepare the Masters for any situation where they would be kept waiting. Though Ashinica and Aris seemed to take the delay in stride, Jastra paced impatiently, her eyes going to the page over and over again, as though her stare would somehow motivate the others to quicker action. Fiona simply stood her ground a few paces from where she announced their arrival, her hands clasped behind her back, her breath gentle and controlled, half meditating, and half completely aware of every motion that went on around her. She could feel the tension that was running through the palace. There was something more than their surprising arrival. It was subtle, a single sour note hidden in the melody and practiced harmony.

When the page finally returned, he bowed uneasily to Fiona and then tried her best to force a smile, two factors that were not lost on Fiona.

"I apologize for the delay, Master Ebonsight," the page said shakily, "but the crown prince wanted to ensure that everything was prepared for a meeting of this importance."

Fiona caught the name.

"The crown prince? Are the Lord and Lady of Iltorp unable to meet with the Masters?"

The page paled.

"The Lord and Lady are indisposed, Master Ebonsight, all the more reason that the crown prince wanted to assure that all was in a state of readiness. Iltorp would hate for there to be any misunderstandings that would strain relations between Iltorp and Jelan. The crown prince wanted me to stress how much he wanted to avoid catastrophic misunderstandings, his words exactly, Master Ebonsight."

Fiona bristled at the words. The discord that she was feeling was growing stronger. However, unlike the page, she was more practiced at masking her displeasure.

"Let me gather the other Masters, and then you can lead us into the presence of the crown prince."

Fiona turned and her eyes first caught Aris' who had heard the entire conversation. Fiona's daughter opened her mouth as though to speak, but Fiona cut off the question with a narrow-eyed gaze. After taking several steps over to where Ashinica sat, Fiona stopped and waited for Jastra and Aris to join them. When Fiona finally did speak, she did so with low conspiratorial tones.

"Be vigilant. Things here are not what they seem."

Finally Aris spoke, observing the calm and quite tone that her mother had used.

"What was all of that about a catastrophic misunderstanding? It seemed almost like a threat."

Fiona frowned.

"That was meant for me. It was a reminder about our banishment from the Imperial Court. Whomever this crown prince is, he is certainly not a friend. He wanted me to know that we are here on his terms."

Jastra frowned.

"Could he be a threat?"

The question had but one implication. Would the Masters be able to use their abilities to protect themselves, and should they prepare themselves for a fight?

"We must be prepared for all eventualities. The safety of the students and the adherence to the covenants are the only concern here. Aris, no matter what happens you must ensure that the students are safe, even if it means leaving the rest of us behind. That is an order from the Grand Master and not up for discussion. Now, shall we go before the crown prince starts to become concerned about our breech of etiquette?"

Fiona turned without waiting for an answer, and the other three members of the Master's Council fell in behind her without further discussion. The page acknowledged the four women with a curt nod and then turned to lead them through the corridors of the inner palace to the receiving hall for the Kingdom of Iltorp. When they reached the large heavy wooden doors, the page paused for a long moment as though gathering himself before pushing at the center seam of the doors to open them. Guards on the inside of the room drew back the doors after the initial breech, and the page stepped to one side, motioning for the Masters to continue into the hall. Fiona nodded in the page's direction one final time before stepping across the threshold.

The receiving hall was well lit with large braziers and torches scattered through the room to maximize the light. The hall itself was not overly large as one would expect, but it was large enough to hold a great many people at once. Tapestries hung throughout the room depicting the great victories of the Cadarian Empire, mostly focusing on the archers who made the difference in the early campaigns of the Founding Wars. There was a long green carpet that ran from the doors to the small flight of three steps that led to the dais. Where Fiona had expected to see twin thrones sitting on top of the dais, she was shocked to see that one had been knocked onto its side and the other moved to a more central position. Sitting upon that throne, though more lounging than sitting, was a young man who couldn't have been older than thirty. One leg was draped over the arm of the throne while the other foot was propped between the arm and the front edge. The young man had short blond hair that stood mostly straight up, but also fanned out in all directions. He wore no finery, with the exception of very high-quality riding boots, but the rest of his dress would have been more readily found on that of a farmer, a simple shirt and pant. The shirt laced up the front from the middle of the chest to the collar, but all of the laces were removed from the shirt and it hung loose. In the young man's hands was an antique lute by its styling. As the Masters approached the young man continued to pick at the lute without even looking up. Several strides from the dais the Masters stopped in unison and bowed as little as would be considered respectful. They waited for several long moments to be acknowledged by the man who could only be the crown prince. After what was a borderline insulting period of time, the young man on the throne finally spoke, but he did so still looking down at the lute in his lap.

"The royal family of Iltorp bids welcome to the Masters of the Academy of Arcane Arts," the young man said, his voice filled with a mixture of amusement and contempt. "I apologize that the Lord and Lady of Iltorp will not be available to witness this momentous occasion, but there have been, shall we say, events that have conspired to relieve them of their positions here in the capitol. So, for now, I am the voice of Iltorp."

Finally the young man looked up and locked his cold blue eyes on Fiona.

"To what do we owe the honor of this visit?"

The bemusement in the man's voice was gone, replaced by a tone like cold iron. Fiona did her best to stifle a shiver.

"My lord," Fiona answered, trying to remain respectful given the circumstances, "as you may or may not be aware, the Academy of Arcane Arts in Jelan came under attack by unknown forces that were bent on either our recruitment or destruction, including agents from both the loyal armies of the Emperor of Cadaria as well as those of the rebellion under the command of Marlae Lorien. We were forced at last to flee from Jelan, and we were told that we would be given safe haven in the estate of the Serpentine Knight. However, upon arriving at the Serpentine Knight's estate, it became clear that something had occurred there and neither Sir Vallic nor his companion were to be found. Thus we have come here, seeking asylum from the crown prince in his kingdom."

After her final word, Fiona bowed low, a gesture that was echoed by the other Masters. After straightening Fiona expected to meet the crown prince's eyes once again, but instead his glance had moved from Fiona to Aris.

"And is it just the leadership of the Academy that escaped these usurpers, or did the whole of the student body survive as well?"

The crown prince continued to gaze at Aris even as Fiona spoke.

"We were able to evacuate all of the students in time. We have no idea what happened to the buildings of the Academy themselves, but we were forced to destroy many records and seal away many artifacts so that they could not be used for ill. Our first priority of course was to the children. We would not have abandoned them, my lord."

Finally the crown prince's eyes returned to Fiona.

"Of course."

The young man fell silent for many moments, but then he put his lute down beside the throne and got to his feet. Having a better look at the man, Fiona was surprised at the broadness of his shoulders and how well developed he was muscularly. He did not hold himself like a nobleman. Fear began to race through Fiona's veins. Had there been a coup? Had this upstart taken the reins of power in the Serpentine Knight's absence? Had this usurper been behind the unrest at the Serpentine Knight's estate? A thousand horrible thoughts whirled through Fiona's mind, and when a wide smile came to the young man's face, she felt the knots growing in the pit of her stomach.

"This world has seen great upheavals over the last few months. The attempt on Emperor Kaitain's life, the assault on the Heart of Stone, the destruction of the Imperial Palace, the devastation in Rashaleb, the death of the entire royal family in Thorigald. We have even heard rumors that the Citadel of the Dark Gods has been destroyed. Now we hear about the assault on the Academy of Arcane Arts. The world is coming apart at the seams, and it's only a matter of time before the madness finds its way here. But for now, Iltorp seems to be in the eye of the storm, and as is the way of our people, we will give aid where it is needed. Of course we will grant asylum to the survivors of the Academy, and we will welcome you with open arms."

The words did nothing to allay Fiona's disquiet, and though she forced a smile she did not feel its warmth.

"But," the young man continued, "there would need to be conditions to this asylum. If indeed it is true that you are being chased by so many, including the Emperor, there would need to be something to legitimize this arrangement."

Fiona's blood ran cold. Thankfully it was Jastra, who had a reputation for volatility and a penchant for ignoring the niceties of court who spoke up.

"What kind of arrangement could give us the legitimacy you feel we need in these circumstances? What could possibly protect us here from the wrath of the Emperor?"

The young man smiled and shook his head.

"You may all be regarded as the most gifted and intelligent people in Cadaria, but it is shocking how limited your sight and understanding are."

Ashinica took hold of Jastra's arm, trying desperately to keep the situation from escalating and spinning wildly out of control. The young man's smile disappeared and a more stoic and dangerous look fell over his features as he spoke again.

"New forces are taking power on this world, forces far beyond the understanding of self-important creatures like your Emperor Kaitain Lorien, or like the man and woman who used to rule Iltorp. Petty mortal squabbles are no longer at issue. People like yourselves, Masters of that reality which you are able to grasp, could be useful and perhaps even impactful in the battles that are to come. That is, if you shed this useless naiveté about the nature of power and the impact it can have. I am offering you a chance to save your students, protect them from harm for however long this conflict lasts, and ensure that they have a future beyond being victims. In exchange for my magnanimity, I ask that the Masters of the Academy and only the Masters abandon your foolish adherence to non-violent uses of your gifts and form an alliance with myself and my patron."

Jastra's look of disgust could no longer be hidden, nor could Ashinica and Aris' look of dismay and shock. Only Fiona seemed to remain calm in the face of the inflammatory statements.

"Naturally, we would want to meet your patron and hear these guarantees as well as the manner in which they will be carried out."

The young man smiled.

"Of course. But he is attending to far more pressing matters at this moment, and I can give you every assurance that everything my patron promises will be delivered, and in such wondrous ways that you will not believe even once you have witnessed them. Dare I call them, miraculous?"

A chuckle came from the young man a moment later, but before anyone could speak, he continued.

"But as I mentioned, this alliance must be legitimized. A token of friendship and trust as it were."

The sinking feeling came to Fiona's stomach.

"And what would this token be?"

"Why the hand of the beautiful Aris Ebonsight in marriage, of course. A union between the Academy and the newly invested ruler of Iltorp would insure that nothing could come between us."

Finally Fiona's resolve cracked, and shock registered on her face. Aris' face went pale.

"Try not to look so mortified, my dear. You don't know how fortunate you are. Within a matter of weeks you will find yourself married to the future ruler of this world and you will be proud to call yourself the wife of Talon Aielin."

Founding a Third Empire

Year Four of the Just Emperor Kaitain "Dragonsbane" Lorien, Creator's Calendar Year 1871

It was just after sundown when the carriage arrived at the makeshift camp set up by the rebel army of Lordhill. Of course, to anyone outside the leadership of Lordhill, this camp was nothing more than a resource scouting party, exploring possible new sites to dig for natural resources. Such scouting parties were not as common as they once were, but with the whole of Cadaria in their fourth year of war, resources for the creation of weapons and armor were becoming more and more scarce. While it was not the key responsibility of the Lordhill defense force to find new sources for these precious resources, it was the responsibility of every member of the Imperial Legion to investigate possible sites. Sentries patrolled the entire perimeter to ensure that no members of the Imperial Legion would stumble on the true purpose of the camp. Since Rhionna was driving the carriage, none of the soldiers stopped them for more than a few moments to ensure that the carriage posed no threat. The camp itself was sparse, manned by no more than three hundred soldiers, large enough to be effective in a fight for a short time, but small enough to escape serious notice. It represented a small fraction of what Lordhill could bring to muster if needs be, but in the end they were not a strong enough force to rival the Imperial Legion, at least not yet. By the time Rhionna was lowering herself out of the seat, Connor and Gabrielle Peregrim had emerged from the command tent, a combination of concerned and relieved looks on their faces. Gabrielle began to approach the door of the carriage, but Rhionna cut her off with a raised hand and shook her head softly. A moment later the blond woman moved to the door and opened it slowly.

"Just keep an open mind," Rhionna said softly.

Once the door opened, the first person who exited the carriage was Quyhn Ravenheart Lorien. Rhionna helped her down from the carriage and Quyhn waited as Chelsea Zarova moved slowly to the doorway. She was still weak from her confrontation with the Dark God Serrina but it seemed that the healing work done by Liara was beginning to help the Knight of the Flashing Blade regain her former strength. Chelsea accepted Rhionna's hand and stepped down, keeping as much of her weight balanced on her own two feet as she could, but it was a struggle. After several moments, Dominique Arias emerged from the carriage, and Connor and Gabrielle both bowed to the reigning Empress of Cadaria, despite her questionable status for the rest of the world. The last two to emerge from the carriage were the twin members of the Dark Gods, Mirana and Liara. There was a slight hesitation from both Connor and Gabrielle when the two young women emerged, but seeing the way that the others held themselves, it was clear that the young women posed no threat. Without a word, Connor motioned toward the entryway to the command tent, and waited as his wife passed first. Chelsea took a step toward the tent and stumbled slightly. Dominique was by her side the next moment, supporting her friend's weight and keeping her safe in the same way that Chelsea had always strived to keep Dominique safe.

Inside the command tent, the rest of Connor's command staff waited. Arent was leaning over a low table on the far side of the tent looking over maps while Strum was sitting in a corner near the entrance flipping through a series of reports. In the center of the tent was a larger table with chairs placed randomly around it. When Connor entered, he and Gabrielle took places at the table and motioned for Arent and Strum to join them. However, when Dominique and the others entered the tent, both Arent and Strum fell to a knee in deference to their Empress. After the appropriate amount of time, both of the men rose and moved to the table, staying on their feet until both Quyhn and Dominique were seated. Liara and Mirana entered the tent last, and without a word joined the others at the table. There was silence for a long time among the group, before Arent finally leaned back in his chair and started whistling an old tune. As always, Arent's whistling was considerably off-key. Strum began laughing, and within a matter of moments the laughter radiated from the table, and Arent leaned forward again knowing that his job of breaking the tension was successful. Connor rested his elbows on the table and then his chin on the back of his folded hands and rested his gaze on Dominique Arias.

"I'm not sure if you remember or not, Empress," Connor said softly, "but we met once. It was just before your wedding. It was one of the few times that I was allowed to leave Lordhill and come to the capitol. There was a long line of us that waited to pay our respects to you. I know by the time I kissed your hand that you had probably seen a thousand people, but you were still gracious and poised. I know you made quite an impression on everyone that day."

While the compliment made Dominique slightly self-conscious and uncomfortable, she knew that it had come from a place of honesty. She smiled as brightly as she could and even felt herself blush a little.

"That seems like a lifetime ago. It was a blur even then, and now it feels more like a dream. I thought there were so many things I would be able to accomplish, so much good that I could do. But now I look at what Cadaria has become, what this world has become… We have a chance now, finally a real chance to do what is right for our people. But we can't do it alone, and that is why our new friends Mirana and Liara are here. Together, we here at this table can begin to shape a future that none of us could have dreamed before today."

Gabrielle moved her gaze from the Empress to the two young women.

"And so how did you two young ladies find your way into our little conspiracy?"

Before either Mirana or Liara could answer, Quyhn interjected.

"Mirana and Liara have brought us the opportunity for an unexpected alliance. Much more than that I cannot tell you until we discuss the opportunity in more detail. But I can tell you that through them, we may be able to negotiate for a peace and alliance with the Dark Gods."

There was a stunned silence around the room. Connor and Gabrielle shared a look for several moments before Strum spoke.

"I'm not sure if you're all out of your mind, or you're brilliant."

Arent picked up on the thought.

"Kaitain is alienating everyone that used to be an ally of the Loriens. Whether it is the Church of the Creator, or the Academy, or us. I'm not sure though if you were to ally with the Dark Gods, it wouldn't make you even less popular than your husband."

Chelsea glared at Arent and started to speak, but Dominique put her hand on Chelsea's arm.

"I appreciate your honesty," Dominique said after a moment. "For so many years, the Dark Gods have been heralded as the enemy of everyone who called Cadaria home. Even with all of the horrible things that we do to one another, and all of the petty squabbles between the Kingdoms, the Dark Gods are still the greatest threat that any of us could ever know. And your point is well taken. Even the monster that my husband has become, what would I look like if I were to ally myself with the Dark Gods? I would be even more of a traitor. I would be a pariah. I would be more than an adulterous whore, I would be a heretic."

Dominique's words were shattering and disheartening, but her brutal honesty not only about the situation but her role in it was refreshing, striking, and disturbing. Connor leaned back in his chair and crossed his arms under his chest. He looked again to his wife and answered her unspoken question with a nod. Gabrielle focused her eyes on Dominique.

"There has been a lot happening in your absence, Empress, and we received more news once we camped here. The world has become stranger and the divisions in our Empire are deepening every single day. And I'm afraid that news is not encouraging. Strum, you have been going through all of the reports coming out of Zevarit and the ones we intercepted from the Imperial Legions, would you care to brief our honored guests?"

Strum rose from the table and recovered the stack of reports that he was leafing through when everyone entered. When he returned to the table, his brow was furrowed with frustration and confusion. He pulled one particular paper from the stack and cleared his throat.

"It seems as though Kaitain's propaganda against the Church of the Creator was more than just words. I have at least a dozen reports of members of the Imperial Legion raiding and destroying property that belonged to the Church. Those people who were living in these abbeys or retreats are then stripped of all their possessions and all of their freedoms and forced into slavery. The women who had dedicated their lives to worship of the Creator have been reduced to whores that are raped repeatedly by soldiers who have been left vindictive and hateful because of the state of the war. I have stacks and stacks of paper detailing Church properties being burned to the ground. Farmers who took up arms to protect the missionaries and the priests who have been ministering to small towns for years being put to death for their crimes. Those farmers' properties are then confiscated, and once the valuables are taken, they are burned to the ground."

Dominique was horrified, but the details continued, this time coming from Arent.

"We intercepted orders from Kaitain's camp to the Army of Stone in Albitonin. Kaitain has ordered the Army of Stone to invade the Heart of Stone, arrest the High Priestess, and to disassemble any standing forces that are loyal only to the Church. Thus far we have been able to keep most of the messengers from the front from getting past us, but it's only a matter of time. Hopefully, the Army of Stone is dedicated enough to the protection of the High Priestess and the legacy of Hannah Ironheart that they will ignore the orders and stand on their own."

Rhionna tilted her head and looked at Arent with puzzlement written all over her face.

"What incentive would the Army of Stone have to take any orders from Kaitain? They separated themselves from his rule when Albitonin became part of Marlae Lorien's rebellion."

Connor took that opportunity to add his voice to the discussion.

"Hannah Ironheart's disappearance, as well as Gregor Quicksilver's is the reason that Kaitain thinks that he can worm his way back in. Kaitain is not a stupid man, no matter how reckless his actions may seem now; they are all done to create an environment of fear. These attacks, this brutality by the Imperial Legion on the lands and people of the Church of the Creator are not random. Kaitain wants the rumors and fear to fill the ranks of everyone who has a tie to the Church. If he sews enough fear, if he creates enough doubt, he can begin to fracture the power base that Hannah worked so hard to create."

Gabrielle picked up where her husband left off.

"When Feyd and Kaitain were just boys, Ender was dealing with the aftermath of Kaldawyn's death, and the fragmentation of the Empire that that death caused. The Knights of the Flashing Blade were spread out through the whole of the Empire trying to hold fragmentary Kingdoms together. There was talk coming from everywhere that some of the royals doubted the rule of the Lorien family. They were wondering very loudly if the Founding Wars should start again, and a new Imperial Family be chosen. That was where Gregor Quicksilver came in. He traveled through all of the Kingdoms preaching patience and tolerance and understanding. He was beloved in a way that neither Kaldawyn nor Ender ever would be. Gregor's faithfulness had exactly the opposite effect that he intended. Of course his words and his actions cooled the talk of a new Founding War, but in its place came calls for Emperor Ender Lorien to step down from his position and give the throne to Gregor Quicksilver."

Here Gabrielle took a long deep breath.

"At the time, Ender was calm, and he dealt with the situation the only way that a sitting Emperor could. He called Gregor to Aldere and spoke with him. Gregor didn't want the throne, didn't want power, and didn't want the love that he had engendered with the people to pull the Empire apart. He offered to resign his position as Knight of the Flashing Blade, and to go into seclusion for the rest of his days. What Ender didn't know was that both Feyd and Kaitain listened to the whole saga, listened as a man that Ender trusted detailed how much more he was loved in the Empire than their father. Feyd was far more understanding, as one would expect, but Kaitain, he immediately hated Gregor. For days all Kaitain would talk about was how the Church would do anything in their power to steal the throne out from under Ender. Gregor was too stupid to take the power that was offered to him, but how long would it be before some other unscrupulous religious fanatic with delusions of grandeur would turn the huddled masses into a fanatical raving mob."

Connor crossed his arms.

"Kaitain's been plotting this for a long time. When he was just a prince being prepared for taking the throne, Kaitain learned everything he could about the types of people who were in the Imperial Legion, and then once he took the throne, he found ways to transfer all of the morally upright officers and soldiers to the most remote postings in Cadaria. He surrounded himself with thugs, barbarians, and those who could be easily controlled. Those who were the most blood-thirsty and coveted power found themselves fast-tracked into leadership positions. The only ones that Kaitain couldn't freeze out were those that were in leadership positions already and were considered untouchable, like the Knights of the Flashing Blade and their lieutenants."

Quyhn frowned.

"Who knew he was that much of a monster?"

Dominique sat straight.

"Kaitain didn't respect the way that his father did things. When Kaitain would come to bed drunk he would ramble and rage for hours about how his father let the people of Cadaria become too comfortable. There were so many threats, and so many dangers, and Ender did not allow his people to see them. His military was soft, and too insular to be of any use when the time came for real war. The Wasting Disease was a blessing as far as Kaitain was concerned. It freed him in a way he never expected. His wife was gone, his father was gone, he had all the power he could ever want, and there was a ready-made war waiting for him. Perhaps there was madness in him. Whatever it was, once he sat upon the throne, the rest of the world could only shudder and suffer."

It was Chelsea's opportunity to add her voice to the conversation.

"Once Kaitain became Emperor, we all saw shifts. What Connor describes at lower levels was more acutely present at the highest levels. Royal family members started disappearing throughout the kingdoms. People who should never have been considered for the Knights of the Flashing Blade were suddenly elevated to the highest levels of Cadarian armies. Tolon Morr didn't have the qualifications to be a general, but he was a powerful warrior. Orren Eldrath and Jaccob Aldora were selected to antagonize the Academy of Arcane Arts. They also seemed to share similar views that the Academy could not remain isolated and that their abilities needed to be used to combat threats to the Cadarian Empire. Devlin Rannoch was an outcast that couldn't be trusted by anyone. But nothing Kaitain could do would infiltrate his will into Albitonin, Thorigald, Saldarine, Oradrim, Zevarit, Menoris, Bellnoc, or Iltorp."

Dominique frowned.

"Until he found out about me."

Chelsea continued.

"Marrying Dominique was designed to drive a deeper wedge between Saldarine and Thorigald. It was meant to put Seraph and I on the defensive. And it worked. Bellnoc would always be in play because it's controlled predominately by the Shadow Guild. Zevarit wasn't going to budge until Gregor was out of the way. That's why the suicide mission to Mythryn. Best case, Gregor would be killed and Kaitain could name whoever he wanted to the post of Ruby Knight, but even if Gregor returned, Kaitain would be able to name him as a traitor. Once that happened, there would be many who would come to Gregor's defense, namely Leonora. That would take down two of the most powerful members of the Knights of the Flashing Blade, and those with the most unimpeachable reputations."

Gabrielle nodded.

"And now that the whole of the Knights of the Flashing Blade have been dissolved and broken, the Cadarian Empire along with it, it gives Kaitain the opportunity to do what no Emperor has ever been able to do, to take direct control over each and every Cadarian Kingdom and unite them under his iron fist."

For all this time, Mirana and Liara had simply been sitting and listening. This was the time they took the opportunity to add their voices to the discussion. Mirana leaned forward and rested her elbows on the table, brought her hand to her chin and slowly spun the ring around her thumb.

"It's interesting listening to all of you talk about your Kaitain Lorien that way. From where we could observe, this Kaitain seemed reckless, stupid and blinded by his need to destroy. From the outside it looked like he was lashing out at anyone he could."

"And we know all about that," Liara added.

"This is just evil," Mirana said.

"And we know all about that too," Liara answered.

"Which is why it was harder and harder for the Dark Gods to stay out of the conflict," Mirana continued. "He was destabilizing everything to force a war."

"A war he could never possibly win," Liara countered.

"And one that would only mean destruction because as much as he understood the politics of his own Empire, he could never understand the politics that kept the Dark Gods from destroying him. He had been raised on the same lie that the rest of the Cadarians have been for generations," Mirana said with disgust filling her voice.

"That one brave Emperor with his shiny golden sword could cut down a member of the Dark Gods," Liara finished.

Gabrielle and Connor's faces were blank, while both Strum and Arent looked on with combinations of puzzlement and disbelief. Dominique smiled and shook her head, while Quyhn simply added.

"They do that," with a smile in her voice. "You get used to it."

Both Mirana and Liara smiled an almost embarrassed smile and finally Mirana continued.

"But this is the reason that Midarin chose to approach you, Dominique," Mirana said with a new conviction in her voice. "The Dark Gods do not want open conflict with the Cadarians. It would benefit no one, and if anything it would be devastating for the whole of Cadaria. The Dark Gods have no interest in ruling Cadaria, but if that was the only way to stop the threat, then just one of them is more than capable of devastating the whole of your Imperial Legion and laying waste to your cities. An alliance that sees the removal of Kaitain and the restoration of a just government that will abide by the conditions of the original treaty of the first Cadarian Emperor is what the Dark Gods are seeking. If such an alliance were offered, the Dark Gods would accept it with the proviso that they would take no aggressive action against any Cadarian interests."

Dominique looked to Quyhn.

"We've spoken about this privately but Connor deserves to hear it all."

Quyhn nodded and turned her attention to Connor and Gabrielle.

"As Dominique and I have discussed, she has no power to negotiate a truce with the Dark Gods, at least not one that could be considered binding in any way. If Kaitain is removed from power, the title would not pass to her, but to me. So I would have to be the one to make any deal. I am willing to have these discussions, and Mirana and Liara here have assured me that the Dark Gods will be willing to have these discussions as well. You are my trusted councilors, and I believe that I owed it to you to hear the proposal and hear your opinion before any course was taken."

Gabrielle and Connor exchanged glances once again, and this time it was Connor who spoke. There was concern in his voice, but his words were not at all what Quyhn had been expecting.

"When I was first assigned to Rashaleb, I was on a night patrol when I ventured too far away from camp. Because of the shifting weather it was too dangerous to go into too many of the uninhabited areas because of possible avalanches and fissures that could open in the ice without warning. But something had caught my attention and I had to know what I saw."

Here Connor paused, and he rubbed his shoulder as though remembering the pain of an old injury.

"I thought I saw a shadow move, the shape of a person moving into what I knew was a clearing between two glacial crags. In order to gain a better understanding of what was going on, I made my way to the top of one of the bluffs so that I could look down upon the clearing. There I saw the mysterious figure, waiting in the middle of nowhere, doing nothing but looking around. A moment later another man just appeared out of thin air. The second man was memorable because he had only one arm."

Connor saw a quick sideways glance pass between the two young women on the far side of the table, but he continued.

"Of course I couldn't make out what the two men were saying to one another, but the one-armed man seemed to just be listening while the other did all the talking. Finally the one-armed man spoke a few words and the other man left. I was going to back away slowly and report what I saw, but the ice under me gave way and I went tumbling down the cliff with rocks and ice falling right on top of me. When I hit the bottom, I was pinned. My legs were crushed and my shoulder was broken and dislocated. By the time anyone from my regiment found me, I would have been long dead. Either I would have bled to death, frozen to death, or have been eaten. I didn't even have the strength to cry out for help. But the one-armed man, he saw the avalanche. He saw me fall. Instead of leaving me for dead, he came to my rescue, and without lifting so much as a finger the weight was shifted off of me and I was freed. Even then I would not have been able to crawl back to camp. The pain was too great. The next thing I knew, the one-armed man was leaning over me just as I lost consciousness. When I woke up, I was back in my own bed, and the only evidence I had that the whole thing wasn't a dream was the throbbing pain in my shoulder that I've had ever since. I've known in my heart for all these years that the one-armed man was a Dark God."

Liara smiled.

"That was our grandfather."

The implication of the statement was clear, but gained no more reaction than a slight smile from Gabrielle. Finally, Connor turned back to Quyhn and nodded. Quyhn smiled and motioned to Liara. The younger of the sisters pushed back from the table and stood.

"Well, I guess I better get going then. I should be back within the day with your answer."

Dominique nodded.

"In the mean time we have a lot of planning to do if we're going to create the foundation of Quyhn's new empire."

Buried Alive

Year Four of the Just Emperor Kaitain "Dragonsbane" Lorien,
Creator's Calendar Year 1871

For most of her life, Jillian Corven had been in the midst of one kind of battle or another. When she was just a young girl, her entire village had been reduced to a charred husk of its former self by a dragon attack. Her mother was gone, her friends were gone, and everything that she knew lay smoking around her. In those days, her mind wasn't equipped to deal with the horrors, and in some ways she never even processed them as tragic. She was alone, she was afraid, and the smell of the burning bodies did nothing more than drive her away. There were only fragments of those images left in her memory, and they did not chill her in the same way that the carnage in the Plains of Steam had. From the moment she became an orphan in the dragon attack to the moment she found herself at the side of a Dark God, Jillian thought she had an understanding of what her life was and what her life would always be. And then the man she first came to know as Dane, and then later by his true name, Logan Ranthall, came into her life and turned everything upside down. Fighting dragons seemed trivial now. She saw one of Dorovar's servants. She saw a power-mad little girl who was a match for a handful of Dark Gods, and she had been in the presence of a woman that had the powers of a Child of the Creator. If she had stopped to think about any of it for more than a few moments, her entire concept of perspective would be destroyed and she would probably be rendered completely useless to anyone. So, somehow, Logan had become her anchor in the sea of absurdity. But nothing she had seen, not the destruction of her village, not the thousands of dead soldiers in the Plains of Steam, not even the news of the destruction of Rashaleb prepared her for what waited on the other side of the portal. Nothing prepared her for the insanity and the devastation in Menoris.

Logan had emerged first from the portal, and when Jillian stepped through, she ran right into the back of him. He had come to a complete halt, and for a few brief seconds she didn't see what had frozen him in his tracks. But the minute her eyes found what should have been the city of Menoris stretched below them, her knees went weak and it felt as though her stomach were going to violently reject the remnants of breakfast. Her head ached and tears poured from the corners of her eyes. The city was simply gone, crushed beneath an unbelievable weight. At the edges of the devastation fires still burned, but nothing stirred. She could not see anything that resembled a survivor, not even wildlife seemed to be spared the unbelievable destruction. Logan still had not moved a muscle, but finally, he reached out and touched her arm for a moment. She thought he was going to hold her hand, attempt to find some support or some kind of sanity in the face of the insane, but instead he pushed her slightly away from him. The next moment Jillian felt the heat as an explosion of green flame seemed to pour from each of his pores, surrounding him in a burning aura. The heat caused Jillian to take another step away from Logan, but at the same time she moved to a position where she could see his face. His eyes were closed and the lines on his face betrayed the effort he was putting into whatever he was doing. What shocked Jillian the most was the stream of blood that was pouring not only from his nose, but also from the corners of his eyes. He extended one hand after what seemed like an eternity and then the brilliant flames intensified, almost completely obscuring Logan from her view. It was the sound of rumbling from below that broke Jillian's concentration on her companion, and she was not prepared for the sight of a broken mountain rising from the ground below. It moved very little for the first few moments, as though the sheer weight was too much to be moved. Finally the whole broken mass was lifted off the ground, and Jillian could see the remains of the city beneath. The grunt from Logan's lips was enough to bring her attention back to him, but the fires were too bright for her to make out any of his features. The roaring green fires flared again, the brilliant green fading, replaced by blinding white. A pulse of the brilliant flames burst forth engulfing the rubble. Jillian had to shield her eyes and when she was finally able to blink away the brilliant spots, the pieces of the mountain were simply gone. Logan had slumped to the ground, and supported himself on his hands and knees. Blood continued to pour from his nose and eyes, but now was joined with a steady stream that oozed from his mouth as he panted for breath. She wasn't sure what she was supposed to do, so she did what seemed the most expedient. She rummaged through her pack for a shirt and knelt beside Logan, dabbing the blood away from his mouth and nose. After several long moments, he was able to gain control of his breathing, and sat back on his knees, looking not at Jillian, but off to the horizon.

"Well, that was probably one of the more stupid things I've ever done," he said with slight amusement in his voice. "It probably should have killed me."

Jillian tried not to let any concern show on her face, and the shock helped that. It would take a long time before her mind could wrap itself around what she had just seen. How was it that anyone, even a member of the Dark Gods, could lift an entire mountain? After a long deep breath, Logan tried to push his way back to his feet, but faltered. He managed to get one foot underneath him, but almost toppled over. Jillian was able to keep him upright, but just barely. When he leaned on her for balance he felt as though he weighed three times what he should, but he only used her for a moment, and the weight was not enough to overwhelm her. Finally he was able to get both feet beneath him and push himself back to a standing position, but his knees were obviously week and his footing unsure. He tested a few short steps before feeling confident enough for a normal stride. Those simple full steps took him to the edge of the cliff that looked down onto the city. He looked back at Jillian and then back to the city several times, as though he was trying to make a decision.

"What's wrong?" she asked finally.

"Not sure I can manage a portal," he said with a little embarrassment in his voice. "And even if I could, I'm not sure my aim would do you much good. If I miss high, I can survive the fall much better than you can, and if

I were to miss low, I can hold my breath long enough to dig out. I'm really afraid that any miscalculation would be fatal for you."

Jillian couldn't suppress her smile.

"Then why don't we just go down the mortal way," she said pointing at a simple trial obviously used by traders and locals. "That is, if you can manage such a mundane thing."

Logan could not help but smile himself. He gave her an exaggerated bow, followed by a sweep of his arm indicating that she should precede him.

"By all means," his voice intoned with a hint of sarcasm. "Ladies first."

She couldn't resist striking him in the shoulder as she passed.

* * * * * * * * * * * *

The Gray Man Pestilence stood looking over the carnage below and marveled with a bemused look on his long gaunt face. His companion wore no expression at all, but that was to be expected from one with the name Death. For a long time Pestilence watched silently as the man and woman picked their way down the narrow path that lead them safely down into the valley where the city of Menoris once stood. Now all that was left was a graveyard.

"He's becoming quite strong, isn't he?"

Pestilence turned his attention to his companion who not surprisingly said nothing at all, but had his red-eyed stare firmly locked on the one known as the Phoenix.

"Though he is still no match for the Master, he could still cause quite a bit of trouble. While Jerah has firmly ordered me to take no action against him, I don't recall you being given the same orders."

Finally Death turned its head to regard Pestilence. Death did not hate Pestilence, but he found the creature's tone trying. Despite its transcendence, it still had the uncanny knack for acting human. Perhaps that was why Jerah was Dorovar's chosen and not Pestilence. But, no matter the scheme that Pestilence was planning to hatch, one thing was clear to Death. The one called the Phoenix was dangerous, and if there was no direct prohibition against Death taking action in the name of the Master, then he would proudly do so. Death knelt and drew his sword, embedding it firmly in the ground and then beginning to concentrate. Though the souls of the wretched mortals had been freed to join the Master's chorus, the bodies could still find some use.

* * * * * * * * * * *

From a distance the carnage had been terrible, but now that she was face to face with it, there were no words to describe just how horrible it all was. Crushed and broken bodies littered what once were the streets, and they were largely indistinguishable because of the piles of rubble and broken buildings that had been spread across the entire face of what had once been one of the most beautiful cities in all of Cadaria. Menoris was not the largest of the capital cities of the Cadarian Kingdoms, but its population numbered nearly one hundred thousand. A large portion of that number was part of the monastic order that had called Menoris home nearly since the inception of the Empire. The Peaks of Patience cast a shadow over them, and in their teachings was a reminder of the greatness of things that came before, and the greatness of the power of nature to create such wonders. Now it was that revered wonder that had destroyed them.

Logan walked silently, his eyes scanning all around him, looking for some hint that there had been fortunate survivors. Here and there he knelt down, picking his way through rubble. Occasionally he found doors that looked as though they led to cellars in some of the larger houses. However each time he found nothing. It was as though the inhabitants of Menoris had no warning, no time to react and to get themselves to safety. One of the worst displays of death was in a ship that had been cast onto the shore. It must have crashed down from a great height, the thick masts shattered into thousands of pieces and the bodies of the sailors were impaled in dozens of places. Logan was clearly steering them toward where the foot of the mountain had been, the home of the monastic order that was both the government and the royalty for the Kingdom of Menoris. Menoris was the only Kingdom of Cadaria that did not have a royal family, and the leadership instead was imparted to the leader of the monastic order, and that power was passed down as each new leader took over for the last. It was a stability that benefited everyone in Menoris, and helped the Kingdom earn its name as the Kingdom of Knowledge and Wisdom. Few called the Kingdom by both names, preferring to shorten the title to the more preferred Kingdom of Knowledge.

The deathly silence was broken suddenly by the sound of a pile of rubble shifting. Both Logan and Jillian found themselves with their hands on their blades and after a long moment looking in the direction the sound had come they looked at one another, and it was Logan who smiled and shook his head.

"Guess I'm getting jumpy in my old age. Though I guess you can't blame a guy who's two thousand years old, give or take."

Jillian flashed him her best flirty smile.

"I suppose last night gives a whole new meaning to cradle robbing then."

Logan's smile widened and there was a slight blush in his cheeks.

"Are you sure you're not related to Aerith? That sounds just like something he would say."

The repartee was interrupted by another sound, this time coming from a pile of debris closer to the pair. However the sound was accompanied by a groan from deep under the pile. Without a word Logan rushed to the pile, practically throwing the massive weight aside to get at the person below. Perhaps there were survivors after all, and the hunt was not in vain. However, as soon as Logan saw the desiccated body he had uncovered, he worried that the sound he had heard had only been a figment of his imagination, wishful thinking manifested. But then the corpse moved. Half of what used to be a man's skull was exposed and several ribs poked out from his side. His jaw hung loose, broken teeth clearly visible in the gaping mouth. The creature's eyes were white, and as it shambled to its feet, it took a piece of wood that lay nearby and wielded it like a club. Logan took a step back, collecting Jillian with his outstretched arm. But she did not move at his urging. At first he thought she had been frozen by the sight of the dead man, but when he looked over his shoulder, he saw what had truly drawn her attention.

All around them the bodies of the fallen were beginning to move. Most were able to get to their feet while others were still trying to free themselves from the rubble that trapped them. All were armed, and while many only carried improvised clubs, some were still wielding the swords and other weapons that they had been carrying before their death. Dozens became hundreds, and within a matter of moments, Logan and Jillian were surrounded, with the ranks of the dead stretching on as far as the eye could see. Now Logan didn't hesitate to draw his sword, and without a word his lashed out with a burst of flame that engulfed several dozen of the creatures. They fell to the ground without a sound, but the victory was short-lived. The force of the blow had been enough to knock them from their feet, but with fire crawling across their mangled bodies, the fallen got back to their feet, renewing their slow advance.

"Well," Logan said wiping some sweat from his brow, "who says after two thousand years you can't see something new?"

Jillian could feel the exhaustion in Logan's voice, and she prepared herself for a fight. No matter what these creatures were, there had to be a way to defeat them. Nothing was invincible, not dragons, not dark gods, and certainly not shambling dead. Logan's voice came again and he put his sword back into the sheathe on his hip.

"Ok, time to be a little more inventive. Picked this up from an old friend."

The next moment Logan extended his hands in front of him. The ground beneath their feet rumbled loudly like thunder coming from under the soil. The sound and movement slowed the advance of the surrounding creatures, and Jillian could feel Logan's whole body trembling. Finally he spread his extended hands apart, and the ground before him began to open into a large fissure. The fissure widened, soil giving way and sending dozens of the creatures toppling into the chasm that was opening beneath their feet. But as many of the creatures fell, the others continued their advance, their pace quickening. Logan changed his tactics, thrusting his hands down toward the ground, and when he raised them again a circular wall of stone several feet thick sprung up around them. For some reason through, Jillian did not feel safe behind their newly constructed defenses. In her mind it was only a matter of time before the creatures either broke through or climbed over.

"Any other ideas?" Jillian asked trying hard not to sound disheartened.

"Oh ye of little faith," Logan said trying to hide his own concern. "Have an idea, but needed to protect us first. If this works, there won't be much left."

If Jillian wanted to ask a question, it was drown out by the rumbling that suddenly began beneath their feet. It was deeper than Logan's last attempt to destroy the creatures, and the whole area sounded like it was being squeezed and tortured by whatever the dark god was doing. It wasn't until the rumbling grew louder that Jillian realized that she was sweating and it was starting to get hotter around them. Then she saw the first geyser of fire shoot into the sky. It was far enough away that none of it would splash down upon them, but it didn't stop Jillian from shaking, or moving closer to Logan. Another geyser flashed into the sky, followed by another, and another. Before long a dozen of the pillars of liquid fire had erupted from the ground. Finally Logan wiped his brow and dropped to his knees. It was clear that the effort, coupled with what it had taken to remove the remainder of the mountain had taxed him to the limit, but he did not allow himself to stay on his knees for too long. By the time Jillian had knelt beside him, he was already looking at the stone wall that surrounded them. He extended his hand and touched the wall. There was a bright flash of light, and suddenly the opaque stone wall had changed into transparent crystal, allowing the two of them to view the carnage that was taking place beyond their circle of protective stone.

What Jillian saw beyond the circle of transparent stone took several moments to adjust to, as it was too ridiculous to be real. But then she had to remind herself that her perception of reality was little better than an ant's perception of the world of humans. All around them the liquid flames were spreading across the ground, engulfing anything that it touched. The creatures that surrounded them were dragged down into the flames as though it were quicksand, and after a few moments were completely devoured by the lava. The ground had belched forth this maelstrom of death and devastation, but Logan was using it cleanse away the destruction wrought by the falling mountain. It would take only a handful of minutes before all of the beasts were consumed as well as the rubble from the fallen homes. The geysers subsided, leaving only the roiling flames and ocean of lava behind. Their island of crystal had remained undisturbed and finally Jillian began to feel safe once again. But suddenly her eyes found something in the distance, in the direction where the foot of the Peaks of Patience had once been. It looked like a shadow for a moment, and then the shadow moved, getting closer to them. After several moments the shadow had a definite shape, that of a man, but even at that distance Jillian could tell that it was no ordinary man, more like a giant. There were no words that found their way to Jillian's tongue, and all she could do was tug at Logan's sleeve and point toward her discovery. She found herself more surprised when he smiled.

"I was hoping he would notice."

Jillian just stared.

"As if someone wouldn't notice this?"

Logan got back to his feet and helped Jillian to hers. His smile was wide and his eyes beamed with pride.

"You don't know my friend. He's a sound sleeper."

As the giant man approached, Jillian got a better look at him. He wore a simple monk's robe with a crimson sash and some crimson embroidery around the cuffs of the sleeves and the bottom. His head was shaven with the exception of long strands of hair that jutted out from the back of his head and fell into a long braid that reached nearly to his feet. It swung from side to side as he walked. He wore no shoes, but everywhere that his feet touched the roiling lava, it turned to shimmering obsidian, smooth and solid. When the man finally made his way to the circle of crystal, he put his hand over his heart and bowed slightly to Logan, then reached down with his massive hands and touched the lava. Darkness swept through the lake of fire bringing it to a frozen end, all converted to the shiny black stone. Once done, Logan put his hand on the circle of crystal, and the protective wall disappeared. The massive man standing well over ten feet in height stepped into the circle and went down to one knee so that Logan and Jillian would not have to crane their necks to look up at him. Despite his size and muscle-laden frame, the giant had a kind and peaceful air about him.

"Jillian, I'd like to you to meet my brother, in more ways than one I suppose. This is the Living Flame, Kamen."

The man that Logan introduced as Kamen bowed his head slightly in Jillian's direction and turned his attention back to Logan.

"You picked an inopportune time to return home, brother. There was no warning, and there were so few that I could save. Twenty brothers were in the Sanctuary of Flame with me, and another dozen acolytes were in the passages. All told there are no more than fifty of the Order still remaining. But perhaps that is why you are here Phoenix. Can you restore your order from the ashes as you did once before?"

Jillian looked from Kamen to Logan who had a pensive look on his face. When he finally realized that Jillian was looking at him, he did his best to smile.

"Kamen is exaggerating. I just helped get the Order on its feet."

There was a slight frown on Kamen's face for a brief moment, but he then put his hand on his heart and bowed his head.

"The Phoenix returns to flames when its life is ended, only to be reborn once more to continue its work. My life before was the Phoenix. Now I am but the flickering flame waiting to be reborn. Only through my deeds on this world may I become the majestic Phoenix once more. I shall walk this world, the flickering flame, to raise up those who cannot rise by themselves. I shall use this flickering flame to bring comfort to those who have none, shelter those who know only the ravages of the world. I am the flickering flame, and yet I am so much more."

Kamen raised his head once more, only this time setting his eyes on Jillian.

"Once I was the Flame, and I was given the power to destroy. When I was brought to this world, destroy was all I knew how to do. The Phoenix, my brother, the only brother to ever show me kindness, found me. He showed me that we are not limited by the path we were born on. He showed me another way. When the wars for control of Cadaria were coming to an end there were soldiers who knew no other way but to kill. Logan brought them here; he showed them that there was another way. A path other than death and destruction. He drew around him those who wanted to be more. And so they were the Order of the Flickering Flame. They embraced the greatness of what the Phoenix offered. And when the Phoenix left them, they redoubled their efforts. They wanted to prove that the flickering flame of their new lives was more powerful than the raging fires of the old. They too hoped to be reborn into something greater, to find a way to become a phoenix themselves. I stayed when Logan left to take his teaching and his love into the world. I continued to work, and through the Order of the Flickering Flame we carved an island of wisdom into the sea of chaos. Now it seems that the forces of darkness have tried to extinguish the flickering flame, and they will only taste the ash when it returns to burn them."

Kamen stood, pulling himself to his full height.

"Where the Phoenix walks, the Flame shall follow. The time for peace has passed, and the time has come to make our enemies burn."

Animosity's Price

Year Four of the Just Emperor Kaitain "Dragonsbane" Lorien, Creator's Calendar Year 1871

Mariti Brightblade stood outside of the home that all of the dragons had known since coming to Espre. She could not stand to set foot inside the ruins of the Great Tree, for she knew that the corpse of her beloved, the body of the greatest of their number still lay there. No member of the dragons would approach his body, they would simply let him lie in state for as long as nature determined that he should. That was the dragon way. They were born out of the Cosmos, and they would return to the Cosmos, each in their own time. So too would be true for Lord Tarot. Soon there would be nothing left of him, not even his bones. But as the stars began to appear overhead, it gave Mariti time to reflect before the rest of the members of the Council arrived, at least those who were still loyal to the cause that Tarot began. How many would come, she wondered. How many would be willing to fight by her side once they learned who they would fight with. But the battle lines were clearly drawn now, and there were not two simple and clean sides. There were the forces of the Creator, the forces of each of the Children, the forces that Dorovar had called to his banner. Now there were those that served the Heretic and those that served the Dark Gods. The battlefield was awash with confusion, and it was clear that each side was trying to play those in the middle off each other. That was why the Spirit came to her. There were alliances to be secured. But the truth was that the Creator had nothing to offer the dragons. The visit was manipulation nothing more. But the woman, Hannah Ironheart, she had something to offer. She saw a better way. The question was whose better way it was. Was it hers, or was it the Heretic's? Perhaps it no longer mattered. The fight had been joined. One of Dorovar's Heralds had fallen, and it had been Hannah Ironheart, and not one of the Servants of the Creator that made it possible. Actions spoke louder in the current climate of war, and it was Hannah Ironheart's actions that had inflamed Mariti to action.

"I never thought I would come back here," said a voice from off in the distance. "And I almost did not. But I felt your call, and I knew that if you were calling, it was important."

Mariti did not have to turn to know the identity of the voice. Diamondvein had been one of the staunchest supporters of Tarot back in the days of the wars, and during the divisions that led to the occupation of Dorovar's world.

"Were this not the most appropriate place for this conversation, old friend, I would not choose to be here either. Any news from the world? I have been occupied as of late and know nothing of the war's progress."

Diamondvein's voice took on a sorrowful quality.

"Something is happening, and it impacts all of us. There is a force, many believe it is tied to Dorovar that is hunting down and wiping us out one by one. Abysm Nightwalker and Agathys Smokespitter both fell in their dens in Galateria. There was no warning, and no sightings of dragon hunters in the area. Dothian the Inevitable was killed when the Peaks of Patience were somehow dropped upon the city of Menoris."

Though she was repulsed by the thought of three of their members falling to unknown forces, the names did not have as much impact as they could. Both Abysm and Agathys were supporters of Shadowweaver and would not have been party to this new conspiracy, and in some aspects their deaths removed opposition from her cause. Dothian would not have supported any side, his goals and motivations had always been his own, and he had never been one to share them. He would have waited until the end of the world and slept through it if he could have. Many millennia ago, when Dorovar's world fell, Dothian lost the will to fight, and lost the will to do anything other than live out his years in peace.

"Glaciarium Magnus and Frigia Shatterbreath must be counted among the lost as well," a new voice added. "They were killed in battle in Rashaleb. It is said that there were Dark Gods in Rashaleb and a great battle. Glaciarium and Frigia were only protecting their homes, and the Dark Gods cut them down as though they were nothing. There was no provocation."

Jovar the Unbreakable was an older member of the race, but was not nearly as old as Mariti. He was somewhat erratic, but usually had the best intentions for his actions. The words he was saying in substance may have been true, but Mariti knew from experience that he was not telling the whole story because he was not interested in the whole story. He was a reactionary. It puzzled Mariti as to why Jovar would support Tarot after all of these years, as his temperament seemed more suited to Shadowweaver's way of thinking, but century after century Jovar resisted Shadowweaver's radical callings.

"facts not clear….." Serentis' voice came from the shadows, "Frigia…..unstable….territorial. quick to judge….quick to anger."

Mariti was relieved to see Serentis. There was little argument that Serentis was the wisest of their ranks, and it was always thought that she could see into the beyond much in the same way as the mortal seers had been able to. She was one of the few members of the dragon race that had been touched with divine power. It was unclear how those dragons came to be, or why they even existed. But the fact was that Serentis had never spoken about what her visions showed her unless it meant there were dire consequences that faced the dragons. She predicted the coming of Dorovar, but no one even listened.

"Whatever happened," Mariti said finally, "they are both great losses to our cause."

Over the next hour over two dozen more dragons appeared in the clearing, and every one that arrived, made Mariti feel that the task before them was less hopeless. However there were some notable absences that concerned her. The war had made it difficult to trust, even in the leadership of the dragon council, and Tarot's death had impacts that few would ever really understand. All told there were twenty five of them, and with another fourteen counted among the dead, a full third of their membership had been accounted for. More Mariti knew would never follow Shadowweaver, but she did not know how many of those would remain neutral in the war to come. Shadowweaver could muster at least equal to their number, and perhaps had more than that. But at the least it was encouraging.

"Why are we here Mariti? I know that the death of Tarot has impacted you, but if you are ready to assume the leadership of our race as Tarot intended, you couldn't have picked a better time."

Aisengard Starlight was a welcome face, loyal and powerful. Mariti measured her words before responding.

"We have sat passive and comfortable in our superiority for too long, and our complacency has allowed threats like the Dark Gods and Dorovar to rise unchecked. Even the mortals hunt us, kill us, and burn our nests. But the ultimate injustice was done here. Dorovar came to our home and killed our leader with his bare hands. He has vowed to destroy every one of us, one by one, to gain his revenge against us. But his power is not absolute. I have watched as one of his Heralds was torn down. It can be done, and he can be defeated. But we cannot do it alone. We have to make alliances with those of like mind to us, those who share common enemies with us, and those who we pose no threat to and who pose no threat to us."

Venya of the Gleaming Eyes was the next to add her voice to the proceedings.

"And who are these allies? Who was powerful enough to fight Dorovar's Heralds on their own terms? We've already heard the stories about the creature called War. And then there is the one called Jerah that had a hand in the deaths of Phantasma, Pandesmos, and Karasut. We know the Servants of the Creator cannot be trusted, and there is no bright light like Pyrrus to align with against Talisia and Emries. I've heard that even Halicon has fallen."

"Halicon gone…..power remains," Serentis intoned. "Pyrrus too….gone but still powerful….have not slipped from the world yet….Emries confident….Talisia schemes….no alliance possible….Raenera waits."

Ossa Skyscraper, one of the smaller of the dragons spoke with a high tinny voice.

"Are we really ready to stand against the Children of the Creator? Has it come to that at last? Stand against Dorovar, stand against the Children. But does that mean we stand against the Servants and the Creator as well?"

Aspertis the Just snorted fire into the air. His scales rippled with divine fire, and was without question possessed of the very fires of the Heavens that the angels wielded in their swords. Aspertis was sometimes called the Dragon of Heaven, or at the very least the Dragon of Divine Fire, however he preferred simply Aspertis the Just.

"We cannot stand against the Creator. We were made by the Creator, no differently than the Children were. He formed us with His own hands and His own thoughts. There is nothing save His providence that can unmake us. But make no mistake, if we stand in opposition to the Children, we may prevail. If we stand in opposition to the Servants, we may win great victories. However, standing against the Creator, standing against the one who made us would be the ruination of us all. There is no victory there. That burden, if there is to be a toppling of the Throne, must come from the mortals. We cannot take part."

Venya answered.

"Those sound like the words of a coward."

Diamondvein came to Aspertis' defense quickly.

"They are the words of someone who has gazed on the Throne, and who has tasted the blood of angels. Aspertis and Mariti are the most accomplished warriors in our ranks. During Talisia's rebellion they waded through whole regiments of angels trying to save Pyrrus. There are many among our breed that I would call a coward, and Aspertis would never be one of them."

Mariti growled.

"This is why we fail," Mariti said coldly. "The animosity that holds between us has always prevented us from acting responsibly. We argue, we bicker, and we try to hold together fragile alliances that have never done anything but prevent all-out war. But it was Tarot's will that truly held us together, and all that is left now that he is gone is old grudges, mistrust, and fear. The cracks between us have finally shattered what had held since the dawn of time. Even during the rebellion we were not this fractured. That is why there must be drastic changes. You are not going to be held to old agreements, old friendships and old grudges. If all you want is to make those who you have battled with for generations suffer, then perhaps you should not be here. I have seen the new way, and this is what I offer to you. The Spirit has already tried to dissuade me from this task. I have gotten threats from every angle possible, but one has stood before me, unafraid of those who seek to destroy us. One who is dedicated to her task and to her lot in this war. She has asked that we fight with her, and I have said that I would rally troops to her banner. And so I have called you here, to tell you of this opportunity and to ask for your help."

Aisengard asked the question that everyone was waiting for the answer to.

"And who is this mysterious ally that offers deliverance from our enemies and salvation from the hands of those who would destroy us?"

Mariti steeled herself for the inevitable tumult that would follow her next words.

"Hannah Ironheart."

There were several roars that came from different direction and the bickering began. Many voices called down the name, a mortal, a servant of the emperor who called himself the bane of dragons. Others supported Mariti, knowing she would not make the suggestion lightly. Finally it was

Serentis' voice that rose above the rest, and as usual, when the serpentine dragon spoke, everyone listened.

"woman linked to heretic….not beholden….new vision….new opportunities….good match."

The words caused a strong reaction from several, none stronger than from Jovar.

"We cannot align with the Heretic. He will lead us to ruin, and any who follow him will share that fate. He is reckless, cares for none other than himself and his goals. How many have died because of him? How many have suffered because of him? He wants to destroy everything, tear everything down that the Creator has made, and doesn't care how he goes about it. That is not our way. We are not mindless thugs that burn everything in our path. How can we say we are the superior creatures in the Cosmos if we bow to that creature?"

Aspertis answered.

"That is what the unenlightened see. Aerith reaps chaos, but his actions are not chaotic. His goal is clear, and by meeting here together, we have all but thrown our weight behind him. Are we agreed that the abomination must be defeated? He and his Heralds? Are we agreed that the Children need to be defeated? Are we agreed that that the Servants must be defeated?"

The round of silence was the greatest indicator that all were agreed. Mariti was glad for Aspertis' support. But she was also concerned. The fate of the dragons could not be controlled by the warriors. She and Aspertis were killers, recognized as killers, and had the blood of angels hanging about them. Tarot's strength as leader was always that he could see all options, whether it be fighting, or bargaining, or simply hiding. Perhaps though, it was time that the dragons stopped worrying about diplomatic solutions, and start using the power they had always boasted they had. Hannah Ironheart gave them that focus. Now that Aspertis had put it on the line, he had opened the door for the dragons to lead the war. The path was clear. However, when Aisengard spoke Mariti was worried that it could all be undone.

"Mariti," he said slowly but firmly, "I will follow you. If that means we stand behind a mortal, then so be it. If it means we stand behind the Heretic, so be it. But I will do this on one condition and one condition only. And I must hear it from you, here and now, with no equivocation that this condition will be met."

She steeled herself and nodded for him to continue.

"There is a pox on our house, a nightmare of our own creation," he said clearly. "Since the days before the rebellion in the Heavens, before the destruction of Dorovar's world, we have been at the mercy of the machinations of three of our own. Shadowweaver, Stormbane, and Derelor have done everything in their power to make sure that every world we sat foot upon burned. They have shaped the choices open to us, they have antagonized the inhabitants of every world, and they have deceived, lied, and bullied their way into every war we have ever fought. They ignored Lord Tarot's orders to avoid Dorovar's world, and they embroiled us in a conflict between Raenera, Emries, and Talisia. They are responsible for the creation of the abomination, and they more than any are the reason that we are without Lord Tarot's leadership today. Shadowweaver made the bargain with Talisia to support her in her rebellion, and his arrogance formed the schism that we are now faced with. He surely stands with her now, plotting his own ascension. I will fight with you. I will fight for you, and I will die for you. All at the orders of a mortal if need be. But I must know that you will not stop, that you will not rest, and that no victory can be declared as long as Shadowweaver, Stormbane, Derelor, and any who proclaim themselves to be loyal to their cause are erased from existence. I would see their broken and bloody bodies at my feet before this war could ever be considered won. If you promise me, if you swear to me that we will destroy this schism, that we will remove this pox from our house, then you have my loyalty."

Mariti considered her words carefully.

"There is no resolution to this war in which Stormbane, Derelor, or Shadowweaver survive. Of that you have my word."

Aisengard nodded. Obviously that oath was good enough for him. Unexpectedly, Ossa was the next to give voice to his concerns.

"And what of our treasures? Are we to surrender our treasures to the mortal in order to fight this war? Should they even know that the treasures exist? I don't want the same fate to befall me as befell Khalas."

Khalas Skydancer trusted a mortal with his sacred treasure, and it had proved to be a blight on Khalas. Once Xaran Firesoul died, and the treasure that he was entrusted with was destroyed, Khalas' life was forfeit. He fell from the sky, his heart stopped and his soul ripped from his body. Such was the fate of any dragon who failed to live up to the responsibility of protecting their sacred charge. It was one thing to lose one's life in a fight, but it was another to lose one's life because of absolute trust offered to another.

"point moot…" Serentis' hissing voice broke in. "enemies know….treasures compromised…. Abomination targeting….. herald possesses two."

Mariti felt her blood go cold. If Serentis was right, and Mariti had no reason to believe anything else, then one of Dorovar's Heralds had taken two treasures from two of their breed. It wouldn't take much doing to figure out which ones were missing, but the clear point was that Dorovar knew they existed and he was targeting the ones he felt would be useful to his cause. It was dangerous to trust the mortals with such power, but since they were trusting the whole of the Cosmos to the mortals, it seemed silly to trifle about the fate of a sacred treasure. But, this was not a debate that Mariti could afford to have. The Sacred Treasures were a line that was very difficult to cross. And so, Mariti would only cross it in situations where she knew she could win.

"A sacrifice of trust is required, but I shall not be the one to mandate such sacrifice. I will be giving my treasure to Hannah Ironheart. I would ask that some of our number make sacrifices as well, to show our investment in this alliance. Aerith himself, his wife, and his two other disciples. But no dragon will be made to give what he cannot be ordered to give. I leave it to your conscience to make a choice you can live, and perhaps die with."

Aspertis was the first to raise his voice yet again.

"I agree there is little choice, Mariti. I shall be one to offer up my treasure. I shall go to meet the one called the Flickering Flame. Together he and I shall work toward our goal. I will leave our brothers and sisters to debate whom else will be willing to give up a piece of their soul. Make no mistake, this war will be a long one, one that will have untold death and destruction attached to it. We will continue until either there are none of us left, or until all of our enemies everywhere have been defeated."

Aspertis turned away from the rest of the group and began to walk away. Just at the edge of Mariti's line of sight, she heard him spread his wings and lift his elegant and massive form into the skies. He looked like a streak of fire in the sky, another addition to the falling stars. The remaining members of the new confederation began to discuss amongst themselves the next course of action. Mariti started to tune them out and found herself facing the Great Tree, the place where Tarot's body lay. She felt as though she were being drawn there. Her thoughts were interrupted by the words of Serentis.

"plan complete....allies found."

Aisengard, Ossa, and Serentis stepped forward to add their sacrifice to the ones that Mariti and Aspertis were willing to give. Mariti was surprised that Serentis would be one of those willing to give up her treasure, but in these days of conflict, she could not afford to take anything for granted. There was a brief conversation about next steps, and who would be responsible for what missions in the coming days. The end times for everyone were on the horizon, and finally the dragons had cast their lot into the war. Regardless of how everything came to pass, at least the dragons would go out fighting and not hiding.

"Venya," Mariti said with all of the confidence she could muster. "I'm afraid I must give you the most unpleasant task. You have always been an organizer among us. You know the tempers and the drives of all of our members better than anyone. I must ask that you search the landscape, search the skies and the seas, and bring any allies you can to the fold. Be careful, and present yourself with care. I loathe that I must ask you to be a spy for our cause, but the faster we identify those who stand against us, and those who stand with us, the better chance we have to win this war."

Venya growled, but finally nodded.

"Information is the only way we will be victorious. It is distasteful, but I agree it is necessary. I shall do as you ask."

No more words were spoken between the allies, and no more words were truly needed. The conspiracy was over, and everyone went their separate ways. Mariti lingered, her eyes returning to the site where her love's fallen body lay. Finally she gave into the feeling and slowly walked to the former home of the dragons. A tremor went through her body as her eyes found the broken body. Tarot's jaw was distended, his neck ripped in half. The pool of blood around him had dried and congealed. Smoke and ash still filled the air, but light was beginning to break through. As Mariti looked at his body, she realized that he looked as though he were cradling something in the middle of his fallen form. As though his last thoughts and last actions were to protect something of great value. She walked slowly to his side, and gently moved one of his great legs out of the way. Beneath the limb Mariti saw something that gave her more hope than she had had in thousands of years. There, shielded from the fires and the blood was a small sapling.

The Seed of Life was Tarot's to protect, the spark that would give birth to another Great Tree. The Seed was the greatest of the dragons' Sacred Treasures, and it had done its deed. It had become the new roots of life on this dying world. In time, a new Seed of Life would sprout, and perhaps with it a new future for everyone and everything.

CHAPTER 80

Chapter LXXXI

Forged in Pain, Broken in Sorrow

Year Four of the Just Emperor Kaitain "Dragonsbane" Lorien,
Creator's Calendar Year 1871

Deep in the Pritan Islands the clear skies gave anyone who looked to the heavens the most spectacular view of the twin suns and the moon's passing through the dual coronas and the shower of shooting stars and meteors that rained down through the sky. Few people ever would have the opportunity to stand in the islands to see this sight as there were only a handful of humans that called the islands home. The man who stood on one of the smallest islands of the chain was not a resident. His home had been destroyed long ago, and there had been no place that he would have considered calling home, but perhaps, if circumstances were different, he could have found peace in this place for a while. There was a shuffle of movement to the man's left, and he turned away from the brilliant heavenly display above. When Dorovar's eyes fell on the woman who had approached, he felt an ancient pang, something unresolved, and something that had been banished from his soul long ago. It was more than fondness and more than familiarity. There was a time, perhaps before the breaking of Dorovar's world, that Faelara's approval was as important to Dorovar as Raenera's. The cold blue of the woman's eyes took Dorovar's thoughts back to a place and time when all he thought about was serving his mistress and forging the path for order that his goddess demanded; before the dragons came, before the coming of death.

Loinn was a beautiful world once, full of cities constructed out of polished white stone and channels of running water that passed down the middle of major streets. Water was a reminder that though the flow of life could change at any moment, that flow could be restricted and altered by the ordered mind. Each of the major cities on Loinn would send a representative to Eas to study the ways of the goddess who would then become the advisor to the leader of that city. A small percentage of the representatives sent to Eas would be given the honor of joining the Adhradair, the friends of the Goddess. The Adhradair were taught by the High Priestess of Eas all of the secrets to serving the will of the Goddess, as well as ensuring that Order reigned and continued to reign on Loinn. When the traitorous dragons came to Loinn, there were thirteen members of the Adhradair. In the end, it was only the Adhradair that stood up to the dragons and fought with all of their hearts and blood. When the last of the Adhradair fell, only Dorovar was left standing. He was beaten, broken, and pushed beyond the edge of death, but the bargains made with the traitorous dragons kept his heart beating, and he stood and watched the last of the winged abominations flee his beautiful world before it cracked down the center and exploded in flames. He floated in nothingness, ghosts and memories his only companions.

Dorovar had been a student of the High Priestess of Eas since he was a boy. Both his mother and father had been members of the Adhradair, and their union had been blessed by the High Priestess to conceive a child who would be as much a child of Raenera and the Adhradair as he was a child of mortals. Every possible moment of every day, Dorovar was bathed in the love and teachings of Raenera and little else. He had already been in the Temples of Order for thirty years when the barely sixteen year old Faelara came into his life. She was naïve but dedicated, and Dorovar took it upon himself to tutor her in the teachings of Raenera. Somewhere in the next ten years, Dorovar's fondness for the girl became more than he could rationally explain. The part of him that had been dedicated to the service of the Goddess for so long could not reconcile the new feelings. In some ways it felt as though his heart and mind had begun to betray the teachings. That his everlasting and incalculable love for Raenera had somehow been diminished when Faelara was near. Had his heart betrayed his devotion to Raenera? Had his burgeoning love for his fellow servant diminished his devotion to his mistress? These questions had forced Dorovar's isolation and spiritual journey. He fasted, taking only water when necessary, spending every moment of the day in fervent prayer. He would wait for a sign.

The sign came in the form of a dream. Raenera herself appeared to Dorovar, reaffirming that his faith was still strong, and that he had been chosen for a task, a task that he believed would lead Loinn into an age of prosperity that even the elders could never have envisioned. Soon it would be proven that Dorovar was correct, but not in the way that he had expected. Dorovar would learn the depth of the betrayal that had been visited upon him, the hell that he had unleashed upon his world, and the wanton destruction that would soon touch every man, woman, and child that called Loinn home. At first the dragons were welcome to Loinn. There were plenty of places for them to settle, a great deal of open space that was not needed by the people who had always called the world home. But soon the wilds and open spaces were not enough for the great beasts. They began encroaching closer and closer to the smaller towns, and it would only be a matter of time until the interests of the humans of Loinn and the interests of the dragons would be at odds. It started quietly, simply, as most terrible and insidious things do, with a young dragon wandering into a grazing field and gorging itself on cattle. At first, the farmer simply waited, hoping that the young dragon would only eat a few of the cows before moving along. Before long half the herd was gone. The farmer never intended to hurt the dragon, never intended to do anything but drive the thing away. He ran out with a shovel, more afraid that the dragon would make a snack of him than any damage he might cause. But the tip of the shovel struck a soft spot, breaking through skin between scales. Blood flowed everywhere, and the creature only had time to rear its head back and scream before slumping to the ground. It was an accident, a horrible terrible accident that would be the spark that ignited a war that would consume the world.

The dragons viewed the death of one of their own, for whatever reason, an insult that could never be reconciled. However, a price would have to be paid, and the only price for blood was more blood. The city of

Tursachan was the first to fall. It took only an hour, and only two adult dragons, but they razed the city to the ground and killed every living creature within the city. However the assault was not merciful even in its speed. The dragons approached from opposite directions, belching streams of fire that set the majority of the buildings in the small town on fire. When the dragons returned scant seconds later, they waded into the town from opposite ends with no fear of the fires that raged around them. With jaws, claws and tails, the dragons ripped, tore, and crushed everything that crossed their path until they met in the center of the town. But it was not enough to simply grind the town into dust, they systematically hunted down every mortal that tried to run from the destruction. They left only two alive, more than enough to spread the story of the death of Tursachan. It was supposed to be an object lesson, it was supposed to be the end of the issue. However there were elements within the race of dragons that lived for conflict, thrived on it. Some welcomed a new war, even one against an opponent who was so hopelessly overmatched. Though the leadership of the dragons preached patience and tolerance, the elements that brought the dragons to Loinn had no intention of allowing the humans to believe that this was their world any longer.

The next incident between humans and dragons was not an accident, nor was it a misunderstanding. A dragon by the name of Jovinian arrived at the pristine white walls of the city of Baristos, one of the larger cities on the southern continent. The leadership of Baristos, consisting of the city's ruling council and high priest met with the dragon outside the walls. The deal that the dragon proposed was simple enough. The people of Baristos would keep Jovinian supplied with food and precious metals and Jovinian would ensure that no other dragons would either extort the people of Baristos or cause them harm. Of course, the offer also came with a warning. Failure to agree to the terms of the bargain, as well as failing to meet those terms would result in the destruction of Baristos and the death of every soul that called the city home. The people of Baristos were left with no choice and entered into the bargain with Jovinian. While the demands started small and easily manageable, as the dragon grew so did its appetites. In a matter of months, the people were on the brink of starvation in order to meet the dragon's demands. By this time however, the leadership of Baristos had determined that the only way to protect the citizens was to bring a violent end to the bargain.

The people of Loinn were not warriors; at least they had not been for generations. There were legends that the first thousand years that men walked upon the face of Loinn, there was nothing but war, and that the foundation of every city was built upon either a great battlefield or a great cemetery. The world had been soaked in blood for a thousand years, until Raenera's wisdom put an end to all wars. In the thousands of years since, Order had put an end to all strife, all war, and all conflict. Everyone knew their place. Everyone followed the path that Order intended for them, without question and without reservation. No one wanted for food or comfort. Work and following the tenants of Order were all the reward and fulfillment that anyone could want. All worked for the greater good of all, not the greater good of themselves. Dragons did not understand duty, did not understand sacrifice. They were greedy, they were hostile, and they did not care for the good of anyone, even others of their own race. They played at unity, but only when it suited them, and only when they faced a grave threat. But the people of Loinn were not a grave threat, and they did not have the knowledge to become one. The high priest of Baristos prayed for guidance from their patron Raenera. He prayed for the knowledge to rise above the threat and restore peace to their people. No answer came. At least not one that the high priest could communicate to his followers. But the fear continued to grow. People worked harder than they had ever worked before to ensure that the tithe to Jovinian was paid. So the high priest called all of the people together and held a special mass to pray for guidance and for protection. The people prayed, and the high priest looked to the heavens, but no message came. The people would not accept a message to be patient and to persevere. They would accept nothing else but a mandate to strike back. These people were not used to suffering or hardship. And so the high priest looked to his people and told them that he had received a sign, and that the people of Baristos were destined to protect themselves and free themselves from the dragon's yoke of oppression.

When Jovinian returned for his tribute, the people met the large dragon at the gates with swords, spears, pitchforks and whatever other weapons they could manage. The whole of the city had gathered, believing that they had been ordained to victory by their Goddess. The dragon laughed at the audacity of the people, giving them one chance to save themselves from their foolishness. However the resolve of the people of Baristos would not be broken, and as one they charged, thinking that they would break like waves against the rock, eventually wearing the large creature down with their tenacity and strength of will. This could not have been farther from the truth. In a matter of minutes the dragon had killed most of the people of Baristos, and then the creature took great pleasure in burning the city to the ground. When Jovinian was done, Baristos was no more, a smoldering pile of rubble. Moreover the dragon destroyed all of the farmlands and ate all of the livestock before burning the grazing grounds, ensuring that no life would walk where Baristos stood for generations.

Days after the tragedy at Baristos, a huge dragon calling itself Nessus the Hovering Rain appeared at the capitol city of Eas, demanding to speak with the leadership council. In the town square the dragon threatened the council citing the terms of the deal between the people and the dragons, and reminding them that any further hostility would be met with outright war. Dorovar himself pleaded with the dragon on behalf of the people of Baristos, claiming it was all a misunderstanding, a misreading of the signs. That the high priest had lied to the people and tragedy had been the result, that the attack against the dragon Jovinian had not been sanctioned by the Goddess. Nessus seemed to accept the explanation but reiterated the threat, and added one stipulation, that the contract between Baristos and Jovinian must be concluded, and that the city of Eas would be responsible for paying the tithe to Jovinian for a year. If they did not, it would be clear that all of the talk of peace would be nothing more than a bluff, and that war was the only option. Dorovar gladly accepted the terms of the agreement and the people of Eas would pay the tribute as demanded. However, the seed of discord had been planted.

Unbeknownst to Dorovar and the High Priestess of Eas, the other members of the Adhradair met to discuss how they would take action against the dragons for their blaspheme. For seven days they sat in prayer and meditation practically begging their Goddess for intervention, for the power to defend their people from the dragons. But no help would come, at least no help from Raenera. Only the traitorous Emries and Talisia appeared to extend their assistance. That proved to be the beginning of the end for everything. No matter what their intentions, no matter how their sin was contrived out of love, it was still a sin against the Goddess. Their vanity caused the destruction of their world, their greed for power caused the death of their physical bodies, and their blaspheme against the Goddess cursed them for eternity to toil in darkness. Now when Dorovar looked into Faelara's clear eyes, whatever tenderness he once felt for her had been replaced by sorrow and a feeling of ultimate betrayal.

"It is time, Dorovar," Faelara said finally. "They have assembled in the clearing as you have asked."

Dorovar nodded, and Faelara turned away without any further interaction. Dorovar could feel the disdain that radiated from the woman, and he could understand how she might feel some malice towards him. Of course such feelings were simply misplaced. Faelara didn't really hate Dorovar, she hated herself. She knew that she had failed herself and the people of their world. In time she would come to understand the truth of her situation and that this was her opportunity to make good on the promise that they once had. As servants of the Goddess they were dedicated to bringing Order to their world, and ensuring that the laws of the Goddess were adhered to at all times. Now, on this new world the servants of the Goddess could bring Order to this chaotic place. Finally Dorovar turned away from the view, and walked slowly toward the clearing, his eyes cast down at the ground.

He heard the grumbling as he approached, but no conversation was held between the former members of the Adhradair. Standing nearest the entrance of the clearing was Faelara. To her right were the twin brother and sister Haricos and Redissa. In life, Redissa had been one of the favorites of the High Priestess, and was considered to be next in line for the position. Before she became a member of the Adhradair, Redissa was a dedicated wife to a member of the leadership council of Eas, but her calling came after the still-born death of her first two children. She felt emptiness in her heart that nothing could fill. She prayed daily for guidance, and eventually those prayers led her to the service of the Goddess in the church. Ten years after entering service, she was selected to join the Adhradair partially on the recommendation of her own brother. Haricos was the closest to a holy warrior of any of the Adhradair. He was strongly built and chose to show his devotion to Order through honing his body into the best physical condition possible. The two had fair features, as they were from the temperate region of Loinn. They both had sandy blond hair with clear and bright blue eyes. As he did in life, Haricos was dressed in full dark armor while Redissa dressed more matronly with a flowing white dress and a shawl around her head and neck. On this world, Haricos had been the soul imprisoned in the Sacred Weapon Gravity, while Redissa had been the soul of the weapon Wisdom.

Zaraven had been a priest from the wetlands to the south of Loinn where all manner of beasts and birds of prey roamed. It was said that the Goddess had gifted Zaraven with the ability to understand the hunters of the world, and when the dragons launched their attacks, it had been Zaraven that had led the armies of Adhradair to greatest success. Like Redissa and Haricos, Zaraven had bright blue eyes, sharp and clear like the hunters he personified, but his hair was dark and thick. Dorovar always remembered Zaraven with a hostile sneer on his lips, and this day was no different. Like an animal, Zaraven crouched low, wearing only a tattered pair of pants, his bare chest showing the wounds of his conflicts. Across his chest were three deep scars that ran from his left shoulder to his right hip, the wound that ended his life, the claws of a dragon named Brux had ended him. The Sacred Weapon that served as his prison had been called Tenacity.

The soul that inhabited the Sacred Weapon Faith had been the most powerful of the Adhradair both before and after the intervention of Emries and Talisia. In his days in the temple, Coriden had been devout and had studied everything he could get his hands on. Coriden was from the southern continent, and his dark skin was complimented by his long white hair. Once the Adhradair had been given divine power, it had been Coriden who had literally moved mountains with his bare hands. His anger was so intense that he ripped out the hearts of dragons with his bare hands, and his skin bristled with power like lightning. As in life, Coriden was dressed from head to toe in white, only his face, neck, and hands exposed.

Dorovar took in the looks from around the clearing before lowering his head once more. There was so much malice here, so many misguided feelings, but this was not the time for old grudges and misconceptions. Finally, Dorovar raised his head and eased back the hood of his cloak.

"So much time has passed since this many of us have stood together. I know that there is much anger in your hearts for the way that you were imprisoned and the way that our world ended, but you must allow me to speak and explain. What you believe was my treachery, what you believe is my carelessness is nothing more than the continuation of what the traitors Talisia and Emries want you to believe."

Dorovar took a long even breath and continued, feeling the hate-filled eyes trained on him, all but Faelara, whose eyes drifted off to the distance.

"After our world was destroyed, and I floated in the nothingness, I could feel the souls of those from our world floating in the debris with me. I could hear their sorrow and their fear. I could feel their pain. It fed me, sustained me, helped me to understand my true purpose. The dragons needed to pay for their treachery. Not one of them, not some of them, but all of them. Just as they eliminated every last living thing on our world and left me alone in the morass of hatred and death, so too will I take the lives of every last dragon until only one remains, and I will look into the eyes of that creature and rip it's still beating heart from its chest and watch as the light goes out of its eyes. But our betrayal is more than the dragons. There is the creature Emries and his twisted lover Talisia. They preyed on our fears and our need. They turned you into blasphemous weapons bent only on revenge. They made us forget our devotion to the Goddess and to Order. They are to blame for what became of you both before and after the loss of our world. It was Talisia that pulled you from the darkness. It was Talisia that gave your souls to the Dark Gods and ensured that you fell to this world, and it was Talisia and Emries that arranged for you to be found by the mad weapon smith and imprisoned in the Sacred Weapons for two millennia."

There was silence for a long moment before Redissa's melodious voice rang out.

"And what of Raenera? What of our Goddess? Do you absolve her for abandoning us? Will you return to worshipping her once your task is complete?"

Dorovar shook his head finally.

"No, there is no going back to those ways. Raenera abandoned us. I know that she too is on this world, and so she too must be made to pay for her crimes. And once they have all paid, there is only one criminal left to bring to justice, the Creator himself."

Haricos walked forward until he stood right in front of Dorovar, staring him dead in the eyes. The clear blue eyes were filled with hate and pain.

"I never liked you," Haricos said. "But you counseled us against accepting power from Emries and Talisia. You counseled us against taking the fight to the dragons, and in the end you begged us to end the war to save the people. We didn't listen to you then, and perhaps we have no choice now but to follow you because of the prison that Talisia crafted for us. But I will follow you. I will do as you ask until the last of the dragons has fallen, and until the Creator is made to pay for his crimes."

With his words, Haricos went to one knee and bowed his head. Redissa was the first to follow the gesture, then Coriden, and Faelara. Zaraven crouched in the same place, his eyes never leaving Dorovar's face for a long time before finally he bowed his head and let one of his knees touch the ground. When Dorovar began to speak again, the reunited members of the Adhradair rose back to their feet.

"My powers are still diminished though I am free from my cage, and we the Adhradair are not complete. There are still more of our brothers and sisters who are imprisoned and must be freed. While my foolish heralds sew destruction and discord through the lands of Cadaria, the trembling masses are primed for the application of Order. We must free these people from their deluded ways, and those who will not accept Order will join my Chorus of Souls. But of utmost importance must be freeing our brethren. Track them. You know what must be done to free them from their prisons. Stop at nothing. And then we will save this world from itself."

After a round of nods, Coriden, Haricos, Zaraven, and Redissa disappeared from the clearing leaving only Faelara and Dorovar.

"Do your Heralds know that they are merely disposable tools?"

"They will serve their purpose," Dorovar replied. "They were beings of sin and vice, and as such they have no place in a world of Order. But they have helped to create the conditions that have allowed for our brothers and sisters to find their freedom. When the time comes, they shall pose no impediment."

Faelara's eyes fell to the ground.

"And the one you allowed me to save?"

Dorovar did his best to suppress a grin.

"The princess and her protector will serve their purpose in due time. Keep watch over her as you have, in the guise that was chosen. Keep her on the path of Order, and do not allow her to stray. The Creator's minions and Emries' former general will pull her in directions that do not benefit us. This must not be allowed to occur."

Faelara's voice was small and submissive.

"Why must it be her?"

Finally the smile curled Dorovar's lips.

"Because she is the embodiment of everything we are fighting against, and it is only fitting that the Empress of Sin become our conduit to toppling the Creator."

Benedictus

Year One of the Divine Empress and Child of the Creator Marlae Tamerlane, Creator's Calendar Year 1871

Disasters and tragedies impact societies differently depending upon the true fabric of the people within the community. Some communities are shattered by tragedy, with everyone pointing fingers at one another trying to assign blame, trying to find sense in the senseless through the faults of others. Other communities pull together, setting aside grudges and petty squabbles to elevate the whole. Albitonin had never seen a true disaster, not in the entirety of its existence as a Cadarian Kingdom, at least not until the tragedy at the Heart of Stone. Now the soul of Albitonin, the High Priestess of the Church of the Creator, Hannah Ironheart had gone missing in the wake of the explosions deep within the Heart itself. Even though the Church of the Creator had yet to remove Hannah from her position or declare that she had been lost during the tragedy, the people of Albitonin had held a week of mourning. Once the mourning period had ended, Hannah Ironheart's hand-picked successor, Baeata Catrinel, was appointed to the position of acting High Priestess. But after her public proclamation to the people of Albitonin, the new High Priestess had retired to quiet meditation and seclusion. However, the time for this separation from her flock was growing shorter and shorter. The proclamations by the supposed rightful Emperor of the Cadarian Empire were turning the faithful of the

Church of the Creator into wanted criminals. If the High Priestess did not tend to both the physical and spiritual health of her flock, it was only a matter of time before someone would take rash action. Already word had reached the Heart of Stone that a number of smaller convents had been savaged by the members of the Imperial Legion, and the clergy there taken into bound servitude, their possessions, and in many cases their very dignity stripped from them. Now word had come from Hedorah that an emissary from the so-called Divine Empress of Cadaria, a woman calling herself Marlae Tamerlane, was on the way to meet with the High Priestess to discuss terms of alliance.

In the darkness of her chambers, Baeata Catrinel sat on her knees, facing the north wall of the chamber, candlelight flickering from one brass candlestick in the corner. Hour after hour she had sat in quiet supplication, waiting for some sign as to the course of action she should take in the days and weeks to come. She had prayed over and over again for a sign as to the health and welfare of Hannah Ironheart, the woman she had spent nearly her entire life idolizing and learning from. However, only silence waited for her in the darkness, and only doubt waited for her in the light. When the familiar knock came at the door at midday, she wondered what day it actually was and how long it had been since the last time she had broken her spiritual fast. The other acolytes tried twice a day to get her to eat, but she felt that she needed to continue to purify herself, only taking water when it was necessary. But now the silence and isolation had become too much to bear. Rising, she felt the muscles in her legs ache. Weakness and pain flooded through her whole body, and if she would have been weaker willed, she would have collapsed from it. Deprived of sleep and of sustenance, she probably looked like a gaunt ghost instead of the leader of the largest church on the face of Cadaria. The knock came again at the door, but instead of waiting, the supplicant simply placed the tray at the door and removed the one from the previous meal.

Baeata moved with gentle and measured steps across the room to her small wardrobe, removing from it a simple robe and pulling it over her shoulders. The commandments of the Creator had spoken of bearing oneself completely to the will of the Creator, so after several days without a sign, Baeata had begun conducting her prayers naked. The exposure, even in the privacy of her own quarters had almost been too much for her, and as she knelt on the cold stone floor, she felt as though all of her shames and all of her sins were written on her body. Her mentor Lady Ironheart had once spoken about the way that people revealed themselves to the Creator was tied to the way that they viewed themselves in the company of others. To see the Creator as a person saw their neighbor created a distance that would not allow them to receive the blessings that they were due. The Creator did not judge in the same way that the eyes of a person did. The Creator could forgive all, and could understand all. However, if people were not able to allow the faults within themselves to be revealed to even their Creator, how could they expect them to be forgiven? They would hold back and hide, taking their greatest sins and regrets with them to the grave. Some at the ends of their lives would find the courage to release their shame, and to be honest with their maker and with themselves. Others were entombed with their sins, and those sins became weights that would not allow their souls to ascend to the heavens. In the end, each human being was responsible for the actions that would lead to their salvation or damnation, and the priests and priestesses of the Church of the Creator could only guide those willing to be honest with themselves and with the Creator. For the longest time Baeata thought that she understood the words, thought she understood what it took to have that kind of honesty with the Creator. However when the time came to kneel with the weight of the entire Church of the Creator on her soul, it was brought into a much more serious clarity.

When she opened the door to her chambers, the light from the outside came flooding in, nearly blinding her. On the floor was a simple wooden tray with a small plate of porridge, bread, and small cuts of meat, along with a jug of water. At the end of the hall an acolyte sat in quiet meditation and came instantly to her feet as soon as she saw the High Priestess's door open. The acolyte moved half way down the hallway and then waited head down, for instructions from the High Priestess. Once Baeata's eyes cleared, she regarded the acolyte, searching for the young woman's name. It took only a moment for the red ringlets to jog Baeata's memory. The young woman's name was Aelind Torral. Aelind had come into the service of the Church of the Creator in a fairly uncommon way. For the first ten years of her life, she had been orphan in the kingdom of Hedorah, her name given to her by the lady who ran the orphanage. Though there was a large presence of the Church of the Creator in Hedorah, the church was not allowed dominion over the orphanages. Each one was wholly owned by one of the foundries in the kingdom to ensure a steady stream of labor. By the time she was six, Aelind was working in the kitchens of the orphanage to help earn her room and food. When she turned ten, she was no longer welcome in the orphanage, and was sent on her way with only the clothes on her back and a few pieces of silver in her pocket. In the Kingdom of Hedorah where graft was a way of life, there was not enough silver for a young girl to find her way, and the charity of others could only carry her for so long. By the time she was eleven she had found work in a brothel cleaning and cooking, and by the time she turned fourteen, her role in the brothel was as a whore. An accident would save her from a life in that place, as a fire broke out in the middle of the night that in a matter of hours would reduce the place to ashes. Aelind didn't know why she was spared and so many others were not, nor did she know how she found her way to the Church of the Creator; all she remembered were a man's eyes staring down at her and a strong pair of arms that lifted her from the ground.

Aelind's second chance would not be wasted. She quickly impressed the reverend mother of Hedorah, a woman named Amallia, and before long she had earned a place in Amallia's personal retinue. From there it was only a few months before she was studying to become a priestess at the Heart of Stone, where she came to the notice of Hannah Ironheart. Hannah Ironheart had a reputation of finding those in the Church that most needed her guidance and those who had the most potential to become important to the Church. Hannah's "special projects" were well known and respected in the Church of the Creator, and all had risen rapidly in the hierarchy, including Baeata, who had gone from a novice to an acolyte in only five years, a full two years faster than the average. Aelind too had made her transition rapidly, besting even Baeata's pace, becoming an acolyte in four years. When Baeata ascended to the role of High Priestess, Aelind became Baeata's personal assistant, a position that ordinarily would have gone to someone within the Church who had been there much longer and had a reputation for wisdom and patience. But, because Aelind was one of Hannah's projects, her relative young age was overlooked by most. There were always petty jealousies to deal with, but none would go so far as to openly question Aelind's worth.

Baeata sighed to herself and suppressed her desire to smile at the red-haired woman. The two had studied together for many years, and had become like sisters. Whenever Baeata went to visit her family in the south of Thorigald, she would take Aelind with her, and the two stayed as close as possible even when Baeata was elevated to Priestess. It was only a matter of time before Aelind would also be promoted to Priestess, and that promotion would threaten to pull the two women apart. Now that Aelind was Baeata's right hand, they would continue to be together at least a while longer.

"Aelind," Baeata said, trying not to let weakness enter her voice, "please have a bath prepared and brought to me here. No attendants. I simply wish my meditation to continue free of the sweat and grime."

Aelind nodded but lingered.

"Was there something else?"

Aelind finally looked up.

"Mother Amallia is on her way here from Hedorah. It is expected that she will arrive within the day. We received the courier this morning. Though the courier said that she will not be arriving by boat so no escort from the docks will be necessary. When I tried to press the courier for more information, he simply repeated that Mother Amallia would be here this evening."

Annoyance flooded through her, but Baeata's control would not allow it to show on her face. The mystery of the method of the Reverend Mother's arrival would have to wait; the important thing was that a revered member of the Church of the Creator was risking travel from Hedorah through a kingdom loyal to Kaitain Lorien in order to meet with the High Priestess. It must have been a grave matter indeed that necessitated the risk.

"Very well. Make the necessary arrangements for someone befitting the Reverend Mother's stature."

Baeata began to turn, and then stopped.

BRIAN C. KERSHNER - 149

"Amallia? That was the woman that you learned from when you first entered the Church, isn't it?"

Aelind nodded.

"What is she like?"

Aelind took a moment to consider before answering.

"She is very dedicated," Aelind almost musical voice replied, "and has spent nearly her entire life in the service of the Creator. But she is also a traditionalist. She has never believed that deviation from the teachings of the Creator can result in anything but ruination of the soul."

Baeata considered that for a moment. Hannah Ironheart, though widely respected in the Church of the Creator, had at times run afoul of the more traditionalist devotees. Hannah had always believed and taught that dedication to the Creator began in the heart, and so long as the heart was dedicated to following the teachings, that the actions could be forgiven. Attending services was a mandated activity by the tenants of the Creator, but Hannah often taught that so long as one dedicated the appropriate amount of time and devotion to the Creator, that such worship could be done anywhere, be it a temple, a battlefield, a tent, or a home. The place was not important, as the truest temple to the Creator's love and will were located in the heart. That was why the holiest place in the Empire was called the Heart of Stone. It was a representation of the heart of everyone who followed the Creator.

"Perhaps we shall have better luck bridging the gap between the progressive and the traditional, Aelind."

As soon as she said it, Baeata knew it sounded prideful. She had not meant it as a condemnation of the actions of her predecessor, but were it anyone other than Aelind, Baeata was sure that was how it would be perceived. To her credit, Aelind simply smiled, laughed and turned to walk back down the hallway to relay Baeata's orders. Baeata too laughed at the foolish thoughts and turned back into her room, collecting the tray before shutting the door behind her. After standing looking into the light for so long, her quarters seemed incredibly dark, even with the lone candle glowing in the corner opposite her bed. Taking a long matchstick from the table beside where the candle burned, she lit the stick from the burning candle and then lit several more that stood on other candlesticks throughout the room. There were also two lanterns that hung in opposite corners of the quarters, but Baeata chose to forgo them. The candles would be enough for her purposes. It would only take a few minutes for the bath to be prepared and brought to her, but she had to prepare herself to meet a very high ranking member of the Church of the Creator. This would not be a simple visit for a blessing or an ordination, it was surely a matter of great import, and one that required the most stringent adherence to protocol. However, this would also be Baeata's first official audience as the High Priestess of the Church of the Creator. Hannah had always told her that making proclamations to the people was the easiest part of being the High Priestess. The people wanted to love her. To those that believed in the Creator and wanted to follow His teachings, the High Priestess was the like the sun in their sky. They would be drawn to her like moths to a flame. Dealing with those already in the service of the Church was a different matter altogether. There were as many views on the "right" way to serve the Creator as there were patterns to be found in snowflakes. There were biases and alliances a plenty, and navigating them was as challenging as navigating a battlefield full of the enemy. The difference was that on a battlefield you almost always knew who the enemy was. And so, the impression that Baeata made in this first meeting would be one that reverberated through the whole of the Church of the Creator.

Hannah Ironheart had made her reputation as a warrior long before she became the most powerful member of the Church of the Creator. She had garnered respect all through the lands of Cadaria and as a member of the Knights of the Flashing Blade. She was seen as a hero of the highest order, not just the most important member of the Church. Baeata had no such luxury to draw upon. Most of the world would not even know her name, even after the announcement of her elevation to the position of High Priestess had been made. She was Hannah's successor, nothing more, with very large shoes to fill, and a shadow that she could never escape. To that end though, Hannah and Baeata had concocted an image that could be used to garner instant respect from those who had always been loyal to Hannah, and had loved her for her militant side. Hannah had secretly had a suit of armor crafted that would function both as protection on a battlefield as well as formal dress befitting someone of Baeata's new status.

CHAPTER 81

As she opened her wardrobe, Baeata's eyes immediately fell to the armor. It had taken several visits from both seamstresses and armor smiths to get the measurements right, and several more fittings before it was done. However, once it was complete, the armor fit Baeata like a second skin. The pants fit snuggly and were made out of leather with sturdy padding protecting the outside of each leg, and a thickened pad protecting each hamstring. With the pants were riding boots that came up to her knee and had been reinforced to give additional protection. A form-fitting leather tunic was next, one that had long sleeves that covered to the back of her hands, and had a single ring that fit over her middle finger and another that fit over her thumb to hold the sleeve in place. Over the tunic was then placed the padded leather breastplate with angelic wing-like ornamentation that stretched from the middle of her stomach across her chest that allowed some modesty in the tight-fitting attire. The neckline of the armor came halfway up her neck to protect her throat, but would also allow for unfettered range of motion. Leather gloves would run half-way up her forearm, and a high-collared fur cape with leather backing completed the uniform. The cape was held at the neck with a heavy silver chain. Over the time since the armor had been crafted, Baeata had become quite adept at wearing it, and she almost felt natural in it. The real test would be whether or not she would look natural when it mattered most.

After the supplicants had come and gone, Baeata submersed herself in the hot water and let all of the stress and tension within her disappear. The days ahead would be filled with more than enough stress, and she had committed herself to take solace in the peaceful moments as long as she could. By the time the water had gone cold, she had mentally prepared herself for the meeting. She brushed her shoulder-length blond hair back and used a simple pair of wooden sticks to hold it in a bun at the back of her head. She let one lock fall on the left side of her forehead, and took a deep breath before beginning to don her armor. As the layers of protection touched her body, she imagined similar armor surrounding her soul, and when she finally opened the door to her private quarters, she felt ready to face anything.

* * * * * * * * * * *

It was nearly nightfall when there was clamoring outside of the Grand Temple. A swirling blue portal appeared, and guards flooded from all direction with weapons drawn. No one who served at the Heart of Stone wasn't aware of what the portals signified, and after the criminal Aerith Seth and the rest of his confederates had caused the death of so many, the appearance of such portals would be met with suspicion and hostility for quite some time to come. However, as soon as the three figures emerged from the portal, the soldiers all fell back, and many fell to their knees. First through the portal was Reverend Mother Amallia, her dark gray robes and long crimson vestments complimenting her graying hair and aging features. Following a pace behind the Reverend Mother through the portal were two angelic warriors who floated inches above the ground and who carried swords wreathed in flames. The path was immediately cleared, and the trio was escorted from where they emerged to the long flight of stairs that led to the doors of the Grand Temple. The doors opened unbidden, and Amallia entered the massive church with her head bowed. The long carpeted path was flanked on each side by polished wooden pews, and at the very end of the pathway was the dais where the altar stood. Behind the altar stood the acting High Priestess, and to her right was a woman that Amallia recognized all too well. Showing the proper deference, Amallia stopped at the dais and fell to one knee with her head bowed and waited to be acknowledged by the High Priestess. Even as she bowed, she could feel the heat from the flaming swords at her back, and wondered for a long time what the role of the angelic warriors truly was.

"Welcome home, Reverend Mother Amallia," the High Priestess finally said. "I must say that your entrance has caused many a great deal of worry and wonder."

Taking the words as permission to stand, Amallia rose to her feet and brought her eyes up to behold the new High Priestess. The outfit that she was wearing was unusual to be sure, but it made the impression that Baeata was not a woman to be trifled with.

"The manner of my arrival was the topic of much conversation in Hedorah as well, High Priestess. Though I personally opposed appearing with angels at my back, the Divine Empress believed that it was the only way that her words and her requests would be taken seriously. I must admit that there are times that I cannot even believe what I have seen."

Baeata regarded the winged creatures for a long moment before turning her attention back to Amallia.

"These are dark times, Amallia," Baeata said finally, "and the light of the Creator's servants is always welcome in the Heart of Stone. Please, tell me of this Divine Empress, and what requests she may have of the Church of the Creator."

Amallia took a deep breath. The words as she rehearsed them sounded ludicrous to her ears, and now as she was about to give them voice, she wondered if anyone would believe her, or if she would be labeled a madwoman.

"The woman who in her former life had been known as the Celestial Princess, Marlae Lorien, has been touched by the Creator and his power. The sins and vices of her former life have been washed away, and she has been anointed the rightful ruler of this world by the Creator's Will. She has been given a new name, one befitting her divine rebirth, and is now the Divine Empress Marlae Tamerlane. At her command are the armies of the Heavens, demonstrated by the angels that have accompanied me here. The Divine Empress has sent me here to request that the High Priestess of the Church of the Creator return with me to Hedorah for an audience with the Divine Empress herself to discuss the state of the Church as well as the darkness that has befallen the land."

Amallia fell silent for a moment, and Baeata could tell that the next words she was about to speak made her uncomfortable.

"If the High Priestess cannot or will not accept this invitation, the Divine Empress has bade me to tell you that the Divine Empress herself will come to Albitonin, but will do so with an army of angels at her back during high mass and will announce herself from the altar of the Grand Temple. She asks that you consider the ramifications of such an action on the already beleaguered hearts of Albitonin's faithful."

Though Baeata wanted to smile, she could not. The threat, and it could not be called anything else, was a well-constructed one, and one that this new Divine Empress knew that Baeata could not allow to come to fruition. However, though such a deed would allow the Divine Empress to announce herself upon the most holy site in the whole of the Empire, it would also come at a great price. Such an action would unseat Baeata as the religious authority in Cadaria, and would also cast negative light on the nearly-sainted Hannah Ironheart. Inwardly Baeata wondered if the Divine Empress or her advisors had thought of the ramifications of that.

"Reverend Mother Amallia," Baeata said, her voice as warm as she could manage while still keeping the necessary authority, "the Church of the Creator does and has always wanted nothing more than to protect the people of this world, and allow them the opportunity to learn and grow in the light of the Creator's love. You have come here, to the Heart of Stone, with two of the Creator's Servants at your side, and with a message from the one He has anointed as our leader. You speak with the authority of this new leader, and so you speak with the mandate of the Heavens. As the High Priestess of the Church of the Creator, I cannot refuse such a request."

Amallia visibly exhaled in relief, however, as Baeata continued, she could feel a cold horror begin to grip her heart.

"But you have placed me in a delicate position," Baeata continued. "The recognized Emperor of Cadaria, Kaitain Lorien, has decreed that worship of the Creator is a crime, and that the Church of the Creator itself should no longer exist. His decrees also would rob me of all authority to minister to those who desperately need me. It removes my ability to mobilize forces to protect the people from forced slavery, and essentially converts the Army of Stone into an arm of the Imperial Legion. Though thus far they have been honor bound to protect us, I don't know how long my authority alone will keep the Heart of Stone a safe place. Your arrival, while dazzling and emblematic of the authority that the one you serve has, has also reminded those here of the last time a servant of the Creator appeared. The Will came here, to Albitonin, and decreed the death of one who was recognized as a hero by the very same woman who now wears another name. His escape devastated the Heart of Stone and killed hundreds. I can almost feel the fear that is spreading even now. Perhaps it would be better if the Divine Empress were to appear at the Heart of

Stone. Perhaps it would reignite the faith that we could protect the people. Or perhaps it would destroy it once and for all. I am afraid that your appearance has hastened the fall of the Heart of Stone, whether it be by the forces of your Divine Empress, or by the doubt and fear of those whose faith has been shaken. Word will spread that the Divine Empress now speaks for the Creator on this world, and it will further cast doubt on my role as the High Priestess."

Amallia considered for a long moment, but Baeata continued before the Reverend Mother could speak.

"I shall go to meet with the Divine Empress, but I must attach a condition. The Divine Empress must protect the Heart of Stone in my absence. She must ensure that the Grand Temple remains standing and that the High Priestess retains the ability to preach the Word of the Creator to the people. But most importantly, and on this there can be no negotiation, the Divine Empress must confer sainthood on Lady Hannah Ironheart and erase all doubt as to the justness of my leadership of the Church of the Creator."

Resurrecting Hope

Time Immemorial, World of Onea

To call Pramine a town was generous at best. Cedric had been there a number of times during his life, both before and after his days as the famous Lord Lion. There were many small farm towns and rough villages made mostly of tents and wagons at the edges of the region called the Frontier, and it was all on the periphery of the Kingdom of Marcwell. What made Pramine special was the fact that it was one of the few remaining Moridon settlements. The Moridon were a group of people who were touched with the ability to see the way the natural world interacted with the unseen world. Most members of the Moridon were blessed in some way with the ability to allow the unseen world to alter the natural world, in a way that common people referred to as magic. However, there was a small portion of the Moridon that were gifted in a less obvious way. Some could see into the Other Side and speak to those who had departed. Some could see into the past with complete clarity and know exactly what happened around a person or an item. Still others could see glimpses of the future. However, what brought Cedric and the rest of his long-time companions to Pramine was a desire to determine the fate of their friend, Aryx Terian. One of their number, Mailock, was a member of the Moridon, and so he was able to easily arrange for lodging and also to keep the appearance of the Lord Lion in Pramine quiet from all but the highest ranking members of the town's council.

Diana Terian, Aryx's wife, had been the one to go with Mailock to meet with the seer to determine Aryx's fate. Cedric had chosen to stay behind, secure in his small room on the outskirts of the town. Part of him already knew that Aryx was still alive. There was something within him, something about the nature of the *Coromor* that told him that while his friend was alive, he was in a turmoil that was probably worse than death. In a lot of ways, Cedric felt that he was in a similar position.

For so long, Cedric had been carrying the weight as the light of the world. He was a hero the likes of which had not been seen since the time of myths and legends. It felt sometimes as though he had made the transition from mortal man to legend and myth himself. There were times that he couldn't even believe what he and his companions had done. The creature Shau-ling had been a blight upon the world, and his servants, the phasia, killed and maimed with complete disregard for their victims. If the scourge had continued to grow, it would have engulfed the whole of the world, and plunge it into eternal darkness. While at the time it had seemed like a stroke of fortune that had allowed Cedric to stumble upon his position as *Coromor*, the cost had been impossibly high. The woman that he loved had been taken from him, and in some measure, part of his humanity. But it had fueled him, fueled him with the hatred and the power he needed for the road of pain and blood ahead. But as he sat on the edge of the small bed looking out the window, his mind was drawn to more current problems.

Cedric had just spent time with his successor to the mantle of sacrifice and salvation. He had thought that when the second generation of the prophecies began he would feel a measure of relief, that the great weight he had been carrying for so long would finally shift from his shoulders and he would feel as though he could finally stand straight once more. But just the opposite had been the case. He had met Logan Ranthall, his childhood friends, and the woman that he loved. Upon seeing the love in Logan's eyes, Cedric felt a great pain rocket through his chest, as though some invisible hand was squeezing his heart. All he wanted was to ensure that Logan would not suffer the same fate as Cedric had; that he would not end up jaded, distant, and suffering from an illness that had no cure. For years, Cedric had tried to prepare himself for the day that the second *Coromor* would be brought into the war, but there was nothing that could have prepared him for seeing the young man who now carried the weight of the future. If only there was some way that Cedric could spare Logan from what was ahead of him. For the horror that waited.

And still there was something deeper that tugged at Cedric's heart. Something he had hidden for so long, something that no one would understand. It went back to the final day of the battle with Shau-ling, the aftermath of the fight itself. Cedric had thought that everything was lost, that there was no hope, and so he touched the Blaze, touched the life force of the very enemy that stood before him and pulled upon powers that should never have been touched. With this power he was able to defeat his foe, but something within him had become tainted. When it was all over, and it was revealed that his beloved sister had only been gravely wounded and not killed, the true specter of what Cedric had done visited him. The first night back in Marcwell, Cedric had confessed his crime to his sister, confessed everything that burdened his soul. To her credit, Anabel swallowed her horror and stayed with him all night, holding him as he shivered and cried. She advised him to stay silent, to dedicate his life to ensuring that those who followed him would not be forced to make the horrible choices that Cedric was forced to make. That was the only way to cleanse his sin. However, the next morning, Anabel was gone. She wanted only to move on with her life outside of the large shadow that Cedric would cast in the months and years to come. But she did leave behind a note for Cedric, a note that was never far from him. Now that Anabel was dead, taken from him by the forces of the Shadow, Cedric turned the note over and over in his hands, her last keepsake. He didn't need to read the words any longer to know what they said, the message was written on his heart like those scars left behind by Erika's death. One line tugged at his brain over and over again. 'You shall be made to account for the wrongs that you have done. Of that there can be no doubt. But your sins do not define you, nor does the punishment. The foulest taint cannot dampen a good and giving soul.'

The surge of power from the far side of the room indicated the formation of a portal. Part of Cedric wanted to stand up and draw his sword, but he knew there was no purpose in it. When the portal opened, and Aryx Terian stepped through, Cedric hung his head and shook it softly. Without a word, Aryx moved across the room and sat down beside Cedric and looked out the small window.

"I knew you weren't dead."

Cedric's words echoed through the room, and felt as hollow as they sounded.

"You know why I'm here then?"

Cedric nodded.

"It's time for me to be held accountable for my sins."

Aryx put his hand on Cedric's shoulder.

"There is more to it than that, old friend. Much more than you know, and I wish I could tell you it all. Shau-ling is not what he appears to be, and neither am I. I never have been. You were right when you found me that there was something about me that you didn't think you could trust. If it wasn't for the cosmic joke that made me one of your *Erieal*, I would probably have been your enemy all these years. "

Cedric turned and looked Aryx in his cold blue eyes.

"You're not the enemy Aryx," the legendary hero said coldly. "I am, I always have been. I didn't realize it when I was so fueled by hate. But now, now that I have seen Logan, now that I have truly seen what this war has done and is doing to our world, I know the truth."

Aryx stood and extended his hand.

"Then let's go see our new master, and try to find a way out of this that doesn't kill us all."

* * * * * * * * * * *

Year Forty of the Founding Wars, the Creator's Calendar Year 45

Cedric had been tracking an army that had been gathering under the banner of the Lion for several months. They moved quickly, never camped in one place for more than one night, and engaged in hit and run style attacks on much larger armies. They never focused on anything other than armies being led by former members of the phasia, or those armies that were loyal to the warlord Grawn Aplee. It wasn't clear as to whether or not this Lion Army was loyal to Terrik Lorien, but they were certainly assisting him through their actions. Once Cedric had finally tracked them to their camp, he was horrified to see that most of the members of the army were nothing more than teenaged boys that had been lured into battle on the premise of becoming heroes. The army's general was preying on the timbre of the times, inflaming tempers and romanticizing the horrors and dangers of war. The situation was far worse than Cedric could have ever imagined. He had hoped that he would be able to spare most of the army, force them to run once their commander had been killed, but because the commander of this army had turned these boys into fanatics, there was no salvation for them.

Fires and corpses was all that was left of the camp once Cedric had descended upon them like a vengeful god. He broke their ranks with bursts of power unlike they had ever seen, and once it was over, Cedric was left alone with the commander of the force, his oldest friend, the man known as his right arm in the days of the war with the Shadows, Arathorn Geoffry. Cedric wasn't sure if Arathorn's mind had been poised by the times, or if he had been coopted by the nefarious forces that roamed the face of Espre and the Heavens, but when the two locked weapons in mortal combat, there was no doubt that only one of the old friends would be walking away from the battle alive. Arathorn had always had more talent with the sword than Cedric, and had been the match for any creature that had ever dared to cross blades with the man who was probably better suited to be the *Coromor* than Cedric had ever been. But the factor that gave Cedric the edge was that Cedric had been using his powers for far longer than Arathorn had known he had them. Even when Arathorn was a member of the *Erieal* he relied far more on his sword than he ever had on his powers. And so while on Onea, the battle most likely would have ended with Arathorn's blade through Cedric's heart, on the world of Espre, Arathorn was no match for his old friend. Torrents of fire and lightning burned Arathorn to the ground, blackening his skin and clothes. The once hero was a smoking corpse long before he fell face-first to the blood-soaked ground. For many long moments Cedric stood, looking down at Arathorn's body, feelings of pain and guilt running through him. Finally, he dropped to his knees, his sword falling to the ground at his side, a great sigh escaping from the man's chest.

"It's finally over," Cedric said, exhaustion thick in his voice.

"Is that what you really think?"

Cedric's head lifted, and he scanned the area for the familiar voice. Finally he saw the form of the one-armed man walking out of the bright early morning sunlight. Aryx Terian was not a sight that Cedric wanted to see, nor was it one he expected. Rising to his feet, Cedric took hold of his ancient sword and prepared himself for what could only have been a fight.

"You and Diana are supposed to be with the Dark Gods. What are you doing here?"

"Gwydeon, Logan, and I are all trying to do the same as you," Aryx answered. "The phasia and the others who had such power on Onea cannot be allowed to determine the shape of this world. The people, the mortals, must chart their own course."

Cedric exhaled sharply.

"I won't allow any of those who I led into this conflict become horrors. I know that you and Diana have defenses against this madness, but you too will be called to account for your crimes and your connection to that devil Emries."

Aryx frowned.

"You know he's hunting for you."

Cedric nodded.

"Emries wants to use me. Wants to use my power and use what I know for something. But it doesn't have anything to do with this world. It has to do with the Creator, with the Heavens. What Aerith and Logan and the rest did to Emries on Onea, he'll never forget it, and he'll be looking for revenge as long as any of them still draw breath. But that failure has made him want more. He can't stand the fact that it was the rules of the Creator that thwarted his ambition. He can't abide that his brother was chosen over him. Emries won't rest until he can remake all of this in his own image, and then he'll make those who crossed him burn for eternity."

Cedric's voice went quiet after that, but he added in a tone just above a whisper.

"He won't be able to use me if he can't find me."

Aryx took two steps toward his old friend, but Cedric raised his hand and shook his head. Aryx nodded and started to turn away.

"I wasn't talking about Emries."

Sudden understanding came to Cedric, and he raised his head sharply.

"Jeroch wants the same as you, Cedric," Aryx said finally. "And he knows you're a greater threat than any of us should be able to abide. He would be furious if he knew that I was just going to walk away and let you live. But I promise you that he won't rest until he hunts you down and ends you."

Cedric nodded.

"And if there was anyone who deserved to do it, it would be Jeroch. But now is not that time. There is still much more that I must do. Promises I have to keep and a future to plan for. I may not be able to be there to see the end of this game, Aryx, but don't believe for a moment that I won't have a hand in pulling this whole house of cards down."

Aryx turned, but Cedric's voice stopped him.

"Did you know? All those years, did you know who I was?"

When Aryx turned back, the look in his eyes was the only answer Cedric needed.

"It wasn't until after Nightwing, after the memories of the Blaze were returned to me. But then, you were gone, and there was never a time to make amends."

Aryx turned away and created a portal, but before stepping through he turned back one last time and waived to his old friend. Cedric raised his hand and watched Aryx go, knowing that he would never set eyes upon him again.

"Goodbye grandfather," Cedric said to the empty air, "I hope your road ends in peace and happiness."

* * * * * * * * * * * *

Year Four of the Just Emperor Kaitain "Dragonsbane" Lorien,
Creator's Calendar Year 1871

"I can't do it."

Tess Annis slumped to the ground and pounded her fist against the grass-covered plain that she had created only hours before. She looked up into the passive blue eyes of the one who had been teaching her, the man who called himself Emries, and expected him to be angry. There was no such emotion in his eyes, and she watched as a small smile came to his lips. He knelt beside the girl and put a hand on each of her shoulders and massaged them gently.

"You're trying too hard," he said softly and comfortingly. "Remember how you created the lake and the grass and the creatures. All you did was imagine them in your mind, imagine what they looked like and what they felt like, how they would move and what they would be like, and you could make them happen. You could bring them into existence simply because your will is stronger than the will of what you were acting upon. Clear your mind. Remember what I told you, remember that you are only limited by your own belief in yourself."

Tess nodded but didn't feel any better. She knew that she shouldn't be here, and she shouldn't be with this strange man. But he had been so good to her, taken her under his wing and showed her how to use her powers to make the world a better place. That was more than even her father and mother had done. Even Camille seemed afraid of all the things that Tess could do. But Tess knew that Camille was not thinking clearly. That man, Devlin, had poisoned her mind, turned her against all of the things that she knew she should be doing. Made her abandon her responsibilities. Tess knew that wasn't the kind of person that Camille really was. Camille was so dedicated, so beautiful, and so focused on doing what was right. For as long as Tess could remember, all Camille wanted to do was to keep Tess safe. Maybe Tess had been too jealous. But she loved Camille, and Camille had to know that. Those were concerns for another time. As though Emries could hear her thoughts, the man squeezed her shoulders again reassuringly.

"You need to clear the distractions from your mind, my dear. You know that you have the power within yourself to do this. Think about how much better you want to make the world. Think of your family and all of the people you want to protect. Think of Camille. Don't you want her to be proud of you? Remember how you brought her back to life after she tangled with that creature that called itself Death? Don't you want to stop Dorovar and all of his Heralds?"

Rage began to well up within Tess. She hated Dorovar and all of the creatures that served him. They had hurt her Camille. They had hurt a lot of people. But so had the Cadarians. If only she could just let Dorovar and the Cadarians just kill each other off. Then the Dark Gods could be happy and never have to fight again. Then Tess could be happy with Camille.

"That's it my dear girl," Emries said closing his eyes and feeling the emotion rolling from the powerful girl. "The rage and the anger make you powerful, but only if you can control them. Let them fuel you. Let them seep into you. See your power like a fire in your chest, and let what you are feeling make the fire burn hotter and brighter. Feel it build and burn."

The power coming off the girl was palpable. Her skin was practically vibrating and the hairs on the back of her neck were standing. Her hair too seemed to be lifted by an unseen breeze and started to glow with a golden light. In her mind, all that swirled were visions of Dorovar and the creatures that bowed to him. The member of the Knights of the Flashing Blade that had tried to kill Tess's sister. The Servants of the Creator that had hurt Camille and had almost ended her life. Then her vision went elsewhere, it was no longer in her memories, but it went to other places, and other times. She saw through the eyes of the man who touched her. She saw the thousands of men and women that Emries had ordered to their death trying to kill his own brother. She saw the torment that he inflicted upon her father Pike. She saw the heroes who stood up to him. But most of all she could feel his hatred for all those who now called themselves the Dark Gods. Emries wanted them dead. More than that, Emries wanted them to suffer, and he didn't care what he needed to do to accomplish that goal. But there was something else there. Someone that Emries hated even more than the Dark Gods. Hated even more than his own brother. There was a man, a man that Tess had seen before. The man had called himself Aerith Seth. Emries' hate burned brighter than all of the stars in the sky. Emries was right, hate and anger made you strong, but it also made you blind. Perhaps that is what Tess had been all this time. Blind.

Emries could feel a change in the girl, but when she looked back, the infectious smile was back on her face.

"Maybe it's because I can't see what I'm supposed to be making. Do you think you can show me? If you just put your hand on my head and think about it, I'm sure I can see it."

Emries returned the smile but could not help but feel trepidation rise within him. He was still unclear as to exactly what the girl could do, and if he were to open his thoughts to the girl, would she be able to see more than he wanted her to. No matter what power she possessed, he was still a Child of the Creator, and she was untrained in the finer applications of power. She was no match for him.

"Of course, child."

Emries channeled all of his powers into his defenses and then slowly placed his hand on the girl's forehead and closed his eyes, concentrating on the thing that he wanted so desperately for Tess to make. Tess could clearly see the form of the thing in her mind, but that was not what she wanted. She pushed back through Emries' mind, trying to find why this thing was so important to Emries. It didn't take much digging to see the truth. Her eyes widened with understanding, and felt the power begin to

166 – SACRIFICE OF THE FAITHFUL

course through her body. Sensing the change, Emries removed his hand and stepped away from the girl.

She rose to her feet, the golden glow filling her eyes. As the seconds passed, the golden light returned to her hair and then seemed to cascade across her entire body until she was enveloped from head to toe in the golden glow. Then, slowly, Tess extended a hand before her, and the power seemed to extend from her fingertips like a mist that arched to an empty plot of land where it began to coalesce into a solid form. A hollow exterior began to form first, its shape nebulous, serving more as a vessel for the energy to build within. There was the part of the process that Emries was seeing, and then there was the part of the process that Tess was controlling, the essence of life that she was molding. But there was more to it than simply re-creating a living being. All of the things unseen that made the thing what it was were the very pieces that Tess was having the hardest time making real. Through what she had learned from Emries' mind, Tess reached back into the past, looking for the being, trying to pull it through time and space rather than making it from the nothingness. That had been her original mistake. Only the Creator could make life from nothingness. But there were ripples and breaks in reality that Tess could manipulate to pull things backwards and forwards. The form that Emries was seeing was not the creation of life, but rather the creation of a window that that life could be pulled through.

But there were many realities. Tess had seen that in Emries' mind too. Through Emries, Tess had learned that there were times when the Creator had needed to shatter reality, to explore what would have happened if different choices were made, and certain events were not allowed to come to pass. That was where Tess found what she was looking for. She would be able to fulfill Emries request, she would be able to do what she said she would do, she would learn more about her own abilities, but she would also deprive the creature Emries of the leverage that he so desperately wanted. In Emries' mind she saw the control he would be able to exert over what he wanted her to create, and so she would make sure that the leash would not follow the being through the rip in reality. When the golden light finally subsided, a man stood wide-eyed and blinking, sword in hand. He looked first at Tess and then to Emries. When Tess looked over at Emries, she could see the wide beaming smile with just a hint of malice.

"Welcome back from the abyss, old friend," Emries said finally. "We have much work to do."

Cedric Binosear clenched his fists in rage.

Family Thicker than Blood

Year Four of the Just Emperor Kaitain "Dragonsbane" Lorien, Creator's Calendar Year 1871

Rhain Seth's head swam as she wandered the halls of the royal palace of Celidar aimlessly. One of the few friends that she had was gone, lost to the ravages of a power that now inhabited Rhain's body. The mask of the Wrath hung around Rhain's neck and she could feel its power surrounding her body like silken ribbons. The primitive fires of the Blaze, scalding and uncontrolled poked at her skin from the inside, trying to leak through her pores, but her powers as a Dark God, and also as a descendant of both a member of the phasia and the first *Chosen One* offered her a level of protection that even Sabrina had not had at her disposal. The mask of the Wrath bolstered those natural powers, and Rhain could almost see the silken threads like bandages that as time wore on would be the only thing that held her fragile mortal form together against the strain of a Celestial maelstrom. Already Taya had been told the news of their friend's passing, and as expected the pirate queen took the news hard. But Taya was a warrior, more like her father than her simple and quiet mother. Gideon Viruci was well represented by the woman that Taya had become, and the pirate swore that when the time came, she would be ready to follow Rhain wherever she needed to go.

Rhain's footfalls echoed in the dark and empty hall as her thoughts went to Taya. Though technically Taya was Rhain's elder in physical age, Rhain, through a fluke of the multiple lifetimes granted to members of the phasia was actually Taya's aunt. Gideon Viruci was the first born child of Aerith Seth and Bryn Aplee, and Taya was Gideon's only daughter. Though that had been in a dark alternate version of the world of Onea, the world that Aerith and Bryn had once called home. Another perversion inflicted upon the mortals by the endlessly curious and callous Creator. The war on Onea ended, won by neither side truly, and Taya was spared the fate of the other mortals on the world, and allowed to follow her grandparents into a continuation of her life as a resident of the Heavens. Those mortals that survived the devastation on Onea found their memories removed and they were given new memories when their souls were brought to another of the Creator's worlds. As wasteful as the Creator seemed to be at times when it came to disregarding life, the souls on Onea were preserved as a favor to the supposed victor of the battle between immortal brothers, Halicon. With Halicon's memories inhabiting her, Rhain felt the passion that Halicon had for the poor creatures that were caught in a war that they could not understand; lied to by the patron they believed to be the Creator, his perverted brother Emries. That was why Halicon fought so hard to save the humans that had once cursed and feared him. It was not their fault.

Taya had no such forgiveness in her heart. Hate festered in her from the moment she began to learn the truth about the nature of the senseless destruction of her home. Though she had not been in the Heavens during the two civil wars, Rhain was sure that Taya would not have taken a side. Instead she lived with Bryn and Aerith until the very sight of them was nothing more than a reminder of everything she had lost. For so long she remained apart, keeping to herself and only checking in with her estranged family when it became necessary. Only Sabrina seemed to be able to penetrate the seemingly impregnable shell Taya had formed around herself, and perhaps that was because Sabrina had lost nearly everything as well, depending on adopted family as her real family was dead and buried. It wasn't until the crimes of Kaitain Lorien that Taya took a more personal stake in the events of the mortal world and refashioned herself from an immortal refugee into the terror of the open seas. As Taya always said, it's a small step from a thief to a pirate; all it takes is initiative and ambition.

The thought brought a smile to Rhain's face, one that faded altogether once she realized that her feet had stopped in front of her mother's door.

Rhain took a deep breath and centered herself. Though Rhain would not consider her relationship with her mother strained, she would say that she and her mother were far too much alike to ever be friends. Bryn's blood was ruthlessness in physical form, a trait she passed on to her daughter. Unfortunately for Bryn, that ruthlessness was mixed with a healthy dose of irreverence and complete disregard for authority courtesy of her mostly tolerated husband. Rhain was truly the combination of all the best and worst traits of her parents, and she saw the world through the prism of two trained and unrepentant killers who also somehow found such devotion to each other and their extended family through real and genuine love. And now their relationship had been further complicated. Rhain was now the master of the phasia, an order that Bryn had been a member of for thousands of years, one whose tenants she broke to help Aerith find his path into legend. No matter what had transpired, Rhain knew that her mother would never see Rhain as anything other than her daughter who didn't know half of what the more experienced Lady Fox knew, and because of that there would be grudging acknowledgement of Rhain's elevation, but there would never be acceptance. In some ways, the friction would keep Rhain in check with her new powers. She felt the smile come back to her lips a moment later, and she raised her hand to knock at her mother's door, but was preempted by the door opening and her mother's curt voice from within.

"It's about time," Bryn's annoyed voice intoned. "You know how I hate to wait."

Rhain nearly laughed under her breath, but steeled herself for what was going to be an unpleasant confrontation at best. With a simple push, the door opened the rest of the way, and Rhain entered, immediately finding her mother's judgmental eyes waiting for her. Bryn stood in the far corner of the room; her arms crossed at her chest, and a scowl firmly turning the corners of her lips downward. The door closed behind Rhain without any direct intervention, and the two powerful women stood in uneasy silence for several long moments before Rhain started to speak.

"Mother," Rhain started.

Bryn raised her hand and shook her head. Rhain's voice died in her throat the next moment, and the younger woman waited as Bryn took a long deep breath and then began speaking, her gaze falling to the floor.

"I always knew that there is more of your father in you than was healthy, but I never for a moment thought that you would be so reckless as to do something like this. Sabrina had no choice, but you, you had to just dive in head first without understanding how stupid and delusional your decision would be. What in the name of the Light possessed you to do something that only your father would consider prudent?"

Bryn looked hard into her daughter's eyes, and she tried her best to suppress a smile of pride when the younger woman did not falter. Instead Rhain stood proud and began to answer her mother's charges.

"Mother, it had to be done."

Again Bryn dismissed her daughter's words with a wave of her hand, but this time she crossed the room and put both of her hands on Rhain's shoulders.

"My dear," Bryn said, her voice suddenly softening, "of course it had to be done. And I suppose if there was anyone that it should have been; of course it should have been you. But adopting Halicon's power, becoming the Mistress of the Blaze, the Queen of the Phasia, has made you enemies that no amount of power will protect you from. And now you find yourself responsible for the most dysfunctional and treacherous family that has ever been assembled."

Bryn paused, exhaled, and finally smiled.

"I'm proud of you."

For a long moment Rhain didn't know how to react. Her mother had never been one for compliments, and more often than not was dismissive of everything that anyone accomplished. She was a hard woman forged in a difficult time. Rhain smiled, and the two strong women embraced for a very short few moments before Bryn pulled away, smoothed her dress and then gently took hold of her daughters chin.

"It's still reckless and I still blame your father."

Rhain could not suppress a laugh. Bryn feigned a scowl before taking a step back and crossing her arms once again.

"So, what will you do now?"

Rhain exhaled slowly. Her mind whirled with so much information, so much history; she could feel the thoughts of all of the members of the phasia old and new running through her. Some of them were clearer than others, while others were obscured with layers of power that she could not see through. One that was obscured from her, one very close to her heart and was more family than any of the others filled her with worry, but he had his own troubles to wade through before they would see one another again.

"I think I have no choice but to reform the Council, at least briefly. Sabrina followed Halicon's wishes and invested at least one new member of the Brotherhood, and there are still others who have been outside the fight. There is a great storm coming, one that will wipe this world clean if we are not prepared to stand against it."

Bryn frowned again, this time however it was a genuine one.

"I understand, Rhain, but you know that will be a dangerous meeting. You aren't aware of your powers fully yet, and if one of the others, one of the more experienced members of the phasia were to challenge you, I don't know that I would be able to defend you."

Rhain smiled.

"Don't worry mother," Rhain said in her most soothing tones, "you and father taught me enough tricks to give anyone trouble, and with the Blaze fully at my disposal, I can hold anyone off."

Bryn wanted to say something about misplaced confidence, but Rhain was her father's daughter, and no lectures about arrogance would do anything but strengthen Rhain's resolve. But there was one point that Bryn could not let go.

"Just promise me one thing. If you see Emries or Talisia coming, run. You're no match for them, no matter what you have been taught or what you think you can do. Leave them to Logan and Aerith."

Rhain frowned. The next moment her entire body was wreathed in brilliant green flame, and Bryn nearly had to shield her eyes.

"Do you think so little of me, mother? Aerith and Logan may be strong, but I have the powers of a Child of the Creator coursing through me. I have the powers of a member of the Dark Gods, and I have the blood of two of the most powerful creatures to ever walk this world flowing through my veins. If we are going to win this war, it cannot be left to Aerith and Logan alone. Those of us who have only known this world as home have to stand and defend it, no matter the cost. Halicon knew that. That is why he passed his powers to Sabrina, and that's why in turn she passed them to me. The private war is over. The silence is over. If we are going to fight, we are going to do it on our terms, and not those dictated to us by the tyrants that prefer to hide and manipulate their way to victory. You can either stand with me or step aside."

Bryn stood firm and waited as the flames slowly receded from her daughter's form. Even after the flames subsided, the aura of power remained, like a strong breeze that blew from below her, lifting her hair so that it floated above her head. Finally even the aura of power faded and after Rhain looked as though she was going to collapse. The young woman stumbled backward a step before she was able to find her balance once more, and only was able to do so with the help of the edge of the bed. Part of Bryn wanted to go to her daughter to help her find her footing, but the cautious and more callous portion of her won out.

"Remember what your father always said about power."

Rhain's frown was replaced by a defeated sigh.

"Know your limits."

"Aerith may be reckless, may be arrogant, and may be irritating, but he is never foolish when it comes to the application of power. He knows his limits, and he knows when to test them. You must be measured, and you must be controlled. Demonstrations of power are fine for the mundane and the mortals, but for those who understand the application of power, like the phasia that you now command, just covering yourself in the Blaze does nothing more than tax your powers. We've seen Halicon do far worse, and that was not enough to stop his children from rebelling against him. You will not control through fear and intimidation. So break that habit now."

Rhain nodded.

"I'll get Taya and we'll make for Oradrim. Now that I've cleansed her of all of Emries influence, she can help me to deal with any problems that arise and also watch my back. She feels that she owes Sabrina at least that much. Your two troublesome brothers have begun to stir up trouble, and in time they will have to pay for their scheming. We might as well use Saurn's intelligence to our advantage while we can."

Bryn leaned against the wall and had a pensive look on her face.

"Saurn and Jeroch are not to be trusted, Rhain, no matter what your position is now. The most you'll be able to do is keep the members of the Brotherhood from killing each other, especially now that new members have been introduced into mix. Especially with Logan. Never forget that the phasia tried for so long to kill Logan, and he them. In order to succeed in this war, my darling daughter, you must do the one thing that Halicon never managed. You must unite the phasia and force them to work together."

Rhain considered for a moment, but was not given too long to think before Bryn spoke again.

"I will not be joining you in Oradrim, at least not yet. Besides, my being there will complicate your initial meeting with Saurn. Aerith has been keeping things from me for far too long, and I need answers. I can only think of one person that will tell me the truth, so I need to make a short trip before joining you."

Rhain was shocked when Bryn took two steps across the room and wrapped her arms around the younger woman. Instead of pulling away immediately as Rhain expected Bryn held the embrace for quite some time before stepping back and then kissing her daughter on the forehead. Bryn smiled and squeezed Rhain's shoulder for a moment before nodding. Rhain understood that the conversation was over when she heard the door open behind her. Once again Rhain realized how much her mother knew, as the older woman had taught yet another lesson to her child. No matter what power Rhain attained her mother would still be her mother, and Rhain felt comforted that the wisdom and unconditional love would always be there. Without another word, Rhain left the room, suddenly feeling less pensive about her new position and her new powers. She would find Taya, and together they would dive headfirst into uncertain waters.

* * * * * * * * * * * *

Jeroch had spent several days wandering the headquarters of the Shadow Guild, and the more he wandered the more confused and disheartened he became. For so long he had remained hidden in plain sight, a member of the Knights of the Flashing Blade, serving at the leisure of those that could never be his betters. Saurn on the other hand had spent all of his time building up a secret army, one that would be loyal only to him, and could bring to him the one thing that had failed them for so long, information. That had been the hardest truth that Jeroch had come to stare in the face after the destruction of their home in Onea. The phasia had not failed because they were weak, or stupid, or that their enemies had been more capable. No, what the heroes of the world of Onea had was the ability to work together and share information toward the singular goal of defeating Shau-ling and everyone and everything that followed him. The phasia had been divided, hating each other, hating Shau-ling, and in a lot of ways, hating themselves. It wasn't until Aerith Seth and Logan Ranthall opened Jeroch's eyes, that he saw the error of his ways. But Jeroch was a soldier. That was what he had been bred to be from the moment he drew his first breath. He could only change the world with a weapon in his hand. That was why he became part of the military machine that drove the Cadarian Empire. That was why he tried to steer the fate of the world through his presence and through his power. Saurn on the other hand was born to think, and plot, and plan. He played games with the lives and emotions of generations, and he had the patience to wait for hundreds of years for the conditions to be right for his plans to have the optimal result. Now though it seemed as though his brilliance had finally slipped free of the noose of arrogance.

As he often did during his wanderings, Jeroch found himself walking in the direction of Saurn's prize prisoner, the former Court Sorceress to the Emperor of Cadaria, Irene Drage. For over two weeks, since members of the Shadow Guild recovered her from the wreckage of the Imperial Palace at Aldere, Saurn had kept Irene under constant mental and physical duress. Short of the few moments that the woman passed out from the pain of the physical torture, Irene had not been allowed to sleep, and she had only been fed and given water enough to keep her alive. Saurn intended to break her and rend the secrets from her shattered mind, but thus far the woman's resilience had been extraordinary. Perhaps Saurn had been right after all, and the frail-looking woman had indeed been a vessel within which Talisia's power had once resided. If there was even a remnant of the Child of the Creator's essence within the girl, the information they could extract could change the very nature of the war. Of course, it was likely that any methods undertaken to extract the information would be fatal to Irene. On Onea, Jeroch wouldn't have given a second thought to Irene's fate, and he would have ripped the information out of her, and a hundred like her if necessary. But this was not Onea, and Jeroch was not the same man.

Jeroch moved past the two guards and cracked the door open, steeling himself for the horror that he would see and hear. Irene sat in a simple wooden chair, naked, sweating, and shaking. Her hands and feet were bound to the chair, and the chair itself had been secured to the floor to prevent the woman from trying to escape. A gag had been stuffed in the woman's mouth to muffle her screams, but the simple piece of cloth could only do so much. One of Saurn's interrogators had a long thin knife with an impossibly sharp blade that he was heating over an open flame. Once the edge of the blade began to glow, the assassin slowly but precisely drew the dagger across Irene's exposed flesh, leaving a raised bubbling scar. The interrogator asked no questions, and Jeroch knew that none would be asked. None were ever asked. Any information Irene had she would not be conscious of, but as long as her will remained strong she could fight any of Jeroch's attempts to extract the information. What worried Jeroch however was that perhaps his will was no longer strong enough to do what needed to be done. He was just about to turn away from the torture when he felt familiar flows of power coming from deeper in the compound. Without thinking, Jeroch opened himself to the power of the Blaze and ran as fast as his legs would carry him in the direction that the power was coming from. He skidded to a stop when he saw Saurn. Saurn was wreathed in green flames, and he was looking in the direction of a swirling blue portal that was just expanding in to existence. Jeroch took a moment to summon twin blades of energy to his hands and waited for the intruder to reveal himself.

When the shadow appeared in the portal, Saurn was ready to lash out; however, at the last moment his connection to the Blaze was severed. Saurn's eyes cut from the portal to Jeroch, and he watched in horror as the twin energy blades vanished from his older brother's hands. The look of confusion and concern had barely had the time to come to Jeroch's face when the shadow in the portal solidified into a woman's form. Both members of the phasia had visceral responses to the woman who emerged. Jeroch's was one of disgust and irritation, while Saurn's was one of confusion.

"Rhain?" Saurn said slowly.

Rhain looked in Saurn's direction and waved her hand dismissively. A moment later another woman emerged from the portal, this one drawing the same confused looks from Jeroch and Saurn. Taya Viruci was a confounding addition to the proceedings. Rhain turned to Jeroch first.

"Shadow," she said with a strength that Jeroch felt all the way to his toes, "I have temporarily restricted your powers so that you would not do anything foolish like trying to attack me. My hope is that this conversation can be a civil one."

She then turned to Saurn.

"Saurn, I know this must be confusing for you. You have only ever known me as Rhain Feirbran, one of your newly recruited assassins under the direct command of Master Geoffry Aramour. However, my true identity was hidden from you; in fact, it was hidden from everyone but a select few. In truth, I am Rhain Seth. Daughter of Aerith Seth and Bryn Aplee."

Before Saurn could react, Rhain continued.

"My identity and parentage are less important now, as I have recently become the vessel for your maker's power, and thus I am now the Mistress of the Blaze, and the leader of the phasia."

Saurn glared, his heart immediately filling with hate. Jeroch on the other hand looked first at Saurn and then at Rhain before slowly going to one knee and bowing his head. Saurn was confused by Jeroch's easy submission to the words of the simple girl, but then Saurn remembered all of the things he had seen since being reborn on Espre, and he also remembered the goal that lay ahead of them. It took only another moment, and Saurn gathered his robe and also fell to one knee. Rhain did not let them stay kneeling for long, though the part of her that was most like her father wanted to see them bow and scrape for several more hours.

"Arise," she said letting her voice soften as much as she dared. "There is much to do, and none of it can be done with you on the floor."

Jeroch felt the comment as though it had come from Aerith's lips, and it brought a deep frown to his face. Both he and Saurn were back to their feet in a matter of seconds, but neither made a move.

"There is something that must be said here, before we go any farther," Rhain continued. "I am not Halicon, and I am not Sabrina. What's more, this is not Onea, and there are no petty prophecies or power games to be played. The fate of everything we know and have ever known hangs in the balance, and I will brook no defiance or rebellion. We must be united in our cause to stand against the enemies of life and freedom, and any who do not stand with us only stand against us, that includes any members of the phasia that will not work toward the greater good."

She took a deep breath and looked at Jeroch.

"This means no one will act against my father or those who have worn his mantle."

She then looked at Saurn.

"And those new members of the Brotherhood that will be joining us shall be afforded the same courtesy and respect that I will afford you."

Saurn glowered for a brief moment before nodding in ascent. When Rhain looked back in Jeroch's direction, he also nodded.

"Good. Now, let us try something novel in the history of the phasia," Rhain said letting her posture ease, "let's tell the truth."

Chapter LXXXII

Lacuna

Year Four of the Just Emperor Kaitain "Dragonsbane" Lorien, Creator's Calendar Year 1871

The Pritan Island chain lay quiet in the wake of the wars that continued to enflame the whole of Cadaria, and though they lay so close to the southern kingdoms of the embattled empire, so far the pristine islands remained that way. On one of the smaller and more remote islands a waterfall churned, oblivious to the passing of time and seasons. Lying deep in the equatorial zone, even the harshest winters would not slow the flow of water that fell from its rocky heights, nor could the hottest summer shrink its amble banks. One family had chosen this place as its refuge, a quiet utopia in a garden of madness. It seemed as though it had been a hundred years since anyone had stepped foot in the little cottage that stood only a few feet from the waterfall, and as the old door creaked open, Aerith Seth could not shake the feeling that he was home. But though the feelings found his heart, he knew that the feelings were only half-right. Without his wife there waiting for him, chiding him for his sometime mindlessness, staring at him with those eyes that could hold so much malice and at the same time so much love, the home was still empty.

Crossing the smallish room to where the simple bed stood, he slumped down on the edge and looked around the cottage, his eyes finding places where his wife had stood, remembering conversations, fights, and moments that had been indelibly carved into his heart. Directly across from where he sat was a small circular window that let the morning light stream into the room and in the evening allowed the moonlight to stretch long almost reaching the bed. In front of that window was where Bryn had stood, cradling Rhain in her arms, their first born child on this world that they would call their home for almost two millennia. She had surprised him then, cooing to their newly born baby girl and then softly beginning to sing. It wasn't that Aerith had ever doubted that Bryn could sing if she wanted to, but he never imagined that her heart had changed so much from the killer that she had been created to be. Holding that child in her arms, she was no longer the Lady Fox of the phasia, a creature bent on the subjugation of the human race, she was as human and loving and fragile as any mother who wanted nothing but the best for her child. That morning, Aerith held Rhain for the first time, and he cradled her in his lap as he sat cross-legged on the shore of the small stream that emerged from the bottom of the waterfall. She slept most of the time, only waking in short intervals to look up at her father, as he used his power to fashion a cradle for her out of a nearby tree. He had lost count of how many times he started the project over again before he got it just right. Later Bryn would chide him for being so particular, and though he playfully argued with her in his own way, there was something deeper in his heart, something that Bryn knew but would never speak about openly. Rhain was not the first child that Bryn and Aerith had given birth to. Long before their time on Espre, long before the prophecies and the wars that would mark the end of the world they had once called home, Bryn was the wife of another member of the phasia, and Aerith was a general in her army. The affair was no secret, and if it would have been an affair only, Bryn's husband, the violent and irascible Grawn would never have taken action. But once Bryn became pregnant, and it was clear that Aerith was the father, the man known as the Shark could no longer contain his hatred. Aerith was expelled from the Army of the Fox, sent straight into the hands of Aralias Imstra, the Hand of the Light, and the destiny that awaited him at the hands of Saurn Macco and Shau-ling. Bryn for her crime was strangled in the night, Grawn's powerful hands circling her throat, watching as the light was extinguished from her eyes. It was a futile gesture ultimately as Bryn would be reborn in the next generation, her pregnancy intact.

Grawn's anger by that point had abated to some extent, enough to let the baby boy live. For many years, the child was raised by his mother and his "aunt" Ellis Chandara, taught everything he needed to know about being the child of a member of the phasia, and the part that he would play in the war that was coming. Though Grawn, Bryn, and Ellis were outcasts, they knew that war would eventually find them, and by extension their children. However, Emries would forge a different path for Aerith and Bryn's first child, touching Gideon Viruci with his power, making him a member of the *Erieal* of the second generation of the prophecies. It was through the eyes of Logan Ranthall that Aerith learned of his son, learned of the man he had become, and though it broke his heart, he understood why he had been kept in the dark for so long. Gideon was his mother's son, but he had the soul of a hero and he fought hard at Logan's side, making the world better simply through the force of their will. Aerith cried for a long time when Gideon was killed in the palace of Shau-ling, mourning the loss of another of his children.

Gideon had not been Aerith's first child; his dalliances had produced two others, two more who could not shake the tragedy of war. A boy and a girl, twins born from a single night of passion, would become the cornerstones of the first war against Shau-ling. Cedric Binosear, the first *Coromor* of the prophecies, and Anabel Binosear, the strong young woman that served as both Cedric's conscience and support in times of darkness. Cedric would be heralded as the hero while Anabel would disappear from the spotlight, choosing to have a different impact on the world, hiding behind a different name. But they were drawn to one another, just as later Aerith's mantle would draw Logan Ranthall to Trelon and to Anabel. Anabel fell in Trelon, dead at the hands of a member of the phasia that was desperately trying to get to Logan, and in a strange way, when Logan cradled Anabel's limp body in an effort to save her from the burning Palace of Trelon, Aerith felt as though he was holding his baby girl for the first time, and it broke his heart. However more heartbreak was coming, because in the very same battle that claimed Gideon, Cedric fell, and for a long time Aerith grieved, all three of his children dead and gone. The perverse game that he was trapped in, the ideological war between two brothers, had claimed the life of his children and had fated him to watch them die. He had nearly given up on everything when the third war started. So he had invested his powers in a man who seemed as though he could make a difference. Evan Sinn became a surrogate child. Aerith's losses could never be changed, nor could the wounds ever be healed, but Evan gave Aerith something he had never had, a relationship with his progeny. In the time that was left, all Aerith wanted to do was see Bryn once more, hold her once more, and feel the warmth of her skin against his. Then he could let go, let the rest of the world fend for itself and fade into nothingness. But the Creator had other plans. The stakes had been raised, and it was no longer one impudent child against another, it was now the Creator challenging the very existence of every man and woman that walked Onea. Through the Creator's intervention, realities fractured, and the dead walked in a world of darkness called the Dark Mirror. People he had lost, Gideon, Logan, and a granddaughter that had a different name in his world, breathed again. No longer could Aerith stand by, no longer could he leave these people to the whims of spoiled and petulant gods who cared nothing for the fate of the innocent. He resolved to never watch one of his own fall again. He vowed that no matter the cost, and no matter the trial, he would stop the madness that descended around them, and it was partially through his intervention that Emries was defeated and the war for the souls on Onea was won.

They had been given peace, at least for a little while. Aerith and Bryn were happy for a time. They lived together on the island and got to know their granddaughter, Taya Viruci, though after a hundred years or so, she needed to find a place of her own in the world. But those years gave Aerith a taste of the family that he had been dreaming of since his days in the orphanage and in the deadly mines where he had spent most of his formative years. It took many more years of arguments, bribes, cajoling and begging to convince Bryn to start a real family together. Though she too mourned the loss of Gideon, she also did not fully trust that the wars were over. And though she had been right, and though Aerith was keeping the truth from her, he vowed that no matter what he would stand beside her and keep them out of any trouble that was to come. He fully intended to keep that bargain, and he knew that the others would not approach him unless there was no choice. The one exception to that of course was Sabrina.

Taya was still living with Aerith and Bryn when Sabrina first visited. It was late at night and Aerith woke from a deep slumber with a pain in his chest that he could not explain. He had become very adept over the years of moving silently as not to disturb Bryn from her slumber, and he glided across the floor barely touching down, but not drawing on enough power that it would alert Bryn's very sensitive defenses. The door had been another matter altogether. It had taken Aerith a long time to work the squeaking out of the hinges, and even then they would not always cooperate. That night however silence held and Aerith was able to make his way to the stream where he found Sabrina waiting. It was clear that she had been crying, and all Aerith wanted to do was wrap her in his arms and hold her tightly and take away her pain. He didn't know how long they stood there, didn't know how long that she cried, but he could feel her hot tears against his chest and knew that whatever was troubling her was of such intensity that her whole body shook. No words were spoken that night, no peek into the mind of the woman who had so much weight upon her heart. In the weeks to come there were more late night visits, and while there was some conversation, the majority of the visits found the two of them sitting by the stream, Sabrina leaning into Aerith and his arm around her shoulder. Of course, that all changed when she accepted the powers of the Spirit. The visits stopped, but Aerith began to receive more information about the happenings in the Heavens through the connection that the two of them shared. Logan's visit had been unexpected but not unwelcome. He brought with him Gwydeon Sandar, and the three men hatched the plan that would place them all in incredible jeopardy. The goal was laughable at best, suicidal at worst. But it was the only way, but it would take sacrifice.

Of course Aerith knew that the sacrifice would ultimately be his and his alone. He didn't know when it would come, just that it would. However, until it did, he would live every day to its fullest. During her formative years, there was not a minute that Aerith did not spend with his daughter. To Aerith, Rhain was the most precious thing in his universe, and he did everything in his power to show her that. Though Bryn was more forceful in her lessons, Aerith let Rhain explore their world, as well as her own abilities through a lens that was never afforded to him. From the time that Saurn found Aerith in the mines of Quea, the young orphan had been groomed for one purpose alone, to be a weapon. When it came to her lessons, Rhain was very much like her father in that she drank up as much knowledge as she could from whatever source she could. However it became clear early that Rhain was her mother's daughter. Rhain had a taste for human weakness.

In their early days together, Bryn had confided in Aerith one late night as they lay together in the bed normally occupied by her and her husband. Grawn was away, leading troops into battle and was not expected back for several days. The liaison was still dangerous, but Bryn had moved past the point of caring. Though in those days she never would have admitted it, Bryn was in love with Aerith in the same way that he was in love with her. At that point in time though, she was still the hard and vicious Lady Fox and was expected to order the deaths of thousands on a whim. Laying there intertwined, Bryn rested her head on Aerith's chest as Aerith leaned against the thick padded headboard. She mused softly, on the edge of sleep, about the weakness of the human character but the strength of the human heart and soul. In her mind, humans were the ultimate contradiction. Their souls were essentially good, wanting the best for themselves and for those connected to them. The web of the soul stretched across the whole of the human race, and at that basic level each human knew that the only way to truly elevate the piece was to elevate the whole. But the voice of the soul was weak. It could be easily drowned out by the rages of the world and could only be heard when the person was at peace. The heart was supposed to amplify the voice of the soul. It was supposed to pump the voice through the body with every beat, bringing the whole into harmony with the goodness of the soul. However, often the heart was too influenced by the conscious voice, the character of the person, the corruption of the mind with abstracts that could never be reconciled with the common good. That was where Bryn and the other phasia were born and where they were successful in their war. They understood better than any human ever could the tools of greed, lust, hatred, revenge, sloth, sorrow, and jealousy. Strong negative emotions poisoned the heart, sent it pumping bile and poison through the blood, drowning out the voice of the soul. It had been so easy to corrupt so many, and Bryn was a master at it.

It took years for Aerith to learn that while Bryn was able to use these tools to get anything she wanted at any time she wanted, whether through the application of her mind or her body, that she did not have the same level of mastery at the corruption of the soul as Jeroch had. Jeroch had mastered a power that belied explanation and could delve into the broken characters of fallen men and drag them to the side of the Shadows. For a time they were just enslaved men, their will gone, and their only thought to serve Shau-ling and the phasia. But in the early days of the war, their numbers and their ferocity were not enough to counter the zealots that Emries was always able to throw at the phasia and their armies. Emries was an even more practiced usurer of the human mind than a phase could ever be as he understood and knew them to the core. Emries had created the humans, knew their minds, knew what they were capable of and ultimately how best to manipulate them. So Jeroch had to alter the balance of power. Deep in the lands controlled by the Shadow, Jeroch built a great black tower. Men and women were herded into the tower like cattle and were never seen again. However on the battlefields a new kind of warrior appeared, the Jeresei. Once Aerith was expelled from the Army of the Fox, one of the most important missions that he went on for the Hand of the Light was into Jeroch's den of horrors, to the black tower itself. For his own sanity, Aerith had suppressed the memory of the horrors he saw within the tower, the screams of terror and sorrow that filled every inch of that place. But in the end his chore was successful and the black tower was destroyed, effectively ending the creation of Jeresei on Onea. But it had not prevented a whole new race from being created, and hundreds of thousands from being converted into twisted hateful versions of their former selves.

However, as Bryn told him about the weakness of most mortals, she also spoke of the rare exceptions. There were heroes and villains, creatures of strong enough character that rejected most attempts at manipulation, that were able to exert their will on the world the way they saw fit. At the time Bryn explained it as a fluke of nature, but later Aerith understood that these people of stronger character were interventions from outside the normal flow of nature. For a long time Aerith held that it was the Creator placing his hand into the conflict between his children, but after seeing the pettiness of the Creator during the wars at the end of Onea and now again on Espre, Aerith had begun to believe that there was something beyond even the Creator, something that wanted the table to remain balanced and needed agents that could stand on their own. But where had that started? Had Onea been the first world to have these heroes and villains that stood contrary to the will of the Creator and his Children? Surely Dorovar could be counted among these special beings. Was Dorovar just another world's version of Aerith?

Standing from the edge of the bed, Aerith shook away those thoughts and moved to the small circular window and looked out. In his mind's eye he could see his two children running and playing in the sunlight. It brought flooding back the day that Bryn told Aerith that she was with child again. He turned back from the window and could see Bryn sitting on the edge of the bed as he had been only a moment before, a look of annoyance and disgust on her face. Aerith had just returned from swimming with his now nearly ten year old daughter. Bryn only had to say the words "I hate you" for Aerith to know that they were going to have another child. Ayden was a much different child than Rhain had been. In her early years, Rhain had been clingy, and never wanted to be far from one of her parents. Ayden from the moment he could crawl was always off somewhere trying to find adventure. In the beginning it had been easy to keep track of the boy, but as he aged and began to learn about the powers that he had at his disposal, the games of hide and seek became much more challenging. It was Ayden and not Rhain that first discovered how to create portals. Ayden quickly lost the taste for it after his first foray through a portal landed him high in a tree that he could not find his way out of. He was too frightened and uncertain to try to portal his way out. He spent almost a whole day at the top of the tree miles away from the little house before Aerith finally discovered him and brought him home. It was that day that Aerith and Bryn decided that their children were ready for the true lessons about power.

While their parenting styles had been much different, it soon turned out that Bryn and Aerith both shared the same attitude on the teaching of power. There was no room for coddling. Mistakes with power could lead to death and destruction, and neither parent wanted their children to make a tragic mistake that could end their own lives, or the lives of their family members. Lessons were strict, regimented, and neither parent brooked any defiance. Ayden quickly proved to be a natural, though he bristled at the instruction and the rules, much like Aerith would have if the roles would have been reversed. Ayden's problem was that even though he had power to spare his irreverence prevented him from having the same kind of control that his sister exhibited. Aerith had always been irreverent too, but under that shell was always the heart and mind of a killer. Ayden didn't have that killer instinct, and so he would never be the equal of those who did. Rhain was just the opposite. She had her mother's thirst for blood and the control to match, but she did not have enough raw power to be a challenge for those on the level of the phasia or the Dark Gods. She would earn her victories through guile and precision. In sparring, Rhain always would frustrate Ayden, exploiting his weaknesses and scoring far more victories than losses. Eventually Ayden became more brutal in his tactics, overwhelming Rhain with sheer power, but in time Rhain learned to counter those offensives as well. No matter how Aerith and Bryn tried, Ayden would never learn that power alone was not enough. That was why eventually Aerith and Bryn came to the determination that their teaching techniques were not going to be enough to prepare Ayden for what was to come.

Though they lived in isolation, Aerith was able to keep up on the happenings in the world through Taya's visits as well as through his secret meetings with Sabrina, and the steady stream of information coming to him from Logan. So, breaking with his own promises of isolation and non-interference, Aerith left the small island and traveled to Jelan to meet with the Grand Master of the Academy of Arcane Arts. From what Aerith had been able to learn about Alistair Ravenheart, it was clear that the newly minted Grand Master was a good man and was truly invested in ensuring that his students were his first priority. Perhaps in time it was that selfless dedication that had cost him the life of his wife and eventually his own, but at the time, it was clear that the Academy was the right environment for Ayden. Aerith's visit came in the middle of the night, and when the Grand Master and his wife returned to their chambers after a long day, they came in to find Aerith sitting in a high-backed chair, their infant daughter cradled in his arms. Aerith knew that this could inflame both Alistair and Estelle, but he also knew that it would be a great test of their characters. He proved to be right about both of them. While Estelle was obviously disturbed by the sight, Alistair calmly walked to Aerith and extended his hands. Aerith handed baby Quyhn to Alistair without a word, and once the baby was back in her mother's arms, the three sat and talked for several hours. Getting Ayden into the Academy was not a difficult task, but the secrecy of his induction as well as the promise to ensure that he could not be expelled was something else entirely. Aerith had to make some serious promises that day, ones that would probably haunt him for quite some time, but it was necessary if he wanted the best for his son.

With Ayden safely in the bosom of the Academy of Arcane Arts, that left only their daughter, Rhain, and her ultimate disposition. She had blossomed into full womanhood, and in doing so had become more and more like her mother with every passing year. She was vicious, strong, and had the edge to her that made her a killer. But more than that, she had her father's heart and sense of right and wrong. It was a dangerous combination full of contradictions and trials. It had come to Aerith's attention that the Shadow Guild was starting to make some significant noise, and there was something all-too-familiar about their methods and practices. Most from Onea wouldn't have been able to see it, even the remaining members of the phasia, but it was clear to Aerith that Saurn was behind the Shadow Guild in at least some fashion. With Rhain's temperament, she was a natural to pose as an assassin, and getting her infiltrated into the Shadow Guild would take little to no effort. However, it became important ultimately to protect her identity. So Aerith called in one marker that he had hoped never to use. As the Spirit, Sabrina had learned how to manipulate the fabric that stretched between the unconscious minds of all mortals. With Aerith and Bryn's help, Sabrina was able to plant a kind of illness into the collective unconscious, effective destroying any connection between Rhain and her parents. From that moment, Rhain Seth ceased to exist, and Rhain Feirbran was born. Not even Saurn would be able to ferret out her true identity.

That left Aerith and Bryn, together, alone, for the first time in centuries. Perhaps it was because he knew what was coming, or perhaps it was because they had forgotten how to just be together, but a distance began to grow between the two of them. But at least the discomfort was short-lived. Aryx Terian was soon at their doorstep, and whether because of restlessness or a sense of the foreboding future, Bryn agreed to become involved in the world once again. It brought them face to face with Evan Sinn, face to face with a destiny that Aerith had known was coming for a long time, and face to face with the sacrifice he never wanted to make again. Evan was not his blood, but it didn't make him any less family, and in all ways but blood, Evan was Aerith's son. But to save Evan from himself, to save everyone from the Creator, Evan fell, and Aerith was reborn.

Stepping out of the cottage, Aerith looked back and found a large black ball of fur rolling from a crevice in the rock wall that made up one side of the cottage. There was no way to be sure if this was the same Snag that had followed Aerith from Onea, or even how long one of the creatures actually lived. What Aerith did know was that there were tens of thousands of them spread through tunnels on the island. He knelt down and took the ball of fur into his hands. The creature opened to reveal the bright eyes and glistening teeth, its whisper-thin tail wrapping around Aerith's hand in a gesture Aerith had come to understand was like a hug.

"Well my old friend, the time has come," Aerith said calmly. "No more hiding. Hannah needs you. This is home no longer."

There was no acknowledgement that anyone could understand but there was a wave of emotion that pulsed from the creature. A moment later Aerith felt power build up inside the creature and a small portal appeared beside the Snag. Aerith had to laugh to himself as the Snag bounded through the portal.

"I didn't know they could do that."

Finally Aerith stood and looked back at the cottage once more. This had been their home for so long, but if this war was truly coming to an end, there would be no more hiding and no more safe refuge. He had recovered a simple twig from the ground which he rubbed between his fingers gently until it sparked into life with fire. He tossed the twig into the cottage and turned his back, knowing that the fire would engulf the home and eventually remove all traces of it. Reaching into his pocket, Aerith recovered a white stone, the stone that had been keyed for home. With a simple effort, the stone flattened in his hands, and when he dropped it to the ground it shattered like a dinner plate. He needed answers, and there was only one place he knew he could get them. As he pulled another stone from his pocket, he took a deep breath. A fight was coming, one that had been inevitable. But this time, the fight would be on Aerith's terms.

Dominus

*Year One of the Divine Empress and Child of the Creator
Marlae Tamerlane, Creator's Calendar Year 1871*

Reverend Mother Amallia had been waiting for nearly an hour outside the large wooden doors that led to the aptly dubbed War Room in the Divine Empress's wing of the Royal Palace of Hedorah. Upon her return to Hedorah, she had gone immediately to the presence of the Divine Empress and delivered the answer and conditions from the High Priestess of the Church of the Creator, Baeata Catrinel and had then been promptly dismissed. Through the large wooden doors Amallia could hear the raised voices coming from the room, and though she could not make out many of the words, the voice was obviously that of the god Azure. Finally, the doors opened, and the Divine Empress's servant, a woman Amallia knew as Isabella approached Amallia with her head down. Without a word, Isabella motioned toward the entry to the War Room. Amallia nodded to the girl and then moved through the wooden doors, not knowing what to expect on the other side. It took only a brief look around the room to know that her information had caused an explosion of emotion. Azure's face was flushed and his nostrils were still flaring in anger. Terrance Aldora also was flushed, and his eyes were narrowed in the god's direction. The Divine Empress's face was passive, as was the face of her newly minted High Councilor Anabel Binosear. Upon entering the War Room, Amallia bowed deeply and waited to be acknowledged.

"Reverend Mother, please approach."

It was Anabel's voice and not the Divine Empress's, but Amallia obeyed. As soon as she was within two feet of the chair that the Divine Empress sat upon, Amallia stopped, bowed once more, and then waited.

"We have been debating the requests made by the High Priestess for quite some time now, but we have questions about the woman herself. Could you please give us your impressions of this Baeata Catrinel?"

Again it was Anabel who spoke. It almost appeared from the way that the Divine Empress was clenching her jaw that her annoyance with this situation had made it impossible to keep her tone even and passive.

"Baeata is a woman of great faith and great dedication to that faith. To say that she is a true believer would be degrading. Her whole life has been given to worship of the Creator and betterment of the people of this world. She learned at the foot of perhaps the greatest of us, Hannah Ironheart, and internalized those lessons as though they were a new gospel."

Amallia could hear Azure click his tongue behind her.

"More blaspheme from those who have no concept of what true faith is."

Amallia continued undeterred.

"I believe that there is no thought in Baeata for herself. She is utterly devoted to service, and she has contemplated the best course for her flock, and for those who are threatened by Kaitain Lorien's decrees. I believe she feels that she is in an impossible situation with enemies on all sides, and she can only depend on true faith to protect those who need it the most. And if I may, Your Grace, with the stories that I have heard of the atrocities being inflicted upon those who have dedicated their lives to the Church by the men of the Imperial Legions, I cannot fault the High Priestess for her stance."

Amallia bowed her head, but before either Anabel or Marlae could speak, Azure had rounded on Amallia, along with another man that Amallia did not recognize.

"Your words are troubling, Reverend Mother," Azure said coldly. "You sound as though you admire this woman, and side with her blasphemous views. She is the High Priestess, and yet she makes demands of the one anointed by the Creator. Who is it you serve, Amallia? Are you devoted to the Creator and his chosen vessel on this world? Or do you serve this woman who is supposedly the voice of the Church of the Creator?"

Amallia answered quickly, her tone firm and confident.

"My loyalties are not divided. But I question the premise of your question. The High Priestess has said that she recognizes the validity of the Divine Empress's right to rule and the touch of the Creator upon her. As the High Priestess of the Church of the Creator, she will serve her master, the Creator, and because the Divine Empress is His empowered servant, Baeata will bend her will. As for my loyalties, they have never been in dispute. I am a member of the Church of the Creator, and so I serve at the behest of the High Priestess in what capacity she sees fit. And I have been tasked by the Divine Empress to her needs. They are not mutually exclusive as the High Priestess would never countermand an order given by the Divine Empress."

"An interesting point of view," the new arrival said quietly, but with an edge of ice in his voice. "Fanatics and zealots are like rabid dogs. They should all be put down. Many worlds have been better for it."

"You're out of line, Krysis," Terrance thundered. "Your words are bordering on treason."

The one called Krysis turned his gaze to Terrance and bored holes through him. Some could have called the look one of contempt, but Amallia felt something else from it. It felt as though Krysis was looking at Terrance in the same way that a farmer looked at a gopher. Terrance was an annoyance to Krysis and nothing more, and it would only take minor effort to kill Terrance removing the vermin once and for all.

"Mortal conventions of treason are beneath my notice," Krysis scoffed. "My only concern is to ensure that the Creator's interests are served on this primitive rock."

Terrance opened his mouth to speak, but Marlae raised her hand and all of Terrance's protests died in his throat. After a long moment, Marlae rose from her chair which forced everyone except for the angelic guards to one knee. Krysis was the last to go to one knee, and when he did, Amallia felt as though he was doing it as a courtesy, nothing more, and even that was almost beneath him.

"I will consider everything said here before I render my decision. But as this is a sensitive issue not only for the Church of the Creator, but for my budding rule over this land, I shall not toil for long before making my decision. I shall announce it in due course."

Marlae turned away toward her private chambers, but stopped and turned back to where Amallia still bowed.

"Reverend Mother, did Ayden not return with you from Albitonin?"

Amallia was silent for a long moment before she raised her head and locked her eyes on the Divine Empress.

"The Will did not accompany me to Albitonin," Amallia said, trying to keep her voice as even as possible. "He sent two angelic warriors in his stead. He did use a portal to leave Hedorah, but I do not know to where or for what purpose."

"Perhaps," Azure offered, "the Creator assigned a new task for his Chosen that had to be urgently attended to."

Marlae hesitated for only a moment before nodding briefly and continuing out of the room to her private chambers. Anabel pointed first to Terrance and then to Isabella before herself turning and following Marlae out of the room.

* * * * * * * * * * *

Once Marlae was through the door into her private chambers, she pulled her long white gloves off and threw them across the room before slamming herself into the high-backed chair on the far side of the room. Anabel waited at the door, ushering both Terrance and Isabella through before she herself entered the room and closed the door behind her. Like

Marlae, Terrance was fuming, and instead of sitting in one of the nearby chairs, he stood behind it, gripping the back so tightly that his knuckles were turning white. Isabella stayed near the door, keeping her attention divided between what was going on in the room as well as what was going on in the small hallway that connected the private chambers to the War Room. Moments after the door closed, Anabel surprised everyone by leaning against a wall and laughing. Marlae's eyes went wide, and Terrance looked confused, but finally Marlae's features softened and her lips parted into a small smile.

"I'll say one thing for this new High Priestess," Anabel said finally, "she has guts."

Finally Terrance's anger abated enough for him to speak.

"Guts or not," he said slowly, his hands loosening slightly on the back of the chair, "we may not be able to meet her demands. And even if we were to give her everything she wants, how much power is that giving her to negotiate once she gets to Hedorah?"

"That begs the question," Marlae said after a moment of reflection, "being new to the Chosen of the Creator role, do I even have the power to declare someone a saint? Does my voice have that much authority in that regard?"

Anabel nodded.

"The last person that was proclaimed a saint by the Church of the Creator was Kaldawyn Lorien, Ender's father and the tenth Lorien Emperor. Proclaiming each former Emperor a saint was merely a formality, and had it not been for the outbreaks of wars the likes of which haven't been seen in two thousand years, Ender Lorien would have also been proclaimed a saint by now. Now, Gregor Quicksilver is considered a saint by many, and has nearly been proclaimed one several times, but because of the conflict of interest, he hasn't been."

"Conflict of interest?" Terrance asked.

Anabel cocked her head with a look of confusion on her face.

"He's married to the High Priestess."

"Why should that prevent him from being named a saint? If he has done saintly works, shouldn't he be proclaimed a saint no matter who he's married to?"

Anabel smiled.

"You are very young."

Marlae's sigh cut off Terrance's reply.

"Anabel's point is valid," she said, resignation thick in her voice. "Politics is politics, and should I be involving myself in the politics of the Church in such a manner?"

"Your Grace," Isabella's diminutive voice came from the area of the door, "you have already given pardon and sanctuary to all members of the Knights of the Flashing Blade."

Anabel smiled.

"Of course. You have defied your father by letting the Knights of the Flashing Blade know that they have nothing to fear from you. Now you have the opportunity not only to fully embrace the Church of the Creator, but to forge not just an alliance, but a partnership of such strength that no one can drive a wedge. One thing that has become painfully obvious over the entirety of your father's rule; alliances of convenience and alliances of tradition and familiarity are weak and unreliable. People were loyal to the Lorien family because they united these disparate peoples into something cohesive that worked for a greater goal. But now the family has shattered, and along with it, the Empire. Which Lorien should the people trust? You? Your father? Your uncle? Your step-mother? Your step-sister? Who? Your family no longer dominates the consciousness, so people must look at the other forces that have protected their lives and given them something to believe in. You have extended the olive branch to the Knights of the Flashing Blade. If you court and win the support of the Church of the Creator, all that would be left is the Academy of Arcane Arts. More people will flock to your banner. But you must hold the people, not the royalty."

Terrance's eyes lit up with sudden understanding.

"It will be just as it was during the Founding War. The royals will only be concerned with their own fortunes, with their own power. They will have to be removed if they don't submit to the will of the Divine Empress."

Marlae chimed in.

"That could be problematic in the case of some of the more popular royal families. The Mistics in Celidar are a prime example."

Anabel gave a knowing smile and then nodded.

"The Mistics are not your concern. Unite your family. Feyd, Felicia, Quyhn, Dominique. Extend the hand to them, forgive them both as a woman and as the Empress, and you will heal the schism of this Empire. Only Kaitain and the other evil forces will be left, and this war will turn back to the light."

Marlae wanted to grimace. She knew that it was only a matter of time before this would become an issue. The Lorien family was the heart of the Cadarian Empire. If there were only two voices contending for the favor of the people, Marlae trusted that the people would see the evil that Kaitain represented. However, with a multitude of voices, a multitude of directions, the people would never be able to see the truth.

"Isabella," Marlae said after a moment, "there is information floating around these halls that are not coming to my ears because people are afraid still to talk about my family. Find out what is happening with Feyd and Felicia, find out where Dominique and Quyhn are. Bring that information to me. Once I know where they are, we can determine how to approach them. Even if there are those who will turn away from my father's rule, Dominique and Quyhn have gained a great deal of popularity for their charity and their mercy. We must entice them to join my court of their own free will."

Isabella nodded.

"As you wish, Your Grace."

"There is one more hand that you must extend," Anabel said after several moments. "And it's not one that will be popular. But it cannot be discussed now. Once the High Priestess is safely in the fold, then we will address other alliances. For now though, we must bring Baeata here."

Marlae nodded, though it looked more like defeat than it did agreement.

"Isabella," Marlae said after taking a deep breath, "bring Amallia and Azure here. I wish specific information, as well as to give them orders."

Isabella nodded, bowed, and then left the room. Terrence took the opportunity to sit down and take a deep breath. He had butted heads with Azure ever since the god came to Hedorah. Terrance could not help but think that Azure, and now the new arrival Krysis, had agendas of their own. These so-called gods would work with the Divine Empress as long as it served their interests, but no longer. Anabel too moved from her position against the wall to standing behind the chair where Marlae sat. She bent down quickly and recovered the long white gloves that Marlae had discarded and handed them over the younger woman's shoulder. Marlae was almost shocked when the gloves touched her shoulder, but Anabel saw Marlae's cheeks color with embarrassment for a moment before she took the gloves and began to pull them back onto her hands. By the time the door to the private chambers opened again, Marlae had put her long gloves back on and folded her hands in her lap.

The door opened to admit both Reverend Mother Amallia and the god Azure. Isabella bowed at the doorway and then shut the door, with her remaining in the hallway. Both moved to the center of the room and fell to one knee waiting to be addressed by the Divine Empress.

"Azure," Marlae began, "how many angelic warriors do I have at my disposal?"

Azure raised his head and smoothly returned to his feet. Amallia remained on one knee for a moment longer before slowly making her way back to a standing position.

"It is hard to give you an exact number, Your Grace. As you know, the angelic warriors are also at the beck and call of the Creator, and the Creator has many worlds that He is tending to. Therefore any number that I give you would be an approximation at best."

Marlae frowned.

"So the angelic warriors are not a resource that I can depend on?"

Azure clenched his teeth, but before he could make any answer to the question, Marlae waived her hand as if dismissing her own question. She looked over her shoulder at Anabel and then back at Azure.

"In your estimation," Marlae said finally, "how many angelic warriors would it take to secure a building the size of the Heart of Stone?"

A wide frown twisted Azure's lips.

"Are you seriously considering ceding to the demands of this Catrinel woman?"

It was Anabel's regal voice that cut through the room like a fierce wind.

"What the Divine Empress does and does not consider is not to be questioned even by the likes of you, Azure. You may be a god in the Heavens, and you may be tasked with important work by the Creator, but in this court, and in the presence of the Divine Empress you are an advisor and nothing more. You will comport yourself as such."

For a long moment Terrance thought that Azure was going to thunder back at Anabel; that he was going to threaten or dismiss the woman. He remembered how violently Azure had reacted to Anabel's ascension to the position of High Councilor. But instead, Azure simply bowed his head in a gesture of submission. Perhaps this was why Azure had railed so vehemently against the woman. Did she have a power that made her a threat to someone like Azure?

"The building is vast," Azure said finally, "but there are few approaches that any massing army would be able to use to assault the structure. A dozen or so angelic warriors at each of these points could hold the Heart of Stone for quite some time, at least long enough for reinforcements to be dispatched. All told, three such groups, thirty-six angelic warriors in all, should be sufficient to meet the needs of the situation and fulfill the High Priestess's condition."

Marlae nodded.

"Thank you, Azure. Please make the necessary arrangements and have the warriors dispatched immediately. They will communicate plainly that their only role at the Heart of Stone is to protect it from those who would defile it, and to ensure that the High Priestess is able to do her good work in the Creator's name. Two angelic warriors shall also be tasked to protect the High Priestess at all times. These warriors will come from my own personal detail to ensure that they will not be re-tasked except in the most dire of circumstances."

Azure bowed, but Marlae could feel his resistance to the decree.

"Reverend Mother," Marlae intoned after a moment, "please tell me what it is that I need to do to declare Hannah Ironheart a saint in the eyes of the Church of the Creator."

* * * * * * * * * * * *

The Royal Palace of Hedorah had stood like a quiet monument since the initial addresses that marked Marlae Tamerlane as the Divine Empress of Cadaria. Many flocked past trying to catch a glimpse of the angelic warriors that guarded the palace, some out of morbid curiosity, and others out of a sense of religious zeal. Courtly matters had been dispensed with through decrees rather than through audiences, and the gates to the palace had stood closed to the people of Hedorah. So, when the gates to the Royal Palace opened, people from all over Hedorah came as quickly as they could, hoping to be granted admission to see the Divine Empress and her new court. The receiving hall was massive, a complete redesign from the former royal palace, with a large terrace above the hall itself that allowed for the common people of Hedorah to see interactions that they had previously known about only through rumor and gossip. The newly-minted Divine Empress seemed to want all of her subjects to be able to hear the words that would shape Cadaria. The actual floor of the receiving hall was limited to those with powerful political connections. There were leaders of industry, military, and mercantile pursuits, as well as the few foreign dignitaries from the other Kingdoms of Cadaria that had remained after the purge of Hedorah's former ruling families. The graft and shame had been cleansed from the soul of Hedorah, and the royal palace felt as though it radiated pride and truth once more.

The dais at the far end of the receiving hall was reached through three wide steps that covered no more than two feet in height. The Divine Empress sat on a glowing golden throne whose back was in the shape of a dozen angel's wings fanning out in unison. The woman herself was as radiant as the throne she sat upon, dressed in all white from head to toe, nearly every inch of skin covered with silk and lace, her hair immaculate and her bright eyes clear and filled with goodness and wisdom. But however wondrous her appearance, around the room were stationed angels with flaming swords, and the implication was clear that they could be ready at any moment to strike down any threat to the health and safety of the Divine Empress. Once the hall had been appropriately filled, the woman who stood beside the throne, the High Councilor Anabel Binosear raised her voice to speak.

"People of Hedorah, and our honored guests from the other Great Kingdoms of Cadaria. The Divine Empress, on this occasion has ordained that a hero of the people of Cadaria be honored for her great works of sacrifice and selflessness. Lady Hannah Ironheart, the former High Priestess of the Church of the Creator, and Celestine Knight of the Order of the Flashing Blade has dedicated her life to serving those in the Kingdom of Albitonin, the faithful throughout Cadaria, and the Imperial Family. She has faced all of these challenges and hardships without thought for herself and with her only need to serve the will of the Creator. The Divine Empress decrees that this day, in the presence of this assemblage, and in the sight of the Creator, the Lady Hannah Ironheart forevermore be known as Saint Hannah, the Patron Saint of Duty."

There was a deafening silence for many long moments, until finally from the terrace above the cacophony of cheers and applause began to rain down. In a matter of moments all that could be heard was the cheers for Hannah Ironheart and the cheers for the kind and benevolent Divine Empress. Though Marlae wanted to smile, she kept her countenance passive and waived gently with one hand. However, out of the corner of her eye she caught slight movement. She saw Azure and Krysis standing together just at the edge of the receiving hall nearest a door that led to Marlae's private chambers. Azure looked angry, which was to be expected given the situation. Krysis on the other hand had no particular look on his face, but it was his eyes that disturbed Marlae. His bright golden eyes flared with something that could have only been hate.

The Work of the Soul

Jerrica Maldovrin sat with her hands folded in her lap, but could not shake the uneasy feeling in the pit of her stomach. What she had just heard, seen, and felt were without explanation. She was surrounded by people who should not exist, in a place that should not exist, next to a man who was destined for a far different fate than the one he had chosen. Tolon Morr had bravery enough to be sure for the road that lay ahead, but bravery was not what was needed now. The path ahead was filled with pain and death, and no amount of strength would make a difference. Now it would be Jerrica's sight, and the sight of those blessed with the blood of the first Empress that would make the difference. Jerrica was just beginning to understand the lessons that her mother had taught, and the lessons taught by the great Dark Seer. The tapestry was beginning to unravel, and the more of the world that became unstable, the more it would depend upon those who could see the ramifications of all actions. The issue was that all choices led to a single eventuality as far as Jerrica could see at this point. Destruction. Destruction of the world, destruction of all people, destruction of everything that everyone held dear. Those thoughts were still echoing through Jerrica's mind when the red-haired woman who held herself with the confidence and the power of a queen walked into the room, with Gideon and Natalie. At first Jerrica was relieved to see the young woman had survived the battle, but the way that her right arm hung limp at her side and she walked with the slightest limp showed that she had not escaped unscathed. However, there was no concern on the red-haired woman's face, almost as though the attack never happened. She moved gracefully across the room and sat on the front edge of a chair next to the fireplace. She folded her hands in her lap delicately and locked her cold green eyes first on Tolon and then on Jerrica. The young seer could not help but flinch. The power in the woman's glance was palpable.

"It seems, my young friends, that you have come to us at a most auspicious time," the woman said slowly and formally. "For that you are both fortunate, and I fear, unfortunate."

Jerrica could hear Tolon ball his fists.

"What is all of this? Who are you? Who attacked us?"

The red-haired woman held up a hand and averted her gaze from Tolon. He didn't like the idea of being silent, and the sound of his knuckles cracking as he tightened his fists communicated the stress better than anything could. Finally after a moment the woman lowered her hand and continued speaking.

"For all of your bravery and your strength, you humans have never had the capacity to think beyond the moment. That is why you have been so easily led and manipulated over the millennia. Those in power will always prevent you from seeing the truth so long as immediacy is more important. You trade your futures and your freedom for safety and security of the moment. And thus you spend your lives in invisible bondage, chained to those you cannot possibly understand. The ant may curse the farmer for destroying his anthill, but no famer will ever hear it. Though no ant was ever given the power to change his station in the cosmos. And for that humans are made to suffer more than any race of creatures has ever been made to suffer."

By this time Gideon had helped Natalie to a chair near where Jerrica and Tolon sat, and he returned to the doorway where he leaned using a dagger to clean his nails. Jerrica found the activity disturbing to say the least. But perhaps given the circumstances it was the only way that he had to deal with the stress and the absurdity of the situation.

"But to save you all," she continued, "we must not lament your limitations, but rather learn to work within them."

The woman stood and gently smoothed her dress before pulling herself to her full height. A gentle aura of fire appeared around the woman, and feathered wings of pure fire stretched from behind her. Her face changed from something akin to human to something more alien. Her face stretched, her jaw and chin elongating and her skin pale and white. The sockets of her eyes stretched wide and thin, twisting upwards, and the iris shrank with the green color intensifying and beginning to glow as brightly as a star. Her red hair floated up away from her head, igniting into flames that parted in the middle to reveal a golden crown. The woman's limbs also lengthened and thinned, becoming far more delicate. By the time the transformation had completed, the woman had grown to nearly nine feet in height, and the flames of her hair brushed against the ceiling. Tolon stumbled out of his chair, falling to his knees in front of the creature who looked more like his mental image of an angel than any story he had ever heard. Her visage was a combination of incredible beauty and terrible terrifying power. Jerrica kept her seat, not because she wanted to, but because the power radiating from the woman had frozen her limbs. Whatever power she was exuding was touching the power of a seer within her, interfacing with that divine energy. Even Gideon and Natalie seemed impacted by the transformation; though Natalie tried her best not to let her shock register through her cold and measured exterior. Gideon let the dagger fall from his hand and instead of falling to a knee, instead crouched down low, his eyes locked on the woman's altered form. When the woman finally spoke again, her voice came out in several different pitches at once, a dissonant harmony of multiple octaves and voices. The voice was equal parts comforting and terrifying.

"For so long your kind has only seen us the way that we have wished you to see us. You see us as yourselves. You see us as those whose image you were made in. But this cannot be further from the truth. We are Children of the Creator. We are the very essence of the divine. Even those who call themselves gods, or ascended beings or even angels are nothing but pale shadows of true divinity. I am Raenera, the living embodiment of Order, and the steady persistent rhythm that the whole of the Cosmos must bow to. My brothers and sister sew chaos wherever their feet touch. They bring with them war, misery, and death. They know no other way. But here, now, on this world I shall show them the folly of their ways. I shall show their followers the true depth of how far they have been led astray. And in the end even my Father shall be made to realize that this Cosmos must bow to Order."

After the final word left Raenera's lips, the fearsome version of the woman disappeared and was replaced by the more regal and human appearance. She settled back down into the chair by the fireplace and waited as the others in the room regained their senses. It took quite a few moments before Tolon made his way back into a chair, and for Gideon to regain his feet. However, even after that, Jerrica felt pressure on her chest and for a long time felt as though she were holding her breath. It was Jerrica that Raenera first set her eyes upon and first addressed.

"You, my young seer, are the one whom I pity the most. I say pity because there is no other emotion that I possess that better describes the situation that you are in. You are so young, and with so much power and potential, and absolutely no understanding of your role in the world."

Finally Jerrica found her breath once more. She wanted to protest. She wanted to explain everything that she had learned. She felt as though she needed to prove her worth and her understanding of the world. But at the same time Jerrica knew that her words would mean nothing to a Child of the Creator, and in preaching her knowledge, so would only demonstrate her ignorance. The defeat in her mind won out, and she simply bowed her head.

"Great Lady of the Heavens," Jerrica said softly and with as much humility as she could pour into her voice, "please. I have felt drawn here, drawn away from my sisters, drawn away from everything I have ever known. From the day of my birth, the sight has isolated me from the rest of the world. People have sought our powers to improve their station, to gain an advantage over their enemies, or they have sought to silence our voices and steal our powers for their own. There must be a reason for this curse."

Raenera nodded.

"Of course there is a reason my dear. But your abilities, and those of your sisters, and those of the Dark Seer, and those of the countless others that came before, are not a curse. They are a gift, a gift from the Creator, passed down through the blood of the first Empress of Cadaria. A gift, and a responsibility. Through your blood the Creator has given you the visions that He wished you to see, in order to guide this world to this point. There has never been a question that a war was to be fought on this world. And there has never been a question that in our own way, the Children of the Creator would gather forces to their side to fight that war. Talisia has done so in her way, manipulating the good Emperor Lorien into doing what she wished, partially under the guidance of the Great Seers of the past and in spite of the warnings of the Maldovrin sisters. Halicon too brought an army to bear, but he has done so by telling those who had the capacity to understand the truth about this world. He has won arms through loyalty and love. My beloved Pyrrus has no army, and yet he is going to have the most profound effect on this war. Emries for all his bluster and guile perhaps is the most dangerous of us. He will rely on ghosts of the past to fight his war. But none, my dear girl, command the vast army and the vast arms that I will bring to bear. Not even all of the angels in the Heavens could stand against the might I have assembled."

Raenera stood again and moved to where Gideon stood and reached to place a hand on his shoulder. Jerrica thought she saw the man flinch, but if there was a reaction, he covered it quickly.

"But the force that I have gathered to me are nothing more than soldiers, and they have never waged a war on the scale that will be fought. They have never seen the kind of death and destruction that will visit this world in its last days. That is why I gathered these lost children to me. On their former world, they saw the kind of devastation that is coming. Some of them stood against the rising tide of death and fought until their last breath. That is the kind of leadership that my troops will need. But leadership is not enough in the war to come, nor are numbers. No, there must be an advantage created, and advantage that no other force can bring to bear, and one that cannot be negated. That is why we have worked here in secret; why no one could know of our existence, not even those that my forgotten children would have called ally, friend, or family. Nothing could risk the outcome of the war. Nothing."

Jerrica sensed something flowing through the room that she had not perceived before. It was like a strange smell on the wind that lingers for only a second before disappearing, only enough to be perceived but not identified. As Raenera moved from where Gideon stood to the opposite wall, Jerrica caught the feeling again, and this time she was able to understand more fully. Some power was rolling off of Raenera, a power that filled the room and seemed to wrap itself around each and every person in the room. Jerrica wasn't sure if that force was compelling the obedience of the people that Raenera referred to as her forgotten children, but it must have been having some kind of effect. After several long moments waiting at the wall, she pushed on a segment of the wall to reveal a door. Raenera passed through the door without a word, and Jerrica immediately got the feeling that if the woman were to even acknowledge the others in the room to bid them to follow, it would be an action that would be beneath her. It didn't take long for Gideon to move to Natalie's side to help her from her chair and toward the door. When Jerrica rose from her chair, she saw a look in Gideon's eyes that said he didn't expect this meeting to take the turn that it had. Tolon waited at the hidden door and followed Jerrica after she had entered.

The door led to a dark hallway that seemed to stretch on for quite a distance. Mid way down the length of the hallway, Raenera stopped and pushed on yet another hidden door. As before she stepped through without a word leaving those following her to continue in her wake. When Jerrica stepped through the hidden door, she thought she had stepped out of reality into an absurd dream. The room they had stepped into was massive, easily large enough to hold hundreds of thousands of people. Arrayed across the far wall were thousands of suits of armor, and weapons racks filled with weapons of various shapes and sizes. There was enough to outfit the whole of the Imperial Legion three times over. Raenera stepped halfway into the room before turning back to face the others. Jerrica looked over the faces of the others in the room, and saw the same look of shock and bewilderment. Only Gideon seemed to be unfazed by the array of weaponry. Raenera spread her arms wide and began to speak.

"For nearly two millennia I have had my master craftsman working on these weapons and armor. There is enough here to outfit an army large enough to wage the last and largest war this world has ever seen."

Gideon took several steps forward.

"Two millennia? So you've been planning this since the formation of the Cadarian Empire?"

Raenera let her arms fall to her side.

"The Cadarian Empire is nothing but an illusion. Much like everything else on this world, it is a construct to exert control. Ultimately that control is either in the hands of one of my siblings or in the hands of the Creator himself. The time is also immaterial. It took exactly how long it needed to take to outfit my forces given the constraints at hand. Not just anyone could create the armaments I needed, and the circumstances had to be perfect to allow him to finish his work."

Natalie was the one who first understood the implication.

"One man did this?"

In way of an answer, Raenera motioned in the direction of a door at the far end of the massive chamber. The door slid open at her bidding and after a few moments a disheveled man stumbled into the room. He wore a simple gray shirt that was littered with holes and soot. His arms were so tan that they were nearly black, and his white hair was filled with ash. The bags under his eyes were so pronounced that the bags had bags themselves. The whole time he was walking he seemed to be mumbling to himself, in a voice so low that it did not carry. Even when he stopped beside where Raenera stood he continued to mumble and to rock back and forth from his heels to the balls of his feet and back. Raenera put her hand on the man's head and gently stroked his hair. While most would perceive the gesture as one of kindness and sympathy, Jerrica could not shake the feeling that Raenera saw the man more as a pet.

"For a great many years, my dear friend here has been toiling away at the creation of my army's weapons. From a certain point of view, it could be said that he has been doing this against his will, but that would predispose that he has a will at all to exert. I'm afraid that Arturious here has lost every part of his will except that that would compel him to work toward the destruction of the one who has cursed him with his virtual immortality. The one you know as Dorovar."

Gideon was the first one to catch the man's name, and he took two steps forward toward Raenera.

"Arturious? That is Arturious Demascious? The weapon maker who forged the sacred weapons for the Knights of the Flashing Blade?"

Raenera nodded.

"That's impossible," Tolon blurted out. "How can a man who crafted the weapons for the Knights of the Flashing Blade almost two thousand years ago still be alive? Is he a Dark God too?"

"No," Natalie answered first. "Not a Dark God, but certainly not human."

Raenera folded her arms, and at the gesture Arturious slumped to the ground, sitting cross-legged on the floor. He pulled a piece of metal from one of his pockets and began to slowly turn it over in his fingers. Occasionally he would discover a flaw in the metal and he would pick at it with his fingernails, as though he felt through his own will that he could smooth the imperfections.

"Once upon a time, Arturious was human. He was a savant who understood the essence or the soul of the materials that he worked with. He was an artist, the kind that comes along once in a dozen generations. But like every artist, Arturious soon grew bored with his talent, and began to press ever outwards on the boundaries of his abilities. He found new materials to work with, new frontiers to experiment on the fringes of. It was this quest for the unknown and the untried that led him to the place where the Dark Gods fell, the crack in the world that opened the pathway to Dorovar's tomb. But it wasn't the touch of Dorovar that broke Arturious' mind. It was mine."

For the first time Jerrica felt something akin to human emotion coming from the ancient woman. No one had time to say or do anything before Raenera turned away from the group to face the arms and armor arrayed behind her. When she spoke again, there was a hint of remorse in her voice, a gentle waver of shame.

"Long ago, on a world that no longer exists, Dorovar was one of my most devout followers. Like your phasia were to my brother Halicon, so too were those precious few that received my favor on Dorovar's world. But as Emries betrayed you and the other humans on Onea, so too did Emries and Talisia betray me. They brought the scourge of the dragons to my world, turned my own acolytes against me. Turned Dorovar into a false prophet, and ultimately into a monster. But that monster grew out of anyone's control. In the final days of that world, my acolytes were tempted with power. They were touched by my siblings and given what they needed to fight against the dragons on their terms. But the devastation they wrought, the forces they brought to bear not only destroyed their enemies, but also destroyed the world itself. In the end, the last living being on that world was Dorovar. He stood, impotent to change what would happen. All around him the bodies of the men and women that he had known all his life lay, and on that spot he vowed to get revenge for each and every one of those that were lost on that day. To make Emries, Talisia, and the dragons pay for their treachery."

Raenera stayed silent for a long moment.

"And to make me pay for abandoning them when they needed me the most."

Raenera bowed her head and stood silent for almost a minute before turning back. She held her hands folded at her waist, and her face was devoid of expression. Even her eyes were cold. But there was something in her eyes, something beneath the calm surface that Jerrica could just begin to make out. There was a pulse of rage beating within the ancient woman, a rage that would have no limit, and could never be sated. The rage of a mother who had watched her children torn apart.

"But the humiliation did not end there. Talisia was not satisfied with the destruction of my world, or the monster that Dorovar had become. She ensured that when my trusted and beloved acolytes accepted the power that Emries and Talisia offered, that for the rest of eternity their souls would be forfeit and subject to Talisia's perverted will. My beloved sister knew that eventually Dorovar would be captured, and with the nature of his powers the only place he could be imprisoned would be the Vault of Terrors. A prison without a key, because the Vault is not a place, but an imposition of the Creator's will. Dorovar may have a measure of his powers now, but until all of the chains of the Vault are removed, he will never attain his goals. Talisia intends to release those shackles."

Again Raenera turned her attention to Arturious, placing her hand upon his head and smoothing his wild and matted hair back gently.

"This poor unwitting soul was the instrument of that freedom. A course that cannot now be prevented or changed. Dorovar will be free, and it is as much my fault as it is the culmination of Talisia's machinations."

Gideon finally found his voice once again.

"How will Talisia free Dorovar?"

Raenera sighed.

"The process was set in motion long ago. Talisia stole the souls of my greatest acolytes; fourteen of them in all, and took them to the Heavens with her. When she learned the location of Dorovar's prison, she ensured that the souls would make their way here. They were brought by one of the Dark Gods, either without their knowledge, or by a traitor who worked for my sister. Whichever is the case, it matters little now. The souls were left in the walls of the crater, unwelcome surprises waiting for those foolish enough to set foot where no mortal should. But one mortal did. On the rumors of pure veins of obsidian deep in the ground, fertile ground exposed by the fall of the Dark Gods, Arturious journeyed from his safety within the newly founded Imperial Lands of Aldere and ventured to the sight of the Fall. Upon his descent, he was overwhelmed by the souls of my acolytes. Their pain and their power. They warped his mind, filling it with images of the horrors that Dorovar had done. No one should see that much death, and no mind can survive feeling the deaths of so many. Arturious was broken, but in his delusion he did the only thing he knew to do. He crafted weapons to fight the enemy that he knew was coming. But as he forged his weapons, the souls of my followers spoke to him, told him their secrets, and in the forging of the weapons that you know as the Sacred Weapons, imparted the power of their souls within them. Those souls are the keys that will unlock the totality of Dorovar's powers. As each of the weapons is broken, more of his abilities and more of his control will return."

Tolon's eyes narrowed for a moment, and then spoke in an unsteady and unsure voice.

"But, there are only thirteen sacred weapons. You said that there were fourteen souls. Where is the fourteenth weapon?"

Instead of Raenera answering, it was the mad weapon maker's voice that broke the silence.

"Shhh....secret. Couldn't tell. Never tell. Have to prepare. Have to know. He's coming. Dorovar's coming. Can't find it. Never find it. Empress' Legacy. She came. She knew. Came to me. Sought me out. Special task. She saw. She knew. She saw. She knew."

His words came out fast and broken, almost to the point of not being able to be understood. Once he had spoken he continued to mumble the last two phrases over and over again, rocking back and forth, turning the piece of metal over in his hands. Suddenly Jerrica felt everyone's eyes on her. It was then that Raenera smiled.

"So you see, little seer, it is advantageous that you have found your way here. You are going to tell me everything you know about the legacy of your clan, and where your people have hidden the fourteenth Sacred Weapon."

Chapter LXXXIII

My Sister's Keeper

*Year Four of the Just Emperor Kaitain "Dragonsbane" Lorien,
Creator's Calendar Year 1871*

It wasn't until very late in the evening that the royal palace of Celidar was finally quiet. Well-wishers and petitioners had flooded the receiving hall from the moment of Feyd Lorien's proclamation, and it was all that Celidar's small security force with the help of Gabriel Shadowfall could do to keep them all at bay. Despite their ever increasing numbers, the petitioners were well behaved and there were only a few of Kaitain's fanatics that tried to disrupt the proceedings. To Gabriel's great surprise the people of Celidar took care of far more of the interlopers than Gabriel or the soldiers needed to concern themselves with. The people of Celidar truly loved what Jerrard and Erika represented, and they would do anything to protect their lord and lady. But as Gabriel sat at the dinner table with his new employers, he couldn't help but wonder if it was the man and woman that the people loved, or what they represented. Only a few months before, Gabriel Shadowfall was a soldier, with perhaps the most enviable and hated position in the whole of the empire. He was the personal guard of the Celestial Princess of the Cadarian Empire. Despite her teasing and her temper, Marlae was not a terrible charge, though Gabriel often found himself having to make the best of bad situations. But then came the elevation to a member of the Knights of the Flashing Blade, a chance meeting with a rebellious man by the name of Aerith Seth, a rebellion against the rightful emperor, and finally serving at the side of the Dark Gods. He thought back to the fateful meeting with the Empress Dominique Lorien and the Garnet Knight of the Flashing Blade Chelsea Zarova. They had a mission for him, a mission that would change his life. If he would have said no, his life would have ended that moment. During the worst of the madness, Gabriel had wondered if perhaps that would have been the better course. But his mind kept coming back to two individuals. The first of course was Aerith Seth. The man had changed Gabriel's life. Under the irreverence and the disrespect for authority, Gabriel saw that Aerith was not that different from himself. He was a soldier, and he took it as his personal charge to make the world better wherever he was. Of course, the two men had completely different definitions of what constituted better, but at the end of the day, Aerith's methods got results, and Gabriel's thus far had not. Which brought Gabriel's mind to Marlae.

For so long Gabriel looked upon her as a precious jewel locked away in an impregnable block of ice. He tried to remain detached, and perhaps that was why Marlae took such pleasure in tormenting him. Whether it was her strolling around her chambers nude, or it was her flagrant trysts with Rhain Feirbran, Gabriel did his best to always focus on his duty and not the woman. But such discipline would not last forever. However, it was not the flagrant moments that inflamed Gabriel's heart. There were the moments when she passed out on the floor of her chambers from too much drink and Gabriel would pick her up and carry her to her bed. The unguarded moments when Marlae thought no one was looking that she would rage and cry at the sometime unfairness of her station. Those times reminded that there was a woman that lived within the title, and no matter what cruelty or torment she wrapped herself in, the woman would always remain; it was that woman that Gabriel loved. Feyd Lorien clearing his throat shook Gabriel away from his thoughts and brought his focus back to his three companions at the dinner table.

"Somehow I thought having dinner with Dark Gods would be more exciting."

Erika laughed softly.

"Perhaps we thought dining with a member of the Lorien family would be more dangerous. After all, we've been sitting here for quite some time and there hasn't been an assassination attempt yet."

Feyd's smile and genuine laugh filled Gabriel with a sense of comfort.

"The night is young yet," he quipped.

While Feyd and Erika shared the reverie, Jerrard's focus seemed to be elsewhere. His head was turned slightly away from the others, as though he was listening for something. When Erika stopped laughing and turned her attention to the mysterious something, Gabriel stood and put his hand on his sword.

"What is it?"

Jerrard put his hand up.

"It feels like a portal. But it's raw, unpracticed. Almost as though someone is using it for the first time."

Erika nodded silently.

"We normally don't get this much warning," Erika said in answer to Feyd and Gabriel's silent question. "Whoever is creating the portal doesn't know enough to hide the flows of power until the last possible moment."

Jerrard was on his feet and moving toward the door the next moment.

"It will be opening in the receiving hall," he said over his shoulder.

Erika was quickly behind her husband, and Gabriel waited until Feyd too was on his feet and moving before he set off after them. Gabriel's charge was the protection of Feyd Lorien, and while there was no doubt that the Lord and Lady Mystic could take care of themselves there was no doubt that Feyd would have little chance against some of the things that Gabriel had seen. When Gabriel finally skidded to a stop just in front of Feyd Lorien in the receiving hall, the swirling blue portal was just beginning to form. It was several feet off the ground and tilted at an odd angle. A moment later several forms tumbled out of the portal. Two of the group landed unceremoniously on the floor, obviously unconscious, while the other two made an attempt to land on their feet. The young woman was more successful than her companion who while initially landing on his feet promptly fell back and ended up seated on the floor. Immediately the young man began laughing. Felicia Lorien looked down at her companion and her own laughter caught the air. It wasn't for several more moments that Orren Eldrath realized that they weren't alone. He scurried to his feet and bowed first to Feyd Lorien and then to the Lord and Lady of Celidar. Felicia moved quickly to her father and wrapped him in a hug. Jerrard was about to speak, but Erika's hand on his shoulder and the shocked look on her face held him in silence. She sprinted across the room to the fallen pair, and immediately cradled the woman's head in her lap, tears falling from her eyes. Jerrard followed a moment after, his footfalls cautious.

"It's our Taya," Erika said, her voice wavering. "And Storm. It's our children, Jerrard."

Jerrard whirled on Felicia.

"Explain this!"

Jerrard's tone was filled with power, and it nearly shook the room. The young princess was so shocked by the sudden outburst that her voice died in her throat. Orren Eldrath on the other hand was not dissuaded. He tried to answer as quickly as possible.

"We were attacked," Orren said as calmly as he could manage. "Well at least I was. There has been so much in such a short time; it's hard to keep it all straight. Aryx Terian gave me his powers, and then as I was going to bury him, Emries and Draven came out of nowhere and attacked. They wanted information about Logan and Saurn. Of course I wasn't going to tell them anything, but they weren't going to take no for an answer. Emries thrashed me around pretty well until he realized he wasn't going to get the answers that he wanted. Then he left and left me to Draven. Luckily Gwydeon, Midarin, and Felicia showed up when they did. But it was clear that Draven wasn't going to fight them. Someone else showed up then, someone who called himself Nathan Sandar."

Jerrard cursed under his breath.

"A demon wearing Midarin's son's face. One of Emries lackeys. When we learned that Korrd had turned against us, I suppose I should have prepared myself for that creature returning."

"But he wasn't alone," Felicia continued, finally finding her voice. "He brought Storm and Taya as reinforcements. Apparently Emries has enslaved everyone who used to have access to his powers, all of the *Coromors* and every member of the *Erieal*, to his will. Storm and Taya had no choice but to follow Nathan's command and attack us. Taya and I fought each other to a standstill, and Storm and Orren knocked each other out. When I came to, Gwydeon was fighting with a blond woman that it took me some time to recognize. But after the fight was over, which took Gwydeon, Camille, and myself to do, I realized that it was Eldar Merin, and that she had become the new vessel for the Spirit."

Jerrard wanted to curse again, but the information was too staggering for any response. Of course the Creator would have used such an underhanded tactic to try to keep them off balance. But at least the combined powers of Gwydeon, Felicia, and Camille had been enough to defeat her, at least temporarily. What was more disconcerting was Emries' interventions on this world. He had laid in wait for so long, planning and plotting his response to his failures on Onea. Bringing back to the land of the living those who once served him could only serve to further distract his old enemies. If Taya and Storm had been brought onto the field during an invasion of Celidar, would it have been enough to keep Jerrard or Erika from fighting to the fullest of their ability? Already Korrd had distracted Logan to the point of revealing information to Emries, and now the intervention of Nathan Sandar had almost cost Gwydeon and Midarin their lives. Whatever Jerrard thought of Emries or his tactics, he could not help but admit that they were effective.

"Gwydeon wanted us to bring Taya and Storm to Sabrina so that she could remove Emries' influence from them," Orren finished.

"On our way here, I lost the ability to feel Sabrina," Felicia said. "This was the last place I knew she was, so we came here."

Jerrard hung his head.

"Sabrina is gone," Jerrard said finally. "The power that Halicon entrusted her with was too much for her body. And after Tess Annis taxed her even more with her assault, she had no choice but to pass the powers on and surrender her life. She had been through so much."

Felicia turned toward Erika, who was just beginning to regain her composure.

"So what can we do for them?"

Jerrard looked down at his wife and then back up at Felicia and Orren.

"Rhain has Halicon's powers, and she would be able to protect them from Emries influence. But I'm afraid that she has gone to a place that will be difficult to get to, at least for now. Well perhaps not difficult, but certainly dangerous. She has gone to meet with the remaining members of the phasia, and to reform the Council. Taking Taya and Storm into that powder keg is too dangerous for them. Saurn might decide it is too much in their favor to try to extract information from them instead of curing them. Or perhaps Jeroch will simply want to kill them to remove more powered individuals from the field of battle."

Erika frowned and gritted her teeth.

"I'm not losing my children. Not again."

Orren knelt down at Erika's side.

"I'm sorry. We won't let that happen."

Felicia moved to Jerrard and put her hand on Jerrard's shoulder.

"So what other option do we have?"

Erika wiped the tears away from her eyes.

"This doesn't make sense," she said finally. "Our Taya was not a member of the *Erieal* and had no tie to Emries. How could she be turned against us? The Taya from the Dark Mirror reality was the Wind *Erieal*."

Jerrard rubbed his chin. Erika was right. Could Emries have somehow tapped into the power of one of the women's souls in order to gain control of the other's? Somehow it didn't surprise Jerrard that Emries would sink to such depths of depravity.

"Until we can come up with another option, we're going to have to make sure that they are not a threat to themselves or anyone else."

Jerrard knelt by his son first, placing a hand on his chest. Probing deeply into his son's mind, he could instantly feel the malicious presence of Emries upon the boy. There was a perpetual rage that surged through his mind like the waves of the power of Water that Storm controlled. Finally Jerrard channeled the gentle flows of wind into Storm's heart, slowing the beating to a barely perceptible level. It would not be enough to kill the young man, but it would not allow the boy to awaken without intervention from an outside source. Jerrard then moved to Taya's side, and when he placed his hand on her chest and scanned her mind, he felt nothing. Her thoughts were there, but there was no anger, no outside influence, and no divine power. Whatever hold Emries once had on Taya had been removed. Perhaps it was because Rhain had removed Taya's tie to her past. Perhaps once one side of the fragmented soul had been cleansed, the other would have been as well. Inwardly Jerrard cursed his sentimentality. He looked over his should at Felicia.

"I don't feel Emries' pull on Taya's mind. I'm going to chance waking her up. But be ready just in case."

A moment later, the young princess of Cadaria had been replaced by the glistening armor of the creature known as Nightwing. Feyd Lorien's eyes went wide, but a reassuring nod from Gabriel kept Feyd's fear in check. Orren too had sunk back into a fighting posture, and after a curt nod from his direction, Jerrard focused his attention back on his daughter. A moment later, the flows of Wind and Water were mixing inside of the young woman, and her eyes began to flutter. Moments later she was looking up into the eyes of her mother, a weak voice straining through barely opened lips.

"Mother?" the girl said softly. "I had the strangest dream."

* * * * * * * * * * * *

Alise Modrall stalked through the empty halls of the royal palace of Celidar, making sure to stay to the shadows and to keep her footfalls nearly imperceptible. It had been easy enough for her to get into the palace with the rest of the mindless throng who were intent on laying their hands and feasting their eyes on the newest messiah to the scene. Just a day ago many of those blithering idiots thought that the only fate a Dark God deserved was a long slow death. Now the useless sheep all flocked to call the Dark Gods their saviors as soon as they realized that it had been Dark Gods that had been feeding them and patting their heads like the good obedient little pets that they were. As soon as Alise's father, the rightful Emperor, exposed these frauds for what they were, the idiot throng would turn upon the Lord and Lady Mystic like rabid wolves. For now though, Alise had more important endeavors. Kaitain's brother, the favored son Feyd, was being harbored by the Mystics, and so Alise had to make sure that the so-called prince felt her claws before the night was over.

Within a matter of minutes, Alise had made her way to the small servant's access to the receiving hall. From here there would be less shadows to use to conceal her movements and more chance of discovery. However, such things were trivial for someone of Alise's power. It took only a minor use of the powers at her disposal to wrap herself in a cloak of shadows. However, before she was able to cross the large chamber, she felt a trickle of power in the back of her mind. She had learned to sense portals early in her training as an assassin of the Shadow Guild, and the flows of power were unmistakable. It was also unmistakable that the person who created the portal didn't know what they were doing. The aim was dangerous at best, and as the forms tumbled out, it was sheer luck that none of them wound up breaking their necks. But the appearance of the Lord and Lady Mystic, as well as the disgraced Ruby Knight of the Flashing Blade Gabriel Shadowfall along with her target made Alise pause. One of the new arrivals was Felicia Lorien, and the other was the former Sapphire Knight of the Flashing Blade Orren Eldrath. This was an interesting meeting of the minds, and it was also rife with those that Alise's father would like to see killed. So from the shadows Alise watched and listened, gently bending the flowing air in the chamber to bring the distant voices to her ear. She didn't dare use too much power lest she be discovered by the

Dark Gods, but disguising her use of power had become one of the things that had made her such a dangerous assassin. Not even masters of the Shadow Guild could feel her coming, and Alise was sure that the Grand Master would also be easy prey when her father so ordered his assassination. In a matter of minutes, Alise had learned the identity of the unconscious pair, and also learned another important name. Emries. Whoever this Emries was, the Dark Gods were afraid of him. Perhaps this would be information important enough to bring to Kaitain, and perhaps that would help make up for her more recent uncharacteristic failures. However, Alise had no time to dwell on such things. The group was breaking up and they were going to store the sleeping boy Storm in one of the guest rooms under lock and key. It would take little effort for Alise to undo the sleeping spell that Jerrard had put the boy under, and together Alise and Storm would be able to bring the palace down around the rebels' ears.

Alise waited for several long minutes before she chanced leaving her hiding place. Tentatively she moved into the receiving hall, staying against the wall and continuing to wrap the meager shadows around her to conceal her movements. The process was laborious and slow, but she managed to make it all the way across the chamber to the hallway that led deeper into the private wing of the palace. It took a little divining to determine in which direction the prisoner had been taken, but Alise secreted herself into a corner and sent her mind out into the void. She could see the emotions of the people in that wing of the palace. She could feel the mixture of sorrow and elation coming from Lord and Lady Mystic, but Alise knew if she pressed harder that they would feel her presence. There was confusion coming from the girl that had been identified as Taya Mystic. Quiet confidence and a suppressed fear that had to be coming from Orren Eldrath. More confusion but a strange peace came from Gabriel Shadowfall, while Feyd Lorien emitted nothing but bewilderment and a feeling that he was completely out of his depth. For some reason, Alise could not feel the little princess Felicia, but she didn't matter. What Alise wanted was the bright burning rage that radiated from the sleeping Storm. It was like the beacon of a lighthouse burning out across the void. When she closed herself off to the thoughts, she felt as though she had been staring into the sun. Her senses were dulled by the contact with the unbridled rage. It took several minutes before Alise felt that she had recovered enough of her edge to continue to effectively shield her presence.

With more shadows in the private hallways, Alise did not have to exert as much of her abilities to make her way, and within a matter of minutes she was standing in front of the door that led to the sleeping monster. The lock on the door was child's play to someone with her abilities, and the door cracked open after a simple waive of her hand.

"And just what do you think you're doing?"

Alise's blood ran cold. The voice was unmistakable; it was that of the foolish little princess Felicia Lorien. Alise sank into a low stance and turned to face Felicia, her razor-sharp claws appearing instantly at the back of her hands. Her lips twisted into an evil smile. To her credit, the little princess didn't react at all.

"I'm going to kill you in the name of my master Kaitain, and then I'm going to free your captive and use him to tear this rebel stronghold to the ground."

Felicia's eyes went wide.

"I remember you."

Alise smiled.

"You're the one that attacked my father and me outside of Pellatori. The man you knew as Wynne defeated you."

Alise's smile turned to a snarl. That name was like bile in her mouth. But her revenge against that farmer would come in due time. Now she was only concerned with ending the life of the little spoiled princess. However, if Felicia's resolve had been shaken by the familiarity of the assassin that faced her, it did not show in her eyes. Instead there was a steely resolve, one that Alise was puzzled by. It added to Alise's unconscious wonder at why she had not felt the princess's approach.

"Your protector is not here," Alise spat. "So there will be nothing to prevent me from ripping your heart out this time."

Felicia sank into a defensive position and a shimmering blade simply appeared in her hand.

"You'll find I'm more than a match for you now, assassin."

Alise was impressed with the girl. She did not even feel the flows of power that had conjured the blade. However, she would not let her prey see doubt.

"It will take more than parlor tricks to save you, Felicia."

That moment Alise leapt from her crouch, bringing both of her claws to bear. Felicia wheeled herself out of the way, bringing the blade up to intercept part of the assault while dodging the rest. The corridor was narrow, but it still afforded Felicia some mobility. However, Alise was not content with a simple parried strike. She twisted in mid-air, let her boot hit the wall of the corridor and then bounced back at Felicia. Felicia's reflexes were better than Alise expected, and again her attack was parried away. Had she not been deep in enemy territory with those who could feel the application of power, Alise would have used portals to create difficult attacks for the princess to defend against, but the moment she used a single portal, Lord and Lady Mystic would come running. Instead, Alise would confine herself to more conventional methods of attack. However, she would have to finish her opponent quickly. Felicia would have no restrictions on her uses of power, and if she used something large enough to be noticed, Alise would find herself quickly on the defensive and an opportunity she had to surprise the rest of her prey would be lost. Once more Alise leapt at her prey, only this time she feinted high and dove low, one set of blades aimed at the princess's stomach. This time, the blades struck true. However instead of the satisfying feel of steel ripping through flesh, Alise instead heard the sound of metal scraping against metal.

By the time Alise recovered from her attack, she turned to see what had happened. The princess's shirt had been ripped to shreds across the stomach, but instead of ripped and bloody flesh, there was gleaming metal. Alise's confusion was only held at bay by the rising anger that was further ignited by Felicia's sly smile.

"I think you're out of your league, assassin."

This time, it was Alise that smiled.

"I think not."

Alise stood straight and extended her claws. A moment later, they were wrapped with white hot fire. The fire burned so hot that Felicia could feel the sweat begin to bead on her forehead.

"I'm going to teach you a lesson, sister. I'm going to carve traitor into that silly metal skin of yours."

Felicia's eyes went wide in confusion as the assassin charged.

To Rise You Must First Fall

Year Four of the Just Emperor Kaitain "Dragonsbane" Lorien,
Creator's Calendar Year 1871

Logan followed slowly as Kamen led the way across the slippery path of obsidian that led back to an entrance to the caverns that lay below the city. The caverns had been slowly excavated over hundreds of years, creating a place where the initiates and masters of the Order could study and contemplate the nature of everything in the world around them. Through Kamen, the Order had learned truths that were beyond the reach and understanding of normal people, and they got the barest glimpse behind the curtain into the mind of the Creator. But even the masters of the Order of the Flickering Flame did not have the perspective or the knowledge that Jillian had amassed in just a few days at Logan's side. She understood more than nearly any mortal ever could about the true nature of the world and the nature of the beings that claimed the title of the divine. They had traveled half way to the entrance when Logan felt something behind them. There was something familiar about the power, but he barely had time to tackle Jillian to the ground before the sizzling bolt of dark energy shot through the space where her head had been only a split second before. Kamen turned at the commotion, and a bolt of energy struck him in the shoulder. The massive man was not staggered by the blow, but it had left a smoking wound nearly six inches across. A second beam of dark light streamed in but this time the gigantic man was ready. With a single outstretched hand he deflected the blow, sending it crashing harmlessly into rubble at his feet. By this time Logan had scrambled back to his feet and let a crystalline blade unconsciously form in his hand. Standing nearly a hundred yards away was a figure clad in black armor from head to toe. A sickening dark power crawled across the armor, coalescing into pulsing auras around each of the creature's balled fists.

"Corpses may have been no challenge for you, Phoenix, but I am no mere corpse. I am a servant of the great and benevolent Dorovar. Here in this place that has been cleansed by Dorovar's will shall you meet your end. Here your soul shall join the thousands that already sing to Dorovar their praises for saving them from this life of servitude, eternally under the thumb of their so-called Creator. They have been but slaves, as you have been. But I shall break your chains, and before you draw your last breath you shall look into my eyes and thank me for freeing you. You shall finally find peace in Death's embrace."

Logan looked back at Kamen for the briefest moment and then cast his eyes to Jillian. Kamen nodded in ascent to the unspoken command and watched as Logan charged headlong at the servant of Dorovar. His old reflexes taking over, he unconsciously ducked and weaved around the half-dozen bolts of energy that his opponent threw in his direction. A handful of feet from his target, Logan hesitated briefly to gather his feet beneath him, coiling all of his strength and power into one hard lunging strike, much like Gwydeon had taught him a dozen lifetimes ago. The tip of the crystalline sword sped toward the center of the creature's breastplate, but at the last moment Death brought its hand into its body. The tip of the crystalline sword impacted the center of the armored palm, and Logan immediately heard the sound of breaking glass fill his ears. Before he could react there was a bright flash of light and an explosion of power spread outward from the point of impact. Logan didn't have a chance to brace himself for the blow and was sent crashing to the ground. When his vision finally cleared, all he saw in his field of vision was an indistinct black shape hovering over him, but the next moment he felt the cold metallic hand closing around his throat. When the hand began to pull him upward, Logan brought his hands up to clasp at Death's wrist, taking some of the pressure off of his neck. The squeezing wasn't enough to totally restrict his airway, but Logan was beginning to wonder if after all of the power he expended first in lifting the mountain and then in battling the animated corpses if he had enough left within him to take on a Herald of Dorovar. Though perhaps he should have considered all of that before he charged in. Death lifted Logan completely off the ground, his pulsing red eyes boring holes into his opponent.

"So this is the mighty Phoenix? Killer of gods. I'm not impressed."

Logan could feel the hand begin to squeeze harder around his throat, finally cutting off the air supply. Sparks fired at the edges of the field of Logan's vision. In a few moments he would lose consciousness, but before he did he had to mount some kind of attempt to free himself. Reaching deep into himself he tried to find the roaring green flames, but for some reason they were not there. All that seemed to be available to him were the powers that had been granted to him as an ascended being, but even those seemed dampened. A hard squeeze at his throat got Logan's attention and forced him to look back at Death.

"Something wrong, Phoenix?"

Logan's eyes went wide when he saw the evil grin on the face of the creature, its red eyes pulsing faster and with more intensity.

"You didn't think for a moment that Dorovar would not learn about the abilities of his enemies? Through Jerah he has learned all about the powers of the roaring flames you call the Blaze and about its connection to the Child of the Creator called Halicon. No matter who owns the power now, we know how to prevent you from touching it. And as for your powers as a divine being, the touch of the glorious Dorovar has been enabled to disrupt those abilities as well. The gift of our newest Herald, Conquest, to his new master. Even at the height of your powers, Phoenix, you would have not been able to match the powers that Dorovar has gained during his imprisonment, but now, with all of your powers suppressed, you stand no chance."

The look of gloating victory was replaced by shock and surprise the next moment as the cold steel of a blade came crashing down on Death's wrist, severing it cleanly from the rest of the arm. Logan crumpled to the ground, but quickly was able to find his feet again. Jillian stood several feet away, having retreated slightly out of Death's reach after the strike, her sword clutched tightly in both hands. Scaleripper gleamed in her hands, and Logan could almost feel the malice rolling from the blade. Death's expression faded from shock to blank, only its pulsing eyes showing the hate that burned inside of it. The stump still extended, the aura of dark energy intensified, and in a matter of moments a new hand had appeared where the old one had been. However, Death was not content in simply recovering from Jillian's attack. It was on her in a matter of moments, a blade of dark energy forming in its new hand as it closed the distance to her. To Jillian's credit, she had enough knowledge of the sword to parry the incoming thrust, but her mortal reflexes were no match for the Herald of Dorovar. The thrust of the sword was followed by a hard backhand from Death's left hand. Had the blow struck, it would have broken every bone in one side of the woman's face, and may well have had enough force to kill her. However Kamen's huge hand intercepted Death's strike. In one easy motion, Kamen lifted Death off the ground by his fist and then slammed him down to the ground, sending the blade clattering across the slippery obsidian surface. Instead of scrambling to his feet as Kamen expected, Death remained on the slick surface and lashed out with two bolts of power aimed at Kamen's feet. The bolts of power struck not Kamen but the solidified lava at his feet, breaking through the frozen surface. Twin geysers of the super-heated rock erupted from beneath Kamen, and as Death made its way back to its feet, a confident smile twisted its lips as it turned its attention back to the object of its disdain, Logan Ranthall. However, Death had not properly prepared itself for its new adversary, thinking that the columns of fire and rock would cause significant damage to the man who had once been known as the Living Flame.

Kamen emerged from the flames, his simple garments still smoking and in tatters, but the flesh beneath untouched by the intense heat. Lava rolled off of his exposed skin like sweat, and as Death turned its attention back to the huge man, Kamen struck. A hard open-handed blow struck Death on the right side of its helm, and blow hard enough to shatter a normal person's skull, but even the great and powerful Herald of Dorovar found itself staggered. Another series of strikes found an open target in Death's breastplate, and after the Herald fell back, Logan could see where dents had formed in the armor from Kamen's powerful blows. Kamen lunged in, his massive fists raised over his head for a finishing blow, but he did not see the counterattack coming before it was too late. Kamen's fists came down hard, but Death anticipated the blow and its speed, dropping to one knee and channeling all of its strength into a single strike. The flash of black energy made a sickening sound like a tortured moan as it erupted from Death's extended hand and claimed Kamen in the stomach. The energy then erupted through the back of the ancient giant, leaving a massive bloody wound. For a long moment Kamen simply stood, as though he had been frozen mid-blow. Finally the giant fell to his knees and then slumped face-first to the rubble-strewn ground. Anger boiled in the pit of Logan's stomach, but then he saw his old friend's chest rise and fall. It was a shallow breath, but it was a breath. Kamen was still alive, at least for the moment. Logan's attention fully turned back to Death, and for the first time in a long time, Logan felt mortal. If what the boasting Herald said was true, Dorovar had learned how to negate the powers of the Blaze, as well as the powers granted by becoming an ascended being. Despite himself, Logan smiled and began to laugh softly to himself.

Jillian saw Logan begin to laugh, and she could not keep the incredulous look from coming to her face. A man who Logan himself referred to as a friend lay not far from them if not dead on the ragged edge of it, all of their lives hanging in the balance against a foe that seemed to have an answer for every attack that they launched against it, and Logan was laughing. But for some reason, Jillian felt the absurdity of it pass through her and for the briefest moment she felt as though she understood. Death on the other hand only snarled, its red eyes flashing with barely controlled rage. With a single motion of his hand, Logan urged Jillian to take several steps back, which she did after a moment of hesitation. Logan took a deep breath, closed his eyes for a fraction of a second and then locked his suddenly serious gaze on his opponent. Jillian fully expected him to conjure some kind of weapon so that he could fight Death, but instead Logan balled his fists and waited. For a moment, Jillian thought she saw an aura of white outline Logan's body, but it was gone so quickly that she couldn't be sure if she saw it at all, or it was her eyes playing tricks. Finally, Logan's serious stare cracked, and the left corner of his mouth rose into a smirk.

"Dorovar is proving to be a very challenging opponent," Logan said after a long moment, his voice filled with nothing but the most serious tones. "But one thing I think Dorovar did not count on was the fact that some of us perform best when we are challenged and pushed beyond our limits."

Death scoffed.

"Pathetic human. You stood against a Child of the Creator, and were fortunate that he did not erase you from existence, and now you think that you are powerful enough to shake the Cosmos as Dorovar will. Emries and Halicon were fools, too confident in their own abilities to think that mortals could challenge them. You have found Emries and his servants more of a challenge on this world, haven't you? That is because their confidence has been eroded and they have been tested and found themselves lacking. The fortunate outcomes that you were blessed with as a mortal will carry you no farther, and the losses will mount. Now you and your so-called Dark Gods are the overconfident ones. How many have you lost? Where are the great Aryx Terian and his wife? Where is the Voice of the Dark Gods, the youthful Serrina? Where is Evan Sinn? More and more fall to the machinations of my master, and soon enough there will be none of your arrogant brooding filth walking this world. Already traitors walk in your midst, and already they clamor to serve Dorovar, like your friend Pike."

Logan's eyes opened wide for a moment, but then he could only nod to himself. It made sense. Pike had been on a collision course with this destiny from the moment he set foot in the Heavens, and Logan had been at the other end of that path. They were destined to meet on the field of battle, much as it seemed Aerith and Dorovar were meant to collide. Now though the stakes were higher. With Pike at Dorovar's side, all of the secrets of the Dark Gods, their abilities, and their drives were laid bare. It was betrayal so profound that it could not be put into words. But if Dorovar and his servants thought for a moment that they had the advantage, Logan was determined to ensure that they paid for their arrogant presumption. He clenched his fists tighter, so tightly that his nails dug into the tender flesh of his palms. After a moment, blood began to squeeze through his tightly clenched fingers, and the smile on Logan's face widened.

"I think I may have a few tricks up my sleeve for you," Logan said finally. "Let me show you one that I learned from my friend Kamen over there."

The flow of blood that squeezed through Logan's fingers increased the next moment, but instead of falling to the ground below, the blood seemed to crawl up the length of Logan's fingers until it began to coat his hands. An eerie glow came to Logan's eyes, and his lips curled into a malicious and cruel grin.

"Now pay attention," his voice came out thick and gravelly, "because you're only going to see this once."

* * * * * * * * * * *

Deep in the Vault of Terrors, Wolf Ranthall sat cross legged, a large tome spread across his lap. Together he and Darrien Annis were trying their best to piece together what they could about the abilities that Dorovar had gained during his studies of the ancient horrors that were collected in the Vault. Perhaps in time they would be able to find some kind of weakness that they could exploit. However, Dorovar had several thousand years to go over the material that the Creator and his servants had collected in the Vault, and at best Wolf and Darrien would have a few weeks, perhaps a month to find some kind of answer before their absence would either swing the balance of the war, or that their searching would no longer be of use. It was obvious to everyone who understood the nature of the war that it was rapidly approaching its climax, but the resolution was still very much in doubt.

Wolf had been sitting in the same place for several hours, and suddenly his head began to hurt and his eyes lost focus. At first he thought that he was just exhausted, but then he felt as though his stomach were trying to force its way up his chest and his heart raced. When his eyes finally regained focus, it was in time to see the first drop of blood fall from his nose where it struck the book below him. His head pounded and he pushed the book off his lap and tried to get to his feet. But something was wrong. All of the strength had begun to flee from his body, and for just a moment he thought that perhaps the same fate that befell Sabrina after she inherited her power from Halicon was starting to claim him as well.

Reaching into himself, Wolf found the brilliant glowing light that surrounded his soul, the powers that he had inherited from Pyrrus, the powers that held the fractured pieces of Wolf's soul together. Something from the outside had reached in and touched Pyrrus' power. Something was drawing on it, and when Wolf touched the glowing light he could not help but smile at the understanding of the truth.

When Wolf opened his eyes, he could not contain his smile, but the levity was short lived as a soft glow immediately caught his attention from the other side of the room. The large book that had been sitting on his lap now lay on the floor of the dark Vault, still open to the page that Wolf had been reading, but now there was a soft red glow coming from the pages.

* * * * * * * * * * * *

Arin Chandara, the acting commander of the Army of Fire looked over his troops and smiled. In a matter of hours they would launch and crippling strike on the border garrisons that separated the Kingdom of Water, Thorigald from its neighbor to the south the Kingdom of Steam, Iltorp. While the Army of Fire had not had explicit permission to cross through Iltorp or to attack Thorigald, Arin had taken it upon himself to anticipate the desires of the woman who was no in charge of the Kingdom of Fire, Saldarine. As popular as the Wolf of Saldarine was, Chelsea would never condemn an attack on their mortal enemies. Besides, by the time she found out, the war would be over and Arin would be standing in the royal palace. An old vendetta was not the only thing driving the leader of the Army of Fire however. Arin Chandara was more properly known as Korrd Ranthall, and as one of the servants of the Child of the Creator known as Emries, Korrd was ensuring that chaos continued to reign over the countryside. It would keep their enemies off balance, and more importantly it would help to draw out Aerith and his irritating progeny. Korrd looked most forward to crossing blades with his wayward brother, proving once and for all that Korrd was the only one with the strength to do what had to be done with the fate of the Cosmos on the line.

Arin's assistant emerged from a nearby tent with a stack of reports detailing the battle-readiness of his troops. They had lost many to the dragons and to the creature calling itself War on the crossing of the Plains of Steam, but after combining forces with an expeditionary group, the army's ranks had nearly swollen back to full strength. In Korrd's estimation, it would be more than enough to crush any resistance they met until far deeper into the Thorigald countryside. After several moments Korrd realized that he was not holding the reports yet, and when he looked over to his aide, he saw that the man was pale and his eyes were wide. Before Korrd could ask a question, he felt something hot on his upper lip and then on his cheeks. When he wiped his upper lip and looked at his hand, it was covered with blood. A little panic set in, and he wiped his cheek with his other hand again finding blood.

Quickly he rushed into the command tent and found the mirror that hung over a simple basin in the corner. Blood trickled from the corners of both of his eyes as well as both of his nostrils. Suddenly there was a metallic taste on his tongue and blood began to flow from the corners of his mouth as well. Pain boiled in the pit of his stomach and he was forced to his knees. Finally his mind caught up with the forces that were wracking his body and in an instant he understood. The cry of rage gurgled through the blood that filled his mouth, and just before he lost consciousness he managed one word.

"Logan."

* * * * * * * * * * * *

Logan felt as though he were going to fly apart from the inside out. Every inch of his skin burned and even the hair on his head hurt. The exertion was unlike anything he had ever felt before. The two forces that he was trying to hold on to on different sides of the world were threatening to rip him down the middle. A hurricane of power swirled around him, invisible to the naked eye, but Logan could see the flows of power that ripped away at him. Even though Death had effectively negated Logan's ability to use the Blaze against him, the Herald was not able to cut Logan off from its power completely. He was breaking a cardinal rule. Rather than controlling the flow of power that coursed through his body, Logan had broken the dam, and the consuming forces coursed through his veins thicker than blood. While the Blaze was trying to burn him from the inside out, on the outside, Pyrrus' power, the brilliant shimmering light like rain made of bolts of lighting, rolled across his skin. At the same time, white-hot flowing crystalline power pushed against everything, a contribution of power from Emries himself through Logan's brother Korrd. The powers of three of the Children of the Creator were fighting against one another in the air around Logan, and as he reached blood soaked hands out, he caught hold of each of the untamable powers and pulled them into himself.

Volatile elements collided for the first time in millennia and Logan knew he was dying. Only the power that remained from Aerith's mantle was holding his fragile form together. The dissonant powers clashed over and over, creating a cacophony of hate, misery, and death. Finally a harmony began to emerge through the noise. The Blaze and the brilliant energy of Pyrrus' essence found a common key, and their resonating power flared so bright that Logan thought he was on fire. But the explosion of energy seemed to be tempered by incongruent tones of Emries' power, until Aerith's mantle merged with them and created a single focused harmony. Every fiber of Logan's body hummed with a power that shouldn't have been possible, and his hair began to stand on end, lifted by a catastrophic wind. The blood on Logan's hands dripped away, and long slender crystalline blades grew from the man's clenched fists.

Faster than the blink of an eye, the battle was over. Logan crossed the distance to where Death stood, thrust both of the crystalline blades into the center of Death's breastplate and then pulled outward. The Herald of Dorovar's body was split down the middle, and thrown apart with such force that its arms and legs snapped off in the process. Death fell to the ground in pieces, its head hitting the ground last, the violent red light in its eyes extinguished forever. Logan stood over the corpse for a long moment, looking down at the dead eyes before the full force of the exertion hit him. All of the power in him fled, and he crumpled to the ground like a broken doll.

Before his eyes closed, he saw Jillian's face over him, looking down with tears of concern forming in the corners of her eyes. He wanted to reach up and wipe the tears away, but he could not move his arms. In fact, he couldn't feel his arms, and somewhere in the back of his mind he wondered if his arms were even still there. Black crept in on the edges of his vision, and he shut his eyes, drifting off into slumber.

Penitent and Patient

Year Four of the Just Emperor Kaitain "Dragonsbane" Lorien,
Creator's Calendar Year 1871

Arin Ranthall made his way through camp, hearing the screams and cries of prisoners coming from deeper in the area where the soldiers were quartered. Kaitain had kept his word; he would see the will of anyone who believed in the Creator beaten and broken until the belief itself had eroded to nothing. Arin had fought in a bloody war against creatures who desired domination of the flesh, and they drove their defeated enemies before them, demanding servitude at the cost of blood. But Kaitain demanded something that even the most evil of the phasia never dared. Perhaps it took a human being to sink to the depths of depravity necessary for subjugating not the will but the very essence and spirit of another living creature. Kaitain was a being filled with such hate for his own condition that he would not rest until that pain, humiliation and degradation was inflicted upon the rest of the world. Those who worshiped the Creator were only the first convenient target. There would be others, many others, but in order to steal the soul of the world, he would first have to break its faith. Faith was the most powerful weapon the human condition had, and once that was stripped away, only the ravages of mortality remained. For what really would there be without faith? Where was the need for heroism? Where was the need for self-sacrifice and morality? Faith was the reason that Arin's sons had fought their way through hell in an attempt to save their world from the scourge of a living nightmare. Faith was why Arin's grandson had stood proud against gods as their world was torn apart beneath their feet. Now, that faith was being threatened by the very humans Aerith and those loyal to him were trying to protect. It didn't matter if people believed in the Creator or not, and perhaps, as Arin reflected, it was better that they didn't, at least not as blindly as they currently did. Blind faith was as damaging as no faith at all. Aerith strove to open the eyes of those who toiled in blindness, to break them from their shackles, and to lead them into the light that had been denied them so long. But Arin worried that in his zeal to win the war, Aerith was letting too many battles fall to the wrong side of the ledger.

Aerith's greatest strength had been his ability to remain focused on a goal regardless of the horror around him. But perhaps over time that had made him numb to the horror, immune to its ramifications on the world around him. He focused on the single green tree in the distance while the forest burned around him. But that was why he had surrounded himself with people who had perspective that had too long been denied to him. Logan had become Aerith's armor. He was strong, proud, and nothing seemed to penetrate his belief that what they were doing was right. He would sacrifice nothing, and defend everything they believed in, but not at any cost. Logan understood the human part of the equation, and he knew that every soul they lost was a loss that could not be tolerated. Sabrina had been Aerith's soul, a reminder that once he had been more than the monster he had reduced himself to. No one would ever know the depths to which Aerith felt pain at Sabrina's loss. It was one more indignity and one more open wound that scarred the man's heart. Hannah had become Aerith's conscience, a reminder of the cost of every action, while at the same time putting a face on the work he was doing. Perhaps also she was the embodiment of the innocence that he was trying to protect in the world. Which left Arin; the piece of Aerith that still had humanity. Arin in life had only been a solider, a father, and a man. He had never been a god, like Logan had become. He had never touched the divine light of the Creator as Sabrina had, and had never been the lens of the Creator's love as Hannah had been. Powers or no powers, Arin's mentality was still that of a normal man, adrift on a sea of uncertainty; one that threatened to dash him against the rocks of unfathomable power any moment. Now though, there was only one power that concerned Arin, and it was that wielded by the madman Emperor Kaitain Lorien.

Finally Arin made his way to the tent that had been prepared for Ivan Quicksilver, and when he saw the two guards standing firm outside, his stomach turned. He knew what waited for him inside the tent, and he knew the difficulty that it was going to cause not only for his conscience, but also for his ultimate goal. Could he afford to save one soul at the risk of exposing himself? As he approached, the two guards came to attention, and Arin risked again touching the powers of the Blaze. When he spoke, the same coercing tones accompanied his voice, and the two guards were immediately spell-bound.

"You will see that I am not disturbed," Arin said loudly enough that anyone around could hear him.

As he stepped closer to the tent, he lowered his voice so that only the two guards could hear him.

"All you will hear coming from the tent is screaming and moaning. Anything else will fall from your mind as though it never existed. And when the commotion begins in the camp, you will ignore the women in this tent and do nothing to draw attention to their actions."

An evil smile came to the faces of both of the guards, which Arin ignored to the best of his ability as he moved past them into the tent. As he felt the tent flap close behind him, Arin fixed his eyes on the pair of naked women huddled together in the center of the tent floor. The repulsive silver collars gleamed even in the low light of the twin lanterns that hung from the posts of the tent. Arin moved to the bed and pulled two blankets off of the cot and moved toward the women. As soon as he moved closer, the women recoiled from him, and their fear and horror were only lessened slightly when Arin wrapped them in the blankets. Not wanting to make them more uncomfortable then they already were, Arin took three steps backward and then dropped to one knee. The older of the two women, the one that the guard had identified as the high priestess wrapped her sister tighter in the blanket and then turned to face Arin, squaring her shoulders and putting as much defiance as she could muster in her eyes.

"Don't think for a moment that one small kindness can erase the indignity that has been done to the faithful of the Creator. You may subject our bodies to this degradation, but our souls will remain pure."

Arin fought the urge to laugh. Though there was nothing funny about the situation, the mindless rhetoric of the believers struck a chord that Arin could not ignore. Aerith had railed against blind belief long before he knew the truth of the war. Those thoughts were hard to ignore. However, Arin did his best to keep his face passive, and he spread his hands and used his best non-threatening voice.

"Priestess, whatever you think this is, I assure you, it is far worse. Unless you do exactly what I tell you, when I tell you, Kaitain will get exactly what he wants. You will be defiled, broken, and finally executed for your beliefs, and then when we move into Zevarit, he will find another convent or church or pious community and do the same thing all over again. By the time he has slit his third throat or raped his fifth acolyte, he will not remember your faces or the little hovel he pulled you from. His hate and rage has consumed him, and the power of his hate is stronger than the power of your faith."

The priestess looked as though she had been struck.

"There is no force stronger than the belief in the Creator."

Arin's face fell, and he could not hold back his expression of disbelief and disappointment. After a moment he closed his eyes and shook his head. Perhaps he had made a miscalculation with these two. But, he had to try.

"This is not about faith, priestess. Kaitain has turned the Creator into his enemy. And Kaitain has the muscle behind him to make this war work. All of the power is on his side. Hannah Ironheart and Gregor Quicksilver are missing. The new High Priestess is unproven. The paladin core was shaken by the fall of the Heart of Stone. Even if you all prayed, all at once, it would be drowned out by one hateful breath exhaled from Kaitain's black soul."

The words were like a slap in the face, but the priestess to her credit did not flinch.

"This is a different kind of war than has ever been fought. It is a war for souls. It's not the theoretical one that your clergy has been fighting against a great phantom darkness. There is a real darkness, and Kaitain is not even a shadow to this utter eclipse of everything that could shed light on this world. But until the threat that Kaitain poses has been eliminated, we cannot focus on the greater threat, the one that your limited view of the world would never allow you to see. But we have an advantage priestess."

For the first time, that practiced and stoic demeanor cracked.

"What advantage could we have against this nightmare you have just laid out?"

Arin smiled.

"Kaitain made an enemy out of the most numerous and well-funded group of people outside of his own army. If you are united, and you are singular in your purpose, then you can stand against Kaitain, and you will find that you have more allies than you ever dreamed; provided that you shed the naiveté that everything revolves around your precious religion. This experience should tell you that you are not protected. This is not some divine test that you must persevere through. I'm giving you the chance to do everything you ever thought you would do as a priestess of the church. I'm giving you the opportunity to save souls. Not from an evil described in a book thousands of years old, but an evil that is not fifty yards from where you are right now. Save other families from being torn apart. Save other women from being humiliated. Save other men from being hung simply because they bend their knee in faith. Be more than a leader of a flock. Be a shepherd and defend your flock."

The priestess considered for a moment.

"What is it you want me to do?"

Inwardly Arin sighed, and his suddenly serious gaze sent a different kind of shiver running through the proud woman's naked flesh.

"There isn't much time. Listen closely."

* * * * * * * * * * * *

The hour was late, and Calindria paced back and forth near the entryway of the Emperor's tent, her mind filled with a strange sensation that she could not place and could not understand. For the last three hours she had heard the steady string of curses and screams coming from the back section of the tent where the Emperor's bed chambers had been arranged. Calindria knew that Kaitain was taking great joy in his distraction with the queen of the Dark Gods, but his dalliances were becoming more violent with every day that passed. It would only be a matter of time before his recklessness and rage would result in the woman's death. It would be a valuable bargaining chip to lose, but in the end, perhaps it would be better to push the war with the Dark Gods over the tipping point rather than constantly keeping it balanced precariously at the precipice of fragmented peace. However, it was not Kaitain's behavior that troubled her mind. It was the arrival of Ivan Quicksilver. Though she had never laid eyes on the man before, there was something familiar about him. Something that felt as though she had met him before.

Calindria had been serving Talisia in another capacity on the fringes of civilization, searching in vain for what the Dark Seer had called the Legacy of her Clan. Whatever the thing was, it had been hidden well. Rumor had it that it was a weapon. Between the Legacy and the Dragon's Tear, Kaitain had become obsessed with gathering to him everything that had the power to destroy a Dark God. Now that Ivan had returned with tales of killing one himself, Kaitain had been even more fanatical. The very thoughts of a Dark God's blood on his hands consumed the man, and he would make the whole world tremble and crush it beneath his boot to get what he wanted. Calindria had been prepared for a certain level of madness, but when she had been called to Kaitain's side when Korin had been sent on his mission for Talisia, she was not prepared for the creature that she would find wearing the Emperor's crown. The very sight of his twisted and grotesque visage was not nearly as disturbing as the monstrous mind that lay embedded in that deformity. His brilliance and adherence to violence was frightening.

Finally, the flap to the rear section of the tent was pulled back and Kaitain emerged. Calindria's stomach lurched, and she did her best to keep the contents from spilling out onto the floor before her. Kaitain was nude, his body glistening with sweat, but streaked with blood in various stages of freshness. His hands were coated in the red viscous liquid, by far the freshest. There were what looked like hand prints on his chest and arms that were mostly dried, and his inner thighs were bright red. Though every part of her wanted to look away, Calindria instead focused her gaze on the wild and hate-filled eyes of the Emperor, and she was shaken to see the glee beneath the hate. The screaming from the bed chamber had ceased, and all that could be heard was a quiet sobbing and coughing. There was no weapon clear in Kaitain's hands, and it seemed from the ragged shape of his fingernails that he could have done all the damage with his bare hands, an act Calindria knew she could not put past him. He stepped up the makeshift dais and slumped down on the throne, blood smearing across its surfaces. His posture was lewd, his legs splayed wide open, his blood-stained manhood on display for anyone who walked in the tent. The scowl was all Calindria needed to know the mood of her master, and she quickly fell to one knee and waited to be acknowledged.

"Speak."

Calindria remained where she knelt, as the order did not allow for her to stand.

"The scouts have returned, and identified several routes that could be taken to the capitol of Zevarit. The first is the most direct route, which would put us in the capitol within four days. However, as you requested, the scouts have identified two large temples along the direct route that appear to be continuing to minister to the people in clear defiance of your orders. The smallest of these communities would only require a two day detour from the path, however, the larger community would require a greater commitment of time and resources, and would most likely delay our arrival in Zevarit by five days, perhaps a week."

Kaitain's response came in a maniacal laugh.

"Have you understood nothing, Calindria? It doesn't matter how many days it takes. These feeble-minded fools must be made to understand. There is no Creator. There are no great gods in the skies above watching over them and offering protection. We have seen what the heavens have to offer the people. They burst forth with waves of destruction. A giant crater and demons that wear the faces of mortals are all that the Heavens have given to the people of Cadaria. These fools must abandon this hopeless quest for salvation in the skies and give their loyalty, devotion and love to the only one who can save them from their misery on this world. They must worship their Emperor as they do their precious Creator. They must be led out of the veil of mysticism and lies and be made to see the truth of their folly. And there is only one way that lesson can be learned. It is a harsh lesson, which requires harsh applications of truth. Even if it means that application is done at the tip of a sword or the end of a lash. In the morning we will take our crusade into the Kingdom of Blood, and for our task to be done, I am sure that we will make every town live up to that name. We will bleed the misplaced faith out of the devout, and we shall cleanse them in any way we can."

Kaitain laughed long and loud.

"The length of the route doesn't matter," he said finally. "I want every vestige of the worship of the so-called Creator wiped away."

Calindria bowed her head wordlessly. She was about to raise her head and ask for permission to be dismissed when there was a great uproar from outside of the tent. There was a loud indecipherable shout followed by screams and the sounds of dying and open battle. Kaitain pushed himself from the throne and grabbed a set of clothes that lay on a table in the corner of the tent. He pulled them on quickly and then took the Imperial Sword and his mask before darting out into the evening air. Shouts rang out for the Divine Empress Marlae, and Kaitain's blood boiled. In a matter of moments, loyal members of the Imperial Guard were striking down anyone who did not yield, while still others chased after the newly bound slaves who broke and ran for the wilderness. As he watched the commotion around him, Kaitain's blood burned in his veins. He plunged the Imperial Sword deep into the ground and looked skyward, the guttural angry roar ripping from his chest.

"MARLAE!!!!"

* * * * * * * * * * * *

Arin had just barely finished going over the details of his plan when the first shouts went up outside. He had not expected his diversion to begin so soon. There was so much that he hadn't thought through, and perhaps in his rash need to save the slaves, he had done more harm than good. But, there would be time enough to second guess himself if he managed to survive the night. After a moment, Arin reached into his pocket and withdrew a single white stone. Reaching back into his memories, and those that he shared with the others who had worn Aerith's mantle, he found the place that he was looking for. There was a small farm town just outside of Albitonin that was far enough from the Heart of Stone that the power from a small portal would not be noticed, unless Aerith or one of the others just happened to be there. Once he had locked the image of the town in his mind, he channeled as little power as he could manage into the waiting stone. The two women watched in awe as the stone shifted through several colors before finally settling on a deep forest green. When Arin opened his eyes, he extended his hand toward the priestess.

"Remember what I told you," he said firmly. "Once you get far enough away that the camp is not in sight, pull on the edges of the stone until it opens up into a swirling blue gate. Don't hesitate, and don't be afraid. The portal will take you to a town outside of Albitonin. You'll be able to find refuge and help there. Get to the Heart of Stone, tell them what is going on, and get the High Priestess to agree to marshal forces in defense of the people. But whatever you do, don't mention my name, and don't mention how you escaped."

The priestess shook her head.

"How will they ever believe any of this? How will they believe that I managed to make it from the border of Zevarit to Albitonin in one night without being noticed by the Imperial Guard? This plan of yours is folly."

Arin frowned. Again, it was obvious he hadn't thought this through. Once more he reached into the recesses of his mind and it took only a few moments to find the memory that he needed.

"Say whatever you have to say to see the High Priestess. Tell them that you have a message that only she is to hear, a message of great importance from Hannah Ironheart."

The priestess paled at the mention of Hannah's name.

"You know Lady Hannah?"

Arin did his best to suppress the self-satisfied smile.

"You could say we're close."

Again, Arin's mind whirled with thoughts and feelings that he knew were not his, and the sarcastic tone on his voice grated on the simplicity of his nature. Arin was not Aerith, and no matter how much Aerith and Logan had become intertwined, Arin would not fall into that trap. No matter what, Arin was a soldier. He was just following orders. He shook off the irreverence and found the serious tone once more.

"When you gain your audience with the High Priestess, request that before she listens to your message that she check the right arm of the chair in Hannah's quarters. There she will find a secret compartment that holds hand-written copies of passages from the Book of the Creator in Hannah's own hand. They will also bear the signature of the previous High Priestess, as they were written by Hannah when she was only an acolyte. Once the new High Priestess has those in hand, she will know that you are a messenger from Hannah, and she will give credence to your words, regardless of how you got there. Can you remember that?"

To her credit, the young woman asked no further questions, and simply nodded.

"Once I leave, count to five and then slide under the side wall of the tent. The guards out front won't see you, and hopefully I'll be able to shield you long enough for you to get away. "

Arin hurried out of the tent and started barking orders to the guards in the vicinity. He had to still play the part of Ivan Quicksilver, the loyal servant of Emperor Kaitain, but at the same time he had to make sure that the two women got away safely. However, he was not ready for what happened next. The younger of the sisters, the acolyte came running from the opening of the tent, crying and shrieking loud enough for everyone to hear.

"I'm sorry Lord Quicksilver. I tried to stop her but she ran. Please don't punish me any more!"

She fell to her knees sobbing, and for a long moment Arin didn't understand what was going on. And then it clicked. The younger sister was sacrificing herself to keep up the illusion. This way any suspicion would be shifted off of Arin, and he could remain in the good graces of the Emperor, that is if the man actually had any. Once more Arin had been guilty of not thinking far enough ahead. If he didn't start soon, there would be nothing to save him from his shortsightedness. To keep up appearances, Arin backhanded the girl across the face. The slap was not hard, but it made enough of a sound that those watching and listening would think it was real. In the next motion, he took hold of the girl's collar and pulled her toward one of the nearby soldiers.

"Take this useless slave back to my tent. But don't you dare lay a finger on her. After this night is over, she will be lucky to survive my wrath."

The soldier complied without a word, and inwardly Arin hoped they would both survive the night.

* * * * * * * * * * * *

Calindria moved slowly and quietly through the Emperor's tent toward the bedchambers. The whole of the encampment was moving to put down the rebellion and to round up the escaping slaves, and the Emperor's anger would keep him occupied with the traitors for at least a few hours. Whatever Calindria was expecting to find on the other side of the tent flap, what she saw before her was far worse. The ground, sheets, and mattress were all stained dark red, and in the middle of it all, naked and curled up in a ball was Sadrina Annis. Her long dark hair was caked with dirt and sweat, and much of it was stuck to her face, shoulder and back in dried blood. Small jagged cuts littered her body, while cleaner more precise ones seemed to be well on their way to healing. At the sound of footsteps in the bedchamber, Sadrina began to shiver and pulled herself into a tighter ball. Whatever Kaitain had done to her, it had clearly begun to break the woman's will. It took Calindria only a moment to cross the distance, and she knelt beside Sadrina's head and tried her best to smooth the woman's hair out of her face so that she could run a delicate hand over the woman's tear-stained cheek. The touch of the skin caused Sadrina to recoil and look up into Calindria's eyes, her own wide and full of fear. A moment later Calindria cooed to the woman, gently caressing her cheek.

"It's alright, Sadrina, I'm here to help. I'll get you out of here. You just have to be patient and hold on a little bit longer."

Sadrina's mouth worked for a moment and she tried hard to form the woman's name.

"Ca….Ca….."

"Shhh, Sadrina, save your strength," the woman said gently. "My name is Cairyn. My daughter sent me to rescue you."

The Blood of Angry Men

Year Four of the Just Emperor Kaitain "Dragonsbane" Lorien,
Creator's Calendar Year 1871

When Gwydeon Sandar opened his eyes again, he was not face down in the snow-covered landscape as he expected. Instead he was sitting upright, his back propped against a rock outcropping, and he could feel the heat of a small fire warming his impossibly cold body. A small shack stood around them, but there was something curious about its construction. The floor was still cold, as though there was nothing more than solid ice below him, and yet the wind and snow no longer whipped around them. It took little effort to concentrate his powers into his vision, and he realized the truth. Like the fire that roared at his feet, the shelter of stone and mud was a construct. Unseen forces instead of mortar and nail held the roof and walls in place, and Gwydeon was impressed at the control of the person who had crafted the shelter. It was an exercise of power that Gwydeon had never seen before, and it would have come in handy on all the long nights that he was forced to camp out in the elements during his exile. However, during those times he had barely had enough power to light a candle, so it was a moot point. However, it was an impressive trick all the same. He tried to turn his head to look for his wife and daughter, but his body would not respond to his direction. The pain was too great.

"Good," a man's voice said, "you're awake."

Gwydeon felt the presence a moment later. When the man's face finally came into view, it took Gwydeon's eyes several moments to fully focus on it. The battles had taken so much out of him that even his most basic of functions had been almost completely compromised. However, once his eyes did focus, part of him wished that the visage before him hadn't appeared at all.

"Not glad to see me," Aerith Seth said with mock disappointment in his voice. "I guess I shouldn't be surprised. But considering the fact that you and I have barely met over these past few millennia I should have thought that you at least would not hold a grudge. After all, I did just save you and your family from freezing to death."

Gwydeon didn't fully understand the rage that had been lit inside of him. What Aerith said was true. They had rarely had personal dealings with one another, and all Gwydeon knew about Aerith he had learned second and third hand through Sabrina, Logan, and others. But there was one constant that could not be ignored no matter what good the man had done in his very long life. Wherever Aerith was, trouble followed quickly, and no situation was better for his having been part of it. And regardless of the necessity of the war that raged on this world, Gwydeon would never forget, and in part never forgive, that all of the death, all of the suffering, was because of Aerith.

"Thank you," Gwydeon managed, "but I'm never going to be glad to see you."

Aerith sat back against the far wall of the shelter facing Gwydeon. His face was serious, and he nodded gravely at Gwydeon's assertion.

"My family?" Gwydeon asked.

"They're in the next room," Aerith replied. "They didn't fare nearly as well as you did. Camille very nearly lost a wing, and half of the bones in her body are broken. Midarin also is beaten around pretty well. She's lucky that I've been practicing my healing over these centuries, otherwise she'd have some pretty nasty scars. Not that I'd think she'd mind. Women like her though tend to wear their scars on the insides, you know?"

Gwydeon couldn't hide the grimace. He knew in his heart that Aerith was not trying to be cruel, but the comment cut deeper than it probably should have. But the circumstances were what they were, Gwydeon couldn't change that. All he could do in the time they had left was to try to make the most of their time together and if he could not erase the necessity of his absence, he could craft new memories that would make the distance and the loneliness seem further away. Gwydeon was relieved that his wife and daughter were still very much alive, even if it galled him that they now owed their lives to the man who sat before him.

"Midarin is strong," Gwydeon said. "She's had to be to get through this nightmare. We've all had to be."

Aerith considered for a moment and then nodded.

"I want to see them."

Aerith looked Gwydeon in the eyes and then put a single hand up.

"Even if it wouldn't undo all of the work I've done on you over the last few minutes, I think you should let them rest. Alderin is with them, he'll make sure they have everything they need while you and I talk."

Gwydeon arched an eyebrow.

"I ran into him while he was struggling trying to figure out how to navigate portals," Aerith answered Gwydeon's silent question. "Probably would be splattered against some mountain right now if I didn't bring him with me. I guess no one gave him the crash course on the differences between being a Dark God and being a mortal with power. Pretty sloppy of my daughter."

Gwydeon could relate. He had gotten used to having the powers of a Dark God, and once they were robbed from him, he had to teach himself how to be a mortal all over again. However, Alderin had never been a mortal. Had never lived life without power. Through his new connection to the Blaze, Gwydeon had known the moment that Sabrina had died, and had known the moment that Rhain Seth became the new master of the Blaze. Now in some ways Alderin and Gwydeon were brothers, linked through the powers of the Child of the Creator that had once been Gwydeon's sworn enemy. This war continued to redefine irony.

"What do you want, Aerith?"

The ancient man scratched at the scruff on his chin.

"You feel it coming, don't you?"

Gwydeon didn't have to answer. Everyone who had known power as long as Gwydeon and Aerith had could feel it in the air. Forces were gathering in every corner of this world, preparing for the final battles that would determine the fate of Creation. It was no coincidence that Gwydeon in rapid succession had faced Emries' agents, dragons, and a Servant of the Creator, and was now faced with Aerith Seth. The invisible force that held them all together was drawing tighter, forcing them into conflict. Gwydeon could only imagine how the weight tugged at Aerith Seth. Whether by design or through his own arrogance, Aerith had been in the center of the conflict between the Children of the Creator for millennia, and weariness sat in the man's eyes to the depths of his soul.

"I can feel the energies of this place," Aerith said looking off into the nothingness. "Emries has been here, so has your son. And two members of the *Erieal* it feels like. Well, at least two. There is something odd about the powers, something unstable. But so many lines have been blurred, it's not surprising."

Gwydeon gritted his teeth.

"The Spirit was here too."

Aerith nodded.

"I felt it."

"Eldar is its host now."

Aerith's eyes widened for just a moment, and then he nodded with a slight chuckle in his voice.

"I would be flattered if I were you," he said finally. "The Creator must be really worried about you and Pike if he's dusted off Eldar's soul. Under different circumstances, I might call it a desperate move. But the Creator is not desperate, since he holds all the power in this situation. He could destroy everything with a thought, but he's going to let it play out long enough to see who wins, then he'll clean up the mess and start over. That is, unless we stop him."

Gwydeon was finally able to shake his head.

"Still talking about remaking the Cosmos in your image?"

The right corner of Aerith's mouth cocked into a smirk.

"You have to admit it wouldn't ever be boring. But no. It was never about me. It was never about my image. It was about giving this world and all of the others a real chance, free of the Children, free of the Creator, and free of the petty creatures who called themselves gods. Present company excluded of course."

For the first time, Gwydeon saw a glimmer of the humanity that Sabrina had always raved about. For all of his self-aggrandizement, it was clear that Aerith wanted an end to the war, not a perpetuation of it.

"I'm not so sure you should exempt any of us from anything," Gwydeon responded absently.

The comment brought a smile to Aerith's lips.

"See, that's why Sabrina always liked you. You never took this as seriously as so many of the others. You and Logan are the reason we've gotten this far. But you two are also going to be the ones that this comes down hardest on in the days to come. While the Children and Dorovar and I are trying to tear this all down, it's going to be up to you and Logan to hold it all together. At least until it's time to do what needs to be done."

Gwydeon sighed.

"Could you be any more vague and ominous?"

Aerith chuckled to himself.

"This was a courtesy, nothing more," Aerith said finally. "I owed you that much, especially with what is coming."

Gwydeon looked Aerith in the eyes and could feel the torment rolling from the man. He knew so much about the greater conflict, and yet he controlled that information the same way that Sabrina had during those lonely years. She had fed Gwydeon just enough to keep him going, and to keep him involved, but the greater tapestry was always just out of reach.

"All those years ago," Gwydeon started, "when Sabrina came to me in the Heavens and told me about what Talisia had planned, I didn't even think. It was wrong what she was planning, as wrong as what Emries had done on our world. Of course it was laughable to think that she would be able to topple the Creator, but when we saw all of the angels and the dragons that were arrayed with her, how could we not fight? Talisia was smarter than we gave her credit for, and it cost us Pyrrus. After the rebellion and the so-called punishment, I went to Evan. I pleaded with him, but he wouldn't hear me. I could see it in his eyes. The Creator had changed him, had wiped away the hero that you had made him into and turned him into just another pawn. I don't know how Sabrina resisted that, but I'm sure that it had something to do with you and it had something to do with the strength that she developed in the wars against Draven."

Aerith sighed.

"Sabrina was special. There will never be another one like her. I don't know if I would be sitting here with you if it wasn't for her. You may both credit and blame me for this war, but she was the lynch pin, and if she wouldn't have taken the chances that she did when she was the Spirit, you would have all been destroyed when you rebelled."

Gwydeon's eyes widened. He had never thought that their rebellion could have ended any other way.

"It was a calculated risk," Aerith answered the silent response. "Sabrina knew it would be split. Emries and Talisia were banished, Raenera was missing, Halicon was recovering from his wounds, and Pyrrus was dead. So, any decision that was to be made as to your fate would have come down to the Creator, his Servants, and the few gods that had wormed their way into trusted positions; gods like your old friend Azure. Sabrina was going to urge for your expulsion, and we knew that the Wrath would urge for you to be destroyed. It took Sabrina's leverage of the bet and her stepping down as the Spirit to make the decision final. But there was still unrest. The other Servants had to have their memories altered so that instead of you falling by choice, you were cast down. To his last breath, Evan believed that you were defeated and that he threw you down from the Heavens with his bare hands."

Gwydeon was mortified.

"I don't understand."

Aerith shrugged.

"Do you think for a moment that if Evan knew why you were being exiled that he wouldn't have relinquished his position and followed right along behind you? The Creator couldn't have allowed that to happen. It was bad enough that he was losing Sabrina. He couldn't have let Evan go as well."

Gwydeon was confused. He couldn't make the connection that Aerith was trying to lead him to. It was clear that there were many lies and so much disinformation about the origins of this conflict, but Gwydeon had thought that he had ferreted out most of them. But if Sabrina knew this secret, it was one that she took to her grave.

"I still don't understand," Gwydeon finally admitted.

"Good," Aerith responded. "If you did, you would be more of a threat than the Creator already thinks you are, and you probably wouldn't have made it this far. But now, you're somewhat clear of the conflict, at least the bloody part. Well, mostly."

Aerith's eyes moved in the direction of the makeshift door that separated the two rooms of the shack that he had conjured to give Gwydeon and his family a place to rest and recover. Gwydeon's eyes followed Aerith's.

"You know that your daughter is compromised, don't you? She's a threat to you and to everything you're doing."

Rage built in Gwydeon.

"What are you talking about? My daughter is no more a threat to what we're doing than your children are to what you're doing."

Aerith shook his head.

"You don't know what you're talking about, Gwydeon. My children are a threat to what I'm doing. So is my wife. Ultimately, so am I. Why do you think that I've put plans in place to eliminate all of us when the time comes? Already people know what they need to do. Ayden will have to be the first, because he is far more compromised than I thought possible. Dorovar got to him, and then opened the door for the Creator to sink his claws in. The Creator thinks that I don't know yet. That when its time, he'll spring it on me. But I've known it was coming since Evan died. The Creator has to keep a check on me, on my powers. The only way he can do that is to co-opt someone connected to me. At first I thought it was going to be Rhain, but her defenses proved to be enough to make her unpalatable to the Creator's designs. Ayden on the other hand, he's too much like me. He's arrogant, he's sure that he can't lose. He thought because he was my son that it made him untouchable. But none of us are untouchable."

Aerith paused and Gwydeon started to speak, but Aerith cut him off.

"Never forget that your daughter is a divine being. You may be her father, and Midarin may be her mother, but she was born in the Heavens, and at the time you were half-divine yourself as the Brother of Angels. Can you say that the Creator can't pull her strings like he does the angels? But don't feel bad, I have the same doubts about Wolf's kids. They were born in the Heavens too, and no one knows how much pull that has. Suffice it to say you need to keep your eyes open."

Aerith closed his eyes for a moment and took a long deep breath. When he opened his eyes and locked them back on Gwydeon, there was a drastic change in the ancient man's demeanor. Any shred of concern was gone, and the clear eyes of a killer replaced them.

"You're in my way."

There was violence and disgust in the man's tone, but after the initial shock passed, Gwydeon realized that it was not directed at him. It was directed at the situation, and in some ways Aerith directed it back at himself.

"One of the things that I've learned after all these years is that heroes excel at two things: making a nuisance of themselves and getting themselves killed. Right now I need you to be a nuisance somewhere else. The Children and Dorovar are mine to deal with, and they are playing at a level far above you. You got lucky fighting off the Spirit, but your luck won't hold, and if you're caught out in the open without your family to back you up, you're done. This isn't Onea, and this isn't the old days where one devoted man with a sword can make a difference. Here you just end up dead, needlessly. This war doesn't need the Brother of Angels that stood toe to toe with Emries and lived to tell about it. After all the time he's had to plan and perfect his tactics, he'd rip your wings off and feed them to you before you managed to get in a single blow."

Had Gwydeon been a more prideful man, he would have taken offense to Aerith's words. But Gwydeon knew better. There was no malice in what Aerith was saying, and that perhaps made it hurt worse. In the past few hours, Gwydeon had barely survived three battles, and even then it had ended up with him and his family on the edge of death. Before Gwydeon got further into his self-deprecation, Aerith continued.

"Walk away from that Gwydeon. Be the Gwydeon that united a broken world against forces they couldn't understand. Take a stand with the common people against the monster that ravages them. Let your allies who are better suited for this fight do their job. But there is real suffering happening right now, and that is where you can make the most difference. Unite the people against Kaitain, and protect them from what is coming. Keep them out of harm's way, because you know what's going to happen in the end. Remember the panic when our world died. Remember the fires. Remember the screaming. Save these people from that. This world needs you to be that kind of hero. And I need you out of my way."

Gwydeon considered for a long moment, and then spoke.

"And if I don't want to be that kind of hero?"

Aerith's eyes flashed.

"You know I could kill you right now. And even at full strength, I don't think you'd fare much better. Don't make me make that choice, Gwydeon. There are bigger dangers that threaten the people of this world, and Kaitain's ignorance and arrogance are going to bring fire down upon everyone, including himself."

Finally Gwydeon nodded.

"You're right, Aerith. The people have to be protected, and we have to be what we once were. Jerrard and Erika have had the right idea all this time. They hid in plain sight among the people, using their abilities to make their lives better and to protect them from what was coming. Back when Onea was on the brink of destruction, Midarin and I held what little we could together. No matter how much the odds were stacked against us, the people fought. It wasn't Midarin, or me, or powers, or anything like that that kept the phasia from our door. It was faith, and the belief that we could make a difference. The world needs that now."

Aerith got to his feet and moved to where Gwydeon sat and knelt down beside him for a moment.

"Thank you, Gwydeon. I know this is a sacrifice for you, but it's for the best. But don't think you're quite out of this war yet. Before this is all over, I'm going to be asking one more favor of you. I hope by then that you and I are still both strong enough to see it through."

With some effort, Aerith helped Gwydeon get to his feet. Pain flew through every part of Gwydeon's body, but the pain was nothing compared to the confusion and the sudden feeling of incredible loss that suffused him.

"Go and see your family," Aerith said finally. "And remember what I said."

Gwydeon took a tentative first step and then took another toward the makeshift door. Just before he started to open it, he turned back, but

Aerith was already gone, off to fight his battles with the rest of the gods and monsters who pretended to be men. No matter what Gwydeon may have once thought, Aerith was right. Gwydeon was never in that league. He could never have shaken the Heavens the way that Aerith or the Children did. He needed to be where fighting the good fight really mattered. A moment later, Gwydeon was in the other room of the small hut and he found Midarin laying on one side of the room and Camille on the other. Both looked well, considering what they had been through, and Aerith had done a masterful job of healing their considerable wounds. Alderin sat in the corner at Camille's feet. He started to rise when he saw Gwydeon, but the older man motioned for him to stay where he was. Gwydeon knelt by his wife and kissed her gently on the forehead. She groaned slightly and then carefully opened her eyes. The smile was in her eyes long before it curled the corners of her lips.

"You're alive."

Gwydeon smiled down at her.

"You are too. And so is Camille. We were lucky this time."

The smile faded from her features.

"Seems like we're getting lucky too often."

Gwydeon nodded and looked over to where their daughter slept. She looked so peaceful, but at the same time, Gwydeon could not help but hears the doubts that Aerith expressed rolling through his head. Could the ancient man have been right? Was there really something to fear from their own daughter? Gwydeon had only to think of how Emries had corrupted their son, and a shiver of regret and fear ran through him. As if sensing his discomfort, Midarin put her hand on his knee.

"What is it?"

The flows of power that sprung up close to them saved Gwydeon from expressing the thoughts that were rocketing through his head.

"Seems like that will have to wait for a few minutes. We have a visitor."

Midarin reached out with her powers and tried to find the source of the portal, but she could not. She was still exhausted from the battle, and it seemed that it would take some time before the finer points of control would return. While she had never been as adept as others at using her powers for the purposes of detection, she had gleaned enough over the years to make sure she knew who was around her at all times. This weakened, she suddenly felt blind.

"It's Liara," Alderin said getting to his feet. "She wants us to know it's her."

Midarin looked over at the new arrival before looking back at Gwydeon. Her husband smiled at her silent question.

"I can't help it that we collect strays," Gwydeon said smiling, trying to bring levity back to the situation.

Midarin smiled, and even Alderin, who was normally extremely reserved, smiled. Gwydeon helped Midarin to her feet and started toward the door.

"Let's go and see what trouble Liara wants to get us into."

Chapter LXXXIV

Clues in the Darkness

Year Four of the Just Emperor Kaitain "Dragonsbane" Lorien, Creator's Calendar Year 1871

Wolf's head pounded, but he could not feel the pain or the weakness that wracked his body. It was more accurate to say that he did not care to feel the pain or the weakness, as they were threatening to drive consciousness from his body, but the elation of what he was seeing was more than enough to keep him from succumbing to unconsciousness. However, when he tried to cross the distance to the glowing book, his legs rebelled and he toppled to one side, barely catching himself on one of the many dangerous devices that filled the darkened Vault of Terrors. However, as Wolf and Darrien had quickly learned in their study, the power from all of these devices had been drained by Dorovar's evil. Darrien was at Wolf's side before he was able to find his balance again. Despite having been robbed of her powers, Darrien was still a strong young woman and she was able to help Wolf across the chamber to the discarded glowing tome. However, as they both slumped unceremoniously to the ground, Darrien ignored the book and focused on her companion.

"Are you alright? What happened?"

Wolf smiled and nodded. The smile felt weak, and for a moment Wolf wasn't sure that the muscles in his face were even working. As the moments passed he felt weaker and weaker, but at the very least he had stabilized enough to prevent losing consciousness.

"My father has a strange way of making a point," Wolf said.

Darrien's eyebrows arched slightly, and at that moment Wolf realized that his comment had been far more cryptic than he had initially intended. However, there were so many thoughts and strategies that were flowing through Wolf's mind, some his, and some that came from the other fractured members of his psyche. They were all united in one thing though. They now completely understood Dorovar's strategy. It was so simple, so plain; Wolf was shocked that they had not discovered it earlier.

"I know what Dorovar is doing," Wolf said finally. "I finally understand."

Darrien scoffed.

"He's trying to kill everyone and everything. He's trying to get his revenge. He's crazy. We knew that already. We're trying to figure out how to stop him."

Wolf shook his head and took both of Darrien's hands in his.

"No, no, you don't understand. It's far simpler than that. Far more simple and far more terrifying. For so long we've been dealing with long-term twisted machinations like those created by Emries and Talisia and Saurn, but even they couldn't understand the subtle brilliance and cruelty that Dorovar has crafted. He learned long ago how to defeat Emries and Talisia, long before he found his way into prison here. All this place did was give him time to learn how to complete the rest of his plan."

Again Darrien rolled her eyes.

"This Chorus of Souls to sing him into the Heavens. Its madness, like everything else he and his Heralds have been spouting all these years."

Wolf leaned back, his heart heavy.

"I wish it were only madness."

CHAPTER 84

* * * * * * * * * * * *

Dorovar sat cross-legged looking out from a high cliff across the waters to the Empire of Cadaria. From his vantage point on one of the closer islands of the Pritan Island chain, he could just make out the southern coast of the enemy empire. Though his personal vendetta did not directly impact the people who dwelled within, their imprisonment made them unaware of the true desolation of their souls. But ignorance was no excuse. Those who wished true understanding and enlightenment could have pursued it, as others had done. They could have called out with their soul to the powers beyond hoping for an answer. If they were worthy, Dorovar would have found them and freed them from their suffering. Now, though, all of the Cadarian Empire would know salvation, whether they wished it or not. That was the magnanimity of Dorovar. Even the unworthy could be redeemed. From somewhere behind Dorovar the foliage ruffled. He didn't need to look over his shoulder to know who it was; he had felt their coming from the moment they set foot on the island.

"My master," Pestilence intoned.

For several long moments, Dorovar waited. He truly had no words for the disappointment he felt at Pestilence failing to follow his orders, but there was little need for words now. The Heralds were serving their purpose. They could not help but to do so, they could do little else. And for all of Pestilence's supposed attempts at self-determination, he was playing right into his role.

"Report."

Pestilence stood fast, not daring to approach his master with the unfortunate news.

"Famine has fallen. She was destroyed by the combined efforts of Hannah Ironheart and the dragon who now leads the fragmented Council, Mariti Brightblade. This occurred at the battle of the Academy of Arcane Arts outside of Jelan."

Wordlessly Dorovar nodded. He waited for a moment, letting his servant worry about his master's reaction.

"Did Jerah accomplish her goal?"

Of course Dorovar already knew the answer to his question, but he did not need Pestilence to know exactly what it was that he knew or didn't know.

"Jerah's intervention drove Talisia Masile from the field and drew out the one known as the fallen angel. Talisia has tasted your power, my master, and found that she did not have strength to oppose it."

Dorovar inwardly frowned. How little his Herald truly understood. Perhaps he had put too much faith in them. Perhaps they would not be able to fulfill their missions.

"What else?"

Here Pestilence hesitated again. Finally he spoke, his voice filled with doubt and fear.

"Death has been destroyed, outside the ruins of Menoris. Despite Jerah's instructions, I enticed Death into combat with the one known as the Flickering Flame. He was weak and ripe for destruction, but somehow he was able to overcome Death in single combat. However, the Flickering Flame's allies were able to recover the fallen hero before I was able to intervene."

Dorovar scratched his chin in mock displeasure.

"So, two of my Heralds have fallen to the disciples of Aerith Seth."

Pestilence gritted his teeth.

"Yes, my master."

Finally Dorovar cocked his head in his Herald's direction.

"And yet you still stand."

Pestilence was stunned into silence, but when he opened his mouth to speak, Dorovar put up a single finger in dismissal. He turned his attention fully back to the far shores before speaking again.

"War?"

Pestilence straightened.

"He remains hidden in the wilds outside of Thorigald as instructed. He will decimate both armies as soon as they are engaged in battle."

Dorovar nodded.

"Excellent. With Thorigald and Saldarine thrown into chaos once their armies are destroyed, it should assist Conquest in what comes next. But in the meantime, I have learned that another of Aerith Seth's chosen pawns has insinuated himself into Emperor Kaitain's ranks. His name is Arin Ranthall. Find him and destroy him."

Pestilence bowed, confusion filling his mind. Who was Conquest, and why was his master suddenly so fixated on Aerith Seth? A moment later the Herald was gone, but Dorovar knew that he was still not alone.

"A pity that they do not know their true purpose in this war," Coriden said coldly. "Perhaps they would fight better if they were not the naïve believers you wish them to be."

Dorovar turned half-way to face the recently freed member of the Adhradair.

"They are tools, nothing more. Like you."

The white clad Coriden stood for a moment, his eyes void of expression, but after taking a step forward, Dorovar could feel the restrained anger.

"Do you still hate us so much, brother, that you would see us in the same light as your Heralds? Are we simply weapons that will be tossed away once our edges are dulled?"

Dorovar shook his head slightly.

"I do not hate you, Coriden."

Dorovar then turned to look his former colleague in the eye.

"I feel nothing for you at all. I have had millennia for my anger and hatred to run its course. Were it not for the fact that Raenera and Talisia chose to use your souls to restrain my powers and prevent me from taking my revenge, I would have left you trapped in those blades for the remainder of this eternity. Once I remake Creation, there will be no place in it for those who called themselves my brothers. You and the others ceased to be my brothers and sisters when you ignored my advice, turned against me, and left me to die at the hands of the very creatures who tricked you into destroying our world. Emries and Talisia took great pleasure in inflicting torment upon my body as they extolled the wonder of the destruction they had wrought through your hands. No, Coriden. I could no more hate you, than I could hate the hammer used to break a window. You allowed yourselves to become tools, and they used you as indiscriminately as I will use you against them. It is only fitting."

Coriden was incredulous, but his shame drowned out any anger that may have been within him.

"I do you the courtesy because we were once brothers to let you know your purpose. The Heralds need know nothing more than the task of the moment. They will succeed in allowing me to touch the powers that I need to unmake this world and to prevent the so-called heroes from intervening. By the time they realize the true nature of my plans, it will be far too late, all of my former brothers and sisters will be freed, and I will have full access to all of the powers that my Heralds have been gathering. None of them, not the Children, not the heretic, and not even the Dark Gods, will stand against me."

Pride swelled in Dorovar's heart, but he would not give in to such base emotions. He did not have time for them.

"Worry not for the condition of my Heralds. Fulfill your function and free your fellows from their confinement."

Coriden stood straight and then bowed slightly to Dorovar. He turned to walk away and then stopped after two paces. He turned his head back slightly.

"Whatever you may think of us, brother, we did not forsake you. We were blinded by the suffering of our world and would have done anything to save it. Perhaps that was our failing. We wanted too much and thought not enough. We should have heeded your council, but the time for that is long past. As you say, we may now only be tools, but our hearts are still where they have always been."

A moment later Coriden was gone, and Dorovar was left with an unfamiliar feeling in the pit of this stomach.

* * * * * * * * * * * *

Wolf recovered the book and read the newly appeared glowing red passages with an increasingly heavy heart. It had become clear after only a moment that Darrien could not see the writing. What was laid out before him was a nightmare that Wolf had never considered. The Creator had engineered a situation that could ultimately lead to His own downfall, and it seemed that no one in the Heavens or on Espre had begun to see the truth of the peril that faced them all. Finally Wolf shoved the book away and rubbed his eyes. It had felt like only minutes to him, but when he looked over to where Darrien sat, he realized that it had been a great deal longer. Seeing that her companion had finished pouring over the text, Darrien sat straighter.

"So?"

Wolf sighed and shook his head.

"After having millennia to plan, I suppose that anyone could look like a genius, but this plan is so intricate and at the same time so simple I have no other word for it. Dorovar knew that he would be facing those with the powers of the Children of the Creator, so he crafted his Heralds to act like sponges. They would be thrust into battle against those who represented the Children and absorb some of their power. Whether it killed them or not didn't matter. It would allow Dorovar to taste that power and develop defenses for it. That is what all this is. He found a way to absorb and negate the powers of the Children of the Creator."

Darrien shrugged.

"Ok, so he can take out the Children. What does that have to do with his Chorus of Souls thing? How is it going to get him into the Heavens?"

Wolf sighed.

"If he can find a way to negate the powers of the Children, all of them, there is a chance that he can negate the powers of the Creator too. By that time, he'll have neutralized the Children, the Servants, the dragons, and all the Dark Gods. There won't be anything left standing in his way."

Darrien forced her way back to her feet.

"So what? We just lose?"

Wolf smiled.

"You're so much like your father."

Darrien frowned.

"I assume you didn't mean that as a compliment."

Wolf ignored the bait and motioned Darrien over.

"Logan showed me something, and I'm not sure even he realized what he was doing until after. But my father is nothing if not consistent, and he was willing to paint a huge target on his chest to take the pressure off of the rest of us so we could figure things out. Unfortunately, I'm not the only one who got the message, and now I think it will be a race against time to put the pieces together."

Wolf took hold of a piece of metal that lay nearby and drew a circle on the dirt floor. At five points on the circle he drew smaller circles. Each one he then pointed to in turn.

"Emries, Talisia, Halicon, Pyrrus, Raenera," Wolf explained. "Each is connected because they are Children of the Creator. But that isn't the only way they are connected, at least not any more. My father, because of his status as a member of the Brotherhood of Phasia has access to Halicon's power. My uncle, Korrd, through being a *Coromor* has access to Emries power. And I'm the vessel of Pyrrus' power, as well as having some ties to Halicon through deals that have been made to keep Pyrrus' power alive."

Darrien's confused look caused Wolf to smile.

"It's a long story."

Finally, with the piece of metal, Wolf connected three of the smaller circles with straight lines.

"Because we share the same blood, Logan was able to connect the powers of three of the Children of the Creator in order to defeat one of Dorovar's Heralds. In his own headstrong and brash way, he stumbled onto exactly what Dorovar himself was doing through his heralds. Except Dorovar was making all of the connections within himself. If I'm right, we have one chance. We need to complete this puzzle before Dorovar does. So far, he hasn't been able to touch Pyrrus' power, at least not in a way that he could find a way to negate it. He has no conduit to it yet because unlike most of the Children, Pyrrus never invested his powers into a mortal vessel. But because Logan touched it and channeled it, Dorovar has gotten just enough of a taste that he's going to want to find a way to get more."

Darrien nodded, understanding finally filling her eyes.

"Ok, I get it. But how do we turn this to our advantage? I mean, unless you've got some other Ranthall family members lying around that have access to Raenera or Talisia's powers, we don't have much of a plan."

Wolf shook his head.

"It can't be the Ranthalls. Unfortunately Logan proved that too. He connected just three of the Children and it almost killed him. It probably should have killed him, but that has been true of so many things my father has done over the years, it's starting to become pedestrian."

Darrien narrowed her eyes.

"Ok, so it can't be Logan or you. So who?"

Wolf frowned.

"Logan was only able to harness the power and keep himself in one piece because of his connection to Aerith Seth. I don't know what it is about that man's powers, but they seem to have some kind of natural unifying properties. Power just seems to collect around him without any kind of repercussions. If we're going to beat Dorovar at his own game, we're going to have to leverage that. Though personally I find it a little distasteful that he's the one who is going to put all this together, there has been more behind this game than any of us have seen for so long, and yet he has seemingly placed himself in the right position over and over again. He's done it too often for it to be luck."

Darrien again looked lost.

"Aerith has ties to power. Like the Ranthalls, he can touch power through his blood and through his mantle. His daughter is the leader of the phasia now, so that gives him access to Halicon's powers. Thanks to Emries, Aerith is about to have more direct access to the powers of one of the *Coromors* again. But even without Emries intervention, Aerith could theoretically draw on that power through Logan."

Darrien frowned.

"But you said if Logan did that again, it would probably kill him."

Wolf sighed.

"Unfortunately, if Aerith asked, my father would sacrifice himself in order to pull this off. So, already that gives Aerith access to three of the Children. And again, unless I miss my guess, Raenera's powers are about to be in play."

Darrien's quizzical glance caused Wolf to smile.

"I can't tell you how I know. Let's just say that Pyrrus as the youngest of the Children of the Creator had to figure out ways to keep up with his more adventurous brothers and sisters. But Raenera was very fond of Pyrrus and the two shared a very special bond. She's been missing him for quite some time, and that love and need have translated into a kind of code that Pyrrus has learned to read. He can't quite read her mind, but he can certainly interpret her intentions."

Darrien looked down at the simple drawing.

"So that leaves Talisia."

Wolf nodded and scowled.

"And that will not be an easy nut to crack. Talisia is cagey, and she does not trust her powers to just anyone. So, we're just going to have to take them instead."

Darrien smiled a cruel smile.

"After tangling with that daughter of hers, the one who calls herself the Fallen Angel, Seraphina, I like the idea of getting revenge for what she did to Alderin."

Wolf nodded.

"Good, because she is the best chance we have of getting the powers we need. Now, during his imprisonment, Dorovar was playing around with the idea of a device that could trap the essence of a Child of the Creator. He couldn't get it to work because there was an aspect of the way that the Children's powers manifested that he could not correct for. His notes are all there in that book, but they are hidden behind blood magic. He inscribed the notes in his own blood and had it not been for Logan tapping into the powers of three of the Children in the way he did, I probably would have never known the notes were there. But thanks to Pyrrus' knowledge, I think I can make Dorovar's trap work, at least for our purposes. So, you're going to attack this Seraphina, steal some of her powers, and then take them to someone who won't mind having a target on their back, and who has a connection to Aerith."

Wolf smiled, and the well-known Ranthall charm poured through in his next words.

"Easy, right?"

Darrien balked slightly.

"Did you forget the part where Seraphina has the powers of one of the Children of the Creator, and that I have no powers at all? And how are we going to find her and get her in a position to use this little trap of yours?"

Wolf's eyes shown yellow in the low light, flashing brighter than they had moments before.

"My grandfather was a farmer, and he used to say that in order to catch a pest, you needed the right bait. If Talisia thinks that she has the upper hand against Dorovar, than she must at least have some inkling as to what his plan is. So, we have an advantage. What do you think Talisia would do if she learned that someone was walking around using Pyrrus' powers?"

Darrien's look was incredulous.

"You're not saying what I think you're saying, are you?"

Again Wolf smiled.

"You said it yourself, Darrien. You have no powers, and if you are going to try to steal Seraphina's powers, we need to make sure you are at least on even footing."

Something inside Darrien caused her to shiver. Wolf chuckled slightly.

"First things first," he said, a glint of mischief in his eye. "We have a lot of materials to gather, and a lot of questions that still don't have answers. Until we get that trap perfected, there is no reason to do anything else, or put anyone else at risk."

Darrien nodded.

"Now, let's get to work."

The Soul of Conquest

Year Four of the Just Emperor Kaitain "Dragonsbane" Lorien,
Creator's Calendar Year 1871

Pike Rhuiden stood looking up at the hulking form of Gregor Quicksilver and wondered instantly why he hadn't just snuffed the life out of the self-confident man when he had foolishly happened upon the Citadel of the Dark Gods on some fool's errand for the Emperor of Cadaria. Over the next few moments, the winged man descended, their eyes never leaving one another. In life, Gregor had been a large and imposing man, and the powers granted to him by the Creator had only accentuated that characteristic. If nothing else, the Creator knew how to intimidate the mundane into servitude. Those who weren't enslaved due to their native ignorance were cajoled into servitude by the slick and intoxicating words of the chosen messengers of the faith. However, for those few that bucked convention and fought against the words of the Creator, the Voice would appear bellowing threats and charges against blaspheme, reinforcing the power of the beliefs of the faithful and reducing the doubters to quivering piles of awe-stuck human refuse. They would conform, crawling on their hands and knees begging for forgiveness for their vanity or ignorance or whatever it was that caused them to stray from the church, while the others would simply be easy prey for the more devout and fanatical of the believers. Dorovar had once been blinded by such faith; he had prayed, felt, and wanted to know the touch of the divine. But when the divine had touched him, his world died, condemned to rip itself apart by the very creatures he had spent his life praying too. Pike on the other hand had never been a believer. He had come from a long line of believers, but he was too willful for blind belief. He chose instead to believe in his friends and the heroes who battled against the darkness that belief never seemed to banish. But that faith had been rewarded in the same way that Dorovar's had. The heroes that he had revered had been mere puppets to the divine, and eventually the friends that he loved and believed in so much had betrayed him. Now only Dorovar's love suffused Pike's being, and he would use it to tear down everything that the Creator had built, and make him pay for all the worlds that burned in tribute to his love.

Gregor Quicksilver let his feet touch the cool water of the stream, allowing only a second to pass before the huge crystalline blade appeared in his hand wreathed in divine fire. His brilliant wings folded behind him, and the shimmering armor made of heavenly metal encased his body, including a brilliant faceplate. From behind the metal, the voice boomed again, filled with a force that could only have come from the Creator himself.

"Kneel and repent," the Voice commanded. "Admit your crimes and renounce the folly of allegiance to the abomination. Dorovar too shall be brought to heel for his crimes, as shall all of his so-called Heralds. You are merely the first."

A sly smile came to Pike's lips.

"The Creator is worried," Pike said finally. "That's the only reason he would have sent you against me so soon after allying myself with Dorovar. Famine, Pestilence, even Death have done far more damage than I have, but he never sent one of the Servants against them. What is it the Creator is afraid of?"

Pike looked down at his left hand and raised it slowly. The sun glinted off the rings that now graced his fingers.

"Could it be these?" Pike continued. "Is this the reason that the Creator is worried? Dorovar has been targeting dragons all along, but it wasn't until he started taking trophies that the Creator unleashed his minions. But why just you? Why not the Wrath and a flock of warrior angels? Perhaps the

Creator doesn't consider me that much of a threat yet, and he's sent you to nip it in the bud."

Gregor's posture never changed, and the faceplate obscured any facial expressions, but there was something in the lack of response that struck a chord in Pike, and he pressed on.

"Perhaps the Creator's forces are stretched a little too thin these days. Maybe my former allies are finally becoming the nuisance that that Creator always feared we would be. I wonder what he'll do when I rip the beating heart from your chest and tear that ridiculous plate from your face and watch all of the light go out of your eyes."

Gregor's charge came the next moment, and he moved at incredible speed, bringing the massive crystalline blade up and then down with force enough the split a mountain in half. However, Pike had been ready for the move. Before Gregor crossed the distance, Pike allowed an ax assembled from pure soul energy to form in his hands. It glowed an eerie green and seemed alive in his hands, but as the crystalline blade struck against its insubstantial haft, the blow was repelled with a burst of green light and a wail that sent Gregor backwards a full ten feet. If the Voice was shaken by the display of power, it did not deter his next charge, a long thrust which Pike parried to one side and then leapt back as the blade swept back at his knees. Pike's feet barely touched the water before he sprang forward, the blade of his phantasmal ax speeding toward the center of the gleaming breastplate of his foe. Gregor shifted his shoulders and hips, but he was not fast enough to escape damage. The blade of the ax clipped his left shoulder, and the armor cracked under the force of the blow. But the large man would not be deterred. He lashed out as Pike passed, the tip of his blade barely catching Pike's exposed back, drawing a long jagged scar from his right shoulder to his left hip. The blow also caused Pike to lose his balance and tumble forward, his momentum overriding his equilibrium. A moment later he was face down in the stream, cold water rushing over him. Pike remained prone for just a moment longer than necessary, trying to bait Gregor into an attack, but no sound came from Pike's opponent, and when Pike finally scrambled to his feet, Gregor was right where he had been only a moment early, the shoulder crest of his armor cracked, and the expressionless mask staring at the newest herald of Dorovar. Despite the supposed weakness of his opponent, Gregor had held his ground, refusing to be conned into a reckless assault.

"I expected more from a Herald of Dorovar," the Voice taunted. "Perhaps he should have invested his power in recruiting one of your contemporaries. But Dorovar never did try to convert the strong. He always preferred to prey on the weak and stupid."

Anger boiled inside of Pike, but instead of leaping back into the fray, he waited, letting the jibe pass through him. As the Voice, Gregor would have had the knowledge of every battle Pike ever fought, every tactic he ever used, and every tactic that had ever been effective against him. The Creator knew Pike as emotional, reckless, and quick to anger. He had let his temper and passion draw him into unfortunate battles before, and perhaps that was why the Voice was the perfect choice as an opponent. Gregor would be measured, patient, disciplined, all of the things that Pike was not. But that was the old Pike. That was the Pike before Dorovar's touch. Before the voices. Now the Chorus of Souls rang clearly in his ears, and Pike knew all of the ways to defeat the hulking opponent.

Pike darted forward, and immediately Gregor lashed out with a strike that would have separated Pike's head from his body. However by the time the crystalline blade passed through the space where Pike would have been, Pike had rolled forward, popping up to a knee long enough to loose a strike at Gregor's knees which ended up higher than anticipated, colliding with the thick plates that protected the Voice's thighs. Again the armor shattered under the pressure of the strike, but Pike was unable to press the advantage as he had to leap out of the way of a straight downward strike that would have impaled the smaller man. But Gregor did not give Pike the opportunity to breathe or to gather himself. The massive blade chopped down again, and Pike brought the haft of his ax up to block blow after blow. Though the ax was equal to the task, the power of the strikes resonated through Pike's arms, threatening to shake loose his grip on his weapon and leave him totally defenseless. The Chorus of Souls sang in Pike's ears, and he felt their power fill him. Like in the fight against the dragon moments before, the power of the souls suffused his being and then burst forth, this time in a bright flash of green light and a death wail so piercing that Gregor was forced back as though he had been struck hard in the chest by a boulder. The Voice was stunned by the assault, and Pike leapt to his feet and feeling the battle drawing to an end, Pike filled himself with as much of the ghostly power as he could manage, feeling like his head was filled with tens of thousands of voices, all drowning out the fear and pain and worry of the moment. They were all fixed on a single purpose, and that purpose caused the blade of the incandescent weapon that writhed in his hand to glow impossible bright, brighter than the suns above. Gregor saw the strike coming at the last moment, the fog finally lifting from his senses. Whatever Pike had done was unexpected and powerful, but the power of the Voice was able to shake the confusion in time for Gregor to bring his massive blade up to meet the glowing green ax that sped toward the center of his breastplate. The next moment an explosion of force blew through the clearing, the ripples so powerful that it ripped trees free from their roots and shook centuries-old rocks from their moorings at the edges of the waterfall. The cascading water was joined by an avalanche of rock that sealed the entrance to the cave where the corpse of Abysm Nightwalker still lay.

In the core of the explosion time seemed to drag to a halt. The nearly invisible leading edge of Pike's ax struck the haze of divine flame that oozed across the face of the Voice's blade like early morning mist across the surface of a calm lake. Voices screamed from Pike's weapon, as though they had been trapped in a burning building and the fires had just touched their skin for the first time. The screams were joined a second later when the blade of the ax pushed through the roiling fires and stuck home on the flat of the crystalline blade. The sound of a thousand breaking windows, and ten thousand wind chimes struck the air, a concordant cacophony to match the growing screams of pain and anger that emanated from deep in the Chorus of Souls. The force behind Pike's strike was so intense that the ordered and sound structure of the divine blade buckled, eventually sending fissures and fractures through its length. Time dragged further. The furthest advance edge of the ax dug deeply into one of the cracks in the structure of the blade. The sound of breaking glass became louder and more overwhelming, the pained voices of the souls suddenly turning hopeful, a quiet triumph emerging from the torment. Shards of crystal burst free from the hemorrhaging wound in the blade, allowing the phantasmal ax to plunge deeper and deeper. Finally the crumpling mass of divine power could stand no more, rent in two by impossible forces. No longer impeded by the Voice's weapon, the ghostly ax crossed the empty expanse and struck home in the center of the brilliant breastplate. However, the collision with the crystalline blade had robbed too much of the power from Pike's assault, and even the screaming power of the Chorus was not fit to breach the last line of defense between its glowing baleful strength and the rapidly beating heart of the Servant of the Creator.

His life spared for the moment, Gregor ignored the maelstrom of sound and light, focusing all of the power that remained within him. His left hand quickly discarded the tip of the broken blade, lurching forward to clutch the Herald of Dorovar by the throat. But Pike's feet dug firmly into the moist ground, and despite the crushing pain through his larynx, the Herald drew ever deeper on the powers gifted him, willing the blade of his ax deeper and deeper into the metal of the Voice's armor, feeling it begin to crack under the strain. Time stood still. Nothing moved. Sweat beaded on Pike's forehead, every ounce of his power, his pain, his fury concentrated on one point in the center of Gregor's chest. He willed death on his opponent. Gregor too felt the strain of the eternal second. The line between life and death drawing ever narrower. In one last desperate act, Gregor pulled Pike forward, taking some of the strain out of the Herald's strike, and driving the shattered hilt of his crystalline blade into Pike's chest. Time hiccupped. The screams from Pike's ax changed pitch, the wail no longer triumphant, but instead shocked and harried. Disbelief reigned in the cacophony. Pike's face, filled with grim and deadly determination a moment before now filled with shock and disillusionment. Hot viscous blood flowed from the gaping wound in Pike's chest, streaming down the fragment of Gregor's blade, onto the Servant's hand, finally dripping off onto the tortured ground beneath. In his ears, Pike heard his heartbeat, loud and defiant. Soon it took on a tortured drag, becoming uneven and doubtful. Blackness crept in on the edges of Pike's vision, and the next moment, the pulsing green weapon disappeared from Pike's grasp. Gregor released his opponent's throat, and Pike staggered back, taking the remainder of the weapon from Gregor, the majority of it still buried deeply in Pike's chest. Staring wide-eyed at Gregor, but jaw firmly set and recalcitrant, Pike pulled the blade free. The action was met with a torrent of blood flowing free of the gaping wound, and a wave of pain that robbed Pike's legs of the ability to continue to support his weight. The hero of Onea fell to his knees in the blood-soaked ground, his eyes threatening to close under the weight of the pain and blood loss. His heartbeat slowed in his ears, weak and barely audible. The last thing Pike saw before he could no longer resist the weight of his eyelids was a simple shimmer that came from the simple silver band on his finger.

Gregor Quicksilver stood over his fallen opponent, watching as he took his last labored shallow breaths. Finally, with a staccato shudder of quick inhales and exhales, the Herald's final breath escaped his lips accompanied by a trickle of blood at the corner of his mouth. Pike's head lulled to one side before finally drooping, the taut muscles in his neck stopping his head before the chin could come to rest fully on his collarbone. The Servant of the Creator could not help but let his eyes fall down to the gaping wound in Pike's chest. Gregor could clearly see where the fragment of the crystalline blade shattered Pike's sternum and several ribs, and where it had perforated one lung, deflating it into a pulpy mass. Several shards had broken off after colliding with the ribs and shot up into Pike's heart. Gregor could see the shimmering slivers piercing the still organ. With a slow shake of the head, Gregor turned away from his fallen foe. He was less than a step away when he heard a piece of crystal hit the ground. When Gregor whirled back around, his eyes found the gaping chest wound once again, and stared in disbelief as the dead and shriveled heart beat. The first hard contraction forced out another of the crystalline shards, the last falling after the third beat. After the last of the foreign objects was expelled, the heart began a slow steady rhythm. A moment later, the deflated mass began to slowly reform, all wounds in the lung healed, and in a matter of seconds, it had returned to its natural fully-functional form. Next to repair themselves were the ribs and the sternum, followed by the muscles and skin of Pike's chest. The healing done, a long gasp escaped from Pike's lips, and his eyes shot open. Though awe-struck and confused, Gregor did not give his opponent time to get back to his feet. The Voice charged the next moment, a new crystalline blade forming in his hands. The tip of the blade this time aimed not for Pike's chest, but for his throat. At the last possible moment, Pike ducked out of the way, and then sprang forward slamming the heels of both of his hands into Gregor's fractured breastplate. The force of the impact caused Gregor to stagger backwards, and it gave Pike all the opening he needed to get back to his feet. It took only a moment before the eerie glowing green ax returned to Pike's hands, and he let his weight fall back on his back leg, a far more defensive and slow posture than he had fought from in the first act of their battle.

"Do you see, Gregor?" Pike said, his voice raspy, "the Touch of Dorovar cannot be so easily defeated, even by a monstrosity like you. His guidance and power have protected me even from the divine hate that flows through you, and it will seal your fate."

Gregor's answer came in the form of a hard charge. At the last moment, a new crystalline sword appeared in the Voice's hands. The blade flashed in, but just as Pike moved to defend, Gregor dropped the blade low and let his shoulder collide with Pike's newly healed chest. The smaller man shuddered at the impact and was driven back several feet before his heels dug into the muddy ground giving him enough traction to resist. As soon as he felt that he could push his opponent no further, Gregor's wings flashed out, and pushed him backwards. However, this was the moment that Pike was waiting for. He pushed off, springing out like a coiled viper crossing the distance between himself and Gregor faster than should have been possible. The ghostly blade of the ax sliced through the air, meeting feathered wing, and rending it clear of Gregor's body. The massive man had enough balance and control to keep from spinning out of control, instead planting both feet firmly on the ground and lashing out with a burst of divine light in the direction of where Pike had been just a second before. However, Pike had long since changed positions, retreating back several feet. Blood poured from the severed wing stalk, but the torrent only lasted for a moment before Gregor stemmed the tide. However, there would be no time to generate a new wing. Whatever remained of the battle would continue to be fought on the ground. Again Gregor scowled and charged, feinting high and then ducking low. The blade of the crystalline sword grazed Pike's thigh, but Pike spun the ax in his hand, letting the haft parry away Gregor's strike. Pike then spun into Gregor's body, slamming his elbow into the cracked breastplate. The force of the strike created a massive fissure in the armor, revealing gleaming divine light beneath. However, Pike was not fast enough to evade Gregor's hand that claimed him around the throat. In one swift motion, Gregor lifted Pike off the ground by his neck and then slammed his other fist into Pike's stomach repeatedly, causing Pike to lose grip on his weapon. The ax winked out of existence as soon as it was out of his hand.

"Burn!"

Before the word had even finished crossing Gregor's lips, waves of divine fire lurched down Gregor's outstretched arm and consumed Pike. A guttural cry emerged from deep within the Herald as the roiling heaving flames lapped at his skin. But the torment lasted only a moment as phantasmal green light began to leak from every one of Pike's pores, pushing back against the flames. The wail of the souls began anew, swirling around Pike like a chilling wind. Over the torturously long seconds, the divine flame and the wind of the dead battled against one another for supremacy. The fires began to recede, and Pike could feel the strength begin to return to his body. However, Gregor would not be content to let his attack be deterred so easily. The Herald had to be made to pay for his crimes, and that was the task Gregor relished accomplishing.

"I said burn!"

The next moment, Gregor's whole form was completely suffused with light. The physical features of the man were replaced by a translucent figure of pure divinity. The arm of light that grasped Pike by the throat sprouted brilliant tendrils that reinforced the flames in their fight against the spectral energy that poured from within the Herald. Tendrils wound themselves around the arms and legs of the Herald, sapping any strength that had been gained in the moment of respite. But still the souls wailed, the keening growing stronger and stronger. Pike felt as though he was dying, but at the same time, he felt the freedom that lay in the blackness. On the outside, the souls cried out in fury and in pain, but in the darkness they beckoned for Pike to follow them. They wanted him to stop fighting against the pull of the mortal world. That was where the Creator reigned. That was where creatures like the Voice had power. Dorovar had shown Pike another way, another path. It was a path that led to power unlike any that any world had ever seen.

Pike surrendered to the call of the voices. In the blackness that fell over his vision, he felt trapped and damned, but once the fear began to fade, Pike realized that there was more than just darkness. A green glow suffused everything. He saw every rock and every tree, and around them all of the souls of the dead who had met their end there. Some had been freed from their mortal forms by the dragon that had made his den here, but a great many more had fallen from a myriad of other reasons. Some from old age, some from war, or famine, or a horrible accident. They all cried out to Pike, and he could hear them cursing the Creator with their last breath for their misfortune. Mothers cried out for their dead children, wanting to know why they were taken so soon. Children screamed for their dead fathers, wanting the angels to bring him back to them. The old and infirm, laying on their death beds wanting to know why they were made to suffer for so long. But there were no answers. Not for any of them. One by one, the spirits turned their attention to Pike, astonished that someone could hear their pain. His pain cried out to them, and they to him. Their dead eyes shifted from Pike to the being of light that assaulted him. The Creator was making Pike suffer, and through Pike they could have retribution for the indifference the Creator showed them. One by one, the sprits lent their power to the Chorus that Pike already touched. Whether they were giving themselves to Dorovar or they were simply seeking their own vengeance in a way that was finally open to them did not matter. They knew only one emotion now, blind rage.

The baleful song grew louder and more intense, beginning to shake the ground and the walls of rock around them. The wail was having a direct impact on the form of pure light as well. The two forces began to resonate with one another, the wail causing the brilliance to buckle under its weight. As the keening call intensified, the tendrils of light began to recede as the Voice struggled to keep its physical form intact against the spectral assault. However, nothing the Voice would do could prevent its fate. One great burst of sound shattered the Servants control, and the suffusion of light faded accompanied by a peel of thunder. Gregor collapsed, falling to his knees completely drained of all power. Not giving his opponent any time to recover, the ax was back in Pike's hands the next moment, and with a single precise strike, the blade of the phantasmal ax struck true, cleaving Gregor's head from his body. The strike was so precise that while the head tumbled away from the body, the decapitated form remained upright, weight shifted back and perfectly balanced. Blood flowed from the neck in all directions, like some gruesome fountain. Finally something shifted within the lifeless form, and the body of the former Servant of the Creator, and former Knight of the Flashing Blade slumped to one side.

For several long moments, Pike simply stood. He was not looking at his victim, nor was he looking at mass of spirits that whirled around him, gleefully adding their joyous voices to the Chorus of Souls. Instead Pike's view was turned north, turned to his next target. He had never heard of the place known as Glacier's Rift until he heard Dorovar speak of it, but what he did know was that enemies of Dorovar's called the place home, and that was enough. Dorovar had shown Pike the way, but it wasn't until Pike had surrendered to that power that he truly understood what it meant to be a Herald. Yes he had been betrayed, yes he had been left behind by those he loved and trusted, but none of that mattered now. All that mattered was doing what he was made to do. He was no longer Pike Rhuiden. He was Conquest. Power rushed through him, a new power unlike he had ever felt in his life as a member of the *Erieal* or as a Dark God. This was true power, and at that moment he knew his thoughts could shake the world. Dorovar had shown him the path, the path that he was always meant for, the path of a true hero. He would unseat the Creator. He would save all of humanity from their yoke of oppression. At last he had taken his rightful place in the narrative of the Cosmos.

Reaching out toward the ground, Conquest felt the bones of the fallen below him. With minimal effort he pulled some of them free of their tombs, erecting a single spike of bone that rose out of the ground ten feet high. A moment later, the head of the Voice lifted from the ground and impaled itself upon the spike, a final insult paid from the newest Herald to those that stood against his master. A portal opened the next instant, and Conquest was gone, leaving only the monument of his victory to tell the tale.

Wind of the Soul

Year Four of the Just Emperor Kaitain "Dragonsbane" Lorien, Creator's Calendar Year 1871

Aris Ebonsight stood dumbfounded looking up at the young man who called himself the Crown Prince of Iltorp. He sat idly, one leg draped over the arm of the throne, lounging back cleaning his nails as though he had just asked for a drink of water rather than the hand of one of the most powerful women in Cadaria. More than his words, there was something about the very essence of the man that made Aris instantly dislike him. It wasn't his arrogance, or his casual manner, because in some ways Aris had always found that enticing. Perhaps that was why she had a brief flirtation with Ayden Seth and all of the baggage that his constantly flippant attitude brought with it. No, there was something more to this Talon Aielin. Deep beneath his words there was dishonesty, a malice that could not be ignored. Before any of the other Masters, including her mother could speak, Aris took several steps forward toward the dais, bowing slightly before she spoke. Suddenly she remembered the last time that she was in the presence of someone with authority. She and her mother stood in front of the newly crowned Emperor Lorien, and as a result of that conversation, the Academy of Arcane Arts was cut off from the love and support of the Throne. It would later lead to the battle over control of the Academy and its eventual abandonment. Now, as Aris gave rise to her words once more, she worried what the outcome would be.

"Lord Talon," Aris said, letting calm fill her voice, "while I am flattered by the offer to become your wife and cement an alliance between the Academy of Arcane Arts and the royal family of Iltorp; you must understand that I have concerns."

Talon looked down his nose at Aris for a long moment before taking his leg off the arm of the throne and sitting forward, his elbows resting on his knees. Interlacing his fingers under his chin, Talon's eyes glistened with amusement.

"And pray tell, Master Ebonsight, what are these concerns?"

The innocent question dripped venom from his lips and tongue and as the words traveled the distance between Talon and Aris, the young woman felt them like an assault. A moment later a wave of dread passed over her heart and mind, and she felt as though the words were draining all of her will to resist. If she hadn't known any better, she would have sworn that the man had used some form of magic against her, but despite all her best efforts she could not see the flows of power if there were any. Or perhaps the truth was that the ability the man was using was so far beyond her, like those of the Dark Gods, that she could not understand them. However, knowing that the assault was happening gave Aris the time and the opportunity to erect some kind of defense. Without knowing exactly what was happening Aris' options were severely limited, but what she could do was flood herself with the flows of Fire and Wind, keeping her heart rate up, and the blood pumping through her system. The tactic would ward off apathy and weakness, but it would leave her open to her fear responses being manipulated. She hoped that her gamble would pay off.

"First and foremost, Lord Talon, I know that the royal family of Iltorp has no sons, which has been a significant issue for some time. Sir Vallic Ultiv has been trying to broker a marriage with either a noble from Thorigald or Saldarine without success. The two oldest daughters of the royal family would have to be married at almost the same time to the princes of the Kingdoms of Fire and Water in order for the Kingdom of Steam to become the neutral bridge between two kingdoms that have hated each other for centuries. How is it sir that you have come to be the Crown Prince of this kingdom?"

Aris could feel the man's smile behind his interlaced fingers. He straightened slightly, enough so that his mouth and chin were visible above his hands.

"I admire the fact that you are so well informed about the make-up and political dispositions of the royal families, Master Ebonsight. I'm sure in the world that you know, and the world that you have been raised in such information is important when negotiating treaties or looking for recruits to your academy. I personally have never had much use for royalty. Every interaction I have ever had with so-called royals has ended badly for the royals. The situation was no different here in Iltorp. The great and powerful Serpentine Knight Vallic Ultiv was part of the problem, and it was through his strength and influence that the shadow royals retained their power. This dream that you speak of, this desire for an uneasy alliance between three kingdoms that have been the most volatile in the west of Cadaria, is nothing more than a fantasy. It was a fantasy concocted by a brutal and manipulative scoundrel who wanted nothing more than to give the royalty a bauble to play with while the real decisions regarding the future of Cadaria were made outside of the halls of supposed power. But what no one realized, what no one could guess was that the true power in Iltorp was in the hands of a great villain. Though he wore the name Vallic Ultiv to the whole of Cadaria, he had another name. A cursed name. His true name and title. He was the Shadow, Jeroch Yetre, first-born of the Brotherhood of the Phasia."

There were blank looks on the faces of the Masters, looks that made Talon smile with self-satisfaction. These women, these supposedly learned women who were so secure in their knowledge of how the world truly worked, the powers that flowed through every tree and even the air itself. There were none living who knew the secrets that they knew, and yet, they were about to be faced with just how ignorant they truly were. Talon's smile widened as he spoke again.

"You would call him a Dark God."

The explosion that came the next moment was from Jastra Mythryn.

"Lies! How dare you impugn the reputation of one of the longest reigning members of the Knights of the Flashing Blade!"

Ashinica and Fiona struggled to hold Jastra back, but her rancor was diffused the next moment as Talon began laughing and reclined back on the throne once again, clapping his hands in delight.

"You see? You see how easy it has been for one of your greatest enemies to infiltrate the ranks of your sainted Knights and use that reputation to lie, scheme, and cheat his way into every corridor of power that would open to him. How many more of your precious knights are also members of that cursed group of fallen villains? How many of them are in league with the Dark Continent? You know of course that Hannah Ironheart's own sister is married to the leader of the Dark Gods. Where do you think her loyalties truly lie? What would you think if I told you that Gregor Quicksilver's father did not die on a mission to the Dark Continent, but instead chose to betray his lord and master the Emperor in favor of his own survival at the heel of one of the Dark Gods? I'm sure he made a nice and obedient pet."

Talon's words struck chords in each of the Masters, filling them with doubt. Though the doubt was not fueled by the words alone. Aris could feel the same waves of emotion on the air, and they fought against the defenses that Aris had erected. It seemed that her fellow Masters had not picked up on the flows of power as quickly as Aris had, and their minds and hearts were being weighted down. Perhaps because she was the Master of Air she had been more capable to detect the poison. Perhaps that was why this Talon Aielin wanted her hand in marriage; because he knew that she was the real threat to his schemes. Whatever his motives, he had not yet finished his character assassination of the Knights of the Flashing Blade, and thundered on with glee, the fog of dread and defeat becoming thicker with every uttered word.

"And then there is Natalia Pressen, the knight who has so many allegiances that even she doesn't know who she's working for. But no matter what anyone thinks, the Dark Gods have run the Shadow Guild from the moment that it came into existence. So even if she was on a mission for the Emperor it was at the allowance of the Grand Master of the Shadow Guild, the Viper himself. Devlin Rannoch, the half-dragon, half-man, all compromised would-be hero. Kaitain appointed him to the Knights to destabilize the whole group, but even Kaitain couldn't have foreseen the true traitor that Devlin would become. How could anyone have known that Devlin's lover was a member of the Dark Gods? Jaccob Aldora spent his last days at the side of a Dark God, and spent his last breath cursing the Creator. Perhaps the most disappointing is the seemingly untouchable Leonora Wastri. If only everyone knew that she spent her formative years as the student and the lover of one of the most traitorous and delusional of all the Dark Gods. What do you think of your all-powerful Knights of the Flashing Blade now? Do you think that it is their power that will save you from the horrible threat of the Dark Gods? How could they when that is where their orders come from?"

Talon let the words sink in for a long moment before locking his eyes back on Aris.

"In answer to your question, my dear young lady, I have taken control of this kingdom to save it. It had to be saved from the stain of the Dark Gods. And any kingdom whose royalty has been supplanted by the treachery of the Knights of the Flashing Blade and the Dark Gods must be removed and the power returned to the people. But in that vacuum there must be strong resourceful and respected people to take control. That is where you Masters can be most useful. Why shouldn't the Master of Fire be in command of the Kingdom of Fire? Why shouldn't the Master of Water be in command of the Kingdom of Water? Why shouldn't the Master of Stone be in command of the Kingdom of Stone? And why should not the Master of Energy rule any kingdom she wishes? These conventions that you have limited yourself to for so long have not simply prevented you from being a threat to the Empire, what it has truly done is prevented you from taking the true leadership position that you were always intended to have. What has held you back has not been prudence, it has been fear."

Aris felt a new pattern permeate the air. Greed, power, and need wove itself into the fabric of doubt and weakness. The combination created confusion and a thirst that could seemingly not be quenched. It was a brutal assault of manipulation, one so strong that even Aris was having difficulty resisting the waves of charged emotion. She could practically feel the power resonating through her body, and her mind was unable to resist the images flashing across her mind's eye of power, prestige and the trappings that were usually only reserved for the most avaricious of dreams. However, the emotions flooding the air like the stench of rotting meat could not have done their job alone. Talon was speaking the words that created the images, and he was playing his audience as masterfully as any bard. And even as he spoke his next words, Aris felt her own emotions being plucked like the tense strings of a finely crafted lyre.

"My patron can make your wildest dreams come true, and all he asks in return is that you shed this archaic naiveté and use the abilities that you have developed to aid him and your fellow mortals in their battle against the blasphemous horde that wants only their destruction. Fight, urge your students to fight and make this world tremble with your power. How little is that to give for all of the things that my patron can offer?"

The next moment, the doors to the throne room creaked open, and as new light from the advancing sunset flooded into the room, it served as an eerie backlight to the figure that strode through the opening. The long brown hair, the plain but imposing armor, and the large mace with the feel of something vicious and alive, they were all the well-known visual identifiers of the woman known as the Celestine Knight of the Flashing Blade, Hannah Ironheart. However, what the woman was most known for, both by her admirers and her adversaries were the stormy blue-gray eyes that spoke of the power that coursed through the woman's body, the power granted to her by her faith and devotion. Wordlessly, Hannah marched down the long carpeted path to the dais, stopping just short of where Aris Ebonsight stood. She took one long look at the man sitting on the throne before speaking.

"Your patron is nothing more than a pretender and a charlatan. He has trod on the Creator's name for so long; he may actually believe that he is the Creator. But the Masters of the Academy of Arcane Arts are under my protection, as are all of their students. They need nothing from a puppet like you."

The strong words of the imposing woman were enough to break the little hold that Talon's spell held over Aris' heart. Hannah also seemed to have an effect on the befuddled minds of the other Masters as Aris could see a spark begin to return to their eyes. It was a light of defiance and pride. If Talon was impacted by the woman's presence, it didn't show on his face. On the contrary, he lounged back as casually as ever as though he had been expecting her.

"And what of your patron, Hannah Ironheart?" Talon asked. "Is he any less a pretender? Constantly spouting his rhetoric about changing the world, and yet he barely lifts a finger to make a difference himself. Always he lets others do the work for him, afraid to get his hands dirty, putting everyone else at risk for his ideals. He is the pretender if there ever was one."

Hannah smiled.

"Aerith knows what he is, and those that follow him now do so because they believe in him and in his cause. Can you say the same thing, Talon? Are you working for Emries because you want to be, or because he is holding your strings so tightly?"

Finally Talon was moved to do more than simply smirk. He was on his feet the next moment, a spear made of pure crystal appearing in his hands.

"Coming here was a mistake, Hannah," Talon said finally. "I was content to simply turn the Masters and their students to Emries' cause, but now that you are here, I'm going to take the opportunity to remove one of Aerith's little pets from this war. I wonder how he'll react once he learns that I cut you open and left your body out to rot. But your interruption has also interfered with my ability to manipulate the Academy, so I shall have no choice but to eliminate them too. Perhaps that is for the best. At least I know that they won't fight back. And you, little knight, will be able to do nothing to stop me."

Rather than making a move himself, Talon motioned in the direction of the sides of the throne room and dozens of heavily armed soldiers flooded into the room. Their armor was emblazoned not with the symbol of the Kingdom of Iltorp, but rather with the crest of a springing lion. Hannah's blood burned instantly, but she didn't immediately understand why. It wasn't until the memories from Aerith and Logan flooded in the fill the gap that she realized the insult that was being perpetrated. Cedric Binosear in life had been the Lord Lion, the first to be duped into Emries' false prophecies. For Emries to invoke his name in this place and in this time was nothing more than a slap in the face of every one of the Dark Gods. But more than that, it was another petty mind game, meant to illicit enough of a response to keep them all off balance. Hannah however had no tie to Cedric or his sacrifices; all she saw was another enemy to defeat. That thought stopped her cold. Again Aerith's influence was strong, urging her to take on incredible odds simply because she could. However, she would not be possessed to move to such rash acts. Reaching out with the new abilities that Aerith had granted her she began to realize that the soldiers were not acting of their own volition. There were no thoughts coming from the men, no emotions, and no sense that they had any awareness of where they were. Hannah reached into the mind of one of the soldiers and was disturbed to find the man's mind was empty except for one thought that screamed in a voice that Hannah instantly recognized as possessed of divine power. That word was simply 'obey'. As Hannah pulled away from the soldiers' mind, she saw the glimmer of recognition in Talon's eyes.

"I see you understand," he said after a moment. "These are just the first. With Nathan and Draven's help we converted thousands. Korrd so far has chosen to lead his forces through the force of his own will, but in time those soldiers that survive his next offensive will be converted to mindless slaves. Now, say goodbye to your pathetic rebellion."

Talon pointed his spear in Hannah's direction.

"Kill them all, then level the keep of the Serpentine Knight and eliminate the refugees there and anyone else that stands in your way."

As one, the three dozen soldiers advanced, brandishing their weapons. As much as it pained Hannah to fight men whose wills had been subverted, she realized that she might not have any choice in the matter. A moment later though, she was given a second option. She felt hundreds of tiny flows of power all around her, and then she saw dozens upon dozens of portals no larger than a foot in diameter open all around the throne room. Out of the portals balls of fur began to pour out, blanketing the floor like a massive rug made of patches of white, brown, and black. A larger portal, but still only about two feet across opened beside Hannah and a much larger black ball of fur emerged. This one however was trailing a whisper thin tail and had a wide mouth filled with razor-sharp teeth and brilliant eyes that gleamed with intelligence. Hannah knew immediately what the creatures were, and when the large black ball bounded from the ground onto Hannah's shoulder, she felt a wave of ease fill her. The Snags had come to protect her from the threat and to give her time to escape. The appearance of the blanket of Snags had caused the advancing troops to pause, waiting for further command from Talon. Talon for his part looked somewhat dismayed at the arrival of the Snags.

"Not these things again," he growled. "Advance. Kill them all."

Before the soldiers could take another step forward, the Snags began to bounce in a rhythm that only they understood, and Hannah took that as the signal to flee. Reaching out, she took Aris by the arm and pulled her toward the doors to the throne room. The other Masters, struck dumb with the unexplainable sight fell in as the two women ran past. Once they were moving the right direction, Hannah released Aris' arm and brought Spirit to bear ready to counter the assault of any of the other mindless warriors that would attempt to block their escape. As the small group fled, Hannah saw flashes of movement appear at the corners of her vision, however, every time she turned to face the on-coming opponent, one of the powerful balls of fur would leap in from the opposite direction and either whirl through with impossibly sharp tail or crushing bite. Not a single soldier was able to able to strike a blow during their flight through the halls of the palace, and as they broke through the front gates and down the long flight of steps that led to the palace and tasted the advancing evening air, for a long moment they felt as though they were going to make an escape. However, such was not the case. Waiting in the courtyard outside the palace were almost five hundred more troops, standing in formation. As soon as they saw the five women, the soldiers raised their weapons. Even as Hannah processed the tactical nightmare they had stumbled into, the most diminutive of the Masters, Ashinica Maupin extended her hands toward the detachment of soldiers. A moment later, the ground began to shake. Jastra reached out and took hold of Ashinica's arm.

"You can't, it violates the code."

Ashinica pulled her arm free.

"Damn the code. This is our lives we're talking about. We can defend ourselves. We have a responsibility to our students, and we can't protect them if we die here."

The ground rumbled again the next moment, chunks of cobblestone breaking off from the greater whole as they lurched and twisted under the strain. Cracks began to form in the ground, and the soldiers shifted to try to keep their balance. What happened next caused Hannah to look over her shoulder at the oldest of the Masters. Gouts of flames leapt up from the cracks Ashinica created. Try as they might the soldiers were unable to avoid all of the attacks and many dropped their weapons attempting to shield their faces from the heat. Aris Ebonsight added her powers next, creating a great wind that whipped around the soldiers, surrounding them in oppressive heat and scorching flame. The final strike came when Jastra sighed hard and extended a single hand toward the conflagration. Something detonated in the center of the maelstrom, a great light suffusing the entire courtyard. Hannah had to shield her eyes, but when the light faded, Hannah was astonished to see that all that remained of the detachment of soldiers were smoking corpses. By this time a group of the bouncing and menacing Snags emerged from the palace, and they flanked the women as they fled the palace ground. Even as they ran, more soldiers were claimed by the Snags, but many more commoners joined the retreat. Hannah could feel their fear, and understood immediately that the new regime in Iltorp had been consecrated through fear and intimidation by the mindless soldiers. The ever growing-group finally reached the edge of the city of Iltorp with roughly two hundred men, women, and children in tow and an escort of easily a thousand Snags. However, as difficult and bloody as their escape had been to that point, they were not ready for what greeted them in the space between the capitol city and the Keep of the Serpentine Knight.

It was immediately apparent that in the time that the Masters were kept waiting for their audience, the so-called crown prince had assembled his massive army. Ranks and ranks of men stood ready to be loosed on their target, several thousand strong of single-minded destructive force. They would fight to the last man, killing everything in their path, and would be overwhelming through sheer number. There were screams that came from the civilians, and Hannah could feel the great fear coming from them.

While the Masters had been impressive in dispatching a few hundred soldiers in an enclosed area, Hannah knew that they had never pushed their powers to deal with an on-rushing army of thousands, and that if they encountered a distraction it would make any attempt defense futile. Hannah inwardly wondered if even Aerith or Logan could handle so many while still protecting the innocent. Before Hannah could go any further in her processing of the situation there was a deafening eruption of thunder overhead. But as Hannah looked skyward, she did not see gathering storm clouds or flashing of lightning, instead she saw huge winged creatures that threatened to blacken the sky with their mass and number. As the moments passed, more of the gargantuan creatures came into view, and the first sped toward the ground, crashing directly into the middle of the ranks of soldiers. Hundreds died in the first assault, and as another touched down, and then another, the battle was joined in earnest. In less than a minute six dragons had plunged into the ranks of the soldiers, and hundreds were already dead. As the stunned assemblage watched the death and destruction, the protective barrier of Snags increased in size. With morbid curiosity Hannah suddenly wondered how the diminutive but powerful creatures would manage against something as overwhelming as a dragon. Those thoughts were purged from Hannah's mind the next moment as another dragon touched down, albeit less violently several feet from where Hannah stood. The knight was forced to smile as the gleaming claws and piercing eyes of Mariti Brightblade came into view.

"Hannah Ironheart," the dragon growled, "I have met with my brothers and sisters, and we have discussed your offer of alliance."

For a brief moment Mariti looked back at the onslaught that raged behind her before turning back to lock eyes with Hannah.

"We have accepted."

Authenteo

Year One of the Divine Empress and Child of the Creator
Marlae Tamerlane, Creator's Calendar Year 1871

It had only been a few hours since the Divine Empress's address that
turned Hannah Ironheart from a simple servant of the Creator into a saint,
and Krysis sat in his quarters staring at the wall fuming. The show had
been artfully planned, and would have had the desired effects on the
masses, but it was nothing more than a show. Saints were an invention of
the mortals to reward those they believed to be pious. But mortals were
inherently flawed simply by the fact that they were made by a Child of the
Creator and not the Creator Himself. Emries was an arrogant controlling
demagogue who wanted nothing more than to rule everything. But his
control took the form of ensuring that he was the only person that knew
what was going on at any given time, and the people who followed him
were operating under the influence of delusions and lies at all times.
Emries told his followers what they needed to know and nothing more, and
most of that time the information was either outright lies or at least tailored
to elicit a particular response. It was a brilliant strategy really. And it had
worked rather effectively, until even Emries could not keep the lies he was
telling straight. That allowed the people he was trying so hard to
manipulate to begin to manipulate him. What remained in the wake of
Emries' fall were a trail of broken followers, caught between the misery of

life without the power that their patron had bestowed upon them and an existence fraught with enemies who craved their deaths because of who they once so faithfully served. Thus there were creatures like Azure floating around the Cosmos trying desperately to attach themselves to anything that would redeem them in the eyes of the Creator. Now Azure was demeaning himself by serving a mortal. The worst part for him was the fact that he knew that his former patron was out there gathering an army.

Azure was once a general. He led Emries' forces into battle and yearned to do so again. Battle was being waged out in the world, and Azure had been reduced to the lowest form of life, a politician. Now Azure spent his days and nights trying to outmaneuver a little girl and the weaklings who gathered around her. Emries was a master at manipulation, and Azure was nothing more than a novice who saw himself as powerful. But really, Azure was a spoiled child who had all of his toys taken away from him, and now he was doing everything he could possibly do to hurt those who he felt were responsible. He wanted to make the Dark Gods pay, he wanted to make them suffer, and right now the best way he could do that was to pervert the will of the newly minted Divine Empress, and make her see them as a threat. However, once the woman Anabel Binosear came into the picture, such a resolution became impossible. Anabel was a member of the Dark Gods, at least by extension, and she was far superior in the realm of politics than all of the people around the Divine Empress. Azure was out of his depth, and with this latest failure that culminated in the sanctifying of Hannah Ironheart, he was now impotent to control the actions of anyone.

Krysis was under no such delusions about his role in the world, or about how he could be most effective in executing his duties. He had been dispatched by the Creator as a military consultant to the Divine Empress, as a show of faith in her ability to remedy the dysfunctions that plagued the world. At least, that is what everyone would tell the little brat. The Creator didn't care about the politics of this world, or any world. His only interest was in the fate of his Children and of his Servants. The rest was simply collateral damage. Krysis had much more important tasks to accomplish, and many more people to punish for their wrongdoing.

Krysis moved to the far side of his room and lifted the mirror from off of the wall and set it on the floor. A moment later he was channeling a mere trickle of power to create a swirling blue portal. Once the portal had formed fully, Krysis lifted the mirror and gently pushed it into the portal, holding it in place until he felt the slight pull from the portal ease. Krysis stepped away from the portal and quickly fell to one knee with his head bowed. For several moments the mirror hung there, with no reaction to the still swirling portal, but finally the glass of the mirror began to glow. When the glow receded, the mirror was black. The blackness began to fade and the image of a woman appeared. The woman had a deep frown and her eyes stared coldly into the void.

"Report, Krysis."

Though he remained on one knee, Krysis raised his head and locked eyes with the woman.

"Azure and the others are chasing their tails as expected. They want to remain focused on the problem of Kaitain. However, the newest addition, this Anabel Binosear, she sees more than any of them. She wants to unite the world under a single banner, and it seems that her favor is growing. Before long the girl will listen to no one other than her."

The woman in the mirror pondered for a moment.

"Can you help to steer them away from my interests."

Krysis tilted his head.

"I am doing my best to ensure that the areas of concern are more enticing than any location you choose to work in. But at some point this Anabel Binosear could complicate matters. If she tries to advocate for alliance with the Dark Gods…"

The woman thundered.

"That cannot be allowed to come to pass. Under no circumstances can that woman be allowed to give the Dark Gods a foothold in Cadaria. That will upset all of my plans. If you cannot control this woman, then you must eliminate her."

Krysis frowned.

"I have no expectations that I can control her."

The answer came quickly.

"Eliminate her. Now."

The image in the mirror faded and the portal immediately closed, letting the mirror fall to the ground and shatter. Krysis sighed to himself and waived one hand. The pieces of the mirror began to slowly pull themselves back together and recreate the whole. Once the mirror had been repaired, it levitated from the ground and re-hung itself on the wall. Krysis remained on one knee and sighed once more with his head hung.

"As you command, Lady Talisia."

* * * * * * * * * * * *

Groups of angels were departing the Flying Kingdom of Hedorah all morning, shoring up the defenses of the Heart of Stone in keeping with the agreement made by the Divine Empress Marlae Tamerlane. The High Priestess Baeata Catrinel was expected to arrive as soon as the last of the angelic warriors arrived in Albitonin, and the final arrangements had been agreed upon. However, unlike the public declaration of Hannah Ironheart's sainthood, no meeting between the Divine Empress and the High Priestess would be conducted in the eyes of the common man. Those conversations would shatter the veneer of confidence that the Divine Empress had instilled in her burgeoning empire. No, any talks between the two women of power would happen behind closed doors, and most of those conversations would likely take an unpleasant tone before too long. But the important task was to ensure that these two powerful women could have an open dialogue and have a real chance to forge an agreement between the new Divine Empire and the Church of the Creator. Early in the morning, Marlae Tamerlane entered consultation with her High Councilor and remained in such seclusion for the majority of the day. Not even her other advisors, Terrance Aldora or the divine emissaries Azure and Krysis, were allowed to enter. The only other person that saw the Divine Empress was her personal servant. However, once evening began to descend on Hedorah, and the appearance of Baeata Catrinel became imminent, the

Divine Empress emerged from the seclusion of her private chambers and moved to the more spacious War Room in her private wing. At this time, Terrance Aldora and Reverend Mother Amallia were admitted, but Azure and Krysis were still left waiting on the outside. The High Councilor waited in a private hallway with Isabelle for the portal to open. She was not waiting long, and just at nine bells, a swirling blue portal opened and two women emerged. The High Priestess was dressed in impressive ceremonial armor, while her personal aide, Aelind Torral was dressed very conservatively. Anabel bowed slightly, enough to be respectful, and upon straightening began to speak.

"High Priestess," Anabel said in her most regal voice, "welcome to the court of the Divine Empress, Marlae Tamerlane. The Divine Empress regrets the fact that she could not welcome you herself, but protocol demands that you be met by your equal in power and importance, and for her to welcome you herself would be to give the wrong impression to those who are watching. I'm sure you understand. I am the Divine Empress's High Councilor Anabel Binosear. Welcome to Hedorah."

Baeata nodded, and did her best to disguise her confusion.

"I trust that the travel was not too disorienting."

The High Priestess forced a smile.

"While it certainly does have the advantage of saving time, I can't help but feel a little uneasy traveling by such means. No matter my position, I am just a common woman in the service of the Creator. Being directly touched by divine power is, humbling."

Anabel frowned slightly.

"Then I'm sure being guarded by angelic warriors is almost unbearable."

Aelind stepped forward with her lips twisted into a snarl.

"Are you mocking the High Priestess of the Church of the Creator? First you insult her by saying that she is not good enough to be welcomed by the Divine Empress herself, and now you mock her beliefs and her humility? You should be ashamed of yourself, and you should bow down and beg her forgiveness."

Anabel waited for Baeata to let the words sink in. The High Priestess blushed slightly in embarrassment and then put her hand out on her aide's arm.

"You'll have to forgive Aelind, High Councilor. She speaks her mind at times when it is not prudent, but her heart is always in the right place. In life she was a servant and was never given the ability to have opinions of her own. Lady Ironheart always encouraged her to use her voice whenever she could."

Anabel smiled.

"There is nothing wrong with speaking one's mind, so long as one knows that there are people who would cut out your tongue rather than listen to you. It is a harsh world, with harsh rules, and harsh consequences for those unable or unwilling to abide."

Anabel took a long moment to let her words sink in before she continued.

"I understand your need to protect your patron, Aelind, and I respect that, which is why I shall answer your challenge in this way. I have been in the presence of great heroes, gods, angels, and Children of the Creator. Now I stand at the side of a woman who has been given the ultimate chance to redeem what she once was, and serve at the right hand of the Creator on this world. I choose to show deference, even though she has given me the right to speak my mind. There is nobility and grace in her, and that should be respected. Telling truth to power is a gift Aelind, which you should never squander. But in this place in this time, I would advise that you leave the speaking to the High Priestess, and serve her the best way you can. And that would be by keeping your eyes and ears open at all times, and understand better what is not being said."

Aelind nodded.

"Thank you, High Councilor. I shall endeavor to serve my mistress to the best of my ability and to temper my enthusiasm."

Anabel smiled.

"I'm sure you will," Anabel replied. "Now, High Priestess Baeata Catrinel, I shall lead you to the presence of the Divine Empress."

* * * * * * * * * * *

When the door opened, Marlae wasn't sure what to expect. She knew that Baeata was a formidable woman, which was going to be the case because of the faith that Hannah Ironheart had placed in her. Hannah did not have time for timidity, and because of the fierce woman that she was, there was no doubt that the woman who was her successor would be fierce as well. The woman who entered walked with grace and purpose, and the light gray padded leather armor that she wore gave her the appearance of a warrior. Her blond hair was short and shone brightly, a sign that the woman cared about how she presented herself to her flock. When she was fully in the room, she moved gently to the center of the floor opposite the gilded chair where Marlae sat and waited. Anabel entered the room only a couple of steps behind Baeata, and moved to her side in the center of the floor. She bowed quickly to Marlae, and then raised her voice.

"Divine Empress Marlae Tamerlane, let me present to you the High Priestess of the Church of the Creator, as well as the acting ruler of the Kingdom of Albitonin, Baeata Catrinel."

Baeata bowed deeply and stayed bowed for several seconds before finally straightening and folding her hands behind her back.

"Thank you, Your Grace, for the invitation to meet with you. I am sorry that I could not come directly, and I'm sure you understand that the safety and security of my people had to be my first priority. Please know that I meant no disrespect."

Marlae smiled and sat forward in her chair.

"And the reason that I did not resist your requests is because I understood the need to protect your people, as they are my people as well. There are threats all over this world, and as long as the Heart of Stone is standing, there will be those that wish to tear it down. My former father has dedicated himself to destroying all worship of the Creator, and he will not rest until he has pulled down all of your holy sites, and has brought low all those speaking the word. He and his forces are not content to target the heads of the Church. While most despots would simply cut off the head of the snake and wait for the body to die, Kaitain Lorien is not a simple man in such regard. He will gladly kill Hannah Ironheart, you and me. But he will also destroy every church, every priest, every acolyte, and enslave everyone who dares to bend a knee in prayer."

Marlae let her words sink in for a moment before continuing.

"However, I am heartened by the fact that you recognized that you could not defend the Heart of Stone on your own. It is clear that we need one another, High Priestess Catrinel, and I am hoping that at the conclusion of this conversation that we shall be able to cement an alliance that will last as long as my Empire stands."

Baeata hesitated a beat and then spoke. Her tone was deferent and respectful, but there was an underlying confidence that was easily felt.

"Your Grace," she began slowly, "Kaitain Lorien is a blight upon this world, and his threat extends far beyond those that worship the Creator. He cares nothing for the rights and lives of the common man. He cares nothing for his own power and his warmongering ways. The people tire of war. Your people tire of war. There are many suffering, and many more that have been robbed of any way to feed their families. Hunger and destitution reign in the lands, except among the noble families who still hold some power and sway. There are some reports from kingdoms of record numbers joining the military so that they will be able to ensure that they eat. So far, Celidar and Albitonin are the only kingdoms that are thriving."

A concerned look came to Marlae's face.

"We have not heard such reports."

Instead of Baeata answering, Amallia added her voice to the conversation.

"Your Grace, the Church of the Creator has missionaries in every Kingdom across Cadaria, and chains of messengers to pass this information quickly across the Empire."

Baeata continued.

"Until now, the Church has been hesitant to make these information chains visible to anyone outside the highest ranking members of the Church, but as Amallia has just demonstrated, the Church trusts the investment of the Creator within you, Divine Empress, and so, these resources that we have, are gladly given over to you."

Marlae's hands tensed on the arms of the chair, but before she could speak, Baeata smiled and spoke once more.

"There is no need to worry about the position of the Church of the Creator, Your Grace. The Church of the Creator gladly recognizes that you are the one chosen to lead us, and have been touched by the hand of the divine. To deny that would be to deny everything that we believe in. Consider myself and all who serve the Church at your disposal from now until the end of your Empire."

Marlae smiled, and motioned behind her. The next moment, Isabella emerged with a chair and sat it gently beside where Baeata stood. It was a great gesture of trust and understanding. Baeata bowed and slowly sat, her eyes never leaving the Divine Empress.

"So, Baeata," Anabel ventured, "please share with us the information that your messengers and missionaries have brought to your attention."

Baeata looked over her shoulder, and Aelind moved quickly to her side and handed her several pieces of folded parchment. After taking a moment to review and order the pages, Baeata began to speak.

"To say that the people of Cadaria are fragmented is being kind, Your Grace. The west is in tatters. The war between Saldarine and Thorigald continues to escalate, and there are reports of a massive detachment of the Army of Fire that even now prepares to cross the border and march straight for the capitol. It is unclear as to whether or not the direction for this invasion is coming from Lady Chelsea Zarova, or Kaitain Lorien.

Iltorp has largely kept to itself, but there are reports that there have been changes in the leadership of the royal family. Vallic Ultiv has disappeared and a new prince has been speaking for the royals. Galateria has also remained silent, but thus far the word is that Galateria has no love for Kaitain Lorien and continues to hold it tentative ties to the rebellion that Albitonin began. Unfortunately we have lost all communication with Oradrim and Menoris. Though communication from those locations has always been troublesome, now they are completely silent."

Baeata flipped through a few more pages, and then continued.

"The most disturbing reports are coming from the east. Kaitain Lorien and the Imperial Guard are advancing on Zevarit, and because of the near civil war that has broken out there, it won't take the Imperial Legion long to remove the royals and place the kingdom under Kaitain's direct control. Rashaleb is still largely in ruins, and information coming from that kingdom is fragmented at best. Pellatori continues to be loyal to the rule of Kaitain Lorien, and there is no expectation that will change. Expectation is that the Imperial Legion will march there following its subjugation of Zevarit. Bellnoc remains verbally loyal to Kaitain Lorien, however, with the Shadow Guild largely in control of that kingdom, it's hard to know exactly where they stand. That has always been the one stronghold that missionaries of the Church of the Creator have never been able to infiltrate. Most disturbing is the news coming from Celidar, I'm afraid."

Here Baeata paused and cleared her throat.

"Your uncle, Feyd Lorien, has declared the Kingdom of Celidar a protectorate."

Marlae leaned forward.

"Under his control? Has he declared himself Emperor?"

Baeata frowned.

"No. He has declared that Celidar is under the protection of the Dark Gods. Lord and Lady Mystic have been revealed as Dark Gods, and the people love them."

Terrance was white faced, and Marlae could see that Amallia was praying to herself. However, it was Anabel that added her voice next.

"Though many of you may be disturbed by this news, I am not. I have known Jerrard and Erika for a very long time, and they are good people. They will see to the protection of Celidar, and they will ensure that their people are not casualties of this war."

Suddenly Terrance found his voice.

"Did you know they were Dark Gods?"

There was no hesitation from Anabel.

"Yes."

If there was an explosion of emotion coming, a raised hand from the Divine Empress stropped it from getting out of control.

"Anabel has been forthcoming with me about what she does and does not know about the Dark Gods. Our consultation this morning was about more than the state of my Empire, and was certainly about far more than strategy in meeting with the High Priestess about an alliance. There are many dangers both within and outside of Hedorah's borders, and I would be a fool if I did not consider all options. Though the revelation of Lord and Lady Mystic's status is a surprise to me, Anabel's faith in them allays all fears I would have. It does however make reaching out to them a much more paramount task. We must secure their favor, and thusly bring my uncle into the fold."

Terrance growled.

"They are Dark Gods, Your Grace. How can they be trusted?"

Marlae looked at Anabel and nodded.

"Do you trust me, Terrance?"

Terrance nodded.

"You have done everything in your power to protect the Divine Empress and ensure that this new Empire has a long and fruitful life. I have never seen or sensed any duplicity in you, and though at times you are blunt and borderline disrespectful, I have come to appreciate your honesty."

Anabel smiled.

"Then appreciate when I tell you that there is more nobility in the Dark Gods than you could imagine, and that your Cadarian royals could learn from their dedication to doing what is right. I have advised the Divine Empress to seek an alliance with some members of the Dark Gods, those I trust. Those whom I have had dealings with for almost my entire life. You see, I have more experience than any of you with the Dark Gods, because under your definition, I am one."

Before anyone could react to Anabel's words, the door to the war room burst open, and a hulking angelic warrior charged through. He raised a flaming spear and prepared to throw it. Terrance could see that the weapon was aimed not at the Divine Empress, but at Anabel. Just as the weapon left the angel's hand, Terrance intervened, jumping between the angel and Anabel, taking the tip of the spear in his chest. He fell to the ground, and Anabel reacted the next moment. Even as the angel was forming a flaming sword it its hand, Anabel moved in front of Marlae and erected a shield of transparent energy that covered both the Divine Empress and the High Priestess. With her free hand, Anabel lashed out with a beam of energy that claimed the angel in the shoulder and forced it to drop its flaming weapon. Undeterred, the angelic warrior raised both hands and loosed a stream of divine fire against the shield. In a matter of seconds it started to buckle under the strain. Anabel was beginning to think about how to protect Marlae and get her out of the line of fire when suddenly the assault relented. The angel slumped to the ground, its head rolling clear of its body. Behind the angel, with flaming sword still in hand stood the diminutive Isabella. Anabel released the shield and moved quickly to Terrance's side as more angels streamed into the room. However, instead of attacking, they took defensive positions around the room ensuring that no further assaults would be coming. Anabel looked down into Terrance's eyes, but it was clear he was gone.

CHAPTER 84

* * * * * * * * * * * *

Krysis turned away from the door that led to the Divine Empress's war room. Perhaps he had been foolish to trust such an important mission to a blunt instrument. Next time, however, he would not allow anything to stand in the way of completing his assigned task.

Chapter LXXXV

The Flickering Flame

Year Four of the Just Emperor Kaitain "Dragonsbane" Lorien,
Creator's Calendar Year 1871

When Logan's eyes opened, all he saw was darkness for several long moments before the clouds over his vision began to clear. At first, he could barely make out contrast between light and darkness, and then collections of hazy shadows. The light and shadows simply swirled, and there was no sound, not even a low buzz. Shadows began to resolve into swirls of color and then finally definite shapes. The foreground of his vision cleared into sharp reality, and he could see Jillian's concerned face hovering over him. She must have recognized that his eyes had focused on her face, as a smile came to her lips and relief touched her eyes. She began to speak, but he couldn't hear any sound attached to her words. There was also a lingering red haze at the edges of his vision. Finally, as though a layer of thick cotton had been removed from his ears, her voice began to force its way through the nothingness.

"Are you alright? You've been unconscious for almost a whole day."

He smiled but didn't try to speak. His surroundings were familiar but it was as though his mind was fighting to place what his eyes were telling him. He was certainly not still lying on the harsh ground in the wasteland that used to be Menoris. It was warmer than he expected it to be, and the air was far dryer. As he looked around, he didn't see any signs of the devastation caused by the fall of the Peaks of Patience or the battle with the walking corpses that followed. There was also no sign of Kamen or the remains of the creature that called itself Death. Slowly Logan started to mouth words, but when he tried to exert his voice, no sound came out. His throat felt as though he had spent a month in the desert with no water. He tried to swallow and ignored the pain that rocketed through his throat.

"Where?"

His voice was gravelly and weak and sounded completely alien to his ears, even with the feeling of everything being completely muffled. Jillian leaned down and kissed him gently on the forehead and then put her arms around him and started to lift him into a sitting position. He tried hard to help her, to exert some kind of strength into his muscles, but it was to no avail. When he tried to reach for the powers of the Blaze to heal his body and suffuse himself with the strength that had fled, the brilliant green flame could not be found. The Blaze was fickle, and would not just appear when beckoned, but there was always its ghostly presence there in the darkness of his mind. But there was nothing, not even a hint of the green glow. Next Logan tried to pull upon the powers granted to him by Aerith Seth. Unlike the Blaze, the mantle of the *Chosen One* was not a physical living entity. Aerith's powers were more like a fog that coated every part of Logan. Most of the time, the application of that power was unconscious. If he needed to heal, or conjure a weapon, or increase his speed or agility, it took merely a thought. Some additional effort was required for things like portals or channeling the primal forces of nature, but the power was always at his disposal, conscious or not. Now though, as he thought about the powers, and thought about applying them, there was nothing there. Finally he had no choice but to surrender and allow Jillian to pull him into a sitting position.

When he was finally sitting upright, the details of the place where he was were more apparent. He recognized the chamber as the Heart of Flame. It was the most sacred and protected place for the Order of the Flickering Flame, and lay near the core of the mostly dormant volcano that formed the foundation of the Peaks of Patience. The chambers consisted of long-quiet lava tubes and thermal exhaust vents that formed elaborate catacombs in the mountain's once turbulent interior. Over the past fifteen hundred years, the members of the Order of the Flickering Flame had turned these natural formations of fury and unrest into sanctuaries of ultimate calm and serenity. This place had been Kamen's home ever since Logan found him wandering Espre without purpose. Together they turned a group of disenfranchised and troubled wanderers into one of the most powerful and dedicated forces for the betterment of Espre. Of course it didn't take long for the Order of the Flickering Flame to be targeted by the Church of the Creator. Several members of the church tried to infiltrate the Order, tried to destroy it from the inside. However the people who had joined the Flickering Flame were seeking something better, and knew that they were in the right place, at the right time, to effect the right change in their lives. No practiced words about the Creator were going to change their minds. All these infiltrators did was to further strengthen the resolve of the members of the Order.

"You were laying there, bleeding, and I thought you were dead, and I didn't know what I was supposed to do, and then Kamen just gets up. He still had the hole in his stomach and his back, but he got up off the ground and walked over to me. He picked you up and carried you all the way down here. He's been sitting in the other room meditating the whole time. There are a couple of your Order running around here making sure that there is food and fresh water available when you need it, but you can tell that they are just trying to stay busy because they don't know what else to do. I can't imagine what they are going through. They've lost everything, and yet they still want to be useful."

Logan leaned forward and tried his best to take a long deep breath. Half-way into the breath, his chest spasmed, and he couldn't prevent the ragged cough that shook him. Jillian's arms firmed up, and she held him tightly, wanting both to be a comfort and also to make sure that he didn't injure himself. Finally the coughing subsided, and Logan was able to take a long slow deep breath. His body was still weak, and for the first time since his days on Onea, he felt human. It was like the clock in this body had begun moving again. He no longer felt timeless and immortal, and he certainly didn't feel like a god.

"Kamen said you'd be weak. That I should bring you to him when you finally woke up."

Jillian was trying to be comforting, but her voice betrayed the worry and uncertainty. She had been through a lot in a relatively short amount of time, and had been introduced to a much larger world that most people would never be able to comprehend. Logan reached up and took her hand, squeezing it as tightly as he could manage. As if taking the unspoken direction, Jillian got back to her feet and pulled Logan upright. It took a great deal of effort, but finally Logan was on his feet. As soon as Logan's legs were under him, he could feel the weakness streaming through his legs, and his knees were on the verge of buckling. However once he took a single step, he felt as though his strength were starting to return, at least in some minor measure. He was slowed, and felt as though he weighed ten times more than he should have, but at least he was back on his feet. Jillian led Logan through the passages that he still remembered as though he had just been their yesterday until Logan saw Kamen sitting in the center of a floor, his eyes closed and his head bowed. However, before either Jillian or Logan said a word, Kamen raised his head and smiled.

"The Phoenix has risen."

Logan could not help but smile. As much as he sometimes hated the devotion that the members of the Order had shown him, and as much as sometimes he resented the fact that it had been Kamen that stayed with the Order to guide them while Logan went off to lead his new life as an irritant, he was comforted by the large man's constancy. It also helped him lay the groundwork for the war that was coming. Logan looked to Jillian, and the woman helped him over to the center of the room where he sank down onto his knees.

"You're still stubborn," Logan said after a moment, which brought a wry smile to the giant man's face.

Kamen first looked at Logan and then up at Jillian. She hesitated for a moment unsure what to do, but Logan reached up, took her hand, and pulled her down beside him. Once she was sitting, Logan motioned for Kamen to continue.

"When Halicon made me, like the other original six, we were made to last for eternity. There was nothing on Onea or in the Heavens that would end our lives so long as the Blaze still burned. The Blaze was eternal, and so we were eternal. Even though Halicon is gone, the Blaze still burns. It burned through Sabrina Binosear, and now it burns through Rhain Seth. The irony is not lost on me. Too many of our siblings are gone, Phoenix, and too many of my contemporaries. The Fox and The Shadow still draw breath, but The Leopard and The Shark are gone. Even the redoubtable Aryx Terian has left this eternity to find peace. Perhaps in time the Blaze will no longer burn, and I too will find peace."

A moment later, one of the members of the Order scurried into the room. He knelt down, whispered something in Kamen's ear, and then scurried out again. Logan could practically feel the fear rolling off the man like sweat. Kamen sat, his look pensive, before he finally returned his gaze to Logan.

"It appears as though we have a visitor. The remaining members of the Order were very cautions in approaching him, but he made it very clear that he was not here out of any malice, and meant none of us any harm, but that he was here specifically to meet with the one called Logan Ranthall, the Phoenix."

Logan perked up a little at the name, and then found himself rising back to his feet. He stumbled slightly but Jillian was at his side. Kamen too rose to his feet, but very slowly. The wound in his belly was still visible, but there were threads of fire that were knitting the edges of the wound together. It would probably take several days before Kamen was back at full strength, and then another few weeks before the subtle injuries would finally be healed. He would experience some weakness to be sure, but the largest impact would be on his ability to draw on the powers of the Blaze. The Blaze had a number of side-effects and the largest one was the fact that the Blaze ate living tissue as people drew upon it. Normally it was not enough damage for a person to notice, it was subtle and small. In fact, the Blaze would usually be able to heal the damage as quickly as it was inflicting it. However, the more injured a person was, the harder it was for the Blaze to not worsen the problem. And, the deeper a person drew on the Blaze, the more severe the damage became. In Kamen's condition, there was a good chance that he could kill himself just trying to erect simple defenses. In a fight, Kamen would be a liability. Logan moved to his ancient friend and put his hand on the giant man's shoulder and smiled.

"You need your rest, my stubborn friend, especially for what is to come. I'll need you in one piece for what I have planned, and there are fights enough ahead where the power of the Living Flame will be the only thing that stands between us and failure. What I did, how I defeated Death, it will have opened a lot of eyes. They know what I can do now, and Dorovar will be sending everything he has against me, and so will Emries. They have to stop me before I can tell Aerith how to do what I have done. I've changed this war, and it will only be a matter of time before it all caves in around me."

Kamen nodded his head.

"I shall prepare our brothers. They must know that the time has come to fight. Many are still on pilgrimage. We should gather, but I know not where."

There was only one answer, but it was one that Logan had to chew on for quite some time before he felt comfortable letting it into the open. He had felt it coming ever since Rhain inherited Halicon's powers. And like a moth drawn to a flame, he felt a pull to her. The analogy caused him to smile when it crossed his mind, and then he laughed, which caused him to cough and then laugh harder. The whole thing was a cosmic joke, but it didn't make the next course of action any less clear.

"It's time that the Council was reformed, old friend. Go to Bellnoc, meet with our brothers and sisters, and tell Rhain that she needs to prepare to send out the Call. Don't let her do it until I arrive. Jerah won't be able to resist the Call, even with Dorovar's influence, and I need to be there to keep her from killing all of you. She'll listen to me, at least I hope she will."

Kamen looked first to Jillian and then back to Logan.

"Has Dorovar's touch changed her nature?"

Logan knew immediately what Kamen was referring to, and it was a valid and dangerous question. In life, Caris had been a vindictive, spiteful, and domineering woman. Those qualities made her incredibly dangerous. Now, with the powers that Dorovar had given her, she was the kind of deadly that made even Logan shudder.

"She's let me live at least twice so far. If she lets me speak, I think I can diffuse her. At least, I hope so."

Kamen nodded, and Logan nodded in return. He started to turn toward the passages that led to the surface, but suddenly stopped and turned back to face Kamen.

"Are you well enough to create a portal?"

Kamen hesitated for a moment, and then frowned. Logan nodded and reached into his pocket and pulled out a bright green stone. He flipped it to the giant man who caught it in the palm of his hand as though it were a pebble.

"Just don't pull too hard on the edges. I'm not sure whether you can break it or not."

Kamen chuckled and Logan turned back toward the passages that led to the mysterious visitor above. Jillian waited until Kamen was well out of view before she asked the question that was burning inside of her.

"What did Kamen mean about Jerah's nature?"

Logan considered for a long moment before answering.

"Caris always was a little possessive, and once she was pulled away from the darkness that dominated her soul, she was able to feel some things that she had always denied herself. It's a long story, but in the end, Caris fell in love with me, and I think she is still in love with me, and because of that, Kamen is concerned that Caris will have issues with you."

Jillian almost stumbled, but finally recovered and forced herself to smile.

"Well, I'm not sure I will be able to win a fight over you."

Logan tried to laugh, and squeezed Jillian's hand tightly. There were so many things that Jillian didn't understand, that he wanted her to understand. But Jillian shifted her attention and quickly changed the subject.

"So what is the story with Kamen?"

Logan breathed a bit of a sigh of relief.

"Kamen was one of Halicon's first children, along with Jeroch, Bryn, Ellis, Grawn, and Aryx. When the war with Emries spun out of control, Halicon became afraid of Kamen because of the amount of power that he had available to him, and because Kamen's attitude was more like Aryx's. Aryx left Halicon's service, Grawn, Bryn, and Ellis were forced into exile, and Kamen was tasked with becoming Halicon's personal guard. While technically he was still a member of the phasia, he was released from most of those duties. When my brother and I, along with the rest of our group, assaulted Halicon on our world, Kamen, or the Flame as he was at that point, was the last line of defense. We defeated him, and went on to defeat Halicon. The next generation, Kamen found himself chained to a new member of the phasia named Draven, and Kamen became a member of Draven's Dark Riders. It was because of Kamen that I was able to become a member of the phasia. Frankly what I did was pretty stupid and should have killed me. What I didn't know at the time, was that it was because of me that Kamen was able to break free of the part of him that was the Flame, and he became Kamen again. He feels as though he owes me his freedom and his identity, which is why he was receptive when I approached him about helping me form the Order. Frankly I'm relieved because in his current state, Kamen is not someone I would like to make an enemy of. He possessed perhaps the most raw power of any member of the phasia, and now that he has the abilities comparable to a Dark God, he is truly fearsome."

Jillian frowned.

"But he seems so peaceful. Even when he was fighting Death, he was totally controlled and reserved."

Logan chuckled.

"That's why Kamen is so scary. If he were to ever really let go, ever really embrace his power, he could shake this world. And as long as he's on our side, we have an advantage that neither Emries nor Talisia can truly counter. At least, as far as we know."

Jillian nodded.

"And that's what you're worried about."

Logan stopped and turned to face Jillian.

"As much as we thought we knew about Emries, he's come up with a whole new bag of tricks. And Talisia is almost completely a mystery. When we fought Emries, he was cocky, arrogant, and didn't think we had a chance. This time he's ready, and he won't make the same mistakes. Talisia is pure evil, and when it comes to a fight, she won't stop until everyone that opposes her is crushed. She doesn't know how to pull punches. We're going to need every trick, every reinforcement, and every advantage we can come up with. So far Aerith has been able to stay one step ahead of them, but in time they'll home in on him and dedicate everything they've got to wiping him out. For now, we have the best chance to accomplish the things he can't and won't."

"Won't?" Jillian asked.

"Aerith is a lot of things, but reliable and friendly is not one of them. He doesn't engender a lot of good will, and though he can lead, he can't recruit. He needs us to gather an army. And we'll need to make the choices he never will."

Before Jillian could ask, Logan looked her in the eye and all levity fell away.

"When all is said and done, Ayden, Bryn, Rhain, Aerith, they all have to die. Aerith knows it. Has known it all this time. Hannah doesn't know it yet, but her role in the end will be to end Aerith. I have the hardest job. Bryn and Ayden, they're my responsibility."

Logan turned away and started walking toward the surface. For several long moments Jillian just stood and watched him, suddenly feeling the incredible burden he was carrying. She hurried to him and took his hand, knowing then that no matter what was coming, she would be by his side.

* * * * * * * * * * * *

When Logan and Jillian arrived at the surface, neither of them were prepared for what was waiting for them. Standing taller than a multiple story building, a red-orange scaled dragon stood with its wings pulled back against its body and its long neck craned in the direction of where the Peaks of Patience once stood. As though it felt them approaching, the dragon craned its neck back in their direction, and Logan at once could see the flames burning in the sockets where the creature's eyes should have been. Small flames seemed to dance across the dragon's head and neck, and after a moment, the creature reared itself up to its full height. The dragon spread its wings wide and lifted itself up high, opened its jaws and roared. The roar was met with a burst of flames that seemed to pour from every scale all at the same time. The whole of the dragon was a roaring inferno that produced no smoke but intense heat. The display of power finished, the dragon came back down onto its four clawed feet and the flames abated, except for the dragon's eyes and the small peaks that constantly danced across its head. Finally the dragon fixed its gaze on Logan, and opened its mouth to speak. Its glimmering white teeth were wreathed in white peaks of flame, and its long serpentine tongue appeared as though it was made of pure fire.

"You are Logan Ranthall? The one they call the Phoenix? The core of the Flickering Flame?"

Logan squeezed Jillian's hand and then pulled away. He took two steps toward the dragon and extended his hands out from his body in a show that he was both unarmed and not a threat.

"I am Logan," he said slowly.

The dragon seemed to hesitate for a long moment and then its head drooped.

"I'm not sure what I was expecting, but certainly you do not feel like the heretic that shook worlds."

Logan laughed, and felt the strain radiate through his body.

"I'm having a bit of an off day."

As though he didn't hear, the dragon continued.

"I am Aspertis the Just, one of the members of the Council of Dragons, and have been empowered by our elder, Mariti Brightblade to offer my strength and my assistance to your cause. Not all of the dragons will fight with you, but those who do, will fight to the death to ensure that the abomination and all those loyal to him are destroyed forever."

Logan was taken aback, but tried his best to recover as quickly as possible.

"I'm grateful for your assistance, Aspertis, and to be honest, we need all the help we can get."

"No," the dragon said, "hear it all before you accept. Those of us who are the oldest of our breed were entrusted with great treasures, treasures that showed our dedication to the Creator and the things that we as his oldest creations named. All worlds, all creatures, and all things, save the Children came after us. All things were named by us, and we shall endure long after all things die. To seal our alliance, to show our commitment, I shall offer you my treasure. It is a bond that cannot be broken, and cannot be rescinded once accepted. If you die, so shall I die. If the treasure is lost or destroyed, so shall I be destroyed. I am placing all that I am in your hands, Flickering Flame, and thus I shall protect you as I am protecting my own life."

The dragon's body flared into flames once more, and then on the ground in front of Logan, a small whirling red portal appeared. A moment later, a package floated gently through the portal and settled at Logan's feet. Logan bent and unwrapped the package, revealing a small pair of almost transparent bracers. When he picked them up, they had almost no weight, but definite texture.

"What you hold in your hands," Aspertis said slowly, "is called Flame. They are made of diamond and strengthened in the fires at the heart of the first world the Creator ever fashioned. As you have seen, I can surround my body with a shield of flame that burns so hot that weapons of natural design cannot touch me. Even those made of unnatural ice, metal, and stone will be turned away. Flame allows you to protect yourself in the same manner, wreathing your body in Celestial Flames. Even those creatures that are not normally impacted by this corporeal world will feel the heat and burn of that which surrounds you."

Logan looked at the bracers in his hands, and tried hard not to laugh. Then, as if someone had been reading his mind, a man's voice came from the darkness.

"I'm sure you appreciate the irony."

It took only a moment for Logan to place the voice, and he turned quickly to see the face of his old ally.

"Didn't expect to see you here, Rael."

The black-clad man emerged from the shadows, his dark eyes flashing in the firelight cast by the massive dragon. He had grown a thick beard since the last time Logan had laid eyes on him.

"Nor did I expect to find a dragon here, but these days it seems life is full of surprises. I think there is someone you should meet."

Kingdoms of Conscience

Year Four of the Just Emperor Kaitain "Dragonsbane" Lorien, Creator's Calendar Year 1871

In a darkened tent on the far side of the rebel camp, Mirana Ranthall sat cross-legged on the ground, her eyes closed, concentrating on the environment around her. Ever since the appearance of the Imperial Heir with her unconventional retinue, the tensions in the camp had been high. The appearance of Chelsea Zarova and Dominique Lorien cemented the rebellion in the minds of all of the soldiers. Even though all of the men and women in the Lordhill rebellion were loyal to Connor and Gabrielle Peregrim, there were still some facets of the war that had not been confronted. Now though, it was all so real. Mirana's mind flowed through the camp, feeling the fears and trepidations of the common soldiers. While the leadership of the rebellion had strong emotions, theirs were more fully formed because they had more information available to them. The soldiers on the other hand had no such solace. They had only the orders of their superiors and the trust that engendered. In the days to come that faith would be tested in a way it never had. All those who had talked about rebellion, dreamed of glory, wished for retribution for some past wrong would be granted their chance. How many would fulfill all of the dreams of their heart and become the heroes that they all had envisioned they could be? How many would falter at the moment of truth and fall short? Would they feel the shame of the moment, or would they redeem themselves by doing everything they could? At the end of the day, would it even matter?

Mirana was not as accomplished with her powers as her sister, at least not in the realms of understanding the drives of the human heart and soul. Mirana was far more practical and calculated. She believed in the applications of power to create order and to create true substance. She saw patterns, no matter how complex, and the ways to wind and unwind them. Liara saw the flows of emotion, the patterns on the wind, and could predict how they would be used or manifest. Though she knew she had obvious deficits in the applications of her powers, specifically in the realm of combat, Mirana took every opportunity she could to practice and learn. The only time she had seen real combat was a matter of hours previous when she and Liara fought with their contemporary Serrina. Serrina had sparred with the greatest fighters of the Dark Gods, and easily outmatched the sisters. They had worked together and barely emerged victorious, but only with the assistance of a far more seasoned, if mortal, warrior. In the days to come, if Mirana and Liara were not ready to push their powers to the limit, to tax themselves to the fullest, then this new alliance they were trying to forge would die in its infancy. That was something that Mirana could never allow to happen, no matter what the cost or the consequences could be.

A few moments before the knock came at the small 'no visitors' wooden sign that hung over the tent flap, Mirana felt her visitor coming. She had been expecting one of the leadership to visit her in the intervening time before Liara returned. It made good tactical sense of course. Having access to information about the capabilities of enemies, former enemies, or prospective enemies was a must, and Mirana represented all of the above for the forces of the Lordhill rebellion. The knock was diminutive and hesitant, and Mirana could feel the uncertainty oozing through the intervening space. It was so powerful in fact that Mirana herself felt disconcerted.

"Please come in," Mirana said almost the moment the knock came.

The wave of uncertainty intensified for a fraction of a second, and then what felt like an artificial and practiced calm descended. A moment later the tent flap opened, and Mirana watched as the Imperial Heir, Quyhn

Ravenheart Lorien entered the tent. Just behind the young dark-haired woman, Mirana spied the Imperial Heir's bodyguard. Rhionna Winter standing just beyond the partially opened tent flap, however, the woman did not make any move to follow her charge into the tent. In some ways, it could have been seen as a show of respect from Quyhn to Mirana; that the Imperial Heir did not consider the woman a threat. However, there was something much more realistic at play. Regardless of Mirana's deficit of combat experience, she was still more than a match for a dozen highly trained bodyguards. Rhionna's presence would mean nothing if Mirana wished Quyhn ill. Mirana smiled at the new arrival, but made no move to rise.

"Welcome, Empress," Mirana said brightly. "I am sure I can find you a chair."

Quyhn shook her head a moment before sinking to the ground, leaning on her left hip, and then swinging her legs to her side.

"Please," she said after a short sigh, "I'm not the Empress, I am merely the Imperial Heir, and even should we succeed in destroying Kaitain Lorien and removing his filth from the world there is no guarantee that there will be an empire left for me to rule. I prefer to focus on what lies before us. To that end, please, call me Quyhn."

Mirana nodded slightly.

"How may I help you, Quyhn?"

Mirana saw a momentary sadness pass over Quyhn's features, and had it not been for Mirana's tendency to notice even the smallest changes in the facial expressions of others, it might have gone unnoticed completely. But the young woman had obviously been through more than Mirana had been able to derive from their short time together, and that rushed maturity was easily evident. Mirana was impressed by Quyhn's strength; had been since they first met. However, in the days to come, she would need to impress those who were far more versed in dealing with the trappings of power and prestige. In the end, Mirana believed this was the best course of action of both sides.

"I was hoping you could give me some insight into what to expect from my upcoming meeting."

Mirana smiled and was about to speak when she felt something run through her. It was a feeling of familiarity combined with a sense of surprise. Something had been waiting for Liara in Rashaleb, something that neither of them suspected. Suddenly the possibility of a treaty with the people of Cadaria had become both more possible and more complicated.

"A moment ago, I think that I would have said that the best possible thing for you to do would be to keep an open mind and to be honest and forthright about all of your fears and concerns, as well as all of your hopes. Now though, I think I will say that above all, you simply need to trust yourself and be ready for the most impossible things to suddenly become reality."

Quyhn's puzzled look was suddenly interrupted by a knock at the sign on the tent. A moment later the flap opened to the concerned face of Rhionna Winter

"Something's happening."

Quyhn looked first from her bodyguard to the Dark God.

"They're here," Mirana said softly. "And they wanted to make a memorable entrance."

* * * * * * * * * * * *

Gwydeon and Midarin had barely left the makeshift hut constructed from fragments of wood, stone, and ice, when Liara dashed across the distance and wrapped her arms around them both. Despite the discomfort that the embrace caused, the married couple could not help but laugh at the genuine joy and exhilaration. When Liara finally pulled back, Midarin could see the tears in the young woman's eyes.

"I felt you," Liara said, almost babbling, "but it couldn't be you. But no one else feels like you, even if you aren't really you."

Gwydeon chuckled at the apt if accidentally poignant description.

"It's really me, Liara. It's good to see you again."

Suddenly, remembering the reason that she had come, a worried look came to her face.

"Oh, but this makes everything so much more complicated. If Mir was here, she'd know what to say, what to do."

Midarin laid a concerned and comforting hand on Liara's shoulder.

"Why don't you come inside and we can talk."

Midarin and Gwydeon steered Liara in the direction of the makeshift hut, but as soon as the girl looked at it, she stopped dead in her tracks, and the worried look that dominated her features deepened.

"I can't go in there," she said with uncharacteristic venom in her voice. "He made it. He's been here, I can feel him."

Midarin looked first at Liara and then to Gwydeon. When she saw the frustration in her husband's eyes, she knew that he understood the girl's cryptic words.

"What is she talking about, Gwydeon? Who's been here?"

Gwydeon ground his teeth.

"Aerith."

Midarin rolled her eyes and then looked back at the structure.

"I should have known," she said finally, "but then again, he's probably the reason we're standing here, so I can't complain too much. But wherever he goes, trouble follows."

"And people die," Liara added coldly.

Gwydeon moved his stiff sword shoulder and smiled at Liara.

"Aerith is a lot of things, but a talented healer he isn't. He was able to patch us all up, but we need a little more finesse from someone who knows what they're doing. Camille got the worst of it, and I know she wouldn't trust anyone but you to patch her up. Why don't you come in, just for a minute, put us all back together and tell us what is going on."

Gwydeon could see the conflict cross the young woman's face. She genuinely cared for the well-being of her confederates, and that was beginning to win out over the mysterious disgust for a man, to Gwydeon's knowledge, that Liara had never even laid eyes upon. It was then that Aerith's warning rang out louder in the back of Gwydeon's mind. Liara was a divine being. Aerith opposed everything that was divine. Was the Creator manipulating Liara to hate the man who could very well be the instrument that undid millennia of the Creator's rule? Could the Creator have the ability to manipulate the mind and actions of his own daughter against the interests of her own family? Gwydeon shook himself away from those thoughts and tried to banish the doubt from his eyes. For a moment, Gwydeon thought that there was a flash of recognition in Liara's eyes. The girl had always been perceptive, almost to the point of seeming clairvoyant. Perhaps she knew more than she was letting on, or perhaps the knowing was not hers but that of a malignant external force. Finally Liara relented with a nod, and the trio entered the small hut.

As soon as they crossed the threshold into the hut, Liara first wrapped her uncle Alderin in a quick embrace before moving to Camille's side, her hands hovering over her considerable wounds. The frown and thinly veiled displeasure had long-since disappeared, and now Liara was focused on her task. In only a matter of moments, Liara was helping Camille to sit up, and the two contemporaries shared a brief moment before Liara turned her attention to the elders of the group and began her tale.

"Everything's been in shambles since you left, Midarin," Liara started. "I'm not sure if Camille has had a chance to fill you in, but the Citadel is gone, and everyone is scattered. I think something may have happened to my mother and father because I can't feel them. Pike stormed off after Kaitain after that thug Ivan took Sadrina. The last thing father told us to do was to keep an eye on things happening in Aldere. So, Mir and I did what we were supposed to do, and we wound up following the Empress Dominique and her guard Chelsea. Serrina attacked them, out of nowhere, saying it was on orders from Pike. We defended them like our father and mother would have wanted, and we went with them to meet with the leadership of a rebellion including the Imperial Heir Quyhn Lorien and the leadership of a place called Lordhill. I know we weren't supposed to interfere, but they're willing to work with us to stop the suffering; to stop Kaitain."

Whatever reaction Liara was expecting, she didn't get it. Instead, Midarin and Gwydeon simply looked at one another and for a long moment the two had a silent conversation. It was Midarin who broke the unspoken treatise first.

"I met briefly with Dominique and Chelsea. They are good people and they have good intentions for their people. I'm not sure, all things considered, that we could find better allies in their world."

Gwydeon sighed and nodded.

"But this time, it's going to be more than one city that we need to hold together. We can't just wall ourselves off and push back the tide."

Midarin looked Gwydeon deep in the eyes and felt a phantom pain in her heart. She had not been the one standing beside Gwydeon as hell collapsed in around the people of Brea and the refugees collected from the fallen kingdoms of the world of Onea. She had never held his hand the moment before a battle against one of the phasia, or had to help him make the choices of who would wade out into the endless ranks of monstrosities to gather supplies. No, in her version of reality, there had been no Gwydeon, and she had had to make difficult choices on her own about how best to fight the forces of the Shadow. She had to compete with a ghost, a phantom of herself that she could only vaguely relate to. There were times that he didn't know the difference between the two Midarins and would find himself reminiscing with her about things they never did. In the end though, Midarin had learned to accept and even find humor in the existence of her doppelganger. But it was times like this, the serious times that it still brought a pang to her heart. In some ways, part of their life had been denied to her, and perhaps it had been the millennia long absence that had reopened the old wound. Whatever it was, there was one fact that could not be ignored. Together they were greater than they were apart, and as long as they stood side by side, anything was possible.

"Well, then I guess it's a good thing we have more help this time."

Gwydeon smiled and took his wife's hand, and after a moment turned his attention back to Liara, who had finished tending to Midarin's wounds. He looked first to Liara and gave the girl a nod before casting his eyes past her to his daughter. Camille had gotten back to her feet and was stretching what had to be stiff shoulders.

"Feel up to a little demonstration?"

Camille cocked an eyebrow. Gwydeon got to his feet and made sure that the sword belt was snugly fastened around his waist. There was concern in Midarin's eyes as she rose.

"Gwydeon, what are you doing?"

A sly smile accompanied his answer.

"They wanted an alliance with the Dark Gods; I think that they should get the full effect of what they're asking for. After all, we've spent too long being the enemy. Now it's time to show them exactly what we are. Now, listen close, I'm going to teach you all a little trick I picked up from an old friend."

* * * * * * * * * * * *

Quyhn emerged from the tent quickly followed by Mirana, and almost immediately joined the rest of the camp in looking skyward. High above the camp in the middle of the sky was a bright white ball of glistening power that rivaled both of the suns and the streaks of flame that scarred the heavens. After several long moments, the ball of flame flared and two forms slowly descended. Mirana immediately recognized both of the forms as soon as they were out of the corona of the low-hanging sun. The first Mirana felt long before she saw the rivulets of red hair catch the light, the two sisters were so intertwined that they always knew where the other was. The other form was also easily recognizable because the three had practically grown up together. Alderin Terian was the youngest son of Aryx and Diana Terian, the brother of Lissa Terian, and though they were raised together, Alderin was Mirana and Liara's uncle. A moment later, the light flared brighter and then disappeared completely, leaving a trio of forms hanging in mid-air, all of them with wings holding them aloft.

"What is this?" Quyhn asked, wonder filling her voice.

Mirana could not help but smile.

"This is what you were never allowed to see or know. This is what the Dark Gods truly are."

Held aloft on her angelic white wings, Camille Sandar was the picture of everything divine. The brilliance of the feathers beat against the wind slowly, and yet the woman seemed to be holding herself effortlessly on the breeze. Beside her, Midarin Sandar floated, and the wings that extended from her back were made of pure fire. The brilliant crimson was striking against the darkened sky. Above the mother and daughter duo, the man with black wings hovered, looking down upon the scattering and somewhat panicked soldiers. However, to Mirana the hovering man, Gwydeon Sandar, represented a hope that had been missing from the ranks of the Dark Gods for centuries. Perhaps there was still some nobility left in their cause, and perhaps it was all going to fall upon his wide shoulders. If history was any indication, Gwydeon Sandar, the hero of Onea and the Heavens was more than capable of bearing the massive weight. As soon as the brilliant ball of light disappeared and the trio of Dark Gods revealed, Liara sprinted across the distance and wrapped her sister in a tight embrace.

"Did you see? Can you believe it?"

The trio was already descending toward the ground when Quyhn, flanked by Rhionna, Liara, and Mirana began to approach. Dominique and Chelsea also moved in the direction of the Dark Gods, coming from the direction of the command tent with Connor and Gabrielle in tow. The moment Gwydeon's foot hit the ground he folded his wings back and took two long strides in the direction of the young woman that Liara had indicated as they hovered above the camp. Many of the soldiers approached, not sure if they should draw their weapons and move to intercded and protect the Imperial Heir. As Rhionna made eye contact with the commanders of the detachment, they kept their soldiers back, trusting the Heir's guard to her task. When they were mere feet from one another, Gwydeon stopped and began to address not only Quyhn, but all who were in ear shot.

"I am here to answer the invitation of Quyhn Ravenheart Lorien to discuss the possibility of an alliance between the Dark Gods and the Cadarian people. We mean no harm, and our arrival was purely a demonstration that had we had malicious intent, this conversation would not be necessary."

Quyhn swallowed hard. She had never been involved in any kind of formal negotiations in her strange role as Imperial Heir, and she had never had to make a decision that impacted as many people as a treaty with the Dark Gods would. However, after a quick look in Dominique's direction, Quyhn pulled her shoulders back and took a step forward before answering.

"I am Quyhn Ravenheart Lorien, the Heir to the Empire of Cadaria, and the Voice of the Emperor. However, as the Emperor has gone mad and has declared war against the people of Cadaria whose charge it is for the Emperor to protect, I, as the Imperial Heir, have no choice but to act in his stead and do what is necessary to protect the people. In that capacity, I believe that a return to the traditions that were founded by Terrik Lorien, the first Lorien Emperor of Cadaria is imperative. One of those traditions was a fragile peace with the Dark Gods. If we are to survive the trials ahead, we cannot afford to make more enemies."

Gwydeon smiled and nodded.

"Well said, Princess," a label that Quyhn immediately balked at, "shall we retire and discuss this prospective peace?"

In answer, Quyhn motioned in the direction of the command tent, and waited until the winged trio started in that direction before following herself. By this time, Midarin had released the flows of power that created her wings of flame. As Gwydeon had predicted, it was an impressive, if ultimately useless trick. Several minutes later, the group of six Dark Gods, as well as a group of six members of the Lordhill rebellion was situated in the command tent around a large table. Introductions had already been made around the table and Midarin and Dominique were deeply embroiled in a return to their discussion about the nature of their alliance. At certain points, Camille, Connor, or Gabrielle would add points or suggestions, and Chelsea seemed to keep the group coming back to the military ramifications of the alliance. When there was a lull in the conversation, Gwydeon let his voice enter the negotiations for the first time.

"When I made the agreement with Terrik, I was naïve. I should have understood that eventually our mere presence and lack of aggression would entice the subsequent emperors to try to prove themselves through our blood. However, I never anticipated the situation where I would watch the rise of a monster like Kaitain. How he could fight a war on so many fronts and still be alive and fighting. He has alienated every ally, destroyed his own protection force, and yet he still prospers. I think that perhaps he is a greater threat than even you realize. The Cadarians have not fought an internal war against an enemy like Kaitain since the Founding Wars, and I am ashamed to say that Terrik would not have been Emperor without the intervention of members of the Dark Gods and those loyal to us. So, we put the Loriens in the position of power, and as such we are responsible for what the line ultimately produced."

Silence fell over the table, but it did not last long, as Dominque answered Gwydeon's words.

"Kaitain is a monster of our making, not yours. Unlike the Cadarians, the Dark Gods kept their part of the bargain and left us to our own devices, trusting that we would make the right decision. We didn't, and the result is devastation raging across the countryside, suffering felt by the common people, and families broken at all corners of the Empire. This cannot be allowed to continue, but we also cannot let the betrayal deepen and be dragged into a war we cannot win with beings as powerful as the Dark Gods. Regardless of whether or not Quyhn ever sits on the Imperial Throne as the Empress of Cadaria, we are compelled to do whatever we can to protect the people."

Gwydeon nodded and pushed back from the table. He stood and move to the far corner of the command tent where a map table had been set up. After several moments of examining the map, he turned back to the table.

"So what is your plan?"

Chelsea stood and joined Gwydeon at the map table, quickly followed by Midarin and Quyhn. Her hand moved from their location to the capital of Rashaleb.

"Rashaleb is a natural choice to establish a base. Once done, we can move our allies from Lordhill in to fortify. It is inhospitable territory and difficult to attack, but the natural formations make it a prime location to defend."

Gwydeon frowned and then pointed toward Zevarit and Pellatori.

"But you will be bordered on two sides with enemy kingdoms. Though you will have allies in Celidar to the south, I'm not sure it is enough. You will not be able to help them if Kaitain launches a full assault, and they will not be able to help you in the same way. No, I'm sorry, but defensibility is not enough."

Chelsea crossed her arms. She was irritated, but the man had a point. Midarin though saw the gears turning in the head of her husband. Despite their long separation, she still knew the man.

"What is it, Gwydeon?" Midarin asked, looking down at the map, trying desperately to see what he saw.

Gwydeon smiled.

"When you cannot outfight your opponent, outthink your opponent. The strength of the Cadarian Empire has always been the core that it held in Aldere. The rest of the Cadarian Empire was held together by the strong center. Kaitain knows this, and if another force holds his capitol, his attention will continue to be divided, and he will start to make mistakes."

Gwydeon slammed his fist down on the map where it indicated the Imperial Palace of Aldere.

"The war against Kaitain starts by putting the Imperial Heir on the Throne in Aldere."

First Taste of Vengeance

Year Four of the Just Emperor Kaitain "Dragonsbane" Lorien, Creator's Calendar Year 1871

Jerrica Maldovrin felt the weight of the gaze upon her and for a long moment wondered if her knees would buckle and give under the weight. So much information had been thrown at her in such a short time. The Dark Gods, the brothers, the forgotten children, the war between the Children of the Creator, the woman who was not a woman at all, but a divine being who called herself Raenera. It was all too much. And now Raenera expected that Jerrica would be able to provide information about the legacy of Forer clan, a supposed fourteenth Sacred Weapon. But Jerrica knew she had no such information, at least not in her conscious mind. If anything it would have required the assistance of her two sisters to unlock. How though could she say such things to a Child of the Creator? How could she deny the power that stood before her? It wasn't until Tolon put his hand on her shoulder that she realized she was shivering. It was at that moment though that she realized that her body was not shivering with fear, it was resonating with the mass of power that flooded around her. Unlike being around the brothers, who seemed to drain away her power, being close to the Child of the Creator filled her with warmth that she could not explain. Suddenly she began to see things around her that she had never seen before. Faraway places and strange faces. They were so clear that they could have been standing merely feet away. She saw a giant man and a mountain, a red-haired man and a raven, a shimmering woman standing on an island flanked by angels. She saw a monster in a mask sitting on a throne of blood, and a man whose face was covered by shadow riding atop a golden dragon. For so long her visions had been thus, abstract, unclear, phantoms of the possible, but now, they seemed to have much greater weight and much more meaning. However, without her sisters to help her decode the images, she felt diminished. That was the power and the curse of the Maldovrin Triplets. Without the three together, their visions could never be of use to anyone.

Raenera watched as the young seer's eyes went white, and she could feel the power surge in the mortal's body. It took little effort to enter the woman's mind using her tie to divine power and to watch as the images flooded through. Some of the faces Raenera recognized, but others were confusing and almost contradictory. However, the Child of the Creator was not simply content with seeing what the seer saw. Instead, Raenera looked through Jerrica's mind to find what lay hidden beneath the images. There she found a threat, a deep and monstrous threat, not only to the mortals of Espre, but also to the Children and their Servants. More than just Dorovar and more than just his Heralds. Something new was coming something that had been unleashed by Dorovar's hand. This would complicate Raenera's plans and force her to take drastic steps. She lamented the coming of this end. It was still supposed to be so far off, and it was supposed to serve a greater purpose. Now though, she would have to entrust her sacred task to another. Then another image pushed past. A dragon, no not just a single dragon, but a massive flight of them. Dozens maybe more flying in formation behind a girl. She held a sword in her hand, a sword that glowed with an inner fire, as though it were possessed of something greater; something so powerful that it defied logical explanation. The woman's face was shrouded in shadows and light, and no matter how hard Raenera tried to pierce the shroud she could not. Suddenly it felt as though the woman was looking right back at Raenera, and the Child of the Creator could feel rather than see the smile that came to her lips. It was cruel smile, and it poured malice before her like a fog. The malignant creeping haze choked off all light and hope, exuding only fear and decay. As the fog passed, thousands died in its wake, armies of men and beasts laid waste. Above the dragons themselves shed their skins like diseased snakes, flesh, muscle, and gore dripping from exposed skeletons, until there was nothing left but the ghastly apparitions of the great beasts hanging in the air through some unknown force. Eventually they too crashed to the ground, leaving only the woman and her gleaming sword. But even that was no longer clear through the miasma. The whole scene had become tinged with a sheen of blood, obscuring all detail, but leaving the impression of devastation behind. That moment a new force plunged through Raenera's thoughts, a white hot spike of danger to shake her away from her cloudy and confused vision.

When Raenera opened her eyes, she was mildly shocked to see that the little seer had collapsed. Blood flood from her nose and from the corners of her eyes where it mixed with a thick froth that billowed from her mouth. Blood also poured from her ears, and the spasms that racked her body were so strong that her fingernails had dug deep into the palms of her hands loosing blood there as well. Raenera had not intended to inflict such harm on the girl with her touch, and was disappointed that she had focused so much effort on bringing the fragile little girl to Glacier's Rift. Perhaps that had been a miscalculation. One had been easy enough to lure away, planting thoughts here and there nudging her out of the nest, but Raenera had expected the girl to have power on the level of Jehna Feris, not to be leashed to her sisters for any true vision. No matter. For the time being Raenera had learned all that she could learn. Perhaps if they had more time, she would be able to ring more information out of the mortal's mind before she expired, but even that was a risky proposition. It was more likely that if Raenera or anyone else with power tried to touch the girl's mind again, she would die suddenly and horribly. The new threat filling her mind, Raenera turned to Gideon.

"One of the abomination's Heralds has crossed the wasteland and is approaching the gates. He must be delayed at all costs until you can take the weapons to meet with our troops in their hiding place. You must be ready to lead them as we have discussed often."

Gideon's eyes went wide, but suddenly he felt the soothing calm enter his mind. He had known for some time that Raenera had been manipulating him, in the same way that his mother had once done. Though this was far stronger. Raenera then shifted her gaze to Natalie.

"Take the others and delay our visitor until I have sent Gideon on his way with our forces. Stop at nothing. Bring the whole mountain down upon him if you must. Whatever it takes."

Natalie took two steps toward the secret staircase before the feeling of impending doom set in. She could not shake the feeling that she was being sent on a suicide mission. However, if they could hold out as they had done before against the thing that called itself Korin Melcab, Raenera would have time to ensure that all of their plans would come to fruition, and then she too could join the battle. All they needed was time. With a curt nod in Gideon's direction, Natalie scurried up the stairs to see to the defense of Glacier's Rift. Again Raenera's eyes shifted to Gideon.

"Once you have left this place, you can never return. Take with you the seer. Perhaps she shall mean more to you than she has to me. There is information inside of her that could turn the tide of this war, but it is sealed behind walls that she cannot defeat alone. You may need to seek out her sisters, though that too could be perilous."

It was then that Raenera let her eyes fall to the strong man who knelt at Jerrica's side. The will inside of him was strong to be sure, but would that be enough for the trial that faced them. Would the bravery win out or would the coward hide behind his love.

"Knight of the Flashing Blade, champion of an emperor. I call upon you to defend this place. Will you stand at the defenses with the rest of these lost children so that you can assure your beloved's escape, or will you stay by her side, a last line of defense that cannot possibly hold?"

Tolon stood, and he could feel the anger and hate coursing through his veins. The challenge to his honor was clear, but before he said something that he knew he would regret, a calm came over him. It was the same calm that descended in the moments before a fight in the gladiatorial arena. It was the acceptance of death, the knowledge that the next moment could be his last. If he lived past the last moment, it meant only that on that day his will was stronger than the spirit of death. As a warrior who battled against death as surely as he battled against his opponent on the other side of the arena, he knew that he could not cheat the reaper forever. Duty demanded that he do everything in his power to protect his charge, and the best place that he could do that was on the battlefield above, not cowering in a hole hoping not to be discovered. If his death was required to secure the future, then so be it. No words were needed, and he gave a curt nod in Gideon's direction before turning and sprinting up the stairs. Once he was out of sight and out of earshot, Raenera sighed and shook her head.

"Foolishness. He will make no difference on the battlefield, and yet he will throw his life away for something as trivial and futile as love."

Gideon's jaw hung loose and he could not find the words to match his disbelief.

"But..."

Raenera cut off Gideon's words with a raised hand.

"But nothing. Mortals. This is what I have been trying to teach you, Gideon. Have you not listened? Attachment, sentimentality, love; the things your race fights so passionately for, in the end are the very things that have kept you chained to the wills of those who have no regard for such weakness. Only the true motivations matter. The application of true and perfect Order. The total subjugation of all Chaos. Purging Evil. Minimizing Good. These are the things that push a civilization forward, and these are the things that I have been fighting my brothers and sister over for eons. Did you think for a moment that one mortal's life was more important than the restoration of Order in the Cosmos? I would sacrifice a million Tolon Morrs to advance my agenda. As would my brothers. As would my wretched sister. Mortals are nothing, weak barely conscious cattle mewling not to be given food or a place to sleep, but for the kind of enlightenment that can only come from the touch and guidance of the divine. And I will gladly give that guidance in return for the kind of obedience demanded by perfect Order. Through the devotion that I will sculpt in your minds and in your flesh, I shall create a new dawn for your race, and I shall finally see an end to this pointless ideological war. My father will see the truth, as shall my brothers and sisters when they fall before the scythe of Order; the scythe my dear Gideon that you will wield for me. You shall separate weak from chaff."

* * * * * * * * * * *

Conquest stood on top of a low hill at the edge of the Frozen Wastes, looking down at the large manor-house that Dorovar had called Glacier's Rift. Even from this distance he could feel the surges of power that emanated from inside of the structure, some of them very familiar. The most powerful however was different than anything Conquest had ever felt before, and he knew instantly that was his target. However, to reach his goal, he would have to deal with the ants that now seemed to flood from the open doors of the structure. Since fully embracing the new powers that Dorovar had granted him, Conquest began to push past the limitations of his formerly mortal shell. The acuity of his vision had begun to sharpen, and even at this great distance he could clearly make out the forms that were emerging from the large wooden doors. His mind made many connections as he scanned the faces of his soon to be opponents, and it was only when the seventh of the small band of defenders emerged that Conquest felt the anger begin to surge in the pit of his stomach. An old grudge would be settled once and for all, and Conquest was glad for the opportunity. Though he could have crossed the distance on foot quickly enough, Conquest wished to have a much greater impact on his opponents. The portal opened under his feet the next moment, and nearly instantly Conquest dropped through the other end, nearly a mile above the surface. As he sped toward the ground, Conquest allowed twin phantasmal axes to appear in his hands and the eerie green spectral forces to wrap themselves around his body. The latter was not needed to survive the fall, but for the demonstration of power that he had planned to have the full effect, it would strike fear into the hearts of his opponents. Moments before impact with the ground, Conquest crossed his arms in front of his chest and brought his chin to his chest.

When Conquest struck the ground, it sent shockwaves in all directions. The ground was frozen solid, and the force that Conquest was wrapped in did not allow for the creation of a great crater, despite the speed and force of the impact. Instead great fissures opened in all directions like the web of a spider. At the same time, the spectral force flared in all directions, coalescing into a fog of spectral bodies that cried and sang and screamed. The curtain of phantasms intensified as Conquest rose to his feet and brought both axes to bear. The would-be defenders, knocked off their feet by the shockwave of Conquest's impact, slowly made their way back to their feet, one of them raising his sword to point it directly at the center of

Conquest's chest. The gesture made a malevolent smile come to Conquest's lips, and malice to fill his veins.

"What are you doing here, Pike?" Hawk screamed over the din of ghostly voices. "No Dark God is welcome on Glacier's Rift. Leave now, or we will be forced to destroy you."

An evil laugh rippled from Conquest.

"Pike Rhuiden is dead, Hawk. Only Conquest remains. I am the greatest of Dorovar's Heralds, and I have come to tear down your little palace in the snow. Dorovar has ordered your deaths, and I shall take great pleasure in destroying all of you."

Conquest pointed the blade of one of his axes in Hawk's direction.

"But I shall enjoy taking your head the most, Hawk. It's been too long since I watched you die the first time, and it was much too fast."

Hawk gritted his teeth.

"You'll find me a much more difficult opponent this time, Pike, or whatever you're calling yourself now. And believe me; I've been waiting for retribution for a long time."

Despite Hawk's words, he was not the first to charge across the distance to face Pike. That honor went to the young woman whom Conquest immediately recognized as Leane Torne. Though she would be the first to die, Conquest knew that her fate was truly not her own, and like the mortals that he freed from their enslaved shells, Leane too deserved to find a place in Dorovar's Chorus. On Onea she had been simply a soldier until her body was stolen by the harlot known as Caris. Caris' touch imprinted upon Leane forever, making her a pawn in this war just as surely as any child of the phasia. Caris had been redeemed by the touch of Dorovar, and she had become the hauntingly beautiful and deadly Jerah, now too her former vessel would find redemption in the Chorus of Souls.

Conquest braced himself as the first slash of the blade made entirely of flames passed mere inches from his face. After the conflicts with the dragons and the Servant of the Creator, these would-be warriors would honestly pose little threat to what Conquest had become. Perhaps, though, as stepping into a colony of bees could prove fatal simply through the mass of wounds, these insects could collectively damage the great Herald. Better to end the fighting quickly than to give them the chance to build foolish hope. More slashes crossed the distance between Leane and Conquest. Her skill was exemplary, but she was no match for the speed of Conquest. The battle was over long before Leane realized it. She ducked in, hoping that her high feint would buy her the precious moment she needed to strike a critical blow, but it had only proved to bring her into range of Conquest's ax. Conquest blocked the thrusting blade with the haft of his ax, at the same time driving her down and forward into the path of his other ax's downward strike. The phantasmal ax easily ripped through the soft flesh of Leane's neck, severing her spine, and cleaving her head from her body. Leane fell without a sound, her life stolen before she knew the battle was over, and her newly-freed soul screaming in a bitter mix of anguish and joy as it rose to join the rest of the Chorus. As Conquest turned his attention to the rest of the on-rushing defenders, he knew that he would not offer them the same mercy that he had just given the one innocent among them.

As two of the men charged in, namely Jared Vale and Hawk Yetre, the two remaining women and a third man, Michael Yarrow began sending stream after stream of fire, ice shards, and a hail of stones in Conquest's direction. The streams of power outpaced the two men, and at the last possible moment, Conquest wrapped himself in a shield of soul energy, sending the waves of power back in the direction of the on-rushing combatants. Hawk was able to slide underneath a stream of fire before popping back to his feet and continuing his charge. Jared was not so lucky. As he attempted to dodge a hail of stones, he was blindsided by a large shard of ice that ripped through his left shoulder. The blow was strong enough the send the young man tumbling to the ground. When the torrent of power relented for a moment, Conquest sent one of the phantasmal axes hurtling through the air in the direction that the attacks came from. Again Hawk had to dodge the attack, but Michael Yarrow was not as lucky. The ax was upon him before he could both halt his attack and dodge out of the way. The blade of the ax collided with Michael's chest, instantly cleaving his sternum and rupturing his heart. The force of the impact sent him flying backwards several feet, but the man was dead long before he ever hit the ground. The death of their comrade seemed to redouble the efforts of the two women, and streams of fire and ice came in rapid and deadly succession.

Conquest knew that allowing his attention to be so divided could potentially lead to distraction and damage. That could not be allowed in the grander scheme of things. Choosing to move for the first time in the battle, Conquest lurched forward in Hawk's direction, taking hold of the haft of his ax in both hands. At the same time, Conquest let a stream of spectral energy flow from the aura around him. Jessica Chandara was the first victim of the spectral energy. It wrapped itself around her like blanket, contracting quickly over the next few seconds until the sound of breaking bones and her tormented screams grew loud enough to rival the Chorus. Natalie Yetre ceased attempting to give her brother cover as he approached the Herald, and instead turned the streams of fire in an attempt to intercept the ghostly force that was bearing down on her. But regardless of how strong and how wide the fan of fire ranged, the eerie green force advanced. When the force was finally upon her, Natalie drew as deeply as she dared on the forces at her disposal, pouring everything she had into the massive gout of fire that emerged from her outstretched hands. Finally it seemed that the fires were pushing the wave of spectral energy back, but at the last moment the green energy split at the point of contact and a moment later was wrapped around her throat. But the wave of souls was not content in simply choking the life out of the woman, instead it ripped her backwards breaking her neck in a single hard jolt, and by the time Natalie hit the ground, her last breath had already been forcibly expelled from her lungs.

Hawk Yetre was on his opponent driving forward as hard as he could. His sword flared out, intent on claiming his opponent square in the chest. The strike was quick and accurate, but it was not strong or fast enough to push through Conquest's defenses. Conquest parried the blow aside and countered with a backhand that easily shattered Hawk's right cheekbone. As Hawk faltered, Conquest took hold of his hair and pulled his head down, bringing a knee up to meet Hawk's face. The sound of breaking bones would have been sickening to an average person, but Conquest felt nothing at all. As he pulled Hawk's broken face back into view, there was little still recognizable of the man. His breathing was labored, and it would be only a matter of time before he choked to death on his own blood. With one quick motion, Hawk's neck snapped, and Conquest watched as the light and life fled from his opponent's eyes. The last of the defenders still on their feet stood close to the doors of the structure, the last line of defense, a long spear clutched in his hands. As Conquest moved in the man's direction, he stopped at the side of the fallen Jared Vale. Blood flowed freely from the gaping wound in his side, and rather than letting the man suffer longer than necessary, Conquest brought a foot down hard on Jared's chest, crushing his ribs and sternum, as well as the heart and lungs that lay beneath. Death was nearly instant. A moment later, Conquest had crossed the distance to the doors and he stood before the final defender. It took merely a moment for recognition to flash in Conquest's eyes.

"Tolon Morr, Knight of the Flashing Blade. How surprising it is to see you here."

Before Tolon could react, Conquest was upon him. The spear easily rent from his grasp, and the Herald's hand wrapped around his throat. In one hard motion, Tolon was slammed against the wall. Conquest stared into the knight's eyes, no expression on his face, and only death in his eyes.

"Where is your Sacred Weapon, Knight of the Flashing Blade? Tell me where it is and I promise you that you will feel no pain when death takes you."

Tolon gasped for air and tried to speak but no words would emerge. Conquest loosened his grip slightly and stared intently, waiting for the answer to his question.

"Gone," Tolon managed finally. "One of the brothers took it."

Conquest frowned.

"What brothers?"

Tolon tried to swallow, but it was no use. Finally he was able to croak out an answer.

"Logan and Korrd."

Fires rose inside of Conquest. He could not believe the two Ranthalls still lived, and what's more, they were now in possession of one of the

Sacred Weapons. This could not be allowed. This was blaspheme of the highest order. Before he realized what he was doing, the fires of rage inside of Conquest had been translated into actual flames by the Chorus of Souls, and the terrible screams of pain and torment that wrenched from Tolon Morr's burning body shook Conquest back to the present. But there was no need to grant the former knight mercy now. His end would come soon enough, and he proved the need for his suffering through failure in his duty. His end ultimately mattered little. The now smoldering corpse discarded, Conquest ripped the massive wooden doors from their hinges and plunged headlong into the place known as Glacier's Rift, looking for his remaining prey.

* * * * * * * * * * * *

Nearly all of the weapons and armor had been moved through portals to their new safe location when Raenera turned to Gideon with palpable sadness in her eyes.

"They have all fallen," she said finally. "All of my lost children have fallen to the Herald."

The implication was clear. For so long they had been Gideon's family, and they had been robbed from him, snuffed out in a matter of moments by a monster. As much as he wanted to stay and fight, to get retribution, Gideon knew that there were greater concerns than one battle. More important things than vengeance. It took only a moment for Gideon to collect the unconscious form of Jerrica Maldovrin and make for the still-open portal. Just before he stepped through, Raenera took him by the arm.

"Remember what you were told. Remember what you must do. Protect Arturious until he completes his work, and then end his suffering. You are now my voice upon this world, my high priest of Order. Do not fail me."

Gideon nodded and stepped through the portal without another word. Once through, Raenera flicked her hand in the direction of the portal and it instantly winked out of existence. Above her she heard the structure of the manor groan under the destruction being wrought by the Herald, and she prepared herself for the first dual she had fought in millennia.

Fire, Stone, and Blood

Year Four of the Just Emperor Kaitain "Dragonsbane" Lorien, Creator's Calendar Year 1871

A soft giggle and the sweet smell of freshly sliced fruit shook Korrd from his momentary unconsciousness, and he opened his eyes and felt his lips go wide with a smile. He would have recognized the place had he been drunk and half-blind. The bar was called the *Crooked Smock*, and it was one of the more reputable drinking establishments in Brea. At least, that was true as long as the sun was up. Once the sun went down however, this was the place that husbands with wandering eyes and wandering hands spent their evenings away from their palatial estates and nagging wives. It was where a great many backroom deals determining the fate of kings and kingdoms were made, and it was the place that Korrd felt most comfortable after he had been proclaimed as the *Coromor* in one of Saurn's diabolical plots to lure Logan out of hiding. Little did Saurn know how true his words had been and once the two brothers were united, the revelation of their actual roles in the war between Light and Darkness became clear. Now though, Korrd knew that he had a moment of solace and a moment where the war could not touch him. It was a moment that he would never have again, his last moment of peace in this or any world. Taking a deep breath of the sweet smell, his nose caught something sour and just as his eyes began to open; the sweet had been almost completely eclipsed. He looked down at the serving girl who had been sitting on his lap, and when her face turned up, a shiver of revulsion rocketed through Korrd. Where a moment before her face had been tan and beautiful, now her visage was warped, desiccated and devoid of any life. The brilliant and intoxicating blue eyes were now glazed over with a sheen of white, no spark there to break through the haze. Grey wrinkled skin cold as the grave brushed against his hand, and the corpse that was once a vital young girl stared up at him, mouth agape. Frozen in his chair, Korrd's eyes darted around the room from patron to patron and one by one their cold dead eyes turned to meet his, a room full of corpses. He wanted to close his eyes, wanted to shut away the growing nightmare, but all he could do was watch as the dozen corpses became two dozen, and then three. Every seat in the bar was soon filled with the dead, all of them looking in his direction, their gaze accusatory. He didn't recognize any of the faces, but he knew what the dream was trying to tell him. He had been the cause of so much death, and he would continue to be. Whatever he had once been, Korrd had become a weapon. Whether it was serving Saurn or Emries or the Creator, the truth was the same. Wherever his boots tread, death followed.

Korrd was thrust back into consciousness as a bowl of cold water was splashed over his face. He was back in the command tent of the Army of Fire, and his second in command was rousing him back from the edge. He didn't hear his second's words as he pulled himself back to his feet, his hand immediately going to his nose where the blood still flowed. Logan had done something terrible to him, that much Korrd knew, but exactly what had been done was unclear. Korrd's chest ached, and his mind was scrambled at best. With a wave of his hand, Korrd dismissed his second, and as soon as he was alone, Korrd dropped back to his knees. Weakness flooded through his body, and it was hard enough to breathe let alone stand. The numbness in his head was beginning to ease, and as the moments passed, he started to piece together what must have happened. Logan had found a way to tap into the powers that Emries had given to Korrd upon his resurrection from the void. Because they shared the same blood, the brothers were connected, and in theory each could draw upon the world-shattering powers of the other. But why had Logan chanced such a thing? Surely he knew that such a maneuver could kill them both. But maybe Logan was that desperate. Maybe he knew that a murder suicide through overloading their powers was the only possible way that Korrd could be defeated. Well, no matter his goals, Korrd still lived, and he would have to devise a protection to keep Logan's attempts from working ever again. However, there in the back of Korrd's mind he felt something else, another power, one that he had never felt before. It was faint, but it was there. Where the Blaze flickered, there was a faint golden glow, one that slid away from his thoughts when they moved in its direction. Korrd was sure it had not been there before Logan's attack. Perhaps it was a trap, a clever and cunning plan to get Korrd to burn himself up from the inside. But so far Korrd had resisted touching any power other than the brilliant white energy that had been a gift from his lord Emries. He had not needed more, and he would not need more to finish off Logan or his patron Aerith Seth. Soon all the battles would be over, and Korrd would take his rightful place at Emries' side in the remade Heavens.

Drawing on the brilliant power, Korrd forced himself back to his feet and felt himself renewed. It would take some time before he would be back to full strength, but that strength would not be needed for the next day's assault. As he leaned over the map table, looking down at the blood-soaked battle plan, he smiled. The Army of Water was in disarray. Rumors swirled that days after he had seized control of Thorigald from the royal families that the disgraced Knight of the Flashing Blade Seraph Kore had simply disappeared. His generals now sniped at each other and squabbled for control over the increasingly fragmented forces that had once been considered the most impregnable in the empire. Now, a massive strike by the forces of the Army of Fire would crush the defenses around Thorigald and in a matter of days, the banner of Saldarine would fly over the capitol of their ancient enemy. Emperor Lorien would be pleased with their progress. Perhaps he would be pleased enough to revoke the death order that had been levied against Chelsea Zarova.

Despite himself, Korrd still cared for Chelsea, and wanted her back safely in Saldarine. But, that would not happen. Chelsea had chosen her path, one that would never be able to be deviated from. Dominique had corrupted her heart, and for that the two women would burn. Sighing to himself, Korrd moved away from the map table to the basin that sat in the corner of the command tent. He was just about to splash cold water on his face when he felt a trickle of power in the back of his mind. It was familiar, powerful, and cold. A bolt of energy shattered the basin less than a moment after Korrd leapt away, and as he came back to his feet, Korrd let a crystalline blade form in his right hand and turned in the direction of the attack. At the moment there was nothing more than a blinding light. Another bolt of power emerged from the light, and Korrd rolled out of the way. It left a smoldering crater in the ground, and Korrd knew that whatever he was dealing with could not be taken lightly. He had expected his soldiers to come running the next moment, the sound of battle coming from inside the tent would have been unmistakable, but as Korrd came back to his feet again, he was disappointed at the lack of intervention. Though the soldiers would have been hopelessly overmatched, at least they would have provided a second or two of distraction for Korrd to try and seize the advantage over his invisible foe. Another volley of energetic bolts came flying at Korrd, this time a trio instead of a single strike. There was nowhere for Korrd to flee to, and no time to open a portal, so he caught one of the bolts with the blade of his crystalline weapon and leapt back in time for the other two to leave smoldering craters where his feet had been a moment earlier. The cloud of light at the far end of the tent flared again, and before the next volley emerged Korrd channeled his powers, forming two portals, one at his feet and one to his right. Just before he fell through the portal below him, Korrd hurled the sword through the portal to his right, the destination of which opened a split-second later behind the cloud of light. Just before Korrd fell completely through the portal, he thought he heard a grunt of pain and saw the crystalline blade clatter to the ground, its tip stained red.

A moment later Korrd dropped out of the swirling blue portal into the middle of the Army of Fire's camp. All around him men stood, but on closer inspection he realized that they were frozen in place. Time around Korrd and his assailant had stopped, and each one of Korrd's soldiers was locked mid-action in the moment before the first blow was struck. There would be no distractions or reinforcements coming, and Korrd would have to face the danger alone. Twin crystalline swords formed in Korrd's hands the next moment, and he prepared for the next assault. For several long moments nothing came, and Korrd felt his nerves becoming frayed as the time passed. He did not like being on the defensive, and he always felt that he fought best when he was dictating the pace of combat. That had always proved to be the key difference between Gwydeon and Korrd. Even though Gwydeon had taught Korrd almost everything he knew about swordplay, the one place that Gwydeon had always been able to best Korrd was with his seemingly limitless and unflappable patience. Like Korrd, Gwydeon could dictate the pace of combat if he chose to, but he preferred to react and use his opponent's mistakes against them. Korrd on the other hand preferred to always push and force mistakes rather than waiting for them to come. The issue that Gwydeon always exposed in Korrd was that impatience often leads to frustration which led to making careless decisions in the heat of combat. However, power tended to cover those mistakes. With the power of Emries at Korrd's disposal, there were few on any world that would be able to withstand Korrd's assault for long. His new adversary would soon learn the folly of his challenging the superior warrior.

Finally the flap of the command tent opened, and a young man stepped through, the unmistakable haze of power clinging to him. Though it wasn't a face that Korrd was familiar with, it didn't take long for Emries' memories to fill the gap. The boy had once been Ayden Seth, the son of the abomination Aerith Seth, but he had since taken on a new identity, one that burned Korrd to the core. The Creator had given Ayden a new name and a new position. Ayden Seth was now Ayden Crill, the Will of the Creator, one of the fearsome Servants who enforced the mandates of the Creator across all of His worlds. A moment later, Ayden's massive wings became visible, and his glistening armor appeared. Ayden may have been the Will, but underneath was still the headstrong and reckless boy that had found himself impaled on Emries blade mere weeks earlier. Power would only serve to make him more reckless. Was this some errand of the Creator that the Will had been tasked with, or was Ayden continuing his personal grudge against Emries? It mattered little to Korrd. The boy had chosen the wrong opponent to test out his new powers against.

"Korrd Ranthall," the boy called, the massive crystalline sword beginning to take shape in his hands, "you have been judged guilty of consorting with the enemies of the Divine Empress, Marlae Tamerlane. For that your sentence is death."

Korrd frowned. Tamerlane? What madness was this?

"The Creator has gone too far," Korrd said, his voice little more than a growl. "Giving a whore the name of one of the most honorable women I have ever known is one thing, but to desecrate the memory of a good woman and an even better man by letting you have their name is insulting to anyone who ever knew them. For that alone you should die, but the fact that you are one of the Servants, and that you are the son of the most notorious charlatan in the history of creation will make this even more satisfying."

Ayden set his feet, his face expressionless, but his eyes full of divine fire.

"My parentage is of little matter now. The Creator is the only father I need. All other debts shall be paid in time. But I assure you, should you ever call the Divine Empress a whore again, dying will be welcome release from the hell I will inflict on your body and your soul."

Korrd flashed a toothy malicious grin.

"A little sweet on the spoiled bitch are we? Well, she's spread her legs for worse I suppose."

The aura around Ayden exploded, changing from white to red. The massive white wings beat against the air, and Ayden charged the next moment, his massive sword crashing down upon where Korrd stood. The former *Coromor* brought his twin blades up to block the assault, while at the same time channeling all of the power he could muster into his body making it as hard and unyielding as diamond. Korrd had not underestimated with strength of the boy, but whatever Logan had done to Korrd had made him unable to adequately protect himself. The sound like a thousand breaking windows resounded through the still countryside, and Korrd was sent flying backwards. Blood streamed from a cut on Korrd's forehead where the massive blade had finally struck true, and more flowed from his nose due to the exertion of power. But Korrd was nowhere near defeated. He tucked his knees to his chest as he fell backwards, speeding to the ground with unnatural velocity. A moment before impact a portal opened, barely the blink of an eye later, Korrd had reappeared above Ayden, falling downward, a spear of pure energy forming in his hands. However, Ayden had been prepared for the tactic, and a hard beat of his wings sent him clear of the falling strike. But like a coiled spring, the moment Korrd's feet hit the ground, he refocused his kinetic energy, sending himself and the spear like an arrow shot from a massive bow at Ayden. The massive crystalline blade too unwieldy to be brought to bear for an effective defense, Ayden dropped the sword and wrapped himself in a shield of divine power. Korrd had expected the tactic, and instead of striking at Ayden directly, struck the ground at his feet, opening a fissure that should have swallowed the boy. Ayden released the shield as he fell, beating his wings wildly. Korrd seized the opportunity, launching forward again, spear at the ready, and struck true. The blade of energy pierced the heavily armored shoulder of the Will, drawing a cry of pain and a stream of blood. However, Korrd would not escape the assault unscathed. From deep within Ayden, a burst of force exploded in all directions, and Korrd felt as though he had been slammed into a brick wall while running at full speed. The force of the blow propelled Korrd backwards, and his senses were so scrambled that he could not mount a defense or an effective counter. He landed on the ground, his right arm broken and his left hip dislocated. Pain wracked his body, but luckily the damage and distraction he had inflicted on his opponent had been enough to forestall an assault.

"It is enough that you are a Dark God," Ayden said, pulling the spear from his shoulder, "but the fact that you are in league with one of the rebellious Children seals your fate. To think that the first execution I carry out would be one of the Ranthall brothers. Soon enough I shall pay your brother a visit, and his little cult of the phoenix will be put down."

Korrd concentrated his powers on knitting his broken body, choosing to take a page out of Logan and Aerith's book to buy time.

"I'd like to see that. Maybe you could let me live and go after my little brother instead. I'd even help you."

Ayden scoffed.

"You'd help long enough to get yourself into a position to kill both of us. No matter what you may think of yourself, Korrd Ranthall, you are no hero. You never were. You were a convenient pawn of those who had more power and more understanding than a flea like you could manage. And when they were done with you, they just let you die. The fact that your brother was able to escape his fate just proves that Aerith is a bigger fool than Emries is. Emries knew how to clean up loose ends by ensuring the death of his followers. In time, once you've served your purpose on this world, he'll cast you away again. But rather than wait for you to fulfill some sick and twisted machination on his behalf, I shall dispose of you now, and then eliminate the other pawn, the one who calls himself Nathan Sandar. Then it will be time for Emries to be called to account for his treachery over these millennia."

Korrd laughed as he pulled himself back to his feet. He was still not strong enough to fight, but if the surprise he was planning worked, he wouldn't have to fight at all.

"You can deny your parentage all you want, Ayden," Korrd taunted, "but that sounds like the hubris that has made Aerith the thorn in everyone's side for as long as he's drawn breath. Do you think that a Servant can go toe to toe with a Child of the Creator and actually win? Emries gutted you once, and don't think for a second that he won't do it again."

Ayden held his ground, and Korrd could feel the power again beginning to build inside the Will's form.

"That was before the divine protection of the Creator was lifted, and before the Creator chose his new emissary. The Divine Empress will ensure that the future for those who are faithful to the teachings of the Creator will never again need the intervention or meddling of the so-called Children. Their time, like yours is at an end."

Korrd frowned.

"I hate zealots. Zealots only know one way, and that way invariably leads to blood."

Ayden snorted.

"You should look in the mirror then, Korrd. Your way leads to nothing but blood; no different than mine."

Korrd never heard Ayden's words. He was already well into his assault by the time the youth opened his mouth. A straight-forward attack came as soon as the last words were out of Ayden's mouth, a stream of fire aimed right at Ayden's heart. Instead of moving out of the way, Ayden extended a hand and blocked the pedestrian attack. However, that was exactly what

Korrd was counting on. With his attention focused on the stream of fire, Ayden never felt Korrd's true attack until it was far too late. Twin portals opened the next moment, but instead of Korrd using them to move behind or beside his opponent, he instead used them in a new lethal way. The two portals appeared side by side at the root of Ayden's right wing. A moment after they opened they closed again, severing the wing at the root. Ayden howled in pain as the massive wing dropped to the ground, and viscous red blood poured from the gaping wound. The pain was too much for even a Servant of the Creator to ignore, and Ayden fell backwards, blood pooling all around him. That moment, Ayden sensed that Korrd was about to move in for the kill. However, Ayden had not come to the battle without a contingency plan. He knew that Korrd Ranthall was a powerful opponent, and it would have been foolish to think that such a man would die easily. Ayden would not make the same mistake that he made against Emries. The wordless order was sent out into the Heavens, and mere seconds later six swirling white portals appeared and warrior angels with flaming swords stepped through. Korrd's hands were filled with weapons again before the last of the angels emerged from the portals.

"I should have known you didn't have the guts to face me one on one," Korrd chided.

Ayden growled.

"There is nothing to be gained in fighting honorably against an opponent who has no honor."

Two of the angels charged at once, their searing hot swords passing dangerously close to Korrd's exposed flesh. Instead of dodging out of the way of the assault, Korrd barreled forward, one of his crystalline swords slashing upwards across the chest of one of the angels, sending a plume of blood into the air. However, the recklessness of the attack had left Korrd off-balance, and he was just barely able to erect a shield of power around himself before one of the angels' flaming swords was upon him. Instead of causing serious damage, the assault merely knocked Korrd off his feet and sent him sprawling face first to the ground. However, by the time he was able to turn over, one of the angels was upon him, stabbing downward at Korrd's head. A hard kick with his leg allowed Korrd to alter the trajectory of the blade enough that it buried into the ground instead of his scalp, but the divine fire that wreathed the blade was more than hot enough to scorch the flesh of his cheek. Another kick at the angel's knee sent him backwards, but Korrd could barely get to his feet before another of the angels was slashing at his chest. A backwards jump got him away from the assault, but also put him close enough to one of the other angels, who quickly slashed at Korrd's unprotected back, leaving a smoking scar from his right shoulder to his left hip. The shock of the blow propelled Korrd forward right into the strike of another of the flaming swords. This blow was straight across Korrd's chest, and had it been just a few inches deeper, Korrd's life would have been over. But Emries' chosen champion would not be defeated so easily.

Reaching deep inside himself, Korrd pulled on all the power he could manage and sent a massive wave of brilliant white energy in all directions. It cut through the angel in front of him like a scythe through winter wheat. When Korrd whirled round and found the other angel still behind him and advancing, the power flowed from his fingertips enveloping the divine servant and ripping him from existence. Korrd felt the next strike coming and he reached out in time to catch the flaming blade before it could score a fatal blow. Every nerve in Korrd's body exploded in pain, and he could smell the flesh of his palm burning. But instead of giving into the pain, Korrd ripped the blade out of the angel's hand, sending a plume of blood erupting from his own hand, and then Korrd turned the blade on its wielder. With his free hand, Korrd took hold of the hilt and with both hands jabbed the blade into the angel's throat. The blow caused the angel to fall backwards, but Korrd toppled with it, and when the angel's back hit the ground, the weight of Korrd's body forced the blade of the flaming sword through the neck of the angel, severing its head from its body.

All Korrd wanted to do was close his eyes and sleep for a month. But he knew that the battle was not yet over and two more angels were stalking him, and it would not take them long to strike. These creatures were not like any that Korrd had ever faced. They had no emotions, could not be made to panic or doubt. They were truly instruments of war and destruction. They killed, that was all they were programmed to do, and there could be no deviation from that programming. Pulling himself away from the body of the fallen angel, Korrd came back to his feet brandishing the flaming sword. His arms felt as though they weighed several hundred pounds each, and he didn't know if he was going to be able to lift them to defend himself. The two angels were advancing quickly, but before they could reach Korrd, a wall of rock shot up between the angels and Korrd, blocking their advance. Shielded from Korrd's view, a volley of fire rained down from above onto the angels and prevented them from escaping the wall of rock that sped in behind them. The two walls of rock collided at terrific speed, crushing the angels, and reducing them to mere smears of blood and gore. As quickly as the walls of rock appeared, they disappeared, and Korrd was faced with two familiar men striding toward him.

The older man was clad in blood red armor, his hair beginning to gray at the temples and white beginning to show in his beard. There was a knowing look in his eyes, a look that came from a long adventure that had ended in both torment and hollow victory. Like his companion, the blond man also was dressed in armor, but its lighter tones harkened back to a kingdom in turmoil on another world long ago. Despite himself, Korrd found himself smiling as he dropped the flaming sword into the growing pool of blood at his feet. The danger was over, and Korrd no longer felt Ayden's presence. The boy had turned tail and run as soon as he saw that Korrd had gained the upper hand against his attack dogs. But soon enough Korrd and the would-be Will of the Creator would lock horns once again.

"You never seem to be far from the danger, old friend," the man in red armor quipped. "But I suppose that the Ranthall name makes it impossible to be anywhere else."

"Spoken like a true Ranthall," the blond man retorted, his hand resting on the hilt of his sword. "Emries thought you could use a little help considering our enemies seem to be massing."

Korrd smiled.

"Gwillim, Arin, it's good to see you both again, and your timing is impeccable. Though, you didn't have to wait until the last minute."

Gwillim Crill frowned.

"We thought you had it under control."

Arin Domae nodded.

"At least until that last one got the drop on you."

It was then that Korrd noticed that the soldiers around them had begun moving again, and they all were gawking at the bodies of the dead angels that lay on the ground at their feet. Before Korrd could say a word a great cheer came from the ranks.

"Not even angels can kill our commander!"

Cheers went up all around as Korrd motioned for Arin and Gwillim to follow him back to the command tent. Gwillim clapped Korrd on the shoulder and smiled.

"Angels are nothing," he said with venom coming to his voice. "Soon we'll be hunting gods."

Chapter LXXXVI

Lies My Father Told Me

Year Four of the Just Emperor Kaitain "Dragonsbane" Lorien, Creator's Calendar Year 1871

The Creator's domain was a confounding and often chaotic place; a mass of planets, stars, moons, and life that spun and moved to a time all its own, often completely unaware of the mass of life teeming around it. But there were spaces between the worlds and the suns and the life that operated on a level that could not be seen by anyone who did not know the true touch of the Divine. One of these places was the Vault of Terror, a place that was not truly a place at all, but was more like an absence of form. It was a prison, a storage area for those things deemed too dangerous to find their way into the hands of petty mortals. There were other places, other pockets of reality however that the Creator chose to store things that could no longer be trusted in the reality that He chose to allow to exist. Like all of these spaces, it had no true name, but the Children of the Creator often referred to it as the Tomb. Unlike traveling from place to place on Espre, it was not as simple as opening a portal and envisioning the destination to get to the Tomb. So, as Bryn stepped out of the twisting white permanent portal that weaved through the darker parts of Creation, she felt as though her whole body was frozen though her insides felt as though they were on fire. The light in the Tomb was blinding, and it took quite some time for her vision to adjust, and even then the haze was so thick and disorienting that it was nearly impossible to make out the features in the area. However, finally, through the seemingly endless void of white, Bryn's eyes found something in the nothingness, a hazy almost insubstantial island of color. As Bryn took her first unsteady step through the field of white, she had to fight to keep her balance. Everything about the place seemed to shift and shudder as though she were standing in the belly of some great beast. Even the ground, if that was what it was at all, gave considerably with every movement. Finally though, Bryn found a rhythm for her steps that allowed her to make progress toward her goal.

Though the distance did not seem long, to Bryn it felt as though she walked several miles over several hours before she finally stood within arm's reach of her goal. Unlike the rest of the area that she traversed, the ground of this area seemed solid, like a round marble slab in the middle of a swamp. Arrayed around the perimeter of the slab were low benches, and in the center was a wider bench on which a young woman sat, staring out into the nothingness. When Bryn approached, the woman had her back turned, but the moment that Bryn's foot found the circle of marble, the woman turned, her eyes brilliant and filled with a mixture of concern and confusion.

"You should not be here," said the woman's voice devoid of emotion but full of strength. "Were you to be discovered, your life would surely be forfeit."

For a long moment, Bryn just stood there looking at the strange woman. Finally, she sank down onto one of the benches and the two just stared at one another. There was a fog that filled Bryn's mind, and it felt instantly as though she had made some grave mistake. Then, as though she suddenly remembered something long forgotten, her eyes went wide.

"I know you."

The statement was simple, but more powerful than even Bryn realized. The woman on the wide bench turned her full body to face Bryn and waved a dismissive hand.

"No, you don't. You've made a simple mistake. Now, you should stand up, turn around, and go back the way you came before you are discovered. I promise that I will not speak of this, and you should not either. Go now, before you commit to a course that you cannot possibly escape."

A wave of uncertainty passed through Bryn and again the woman's face seemed unfamiliar. Perhaps she had been mistaken all along, and the trip had been nothing but folly. Bryn had been kept in the dark all this time, by her husband, her daughter, and even the girl Sabrina, who had seemed to know so much from the very beginning. That was when Bryn's mind seemed to start working again, breaking away from the morass that had set in. The lies they all fought against were older than Espre, older even than Onea, and it was in that truth that Bryn started to see through the lie that sat before her, the lie that the woman was trying to communicate through Bryn's own eyes.

"No," Bryn said locking her eyes on the woman's suddenly sharpening features. "I'm not going to accept that. I know who you are. You're Liette."

The woman's eyes narrowed.

"A name," she said dismissively. "What does a name mean if you know nothing more? I am sure there are a thousand women who have worn that name across a thousand worlds. Perhaps you would be safer in your ignorance, for as much as you think you know who I am, I know who you are, Bryn Aplee Seth, wife of Aerith Seth, mother of Gideon Viruci, Ayden and Rhain Seth, daughter of Halicon, and first born daughter of the Brotherhood of Phasia. I know the horrors that you have visited upon your birth world, and I know the horror that you will soon visit upon your adopted home. Turn back now before you join your husband in damning us all to fire."

Bryn's blood ran cold. She felt as though the woman was looking right through her to her soul, and that there was an underlying tide of malice in the words. However, Bryn felt at that moment that the words were yet another attempt to dissuade Bryn from lingering within the Tomb and discovering what she came to discover.

"I know more than your name," Bryn said finally, finding her strength once again. "Liette Forer."

The woman's eyes went wide for a fraction of a moment and then softened again. There was a bit of defeat behind the fire, but it only lasted for a moment before the cold exterior returned.

"Interesting."

The word hung in the air for what seemed like forever and then the woman nodded in defeat before folding her hands in her lap.

"Tell me what you think you know," the woman said.

Bryn sat quietly for a moment gathering her thoughts. Even as the memories came into her mind, they tried to slide away; as though some force was doing everything it could to hide the woman's identity and history.

"You were on Onea. I'm not completely sure why. It had something to do with the Creator, and it had something to do with making sure that the war between Emries and Halicon came to a resolution and that Onea did not fall into darkness. But there was more to it than that. There were so many lies, so many uncertainties. But I know you had some connection to Midarin Rice and Aryx Terian."

Suddenly something that felt like a memory rocketed through Bryn's mind.

"You were Midarin's daughter. They changed your name to hide your identity."

The woman did not respond.

"But that wasn't all, was it?"

The question was rhetorical, but Bryn was hoping that the question itself would have sparked some kind of response from the woman. However, the woman's cold dark eyes and silence were the only response. But Bryn had already found the memory that she had been searching for.

"You have been on Espre too. After the Founding Wars were over, you suddenly appeared as the wife of Terrik Lorien, and the first Empress of the Kingdom of Cadaria. You were also the one who commissioned the creation of the Sacred Weapons for the Knights of the Flashing Blade, and were also the first of the Seers."

Finally the icy exterior cracked. The woman sighed and shook her head slightly before returning her gaze to her visitor. However, the woman's features changed dramatically over the next few moments. She took on an alien appearance with solid crimson eyes. Her hair also seemed to change in that moment, all the softness and life gone, taking on a more straw-like appearance and sheen. Also, her jaw elongated, hollowing out her cheeks and making her cheekbones much more prominent. The change also caused her mouth to draw wider, with thin almost imperceptible lips. This new appearance shook Bryn's resolve, and instantly inside of her grew the desire to run, to flee, and to get as far away from the beautiful monstrosity as possible. But the answers were too important. It was worth any risk, because without the answers, without the truth, there could be no true victory in the dire war that was about to dawn.

"I allow you to see my true appearance to help you to understand the true gravity of your arrogance. To demand such answers, to invoke the consequences, you are either truly brave, or so foolish that you barely qualify as intelligent. But as puzzled as I am, I am also merciful. Turn around now, walk away, and go back to your dying world. Make what difference you can. Cry and sob as you watch your childrens' lives ripped from them and the light go out of the eyes of every single person you ever loved or cared about. Abandon this folly of a quest to save what cannot be saved. Accept the futility of your existence and do what you were meant to do. Cower and die like a good mortal, it is all you were ever meant to do."

Bryn should have been outraged. She should have screamed at the top of her lungs at the insult. Something however restrained her. It was a fear, a deep intense overriding fear that kept her mute. All of the words that assailed her from the alien woman's mouth were cold, logical, and above all, true. She had been shaken to the core, made to face her worst fears, and the folly of her nature. While the words had impact, there was a wave of emotion that accompanied them. There was the unspoken assault, waves upon waves of crippling doubt that broke against Bryn's resolve like a quickly eroding beach in the face of a strong tide. And yet she remained. Her legs trembled, her quiet pulseless heart ached in her chest. Breath and words caught in her throat, but Bryn remained anchored to her spot on the small bench, shaking like a leaf in a hurricane, but refusing to be torn from her branch.

"I want what I came for," Bryn said finally, her voice unconsciously trembling.

Bryn felt rather than saw the woman frown. Finally though came the nod of ascent, and the waves of doubt and fear relented. The woman straightened again, her eyes still deep crimson and full of power, and when her voice rang out again, it was not filled with the same awe-inspiring and fear-inducing power; it was instead soft and almost matronly.

"I will give you the information you are seeking on two conditions. The first is that no matter what I tell you, you must stay until the whole tale is told. Whether you wish to hear more or not."

Bryn nodded, puzzled.

"And the second?"

"I want to know how you found me, and how you know who I was in the mortal world."

Bryn's expression was blank. She didn't understand the condition or even how it was relevant. As though picking up on the confusion, the woman continued.

"Once my time on Espre was done, and my assignment complete, the Creator wiped all knowledge of my existence from the minds of every creature that roamed the face of Espre, including the dragons. The history of my deeds would remain, but were any creature to see me, they would not recognize me. More importantly, those of you who once called Onea home would never make the connection between the Liette Forer that called that world home, and the woman who later became Liette Lorien. It would be a coincidence of name, nothing more. So I ask you again, how do you know who I was in the mortal world?"

Bryn's face did not belie the shame that suddenly rose inside her.

"I wish I could say that I knew who you were more than a day ago, but I did not. My daughter, Rhain, has become the vessel for the powers of Halicon, and through that she has also become the host for all of his knowledge. I knew that there were so many lies and so many obfuscations in this war between the Creator and the Children, that we needed information in order to find a path to victory. My daughter is strong, but she is inexperienced. So, before I left Celidar I met with my daughter and when we embraced, I used the moment of contact to scan her mind. I know enough to bypass her defenses. It was in her mind that I found information about the Tomb, and how to get here, though I'm not sure that she herself was aware. I was surprised when I set my eyes on you that my own memories had suddenly returned."

The woman nodded.

"I should have suspected as much. The Creator could not have removed my existence from the minds of the Children, or those who inherited their powers."

She then looked off into the distance.

"Or perhaps He could. Perhaps his plan all along was for one of you to find me, and put the final pieces of the puzzle together. Only the Creator knows his mind or his intentions, I can only speculate. The fact that I have even been kept alive to be able to answer your question is a testament to that possibility. But then, that was my purpose on Onea. I was to ensure that the balance was kept, and that there was a resolution to the conundrum that your kind created."

Bryn scowled.

"So I was led here. Fulfilling another of the Creator's tasks."

The woman's eyes flashed.

"He is the Creator. Why does it surprise you that He would know your actions before you do? Why shouldn't it be that you or any of the other mortals would be completely at his whim? The arrogance continues to astound me. Only one of you has proven to be a confounding influence on the direction of the Creator's Design. Which leads to the true purpose of your visit here. The truth."

Bryn gritted her teeth unconsciously.

"I didn't even ask you a question yet."

The sigh that came from the alien woman the next moment had clear implication, her patience was wearing thin.

"As I said," she said finally, "arrogance. You know that you have been lied to. You know that you want the truth, but I say to you that as intelligent as you think you are, you have no concept of what it is you should ask. I have no desire to wait as you puzzle and fumble through the possibilities to approach an understanding. And thus I will tell you the truth you need to know, without requiring you to know you wish for it."

Bryn bristled at the woman's words. Of course she had been talked down to before; by her brothers in the phasia most certainly. But it was only when Halicon's calm and superior tone flowed through her did Bryn ever truly feel that she was nothing more than a petulant child. This woman, obviously touched by the hand of the divine, made Bryn feel the same way, and she hated it. But for the sake of all, Bryn sat, nodded, and waited to be spoon-fed.

"These creatures that you call the Children of the Creator are less his children and more aspects of His Will. For all that the Creator understands, He, like the Cosmos that spawned Him, strives to more fully understand Himself and His creations."

Bryn felt her mind begin to boil with questions.

"Something made the Creator?"

As though the information was so obvious that she had not expected a question to be asked, the woman simply stared at Bryn. Finally she nodded and sighed.

"There is more to the Cosmos than just the Creator and that which the Creator made. Thus the Creator must have come from somewhere, and that somewhere is the Cosmos itself. The Cosmos spawned the Creator, or perhaps the Cosmos and the Creator were spawned simultaneously. Regardless, they operate independently from one another with one goal, to understand themselves and all within their reach. The Creator has attempted to do this though making first his Children, then the dragons, then worlds, and sub-creatures like humans. You are all extensions of this need to understand. The greatest expression of this understanding, at least as far as the Creator is concerned, is through conflict. Conflict has allowed the Creator to discover so much about the nature of the Cosmos and of Himself. But like every true seeker of knowledge, greater understanding comes from constantly changing and increasing the scope of their examination and endeavor. And thus, for the Creator, this required an escalation in conflict."

Bryn was in awe, but it was not at the sudden understanding of the true nature of everything she had ever known, but it was true horror at the enormity of what they were facing. Ignoring the visceral reaction of her companion, the woman continued.

"From their first breaths, the Children have sought to subjugate each other through the application of their core ideologies. In time, simply proving the abstract of their ideology without practical application became pointless. They sought to show one another the breadth of their superiority, and did so by creating worlds in which their dogmatic control was absolute. But these colonies of absolutes instead of serving as proofs became breeding grounds for greater strife. The Children became dissatisfied in comparing their designs for a perfect Cosmos, and instead took to proving why the ideologies of the other Children were inferior. These conflicts, as most conflicts do, started in the abstract. Millennia of posits and suppositions, debated in what has now become the Heavens among the Children. The boredom and frustration with the abstract again took over, and the scattered worlds became the new battlegrounds, where one of the Children established their dominion, and the others tried to tear it away. Greater and greater these clashes became, the conflict escalating and the destruction and loss of mundane life incalculable."

Bryn's mind was filled with the sheer enormity of the scale that the woman was describing. How many died? How many worlds had been sacrificed to prove a point? What kind of monsters were these Children, and would they even have seen themselves as monsters? The woman continued; her dispassionate tone as disturbing as the words that accompanied it.

"So the debate became whether intelligence would change the outcome of the conflicts. Over millennia, new creatures came into existence, each with ever increasing levels of intelligence; all becoming extinct at the expense of the greater ideological debate. Billions were sacrificed. Hundreds of billions. And yet, as the nature of conflict demands, the conflict continued to grow. Worlds died, suns blinked out of existence, and whole races were born and destroyed in the blink of an eye. Then everything changed."

Bryn's frown belied the sickness she felt in the pit of her stomach.

"Humans."

"Given what you and your race refer to as intelligence, I am sure that is considered insightful. In this case however, it is less so. But that in and of itself is the problem. Intelligence. You, your human brothers and sisters, over thousands of years have finally progressed to the point that you can do what no other creature, save the dragons, have been able to do. You can perceive the nature of things. The dragons understand because they have seen, you humans are able to understand because of your capacity to grasp and take as real those things you have never seen, felt, or even know to exist. You have a thirst to know, to conquer ignorance, and to pierce the veil between reality and dream. But you have been nothing more than the shiny new toy in the sandbox for millennia, a speck in time. And yet you have progressed so much farther than all the others that you can now touch the pattern of the divine. Know that there are mysteries to be solved, and not simply that you are at the mercy of forces like the wind. You seek to change the wind, harness it, make it yours. That need and want translates to everything. Even the divine. And so now you have climbed to the highest peak of your understanding and stare out into the Cosmos and have finally discovered that the Cosmos is staring back."

Bryn was dumbstruck. For the first time she doubted whether or not she wanted to know more. Perhaps that was why the woman's condition held that Bryn had to stay to the end of the tale. How much more intricate would the tale become?

"And so at this moment you find yourself in a quandary that is eons in the making. And yet, why does it matter? Even though you understand, you can only have so much impact on the war. The Children will continue to exist; the conflict will continue to exist. And even if your world is destroyed, even if humanity ceases to exist, the moment after the fall, it will all begin again with a new race on a new world or series of worlds with greater intelligence than even you have. Or perhaps the Children will find that your intelligence was a hindrance in their little game, and make something not as dangerous. In a matter of weeks, perhaps months, all of this will mean nothing. Or perhaps, something unexpected is at play here. Something even the Creator did not account for. Are you starting to see? Is the possibility beginning to dawn in that relatively pedestrian mind of yours?"

Bryn's eyes widened.

"Aerith."

The frown creased the woman's face, dipping the corners of her thin mouth almost level to the bottom of her pointed chin. The exaggerated expression was grotesque at best.

"Your suspicion may be correct, but your reasoning is completely inadequate. You have all wondered and surmised for thousands of years why a being like your Aerith exists. Where does his power come from? You've assumed it came from Emries. You've assumed it came from the Creator as a balance for his impetuous and disobedient children. You've assumed it was something new created because of his parentage and the time in which he was sired. But the truth is far more frightening for the Creator and for those who understand the truth. That is why Emries has been bent on destroying Aerith and those who carry his mantle. That is why the Creator tried to keep those with Aerith's mantle like Sabrina and Evan close to him and connected to his power. Why first Sabrina and then Rhain were allowed to inherit Halicon's power, why Ayden Seth is now a member of the Servants wearing the mantle of the Will."

The revelation froze Bryn's heart. Two of her children were directly connected to the Creator, and while it had seemed at the time that Rhain's choice was of her own free will, it now was clear that it was yet another manipulation. Ayden on the other hand was a complete surprise, one that filled Bryn with a sense of dread and foreboding.

"And the third of your children has just become leashed to the will of Raenera as the sole inheritor of her power."

Bryn blinked. It was the only reaction she could manage. Gideon was alive? How? When? Where had he been hiding and why? Why was he with Raenera? How had he come to inherit her power? But sitting looking in the woman's eyes, Bryn knew she was asking the wrong questions. The Creator was afraid of Aerith. Why? Where did his power come from and what was its ultimate purpose?

"Very good," the woman said coldly. "You are finally beginning to not think like a human. You are starting to see the game for what it is. See the lines. See the manipulations. Your contemporary Logan has also begun to see, though he does not know what he thinks he knows. It is merely a piece. The one called Wolf, the inheritor of Pyrrus' power also has begun to understand. But he too only sees shadows cast by the greater light. Already they know too much, they are too dangerous, and steps are in place to remove them from the game permanently."

Already there was too much information, but the next words detonated in Bryn's ears.

"The Creator did not grant Aerith his power, nor was it some fluke of faith. The Cosmos itself has bestowed power upon Aerith, a foil, an end to conflict in all its forms. One who thrives on conflict cannot itself learn without a threat. The Cosmos has ensured that there has been a path to challenge and defeat the Creator. That path lies through Aerith, and though he sees, he does not believe. Once he does, he will come into the truth of his role."

The words forced Bryn to her feet, and she staggered back away from the low bench. Her feet had just left the round patch of stone when the woman who was once called Liette stood.

CHAPTER 86

"You fulfilled the conditions of the bargain, Bryn Seth, and you have learned the truth that you needed, whether it was the truth you sought or not. For that, however, you have become a threat to the Creator and to His plan. I'm afraid that He has decreed that you too shall be trapped within this living Tomb for the remainder of eternity."

Suddenly Bryn felt the presence behind her, and when she whirled around, two dozen warrior angels stood barring her path back to the portal, flaming swords in hand. One of the angels lifted a hand and pointed back to the island of stone in the middle of the sea of white ordering Bryn back. Bryn looked back over her shoulder for just a moment and then turned back to the angels. A moment later her hands were wrapped in the writhing green flames of the Blaze.

"My fight does not end here, and this shall not be my Tomb. I shall rip your wings off and carve your hearts out with your own flaming swords."

Bryn's battle cry hit the air as she charged.

Chapter LXXXVII

Salvation Redux

Aerith Seth stood on a peak high above the Heart of Stone and looked down both amazed and horrified by the sight that stretched before him. Despite the amount of damage that both he and Tess Annis did to the Heart of Stone during Aerith's escape from Creator-sanctioned captivity, the massive fortification still stood like a bastion of light in the long night. However, the structure was now ringed by winged angels with flaming swords, defending the holy building from any incursion. Having the creatures so close was a complication, but not one that was insurmountable. Aerith had learned enough over the millennia to shield his powers from those he did not want to feel his presence. Against blunt instruments like the warrior angels, it wasn't difficult. However, for those far more disciplined and aware, even Aerith's practices defenses could not keep him out of view forever. But he had not come back to Albitonin to hide. Emries had gone on the offense, and if there was anywhere that he would strike next, it would be the Heart of Stone. The so-called Emperor Kaitain Lorien had already started his offensive against the worship of the Creator, but if Emries was able to knock down the central building of the religion of the Creator, then it would sew more dissention and chaos amongst the believers. All Emries wanted was turmoil. He needed all of his enemies off-balance while he moved his pieces into position, and then both he and Talisia would move in for the kill. They would remove Kaitain from power or co-opt him and his army until they no longer served their purpose. But being the coward that he was, Emries would never risk moving on the Heart of Stone himself. No, he would send one of his lackeys. In a way, Emries' own tendencies had assured who that lackey would be.

As much as his vanity and pride demanded it, Emries knew that he was not yet ready to move directly against Logan or Aerith. Recent events had also proven that his agents were not even ready to go up against Gwydeon and Midarin. That had to be galling for Emries, and as such he would need his agent to redeem himself. Nathan Sandar was the only choice to break the Heart of Stone, and so Aerith waited, sitting high in the mountains for the man that he once crossed blades with long ago on a dying world. Luckily for Aerith and his waning patience, he was not kept waiting long. Only a matter of hours into his vigil, Aerith felt the first flows of a portal beginning to form less than a mile south of where he sat. Smartly the newcomer was letting his portal form in a place that would not be easily felt by the angels that guarded the Heart of Stone. Aerith didn't need to use a portal, nor did he need to channel much power to float down the southeastern face of the mountain. He was half way down the mountain when he finally saw the white-clad young man who waited for him. Nathan Sandar for all of his faults was certainly not stupid, and it would have taken little for him to recognize Aerith's powers as soon as he appeared in Albitonin. To the boy's credit, he didn't turn tail and run back to his patron. The boy stood his ground, swords of white-hot flame in both hands, his eyes tracking Aerith's progress down the mountain face. Aerith finally let his feet touch the ground merely two dozen paces from where Nathan stood, but unlike his adversary, Aerith did not produce a weapon.

"It's been a long time, old man," Nathan said finally.

Aerith quietly nodded. He remembered the duel as though it had happened only yesterday. Nathan had long since been corrupted by Emries touch, and though Aerith had only a fraction of his powers, he was able to delay the boy and buy time for Logan and the others to make a run at ending the war in the right way. Unfortunately, Aerith had been robbed of the chance to finish Nathan off. The boy had outmaneuvered him briefly and sent him via portal far away, knowing that the much older warrior didn't have the power left to portal back. The odds still may not have been even, but at least this time, Aerith would be able to ensure that the battle would have a definitive winner and loser.

"Yes it has, Nathan," Aerith responded. "Though I can't imagine that you would have wanted this rematch if you had a choice. I mean, the last time we tangled, you barely got out alive, and if I would have had my powers, it would have ended a lot differently. Now though, you have to know, you're no match for me."

A lance of power shot from somewhere in the haze around the younger man the next moment, and Aerith slid to his left at seemingly the last moment to avoid the strike. Aerith never even felt the flows of power that created the blast until it was almost on top of him.

"I've had a long time to practice, old man. And you'll find I'm full of surprises this time."

A portal appeared in front of Nathan the next moment and he sprinted forward, Aerith felt the portal open right behind him the next moment and he was able to duck and roll out of the way as one of Nathan's swords would have pierced through the center of his back while the other would have severed his head from his shoulders. When Aerith turned and prepared to counterattack, Nathan was already gone, having disappeared through another portal. A whistle from high above was the only warning that Aerith got, and a hail of fiery meteors tumbled from the sky. The first struck inches from where Aerith knelt, and the shockwave of its collision threw Aerith several feet in the air. The old warrior could feel the heat and the burning as the fires licked at his skin, but as he tumbled backwards and regained his balance, he landed on his feet and with only a thought extinguished the fires that clung to him. Again Nathan had relocated, and a burst of pain blossoming in his shoulder told Aerith where the boy was. The focused beam had stuck between Aerith's left shoulder blade and his spine and emerged just under his collarbone. The wound healed instantly, seared shut by the heat of the strike. The pain was immense, but as Aerith turned to face Nathan once again, he shut out everything but the growing rage in the pit of his stomach.

"You see, Aerith," Nathan's overly-pleased voice rang out, "you cannot hope to match the new skills that I have acquired training with Emries and his other servants. We know every trick of everyone who ever stood against our patron, and the ways to counter them. You cannot hope to stand against me now."

Aerith let a cruel smile curl his lips.

"All your new skills didn't serve you too well against your father, did they?"

As expected, the taunt enticed Nathan into a charge. However, as the younger man crossed the distance, two long portals appeared at his side perpendicular to the ground and less than a foot wide. They appeared at shoulder level and stretched several feet. Once they appeared, Nathan extended his arms to the side so that the blades of his white hot swords entered the portals. The next moment, the portals opened beside Aerith, each vertical and only inches from his sides. The tips of the blades appeared at the top of the portals and as Nathan advanced sped downwards, a searing guillotine aimed to split Aerith in half. Feeling rather than seeing the strike, Aerith threw himself backwards to the ground and then slid forward. He was almost too slow to escape the blades as they crashed to the ground, and the deadly scythe ended barely their own width from the top of Aerith's scalp. The split second that he lay on the ground, Aerith could smell the burning of his own hair and the top of his head, but he would not let such things deter him. In a single deft motion, Aerith sprang to his feet and began his counterattack. Pivoting his body, Aerith stamped down with his right foot onto the smoldering blades, trapping them in place. A heartbeat later he extended his left hand towards Nathan's exposed chest and unleashed a tightly packed ball of pure wind that hit like a hammer blow. Nathan was forced to release his hold on both the portals and his weapons as the assault sent him tumbling backward. Even before the younger man struck the ground, the weapons and the portals had disappeared, and by the time Nathan got back to his feet, Aerith had already retrieved the long and majestic Sacred Weapon Valor from its extra-dimensional hiding place.

Though unwieldy, the massive sword known as Valor had some distinct advantages for someone who was strong and skillful enough to wield it.

Primarily, the length of the weapon gave greater range to every strike, but more importantly to Aerith for this battle were the unusual angles that the strikes would come from. Nathan had never proven to be anything other than a conventional fighter, and the ability to dictate the battle would become critical if Aerith were going to stay true to his word and overmatch the villain. But Nathan had proven an impressive command over his powers thus far, and that could complicate things. Aerith knew how to use his powers offensively, but he had always preferred close combat. But there were a few tricks that he had up his sleeves that would keep the boy on his heels for a few moments.

"Alright," Aerith said stretching his neck from one side to the other, "let's see how you like this."

Aerith held the hilt of the extremely heavy and unwieldy Valor in only his left hand for a moment and concentrated power into his right. When he brought the right hand back to the hilt there was a burst of light and a dozen ghostly copies of Valor appeared hovering around Aerith. The next moment Aerith charged in, and Nathan conjured a new flaming sword to defend himself. Several feet before making contact, Aerith stopped dead in his tracks, letting the ghostly blades dart forward on their own. As each one attacked independently, Nathan flashed his blade to mount a defense, but the phantom Valors disappeared immediately upon contact. Aerith took the opportunity then to launch forward, and Valor's true blade slashed in from a high angle, chopping clear across Nathan's torso from his right shoulder to his left hip. Now realizing the subterfuge, Nathan ignored the ghostly weapons and brought his defenses to bear on the real Valor that sped in on him. Just as Nathan brought his sword up to meet the downward slash, Aerith closed the trap, and Valor jumped from his hands and took the place of one of the ghost images that was behind Nathan. It stuck the back of his left shoulder, hard enough to draw blood, but not enough to disable. It then leapt to another one of the ghosts, slicing deep into Nathan's right leg. It was barely in time on the next leap to cut across Nathan's right hip before leaping back to Aerith's hands. By this time the ghost blade that had been in Aerith's hands had passed through Nathan's block, and the now very solid Valor opened a massive gash across the former *Coromor's* chest. With several large gaping wounds pouring blood in all directions, Nathan had no choice but to use the power left in his flaming sword to create a flare in Aerith's face, temporarily blinding the grizzled warrior and giving the younger man a chance to fall back to a safer distance. By the time Aerith's vision cleared a couple of seconds later, the wounds on Nathans' chest and leg were already pulling themselves together.

"Impressive trick," Nathan said, tapping his temple, "but I've seen how you do it now, and I won't be fooled by it again."

The next moment Aerith released the hilt of Valor and it disappeared back into its insubstantial home. A moment later the two other Sacred Weapons in Aerith's possession, the battle axe Strength and the cruelly curved blade known as Discipline. Though normally Aerith was not fond of using an ax in battle, it would yet again give his opponent something new to defend against. By the time Aerith had rearmed, Nathan had completed most of his healing. Aerith could have pressed the advantage and not given his opponent room, but that would most likely have resulted in a desperate attack by the younger warrior, one that Aerith would not be properly prepared for. Aerith was not opposed to rushing in against an opponent that he knew he could overmatch, but with Nathan, Aerith had to be cagier, more deliberate, and that truly was not his style.

Sensing a shift in momentum, Nathan unleashed a torrent of power, a dozen powerful beams all coming from different directions converging on where Aerith stood. With little effort, Aerith dodged three of the blasts, deflected two more, and had lurched forward before the others posed a danger. He brought Strength crashing down on Nathan, who blocked the blow, but he was out of position for the following slash by Discipline. The tip of the blade opened the boy from hip to hip, creating a gaping bloody wound in his belly that threatened to expose his innards. He tried to leap back, but Aerith pressed his advantage, using the blades of Strength like a hook, he brought them down sharply into Nathan's shoulder and ripped the boy off his feet. A cry of pain ripped from Nathan's chest as he was forced to his knees by the pressure of Aerith's strike and the pain that was flooding through his body. There was too much pain for him to concentrate and knit the massive wound in his belly. Even if Aerith did not finish him quickly there was a danger that he would lose consciousness from the amount of blood pouring from the wound, and then he would simply exsanguinate. But as he looked up at Aerith towering over him and saw the dark steel of Discipline lining up for a final strike, he closed his eyes and waited for the pain to end. The blade sped downward, but at the last possible moment, an invisible force took hold of Aerith around the throat and pulled him backwards. Aerith didn't know what was happening for a long second until he was able to feel the flows of wind wrapped around his neck attempting to choke the life from him. Aerith spun on one heel, and out of the corner of his eye he saw a form several feet away. Needing only that amount of time to sight the new opponent, in one deft motion Aerith raised and then threw Strength as hard as he could manage. The blade crossed the distance in a flash, and with perfect accuracy buried itself wholly into the chest of the mystery attacker. Blood sprayed in all directions, and then there was a terrible cry that came not from the man, but from the weapon that emerged from his chest. The cry grew louder and louder until it was beyond deafening. The axe head split in half and the haft slid to the bloody ground. By the time Aerith turned back to Nathan, the boy was gone, retreated to a safe distance at the top of a hill over a hundred feet away. The wound in his belly had not yet fully healed, and an angry red scar was clearly visible on his pale skin.

"You'll pay for this insult soon enough, old man," the boy cursed, "I'll enjoy ending your life."

Discipline disappeared from Aerith's hand, and the older warrior put both of his hands in the air as a demonstration that he was unarmed.

"Don't tell me you're leaving already," Aerith said in his best mocking tone, "we were just starting to have fun."

Nathan shook his head.

"My task was to be accomplished without alerting any of the local defenses until it was far too late for them to respond. However, thanks to your little display, that has become impossible."

The portal appeared beside Nathan the next moment, but before stepping through he pointed back in the direction of the Heart of Stone.

"But if it's fun you're looking for, old man, I'm sure they would be happy to oblige."

Aerith looked over his shoulder briefly to see a flight of warrior angels heading in their direction. Aerith cursed to himself. With the amount of power being traded by the two men, and the added issue of the death of the Sacred Weapon, it was inevitable that the new guards of the Heart of Stone would be roused to investigate. At the end of the day, perhaps this little adventure wasn't worth the risk after all. Aerith had made the same mistake that he had always thought Emries would make. He had been overconfident, and it was his own actions that allowed him to be outmaneuvered. By the time Aerith looked back, Nathan had already stepped through the portal and fled the battlefield. In time, Nathan would have to finish this battle, but Aerith didn't have time to worry about that. The angels would be on him in a matter of moments, and as much as he didn't want to fight them, he could not leave, at least not yet. Besides, the warrior angels were working for the Creator, and any chance that Aerith had to thin the ranks of his opponent, he had to take it.

There were no more than a dozen angels in the flight, but they would be a challenge even if Aerith wasn't wounded. Whatever the mystery attacker had done, it had been effective, and it had drained much of the energy that Aerith still had in reserve. Aerith crossed the distance between where he stood and where the mystery man lay, and knelt down beside the corpse. It took only a quick scan of the memories that had once belonged to Sabrina Binosear to know the identity of the man. His name had been Rand Merin, the Wind *Erieal* of the third generation on Onea. In life he had been a cousin of Eldar Merin, or perhaps a nephew. Some things about the Merin family tree were unclear, but whatever his lineage, he had been coopted by the enemy. He had obviously laid in wait to assist Nathan should he have found himself in a bad position. Aerith's intention in coming to Albitonin had been to remove one of Emries' pawns from the game, and he had done just that, just not the one he had intended to end. By the time Aerith got back to his feet, the angels were descending out of the sky. It hadn't taken them long to locate the source of the power they felt, and as they touched down to the ground, their flaming swords pulsed with malice and their eyes were locked on Aerith.

"No need to worry, guys," Aerith said motioning down at the fallen body, "I took care of him for you. You can go back to whatever you were doing."

For several long moments the angels simply stood looking at Aerith. Their eyes never shifted to the fallen body. Finally, the lead angel lifted his flaming blade and pointed it in Aerith's direction.

"Heretic."

The voice boomed across the distance, and Aerith felt it not with the intimidation that was intended, but rather with annoyance.

"I should have known that wouldn't have worked. Alright, if we're going to fight, we might as well get on with it."

Aerith wasted no time in letting twin blades of crystal appear in his hands. Now that he had seen one of the Sacred Weapons die, he was not willing to risk either of the other two until he had a better understanding of what they were and why they would break. The simpler weapons would be fine against angels. The creatures charged him en masse, blades of fire darting in at him from every direction. Luckily for Aerith, the angels didn't have the same abilities as some of the Servants, and could not channel their power into anything other than melee weapons. That left them clearly in Aerith's favorite area. One of the flaming blades slashed in hard, intending to end the battle quickly and sever Aerith's head from his body. Using the angel's momentum against it, Aerith spun in flashing one blade high and the other low. The high strike removed the angel's arm at the elbow, while the low strike caught the back of the angel's knee, separating the lower leg from the rest of the body. Even as the angel fell to the ground, Aerith was following up his strike with a downward blow that pierced the angel right through the heart. Unlike common opponents however, the warrior angels did not have a sense of fear, and did not have morale to shake. They knew only one direction, forward. Again they were on Aerith as a group, and unable to find a direction to attack in, Aerith could only go completely defensive, batting away attacks as quickly as his rapidly tiring limbs would allow. Finally there was a hole in one of the angel's defenses, and Aerith spun in, changing the grip on the sword in his right hand so that the blade was downward. He slashed hard across the midsection of the angel, piercing through its gleaming armor and cutting down to the tender flesh beneath. Taking the opportunity afforded to him, Aerith channeled power into the crystalline blade and left it lodged in the angel's breastplate. As he threw himself to the ground, the blade detonated, ripping the angel in half and sending crystal shards spraying in all directions. Several of the angels were wounded by the shrapnel, but it didn't do nearly the amount of damage that Aerith had hoped. Only three of the dozen angels were out of commission and Aerith was truly starting to feel the drain on his reserves. The next moment however, Aerith had to make sure he was not hallucinating.

From above, a massive writhing form descended, a brilliant jade green against the darkening but fire-streaked sky. Though the creature had no wings, Aerith immediately knew that it was a dragon, and its undulations allowed it to glide upon the wind as though it were swimming. The brilliant wide red eyes gleamed in the remaining light, and made the creature look menacing at best, terrifying at worst. With one quick motion the dragon dropped out of the sky onto a group of the angels. Three of them were crushed outright by the weight, killed before they knew what happened to them. Another was ripped in half by a flash of claws, while two more lost heads and wings as the dragon chomped downward, sending blood spraying in all direction. One of the remaining angels attempted to slash at the underbelly of the dragon while the other two advanced on Aerith, undeterred by the interruption. Ignoring the one attacking it directly, the dragon instead spun, letting its tail flash through the air, crashing into the two angels moving toward Aerith. One of the angel's spines snapped under the force of the blow as it hurdled through the air like a broken doll. The other was swept up with the tail and then pounded into the ground, reduced to a pulpy mass of flesh. The last of the angels met its end trampled into the ground while it was still attempting to attack the dragon, reduced to nothingness before it could process the fact that it was dead. When Aerith got back to his feet and turned to face the dragon, he wasn't sure whether the massive beast was there to help him, or just wanted the angels out of the way so it could have Aerith to itself.

"draw attention….too much….not subtle…..easy to find…."

The dragon's voice was less a coherent stream and more a collection of hisses that were left to be interpreted. Aerith released the blades that were still in his hands and put his hands on his hips.

"I've been told I make a loud impression."

The dragon didn't react.

"disciple forged alliance....dragons fight....called Serentis.....bring gift...."

A moment later the dragon produced from a pouch slung under a smaller set of scales on its underbelly a pair of fairly ordinary looking boots. Aerith took the brown leather boots in his hands and looked at them, unable to hide the frown that came to his lips.

"Don't have these in black do you?"

Again the dragon ignored his attempt at humor.

"called Endure....never tire....never sleep...do not breathe....do not eat....like divine your fight...less weakness...."

Aerith regarded the boots while the dragon continued speaking.

"Serentis oldest dragon.....second born.....there at beginning......know things....see things.....you must listen...."

For some reason, the dragon was starting to sound more and more like Aerith's wife.

"Serentis," Aerith said smiling, "I think you and I are going to be very good friends."

Where Intention Burns

Year Four of the Just Emperor Kaitain "Dragonsbane" Lorien, Creator's Calendar Year 1871

Logan Ranthall suddenly found himself yet again in the middle of a conspiracy uniting such disparate forces that it was bordering on the ludicrous. To his right stood one of the proud members of the Brotherhood of Phasia, tasked by their father, one of the Children of the Creator, Halicon, with the destruction or subjugation of every member of the human race. In front of him stood one of the oldest members of the oldest race, Aspertis the Just, who spent most of his long life killing mortals and angels alike in the service of his own goals. Behind Logan stood Jillian Corven, who for most of her life had dedicated herself to eradicating every dragon that walked the face of Espre. Below, in the tunnels were members of the monastic group that Logan himself had formed with another member of the Phasia, Kamen, whose only purpose was to save humanity from the plague of perils that seemed to be massing against it. And then there was Logan himself. He had fought for Emries against Halicon, fought for Halicon against Emries, fought against the Creator for his own sake, now stood against Dorovar, the Creator, and even some of his oldest friends for the sake of saving what could be saved. It was a motley crew, but in the end as long as they could work toward a common goal, they had a chance to do the unthinkable. Logan turned back to Aspertis, his eyes finally adjusting to the brilliant fires that rippled on and through the creature's massive frame.

"Aspertis, since you are new to our little conspiracy, I should introduce you to my confederates here. This is my sometime brother and sometime enemy Rael Starlin, and behind me is Jillian Corven."

Aspertis flashed teeth at Jillian's name.

"Yes, I know the name of the so-called Lady of Cadaria. I know that she and her band of dragon hunters have been the death of many of my younger brothers and sisters. And I know that her sword Scaleripper means death to any who set eyes upon it."

Logan didn't need to see Jillian to know that she was tensing behind him, and that her hand was drifting close to the hilt of her sword. But suddenly Aspertis' features softened, and the fangs disappeared behind crimson and gold scales.

"But I also know the crimes committed against her that drove her to those ends. Evil deeds begat evil acts. I could no more blame her for that which drives her than I can blame Dorovar. I may hate them, but I cannot be just if I did not understand them."

The dragon then turned its glace to Rael.

"And you, Panther, I know of your loss as well. To lose children is a terrible thing, and the fact that it was at the hands of my traitorous brothers and sisters sickens me. Know that those who are loyal to Talisia are my enemies as well, and I shall do all to ensure that their losses are far greater than they themselves can inflict."

Logan's eyes instantly went to Rael. If the man reacted past a simple nod of the head, Logan couldn't tell. Logan had known Rael for a very long time, and both he and Trece had offered a safe haven for Logan during the years when he wanted nothing more than to remain hidden. Logan knew many of their children, and had watched several of them grow into adulthood. However, as sure as Logan was that Rael was hurting on the inside, the man would never let it pierce his exterior. Rael was not bred to be sentimental, he was bred to be a killer, and he was very good at it. He had been the only one to get the best of Gwydeon Sandar back on Onea, and for thousands of years that had been the mark that had elevated Rael above so many others, including even Jeroch. But what many did not know, and Logan only learned through centuries of close contact was that Rael the man was never complete without Trece. She was his emotional stability, and she softened the killer. They were two halves of one person, lethal and functional together, but bordering on lost apart.

Rael's eyes shifted from Logan's back in the direction of the access to the temple below. Logan too let his eyes flow in that direction, and he could not help but shake his head when the giant man's head emerged.

"You're supposed to be resting," Logan said gruffly.

Kamen's impassive face and quiet voice answered.

"And you are supposed to be dead. It seems that we both have issue doing as we should. I felt my brother and sister, and could not leave without seeing them."

Rael's eyes were wide with shock, and he turned instantly to Logan.

"You never told me that Kamen was alive."

By that time Kamen had crossed the distance, and he placed he large hand on Rael's shoulder.

"Blame not the Phoenix, my brother. It was my wish to remain hidden. In the days after my beginning on this world, many sought me, trying to use my power to help them seize control. The Shark, The Cobra, and The Viper all tried, but I would not listen. I feared at once that The Shark would move against me if I refused him a second time. It was then that the Phoenix found me. He agreed to help me hide, to help me stay out of the war that I did not wish to fight. It was soon after that I learned of the hunt for our brothers and sisters, the deaths at the hands of Cedric Binosear and the Shadow. At once I was grateful for my seclusion. For so long I helped Phoenix pick up the pieces of the Founding Wars, taking in those who had lost homes and families. Together we built the Flickering Flame. When Phoenix left to fight the wars of the world, I stayed, holding together the core of that which he ignited. I regretted that I could not see all my brothers and sisters again, but perhaps their ends were the kindest thing that could be given them. Those that remain I fear are lessened for their continued lives. Save those who remained secluded as I have."

Rael nodded wordlessly. Logan turned back to the massive dragon.

"This is my brother Kamen," he said smiling. "He has been known as the Living Flame, and is the heart of the Order of the Flickering Flame."

Logan was shocked to see the dragon gently bow its head.

"I know of this one from Halicon. The Child of the Creator spoke at great length of his sadness at the treatment of one of his children, and the unfairness of it all. He said that he had a gift for you, one that only he could give. Perhaps the knowledge of that gift has been passed down with his powers to their new vessel."

Kamen nodded solemnly.

"You're very well informed," Rael said looking over his shoulder at the dragon.

Aspertis scoffed; a plume of smoke bursting from his nostrils.

"Information has never been difficult for the dragons to come by, especially about those whom the Children have fostered or found so fascinating. Those touched by the Creator too have great significance. But only a few of us, a great few have a close tie to divinity. Those of divine origin can feel the Servants and can nearly hear the will of the Throne. I know because of that connection that two of the Servants have been destroyed. One by your hand, Logan, and one by the hand of your old ally Pike Rhuiden, though he bears a different name now."

Logan braced himself.

"He did it didn't he," Logan said with resignation filling his voice, "he's working for Dorovar."

The dragon's voice was grave.

"He is known now as the Herald Conquest. He is quite formidable and has in single combat snuffed the life from the Voice. Though he did not do it without considerable help. He stole treasures from two of my race, treasure that allowed him to cheat death and to steal the power from the Voice upon his death. It will be very difficult for the Creator to make a new Voice as long as its power is trapped within Conquest."

Suddenly Logan's words seemed to impact the dragon.

"You knew he would come to this?"

Logan could only nod in resignation.

"I feared it as soon as I met Jerah. Dorovar appeals to the missing parts of those he targets. Those with holes in their souls that he promises to fill. I'm afraid that both of them have holes in their souls because of me. And it's one thing I promise I will make right before all of this is over."

Then as if his mind locked onto something the dragon said, his eyes flashed and his head snapped back up.

"So you know who the other two Servants are?"

The dragon nodded slowly.

"Who?"

A small growl escaped the dragon's clenched teeth a moment before he spoke.

"The Spirit now inhabits the one you know as Eldar Merin. The Will has found a home in the son of the heretic, the one you call Ayden Seth."

The names hit Logan like a punch in the stomach.

"And where are they?" Jillian saved Logan from his falter.

"The Sprit has returned to the Heavens to deal with matters for the Creator. It is clear that the loss of two of the Servants has changed the Creator's tactics and He will need time to adjust. The Will has been dispatched to serve at the side of the Creator's chosen vessel on this world, one that he calls the Divine Empress, and who has two of the old gods serving at her side. This woman was once the daughter of the emperor who declared war against our kind. She was known as Marlae Lorien then, she wears a different name now, Marlae Tamerlane."

If the previous revelation was a punch to the gut, the following one threatened to rip it out completely. What had the Creator done? It took several moments for Logan to recover his wits enough to answer the dragon's words, and even as he spoke, Jillian was at his side with her hand finding his again, his discomfort clear to her.

"That complicates things," he said finally. "Rael and I have things to discuss, which I imagine are important family business, and I'm sure that you have many things you must attend to as well, Aspertis."

The dragon spread its wings gently.

"There is a war brewing among my race," the dragon said finally, "one that has been coming for millennia. Soon your skies will darken as my kind take the fight to one another, and those that serve Talisia and Shadowweaver will not care how many mortals burn in the process. We will try to keep as much fight to the dark parts of this world as possible, but in time, there will be no place that will be safe. However, we are now tied to one another, bonded until we are both dead. Should you ever need me, speak my name to my treasure, and I shall come as I am able."

A moment later the dragon beat its huge wings in a single hard downward stroke, and leapt high into the air. It seemed impossible that a creature of such size could so seemingly effortlessly glide upon the breeze, but with only two more strong beats of his wings, Aspertis was high in the sky over the ruined city of Menoris. When Logan turned back to Rael, the younger man had a wry smile on his face.

"And you thought you'd never get married again."

The joke was a rare one for the dry wit of the man known as the Panther, but it was perfectly timed. Logan smiled, but Jillian's intoxicating giggle caused his attempt at control to break and he soon was laughing as well. Kamen's still impregnable expression only allowed a simple smile, and together they followed Rael away from the wide open area to one of the partially ruined structures at the edge of the Flickering Flame's shrine. In the broken home, two women waited, seated at a low table that had been cracked down the middle when a ceiling beam fell on it. The beam had been moved, but the crack remained. As soon as Logan saw the two women, he knew instantly who they were. One because of her long standing connection to Logan, and the other because of her notoriety in the Empire of Cadaria. Trece Starlin stood the moment the group came into view, moving first to Logan and wrapping him in a quick embrace before then giving a much longer hug to Kamen. When Trece moved to stand by her husband, Logan spoke.

"Jillian Corven, this is my sister and Rael's beautiful wife Trece Starlin."

Trece nodded to Jillian, and wasted no time in motioning in the blond woman's direction.

"Logan, I'm sure you know who this is, but let me do proper introductions anyway. Logan Ranthall, Lord Phoenix of the Brotherhood of Phasia and founder of the Order of the Flickering Flame, this is our sister, Leonora Wastri, formerly of the Knights of the Flashing Blade."

The shocks by this point had become so common that Logan didn't even feel surprised. Jillian to her credit had been following the wordplay closely enough to pick on the threads in the introduction.

"Wait, wait, wait… Are you telling me that Leonora Wastri, a Knight of the Flashing Blade, is a Dark God too? How many were there in the Knights?"

Rael, Trece, and Leonora all returned looks of puzzlement. Logan turned to the twins.

"Jeroch."

Rael and Trece nodded in unison, but the name did nothing to allay Leonora's confusion. Rael was the first to attempt to explain. As he did so, the group moved to sit around the broken table.

"No, Jillian, Leonora is not a Dark God. I'm sure in your dealings with Logan you have learned that the Dark Gods and the mortals of your world are not that far apart from one another. In fact, you and Leonora are more like the Dark Gods than they are like those of us who used to be called Phasia. You had mortal mothers and fathers, and were born in to this world in very much the same way. The only difference is the touch of the divine or the near divine. Trece, Kamen, and I were not born to mortal parents; we were made by our father Halicon. We are mortal true, but not human."

Logan picked up the story.

"The Blaze, and not blood, is what makes us family. Touching the Blaze is not impossible for a human, but it is difficult. Those who try would most likely be destroyed if they didn't have help. Which, if what Rael and Trece say is true, that means someone taught Leonora how to touch the Blaze, taught her how to use it, and taught her how to surrender to it so that it wouldn't burn her from the inside out. Hopefully her path to it was less painful than mine."

Rael nodded.

"Your rebirth was painful to be sure," he said somberly, "but it was one of necessity, and without it, who knows how the war for our world and our very souls would have ended. But in answer to your question, Leonora did have a guide, but I shall let her tell you herself. Leonora?"

The young blond woman sighed briefly before speaking.

"I was born in seventeen hundred and seventy in a small village outside of Oradrim. When I was twelve years old, I met a man in the wilds, a transient who just wanted to be left alone. I told him that he could get a hot meal and a bath in the village. He had been wandering for so long, and he needed a rest, so he bartered becoming my tutor for room and board. What my mother didn't expect, and neither did I was that I would become so fond of my tutor that I would fall in love with him. I think in his way he fell in love with me too, but what I found out later was that he never intended to live much past the next sunrise. For years we travelled together, with him teaching me everything he could, and he taught me how to touch the Blaze, and how to fight monsters. His name was Cedric Binosear."

Logan sat back in his chair and let a long sigh hit the air.

"Well, of all the unexpected things I've heard today, that tops the list."

When Logan looked to Rael, he could tell that the man had more to say.

"What?" Logan asked, with as much humor in his voice as he could manage.

Rael first looked over to Trece before speaking.

"Jerah told us to bring Leonora to you."

For the first time all day, Logan felt as though things were starting to break in their direction. If Jerah was willing to send Cedric's disciple to Logan…

"That's good news," Logan said a smile coming to his lips.

Leonora leaned heavily on the table.

"I don't understand."

Logan sat straight.

"If Jerah sent you here, that means there is still part of her that Dorovar hasn't touched. That means our plan still has a chance, and that Aerith and Rhain aren't as crazy as I thought they were. Now the tricky part is what comes next. There are still too many questions, still too many variables, and you three need a serious crash course on the war."

Rael frowned, but Logan persisted.

"I'm sorry old friend. You don't get to sit on the sidelines any more. I know I said I would keep you out of this as long as I could. It's the same promise I made to Kamen. But that time is over. The Children are on the move, and we need to start hitting back."

Trece squeezed her husband's hand and nodded.

"Tell us how we can help."

Logan leaned his elbows on the table.

"So much of this hinges on who makes the next move. And if Emries or Talisia hit before we're ready, we may never be able to counterattack. I think we may have waited too long, and now that all the pieces are back on the board, there is no telling how it's going to play out. We've suffered a lot of losses. Too many really. We didn't count on losing Ellis or Sabrina or Aryx and Diana so early, but it couldn't be helped. We are going to have to make due with what we have left."

Trece frowned.

"I hadn't heard about Ellis."

Logan nodded.

"She and Jeroch had made a good life for themselves in Iltorp. She sacrificed herself so that Bryn and Jeroch could escape an assassin that had been sent by Kaitain to eliminate the Knights of the Flashing Blade. Jillian, Warron, and I had been there only a few days prior. I wish we could have been there to save her."

Rael's ears perked up at Warron's name.

"And where is Warron now?"

Logan smiled.

"With my father."

Trece returned the smile.

"Aerith is a crafty one. Who could have foreseen the return of Arin Ranthall to a game that he never truly had a hand in? How many others remain?"

Logan shook his head.

"Aside from the four of us, Jeroch, Bryn, Caris, and Warron, the only other survivor I know of is Saurn, and you know how cagey he is. Cedric and Jeroch did their work well to cut down the number. However, that is still enough of us to do a lot of damage. I just wish we were the only force loyal to a Child or the Creator."

Kamen crossed his arms where he stood just behind Logan.

"Emries has begun to marshal his forces."

Logan grimaced.

"Led of course by Korrd."

Rael nodded.

"How many of the *Erieal* still live?"

Logan shook his head.

"I don't know. As fanatical as we were about getting rid of the phasia, we should have been looking on the other side of the battlefield too and assumed that all of those loyal to Emries would have been brought back too. It was arrogant to think those in the Dark Gods would have been the only ones."

Leonora took the opportunity to add her voice to the conversation.

"Cedric told me stories about people that he fought against during the Founding Wars. I didn't believe him at first, because they all just seemed like lies until I knew who and what he really was. He said that he hunted down his oldest friends Mailock and Arathorn, and he said that he would have killed Aryx and Diana too if the situation had been different."

Logan looked at Leonora.

"That is very helpful. So out of thirteen, that gives us seven accounted for."

Jillian frowned.

"That doesn't sound very good."

"Seven?" Trece asked.

Logan nodded.

"All four of Cedric's *Erieal*, Arathorn, Mailock, Aryx, and Diana are dead. Pike is accounted for out of Korrd's group, and Lissa and Taya are accounted for from the third generation. If Talon were around he wouldn't have stayed out of sight this long, and neither would Gideon. I can't imagine he wouldn't have been in touch with his mother. Arin Domae was a soldier, and he could have easily disappeared into some army somewhere. Gwillim, Storm, Rand, that's anyone's best guess. I suppose we should assume that all of those who are unaccounted for are still out there, and that they will eventually find their way to Korrd."

"Has there been any word on Talisia, Pyrrus, or Raenera?"

Again Logan could only shake his head.

"Talisia has sent out feelers with her so-called children, but she does most of her work behind the scenes as always. Raenera is a complete mystery, but I don't think she's sitting idly by. Pyrrus is using my son as a vessel."

Trece laughed.

"The Ranthall family never ceases to impress."

Rael frowned.

"And annoy."

Logan smiled.

"We do try our best."

"Unfortunately," Rael said leaning back and crossing his arms, "being annoying is not a plan."

Logan nodded.

"Very true. So, this is what we're going to do. I asked Kamen to go to meet with Rhain. The Council has to reform, but in his weakened state, I was worried. Now that the two of you are here, you can go with him. I'm sure he would welcome the company, and it would give the two of you an opportunity to meet Rhain. She is her mother's daughter, but there is a lot of Aerith in her too. Just keep her from sending out the Call until I get there. I don't want any of you to have to deal with Jerah without me. But it's got to be on my terms. Otherwise things could get out of control."

Rael and Trece both stood.

"And you?" Trece asked.

Logan rose, quickly followed by Jillian.

"I made a promise before I left Celidar, and before I see Rhain again I have to head to Hedorah. Unfortunately, that is much more complicated now. But, thanks to you, I think I have a way in."

Logan's eyes moved to where Leonora Wastri sat, and the former Knight of the Flashing Blade was suddenly possessed with a feeling of deep concern.

Epilogue

What War Begat

Year Four of the Just Emperor Kaitain "Dragonsbane" Lorien,
Creator's Calendar Year 1871

Cedric Binosear stood blinking his eyes against the darkness around him, but the red tinting the edges of his vision would not relent. It took several moments before he even saw the young girl that stood beside Emries, and each and every moment that passed only deepened his rage. Finally he could not contain the anger any longer and he charged across the empty space, his hand coming immediately to Emries' throat. The force of their collision propelled the two together until Emries' back slammed hard against a tree. For a moment, Emries thought that the collision would topple the seemingly ancient trunk, but the roots held firm and the shock of the impact radiated through the whole of Emries' body. Pure hate was etched in Cedric's face and the newly-revived man squeezed hard his former patron's throat and threatened to crush his prey's windpipe. However, a moment later, a soft small hand touched Cedric's arm, and Tess Annis' silent sweetness somehow succeeded in forcing Cedric's iron grip to soften. But even though the grip no longer paused the flow of air to Emries' lungs; it still held Emries firmly in place. The attack was one of frustration, and though it would have been an impressive tactic against most opponents, against Emries it was largely futile. Emries was not human, and despite his anatomical similarity to those creatures, he was a divine being, a Child of the Creator, and didn't need to concern himself with petty things like breathing. The energy of the Cosmos sustained him, and not even the heroic visage of Cedric Binosear could rob his body of sustenance that easily. For several long moments the three stood there; Emries a picture of calm and patience, Cedric a mass of rage and confusion, and Tess the calming influence trying to keep the beast at bay. Finally Tess' influence won out, and Cedric released Emries' throat and took two long steps backward. However, no matter how effective Tess' attempts to keep Cedric from killing Emries may have been, it did not fully quench the soaring flames of hate. Cedric's fists were balled at his sides, and if he could have channeled all of his hate into one focused burst, it would have burned Emries to the ground a thousand times over. Rubbing his throat and feigning injury, Emries first frowned and then smiled a venom-filled smile.

"Always so excitable, Cedric. How you ever defeated my brother with that temper of yours I'll never know, but then again you did have the redoubtable Aryx Terian by your side all those years. Perhaps my greatest mistake was taking his memories away and making him one of my *Erieal*. Would have been much simpler if I would have just killed him when I had the chance."

"Why?" Cedric intoned finally, his tongue clicking unconsciously at the end of the word.

Casually Emries leaned back against the tree and folded his arms.

"My dear Cedric, you have been one of my favorite servants from the moment I graced you with my mantle. That great desire in you to do the best you can no matter the hardship is one of the most easily manipulatable character traits I have yet discovered within humanity. And in you, it was your primary drive. Perhaps that was because the man you thought was your father had such a weak character, and because your mother knew that you and your sister were another man's children. That gave you latitude to learn life on your own terms, and you saw the evil and the inequity of humanity. You knew one day that you would inherit power, and it drove you to make life better for those you could."

The words sent shivers through Cedric, and for the first time it put a dent in the rage.

"You knew Aerith was my father before you bestowed me with your mantle, didn't you? You knew what Aerith was, didn't you?"

Emries smiled.

"It's important to you that you know the truth, isn't it, Cedric?"

It was Tess that answered.

"We all deserve to know where we came from, don't you think?"

Emries looked down at the girl and for a moment wondered if she was talking about Cedric or if she was talking about herself. Regardless of her nature as the Dragon's Tear, and her ability to bend reality, there was so much about the girl that even Emries did not know. Her power was much like that which Aerith Seth possessed. It was more akin to the powers of the Creator than it was to the powers of the Children. Of course Aerith had never fully embraced the power that was inside of him, because those that taught him could not have perceived a power greater than their own. How could Saurn or Bryn or Grawn have taught Aerith anything more than what they knew they were capable of? Should Aerith have fallen into Halicon's clutches early in his life instead of being held up as a sacrifice, perhaps things would have been different. Or perhaps not. So much of Aerith was his personality, his irreverence, and his belief that he could overcome any obstacle. But until an obstacle of sufficient difficulty was placed in his path, his powers never grew. It wasn't until others showed him the way, until others with different personalities such as the thrice damned Logan Ranthall, that Aerith began to question how much he could actually do. Finally, Emries nodded his head and frowned.

"You've seen enough now, Cedric, to know that my brothers and sisters and I have a dynamic and explosive relationship. We all have different ways to prove our methodologies, and eventually one of us will prove to be right. However as much as we want to prove ourselves superior to one another, we want to prove ourselves superior to our Father. And for eons that was what held between us. Then Talisia had the idea of sabotaging each other's worlds. It started subtly at first, and then it progressed to what ultimately happened with Dorovar. I saw what the loss of that world did to Raenera. She was shaken, never the same. For centuries she would not return to the

Heavens. Even Pyrrus could not find her. Rumors were that she walked across different worlds disguised as a native creature, but no one knows for sure. I have not seen my sister since the fall of Dorovar's world. But that loss emboldened me. I wanted nothing more than to sabotage my own personal foil Halicon. Our battles were long and brutal both physically and philosophically. However, Talisia was in my ear. She was beginning to think that our Father was grooming us for something greater, for something more than just supremacy over the other Children. She believed that the Creator wanted one of us to surpass even Him. So, when a new world was created, the Creator gave it to me, and told me to do as I wished. For so long we had been dabbling with creatures of different types. Raenera's version of humans were intelligent, but were not as able to see abstraction. If you consider what Raenera stands for, Order at all costs, it would make sense that she would create something unable to see the folly of her commandments. So I gave my version of humans the ability to see the chaos around them and to adjust and adapt to it. As I went to your world for the first time and saw the first generation of my humans, I again heard Talisia's voice in ear. So instead of giving the book of the Creator's law to these people, I instead presented the laws as my own, and became what I truly was, the Creator of the humans of Onea."

Cedric listened, trying to feel the truth between the bias and the lies. For so long Cedric had seen Emries as a liar and a manipulator and would never trust the words that came out of his mouth. Emries had his own motivations and his own view over what was true and not. Moreover, because Emries had been alive so long and had seen so much, Cedric wondered if it was even possible that a human could understand the point of view of a divine being like a Child of the Creator. Tess on the other hand hung on the man's every word. She felt a kinship, a harmony with the man in white with the icy blue eyes. She wanted so much to believe that she was like him.

"For so long I reigned as the god-king of Onea. There were some minor rebellions, but one huge lightning storm or volcanic eruption put an end to the unrest. But the chaos was there, all around me. As much as the people tried to win and curry my favor, so too did they try to subvert my rule to better themselves and their position. Then the Creator sent Halicon to restore the balance and to force me to make the humans acknowledge the true Creator. When Halicon first appeared, I was not concerned. I knew Halicon's tactics; I knew how he would fight against me. He would try to turn those loyal to me against my rule, he would try to shine the light of truth and hope so that it was brighter than mine. What I was not prepared for was the thing that Halicon became. For the first century, Halicon laid in wait. He listened, he watched. He walked among the people and learned. Then one day Halicon approached me. This was the first I became aware of his presence. He had remained hidden for so long, and I began to question my own abilities upon learning that fact. Halicon demanded that I relinquish control of the world, and to tell the truth about the nature of the Cosmos. Regardless of how shaken I was by Halicon's remaining hidden, I still had my own pride and Talisia's voice fueling me. I refused and told Halicon to go back to the Heavens. Halicon once again gave me the chance to withdraw. When I refused the second time, Halicon turned his back to me and told me that I would regret my decision, and he would make sure that many would suffer for my arrogance."

Emries paused and looked out onto the darkened horizon, his eyes flashing the reflection of the streaks of fire across the sky.

"When my brother reemerged almost twenty years later, he was no longer the Halicon that I had been fighting for so long; he had transformed himself into a creature calling itself Shau-ling. The name crept forth across the land like a shadow, and from that shadow emerged all manner of monsters that shook the faith of even the most faithful of my followers. The raids started small, just creatures attacking in waves, burning small towns and instilling as much fear as possible for the least amount of effort. Then a man calling himself the Shadow appeared. In a night he laid siege to one of my most well-defended strongholds, and with a combination of Kalbraks and Stone, he reduced the defenses to rubble. Then he sent in the Jeresei, and they slaughtered every man, woman, and child that dwelled within the stronghold. Jeroch left it a shattered husk, a monument to the lethality of Shau-ling and his creations. I didn't know how to respond. Never before had my brother sacrificed those he deemed as innocent in our ideological war. But soon the phasia, most specifically Jeroch, made it clear that the humans were nothing more than an infestation to be exterminated. When one of my generals learned that Jeroch was constructing a massive black tower in the center of the broken stronghold, he gathered an army to try to take back what had been lost. His men were shaken, but their anger at the seemingly senseless murder of women and children emboldened them even further. The army marched on the growing black edifice, but they were met not with an opposing force of monsters, but with a single massive man standing in the center of the plains that led to Jeroch's tower. Alone and unarmed, Kamen decimated the oncoming army. He broke their spirits and sent them fleeing in all directions. Where Jeroch had eliminated all that stood against him, Kamen fed on their fear, increasing their terror, showing them the futility of action against them. But as powerful and as vicious as Jeroch and Kamen were, the next to emerge were far worse."

Cedric's eyes shifted from Emries to Tess and he was mortified to see that the girl's eyes were sparkling as she drank in the information. There was no doubt that the phasia were horrible and hateful creatures who were bent on destruction, but by the time that Cedric knew them, they had devolved from the single focus of crushing their enemies to turning on each other like a pack of starving jackals. Thinking of the deadly efficiency that the phasia could bring to bear if they ever had truly worked to each other's strength made Cedric shiver deep down inside. Emries turned his eyes back to Cedric, and for the first time, the former *Coromor* felt something from Emries that could not be called quiet confidence. There was something beneath it; something akin to regret.

"With Jeroch's black tower as the center of Shau-ling's new region of dominion, the bands of creatures started to fan out in all directions. Two large towns to the west were immediately overrun, but the way it was done shattered even more faith in my leadership. In the night, every able bodied man was killed by his wife, his lover, or a female family member. To this day I still don't know how Ellis was able to make it happen, but she infected every female in those two cities with unquenchable jealousy, rage, and murderous desire. Overnight she had decimated the army, removed the leadership, and had assumed power, and all through application of only her intelligence and will. To the east of the black tower, the countryside burned. Bryn unleashed devastation unlike any Onea had ever seen. In the area that would become Trelon, she set forests, farms, towns, and people ablaze, an inferno so massive that its smoke could be seen from anywhere in the world. The region that would become Illimar had a grand city, and the peninsula was twice the size of what you remember. That was until

Grawn came. For weeks ever growing waves battered the shores, the town, and flooded the surrounding lands. By the time he was done, there was nothing left standing. By this time the black tower was completed, and the true sinister plan became apparent. Aryx Terian appeared. He walked into the most populated town to the south of the tower. He stood in the center of town and simply began to speak. Within an hour he had enthralled the whole of the population, and they left everything behind to follow him. They marched north en masse, entering the tower one by one, not a single living human ever emerging again. What did emerge however was a new generation of Jeresei, Kalbraks, and the first Shadowwalkers. The horror stories spread quickly, and I was left facing questions I never thought I would have to answer."

Again Emries paused, and when he spoke again, he shifted his gaze to Tess. It was then that Cedric began to see the goal of Emries' words. It was not for Cedric's benefit. Emries had to set himself up as a tragic figure for the girl. He needed her, and in the same way that Emries had enticed Logan and so many others to his cause, he would do the same with the girl through liberal application of his version of factual events.

"These new creatures, these phasia, were something I never thought I would have to face. As such, those who had faith in my absolute power and my status as the Creator began to wane. But there were four, four men, who were blindly loyal and would have done anything for me. They came to me as one, begging for the chance to take the fight to the newly dawned nightmares. And so I touched them with my power, invested them with everything they would need to fight the phasia on their own level. Then I tasked these men with fighting the largest war the world had ever seen, using any tactic they deemed necessary. Thus the first generation of *Erieal* was born. But the whispers of the common people had already begun. My brother had taken the lessons learned during his centuries of wandering and had begun to wrangle the wills of the people. This was the first time the word *Coromor* began to be uttered. In those days it did not mean 'He who brings change'. No, it was a derogatory term, 'He who brings destruction'. The believers were becoming less and less, and as the war stretched and raged, my *Erieal* began to use the tactics of the phasia against them, compelling the people to fight when they did not wish to. Bending the wills of the elements to destroy everything in their path. Onea was on the verge of tearing itself apart after a century of constant war. But my dear brother had learned his lessons too well, had made his phasia too much like my humans."

Finally the normal pride began to return to Emries' voice, and the sound was a sickening twist in Cedric's gut.

"Kamen began to follow his own leads, ignoring the formerly coordinated assaults. Grawn and Bryn became insular and no longer attempted to take other kingdoms. Ellis disappeared completely, preferring to do her studies and her research out of the eyes of the others. Aryx, who had been leading thousands to their deaths suddenly fought less and less, preferring only to be a soldier on the battlefield rather than a general and a bringer of death. This allowed my *Erieal* to topple Jeroch's black tower and gain the first true victory for my people. The tide began to turn as Shau-ling's forces crumbled. Then my brother began to revert to form. The ruthlessness that had marked the first centuries of our rekindled conflict softened. Kamen was removed from the battlefield and remade as the Living Flame, the guardian of Shau-ling's throne room. Aryx was allowed to walk away from the war, unable to live with the guilt and the shame of the hundreds of thousands that had died at his hands. The tide of the war ebbed. The only one who seemed to be interested in fighting was Jeroch. But the defection of Aryx Terian intrigued me. I had to know what would become of the soldier responsible for so much death."

Emries crossed his arms and again looked out into the nothingness.

"Aryx's humanity drew him to try to make some kind of restitution for his actions. He worked as a common laborer, a farmer, a carpenter; any work he could find. He worked for only food and shelter, much like you did Cedric when you were paying your penance during the Founding Wars. He settled down in a little farm house, got married, and had a child. This was where I found my chance at intervention. My spies had learned that Grawn, Bryn, and Ellis had begun searching for a way to remove Shau-ling and take power for themselves. I knew that Aryx's child would be possessed of some kind of power, but I had no idea what it would be. So days after the child's birth, I tied a portion of my power to its limp little form. I could have snuffed it out with a thought, could have ended the threat that would become Aerith Seth long before he would be truly aware of anything other than the field of his own vision. But unlike my investiture in the *Erieal* giving a portion of my power to Aerith required a sacrifice. It couldn't be a direct tie, or my brother would have been able to feel it, so too probably would Aryx. So I surrendered a small portion of my divinity. What I didn't know then but would find out later when I made Aryx into one of my *Erieal,* that though he was stripped of his position as a member of the phasia, Aryx still retained a measure of power. The first phasia were formed directly from Halicon's divinity, the fountainhead from which the Blaze springs. The combination of my divinity and Halicon's made Aerith special, and as such made all of Aerith's progeny special, though to different degrees."

Finally Emries had gotten to the point, and Cedric listened with renewed interest.

"Gideon, Ayden, and Rhain all suffer from the limitation that Shau-ling enforced on all of his phasia. Though they could combine their powers, the combination was actually weaker than they could have been on their own. It was a way to ensure that the phasia would never become a threat. Their strength was through coordination and cooperation, not combination. With Bryn, all of Aerith's children would be diminished from what his first two children were capable of. You, Cedric, and your sister Anabel, the two of you were special. Though Anne never embraced her powers, you, with my help, were able to draw deeper on my powers than even I expected. Unfortunately, it was your own fear and ignorance that kept you from fully embracing your role as the first in a new line of *Coromors*. Perhaps that was my fault. I did not guide you well enough, and I fell into the trap of embracing the wrong Ranthall brother until it was too late. By the time I was able to take direct interest in one of my successors, it was far too late. Nathan proved to be unable to shoulder the burden, and because of the hasty nature in which he was invested with his power, he could never live up to the example created by Cedric and Korrd. This is why I needed you back, Cedric."

Emries crossed the distance to Cedric and put his hand on the mortal's shoulder. A feeling of comfort and warmth passed through Cedric, but he tried hard to fight against it. He needed to focus his rage, he needed to keep his mind sharp and prevent being manipulated as he had been for his entire life on Onea. He needed to stand strong against Emries.

"As powerful of a warrior as you are, and as accomplished a hero, your time was over. I have my general, and Korrd will serve that purpose well. As long as Logan continues to be the nuisance that he has always been, Korrd will remain driven. I have surrounded Korrd with enough shelter and assistance that he will be an effective foil for anything my brothers and sisters might throw at him. You, Cedric, I have a special and important job for you. I have found for you someone possessed of like power and like disposition. Tess here, the one who brought you back from the void, has more in common with you than any other person that has ever walked on any world. You, Cedric, are the son of a man who was touched by two Children of the Creator and gifted with their divine essence. Though your mother was just a mortal, it did not diminish or limit your powers. Tess here is the daughter of one of my sisters, Raenera. She is also the daughter of Pike Rhuiden, who at the time was a divine being. Her power is different than yours, perhaps more potent because Pike's divine power was a gift directly from the Creator. I need you to shepherd Tess, teach her all of the ways that she can use her gifts to make this world a better place, and to win the war against the evils that want to tear this world apart."

Again the flood of power washed through Cedric. His hate began to dim, and he could feel his mind begin to fill with doubt.

"We must not allow my brothers and sisters to gain the upper hand. We must not allow the dragons and Dorovar to plunge this world into fire, and we must not allow your father to do any more damage than he has already done. You know what I'm saying is true Cedric. Think of Tess as the daughter you never had. I know you wanted to teach that dear girl Leonora, but you knew your time was short and you could not see her in the way you wanted. You were hurting so much and needed a companion. You know Tess is special. See her as your own child and protect her from those who would lead her astray."

Cedric turned his head and looked into the golden glowing eyes of the girl and instantly felt compassion and love for her. He knew he needed to protect her. He knew he needed to guide her. As though she could feel the thoughts running through his mind, she smiled and instantly wrapped her arms around his waist and gave him a long hug. A self-satisfied smile came to Emries lips, and he took a step back.

"Then it's agreed," Emries said finally. "Go where you will, but avoid conflict unless you have no choice. Stay away from the western kingdoms. That is where I will be doing most of my work. And under no circumstances are you to seek out either Logan or your father. That confrontation could end badly for all of us."

Cedric's heartbeat quickened, and he could feel the anger surge inside of him again. Though he would not have argued with Emries, it did feel as though some sanity was trying to pierce the fog.

"I have other matters to attend to," the Child of the Creator said finally, "but soon I will be calling on the two of you for the next part of my plan. And believe me, it will be glorious."

A moment later, Emries was simply gone. Tess took Cedric by the hand and started to lead him in the direction of the lake and forest that she had created only hours ago.

"You look hungry. Let's make some dinner. Can you cook?"

Cedric nodded. The thoughts and feelings that Emries had tried to plant in Cedric's head were powerful, but there was something that Emries did not know, a last line of defense that Cedric had tried to hold onto no matter what Emries did. Emries wanted Cedric to love and care for Tess as though she was his own daughter, emotions that Emries thought he could implant. However, as the two of them walked toward the forest, Cedric's thoughts drifted to his own daughter and prayed that she was still safe.

Appendicies

Dramatis Personae

Connor Peregrim
Lord of Lordhill
Former General in the Imperial Guard

Gabrielle Peregrim
Lady of Lordhill
Cousin of Kaitain Lorien

Arent Fox
General in the Rebel Army of
Lordhill

Strum Anvilguard
General in the Rebel Army of
Lordhill

The Knights of the Flashing Blade
Bernhardt Yeoman
The Moonstone Knight
Kingdom of Iron, Pellatori
Wielder of the Hammer Gravity

Chelsea Zarova
The Garnet Knight
Kingdom of Fire, Saldarine
"The Wolf of Saldarine"
Wife of Seraph Kore
Wielder of the Katars Tenacity
Personal Protector of Dominique
Lorien

Devlin Rannoch
The Onyx Knight
Kingdom of Night, Galateria
Half-Dragon
Wielder of the Kopesh Discipline

Gregor Quicksilver
The Ruby Knight
Kingdom of Blood, Zevarit
Husband of Hannah Ironheart
Paladin of the Church of the Creator
Son of Ivan Quicksilver
Wielder of the Greatsword Valor

Hannah Ironheart
The Celestine Knight
Kingdom of Stone, Albitonin
High Priestess of the Church of the
Creator
Wife of Gregor Quicksilver
Wielder of the Mace Spirit
First *Chosen One* of Espre

Leonora Wastri
The Jade Knight
Kingdom of Soul, Oradrim
Wielder of the Naginata Wisdom
Trained by Cedric Binosear

Jaccob Aldora
The Topaz Knight
The Flying Kingdom, Hedorah
Former Member of the Academy of
Arcane Arts
Wielder of the Double Sword
Temperance

Natalia Pressen
The Sunstone Knight
Kingdom of Gold, Bellnoc
Master of the Shadow Guild
Wielder of the Rapier Perseverance

Orren Eldrath
The Sapphire Knight
Kingdom of Ice, Rashaleb
Former Member of the Academy of
Arcane Arts
Wielder of the Long Sword Courage

Seraph Kore
The Emerald Knight
Kingdom of Water, Thorigald
Husband of Chelsea Zarova
Wielder of Twin Sword Patience

Tolon Morr
The Amethyst Knight
Kingdom of Steel, Celidar
Former Gladiator
Wielder of Battle Axe Strength

Vallic Ultiv
The Serpentine Knight
Kingdom of Steam, Iltorp
Wielder of Scythe Harmony
Alias of Jeroch Yetre

Xaran Firesoul
The Tiger's Eye Knight
Kingdom of Knowledge, Menoris
Blind Since Birth
Wielder of Staff Faith

Gabriel Shadowfall
Member of the Imperial Guard
Personal Guard of Marlae Lorien
The Ruby Knight

Ivan Quicksilver
Former Ruby Knight
Father of Gregor Quicksilver
Advisor to the Dark Court

Tutio Illik
Former Onyx Knight

Heremon Tal
Former Amethyst Knight

The Academy of Arcane Arts
Alistair Ravenheart
Grandmaster of the Academy of
Arcane Arts
Master of Water
Imperial Sorcerer
Husband of Estelle Ravenheart
Father of Quyhn Ravenheart

Estelle Ravenheart
Sorceress
Wife of Alistair Ravenheart
Mother of Quyhn Ravenheart

Fiona Ebonsight
Master of Fire
Mother of Aris Ebonsight

Aris Ebonsight
Master of Air
Daughter of Fiona Ebonsight

Jastra Mythryn
Master of Energy

Ashinica Maupin
Master of Stone
Member of the Imperial Family

DRAMATIS PERSONAE

The Seers

Jehna Feris
The Dark Seer

Jania Maldovrin
Oldest of the Maldovrin Triplets

Jerrica Maldovrin
Youngest of the Maldovrin Triplets

Jordyne Maldovrin
Middle of the Maldovrin Triplets

The Dragon Hunters

Jillian Corven
Self-Titled Lady of Cadaria
Wielder of Scaleripper
Leader of the Dragon Hunters

Kiara Aren
Dragon Hunter
Former Priestess of the Creator

Angelina Lynn Sydor
Dragon Hunter

Jacqueline Escandi
Dragon Hunter
Former Member of the Iron Legion

The Chorus

Dorovar
The Destroyer of Worlds

Pestilence
The Grey Man
Carrier of the Crawling Plague

Famine
Formerly Isabel Relin
Carrier of the Wasting Disease

Death
Formerly Ardis Franel
The Collector of Souls

Jerah
Alias of Caris

Conquest
Alias of Pike Rhuiden

The Hand of Chaos

Dimitri Sulano
The Voice of the Lost

Syren Belloch
The Priestess of Blood

Torda Safrick
The Master of Secrets

Xavier Cormea
The Corruptor of Souls

Erik Relcan
Pursuer of Lost Love
Former Personal Assistant of Hannah
Ironheart

Seraphina Masile
Second in Command of the Hand of
Chaos

Korin Melcab
Captain of the Imperial Guard

APPENDICIES

The Children of the Creator

Emries
The First *Coromor*
Creator of the *Erieal*

Halicon
Formerly known as Shau-ling
Father of the Phasia

Talisia Masile
The Dark Goddess

Pyrrus
God of Light

Raenera
Goddess of Order

The Phasia

Rhain Seth
Mistress of the Blaze
Former Personal Guard of Marlae
Lorien
Daughter of Aerith Seth and Bryn
Aplee

Jeroch Yetre
The Lord Shadow
First Born of the Phasia
Father of Hawk Yetre

Bryn Aplee
The Lady Fox
Member of the Brotherhood of Phasia
Former Lover of Aerith Seth
Wife of Grawn Aplee
Mother of Gideon Viruci

Ellis Chandara
The Lady Leopard
Member of the Brotherhood of Phasia
Mother of Korrd Ranthall

Grawn Aplee
The Lord Shark
Member of the Brotherhood of Phasia
Husband of Bryn Aplee

Warron Ysamaran
AKA Blade
The Lord Boar
Member of the Brotherhood of Phasia

Basille Mystic
The Lord Raven
Member of the Brotherhood of Phasia
Father of Jerrard Mystic

Farax Soar
Creator of the Snags
The Lord Vulture
Member of the Brotherhood of Phasia

The Flame
Kamen
Personal Guardian of Shau-ling
Keeper of the Hall of Terrors
Originally known as Kamen, Member
of the Brotherhood of Phasia

Zarsi Aeron
The Lord Cobra
Member of the Brotherhood of Phasia

Aldridge Farran
The Lord Hawk
Member of the Brotherhood of Phasia

Saurn Macco
The Lord Viper
Member of the Brotherhood of Phasia

Caris Vale
The Lady Wolf
Member of the Brotherhood of Phasia

Erdric Yarrow
The Lord Scorpion
Member of the Brotherhood of Phasia

Taron Steen
The Lord Jackal
Member of the Brotherhood of Phasia

Draven Batoe
The Lord Crow
Member of the Brotherhood of Phasia

Rane Larion
The Lady Falcon
Member of the Brotherhood of Phasia

Stryfe Cadre
The Lord Python
Member of the Brotherhood of Phasia

Grimm Salde
The Lord Bear
Member of the Brotherhood of Phasia

Cash Griffon
The Lady Lynx
Member of the Brotherhood of Phasia

Nightwing
Member of the Dark Riders
Shau-ling's Assassin

Hawk Yetre
Son of Jeroch Yetre and Caris Vale

Natalie Yetre
Daughter of Jeroch Yetre and Ellis
Chandara

Jessica Chandara
Daughter of Ellis Chandara and
Grawn Aplee

The Court of the Dark Gods
Sadrina Annis
Queen of Mythryn
Wife of Pike Rhuiden

Darrien Annis
Half-Dark Goddess
Daughter of Pike Rhuiden

Tess Annis
Half-Dark Goddess
Daughter of Pike Rhuiden

Alderin Terian
Dark God
Son of Aryx and Diana Terian
Protector of Darrien Annis

Camille Sandar
Dark Goddess
Daughter of Gwydeon and Midarin
Sandar
Protector of Tess Annis

Serrina Mistic
Dark Goddess
Voice of the Dark Council
Daughter of Jerrard and Erika Mystic

Mirana Ranthall
Daughter of Wolf Ranthall and Lissa
Terian
Twin of Liara Ranthall

Liara Ranthall
Daughter of Wolf Ranthall and Lissa
Terian
Twin of Mirana Ranthall

The Celestial Court
Marlae Tamerlane
The Divine Empress
Chosen Representative of the Creator
Daughter of Kaitain Lorien

Ayden Seth
Son of Aerith Seth and Bryn Aplee
The Will

Anabel Binosear
Sister of Cedric Binosear
Mother of Cairyn Binosear
Daughter of Aerith Seth
High Council to the Divine Empress

Azure
God of the Heavens
Advisor to the Divine Empress

Krysis
God of the Heavens
Advisor to the Divine Empress

Terrance Aldora
Brother of Jaccob Aldora
Advisor to the Divine Empress

Isabella
Advisor to the Divine Empress

The Dark Gods
Aryx Terian
White Lightning
Fire *Erieal* of the First Generation of
the Prophecies
Husband of Diana Geoffry Terian
Father of Lissa Terian
Father of Alderin Parran
Former Host of Nightwing

Diana Terian Geoffry
Wind *Erieal* of the First Generation of
the Prophecies
Sister of Arathorn Geoffry
Wife of Aryx Terian
Mother of Lissa Terian
Mother of Alderin Parran

Pike Rhuiden
Water *Erieal* of the Second
Generation of the Prophecies
Refugee from the Dark Mirror
First Cousin of Logan Ranthall
Eldar Merin's Former Husband
Husband of Sadrina Annis
Father of Darrien and Tess Annis

Gwydeon Sandar
Brother of Angels
Husband of Midarin Rice Sandar
Father of Nathaniel Sandar
Father of Camille Renar
Also Known as Wynne

Midarin Rice
Wife of Gwydeon Sandar
Mother of Nathaniel Sandar
Mother of Camille Renar

Lissa Terian
Fire *Erieal* of the Third Generation of
the Prophecies
Daughter of Aryx and Diana Terian
Wife of Wolf Ranthall

Sabrina Binosear
Third *Chosen One* of the Prophecies
Refugee from the Dark Mirror
Daughter of Cairyn Binosear

Wolf Ranthall
Son of Logan Ranthall and Elwyne
Tamerlane Ranthall

The Forgotten
Aerith Seth
The First *Chosen One*
Husband of Bryn Aplee
Father of Ayden Seth, Cedric
Binosear, Anabel Binosear, Gideon
Viruci

Taya Viruci
Daughter of Gideon Viruci and Erika
Belnosian
Refugee from the Dark Mirror

Logan Ranthall
AKA Dane Rhuiden
Second *Chosen One* of the Prophecies
Brother of Korrd Ranthall
First Cousin of Pike Rhuiden
Father of Wolf Ranthall
Leader of the Order of the Flickering
Flame
Refugee from the Dark Mirror

Jerrard Mystic
Son of Basille Mystic
Husband of Erika Belnosian
Father of Serrina Mistic

Erika Belnosian Mystic
Wife of Jerrard Mystic
Mother of Serrina Mystic

Other Cast
Cole Breon
Freelance Assassin
The Living Shadow

Liandra Nightshade
Freelance Assassin
Death Blossom

Dane Rhuiden
Monk
Leader of the Order of the Flickering
Flame

Blade
Merchant
Purveyor of Oddities
Alias of Warron Ysamaran

Isa Shar
Companion of Vallic Ultiv
Alias of Ellis Chandara

Evan Sinn
Inheritor of Aerith Seth's power
The Voice of the Creator
Husband of Meredith Heron

Taya Mystic
Daughter of Jerrard and Erika Mystic

Meredith Heron
Emissary of the Creator
Wife of Evan Sinn
Murdered by Dorovar

Tera Dawnrunner
Guardian of the Council of the Winds
Guardian of the East
Last of the Tigrelle

Jander Eveningstar
Guardian of the Council of the Winds

Eldar Merin
The Spirit
Best Friend of Elwyne Tamerlane
Wife of Pike Rhuiden

Leane Torne
General in the Army of Rama
Former Member of the Army of Brea

Nathaniel Sandar
The Lord Ram
Third *Coromor* of the Prophecies
Son of Gwydeon Sandar and Midarin Rice
Brother of Liette Forer

Gwillim Sandar
Earth *Erieal* of the Third Generation of the Prophecies
Son of Korrd Ranthall and Gabrielle Crill
Adopted Son of Midarin Rice

Storm Mystic
Son of Jerrard and Erika Mystic
Water *Erieal* of the Third Generation of the Prophecies

Jared Vale
Son of Caris Vale and Cedric Binosear

Cairyn Binosear
Daughter of Anabel Binosear
Niece of Cedric Binosear
Queen of the Kingdoms of Kandor, Trelon, and Marcwell
Wife of Pike Rhuiden
Mother of Duncan Rhuiden and Sabrina Binosear

Sabrina Binosear
Former Host of the Spirit
Third *Chosen One* of the Prophecies
Sister of Duncan Rhuiden
Daughter of Pike Rhuiden and Cairyn Binosear

Duncan Rhuiden
Heir to the Kingdom of Marcwell
Brother of Sabrina Binosear
Son of Pike Rhuiden and Cairyn Binosear

Talon Aielin
Wind *Erieal* of the Second Generation of the Prophecies
Best Friend of Pike Rhuiden

Arin Domae
Fire *Erieal* of the Second Generation of the Prophecies
Former Soldier of the Army of Brea

Gideon Viruci
Earth *Erieal* of the Second Generation of the Prophecies
Killed in Battle with Shau-ling

Heralds of the Creator

The Voice
Formerly embodied by Evan Sinn
Currently embodies Gregor
Quicksilver

The Will
Currently embodies Ayden Seth

The Wrath
Destroyed by Aerith Seth

The Spirit
Formerly embodied by Sabrina
Binosear
Currently embodies Eldar Merin

The Council of Winds
The Elder Dragon Tarot
Leader of the Council

Mariti Brightblade
Second in Command of the Council
Companion of Tarot

Khalas Skydancer
Friend of Xaran Firesoul

The Demon Dragon Shadowweaver
Chief Opposition to Tarot
Krangoth Granitewill

The Arcane Dragon Serentis

Brux Mightytide

Charnada Ivorytooth
Ally of Shadowweaver

Stormbane the Traitor
Ally of Shadowweaver

Sheyruushk Bottomdweller
Ally of Khalas Skydancer

About the Author

Brian Kershner is a life-long dreamer, writer, and problem-solver. He grew up absorbing anything and everything he could get his hands on, and as a child of the Star Wars era he constantly wanted to see the worlds beyond the little Indiana town he grew up in. There was no adventure too far, and no problem too big.

Emboldened by parents who always supported his curiosity and his thoughtfulness, Brian found himself bounding from Space Camp to Laser Summer Camp to Athletic Training Camp to Piano Lessons to Football Practice to Basketball Practice to Choir Practice and back again. Despite all of the roaming and traveling, his family remained close-knit and supportive.

Though he flirted with the idea of becoming a doctor, Brian's attentions always fell back to the computer world. He got his first computer when he was six, and not long after found his way into a word processing program and began crafting his own fantastic worlds and even more fantastic characters.

As he has grown and changed and experienced life, so too have his characters. He continues to write, craft, and create; whether it is websites for his customers, or characters and worlds for his audience.